The King and Queen of Perfect Normal

a novel

INKBLOT BOOKS

The King and Queen of Perfect Normal

Published by Inkblot Books
www.inkblotbooks.com

ISBN-10: 1932461175
ISBN-13: 9781932461176

Printed in the United States of America

Thanks, Char

Also by K.A. Thompson

Charybdis
As Simple As That
Finding Father Rabbit

It's Not About the Cookies

As Max Thompson

The Psychokitty Speaks Out: Diary of a Mad Housecat

The Psychokitty Speaks Out: Something of Yours Will Meet a
Toothy Death

The Rules: A Guide for People Owned by Cats

Peek inside the author's head at
http://kathompson.blogspot.com

Or meet the Psychokitty at
http://psychokitty.blogspot.com

The King and Queen
of
Perfect Normal

a novel

K.A. Thompson

1

Kevin

It doesn't matter how old you are; if you walk into the kitchen and catch your mom groping your dad, it's a bit disturbing.

I was disturbed with astonishing frequency while I was growing up; by the time I was married with a son of my own, I learned to appreciate that sense of Oneness they have, but appreciating it doesn't make the grand visual of your dad pinned against the breakfast bar with your mom's fingers doing *stuff* to him any less weird.

"They're cute," my sister keeps telling me. "Leave it alone."

"They're not cute, they're horny. Shouldn't they be way past all that?"

"God, Kevin, they're not dead yet. Would you prefer they never touch each other at all?"

I don't think that's an option.

You can tell, without even seeing them touch, that my parents are connected. It's there in every look, how they turn to each other when they're in the same room, the way one tilts their head when they hear the other in another part of the house. In a crowded room, with my mother on one side and my father on the other, you just know—even if they aren't looking at each other—that they belong together. And when you see them together you assume that when they do touch, there's an electric current that threads through skin, pulsing with each heart beat, that seeps down through their toes.

I get that; I *have* that. I understand how they are because it's what I know: having a soul mate, the other half of one's heart, the static that can happen even when skin never touches skin.

But come on.

They're my *parents*.

Face it, anyone with average parents would like to think that you count the number of kids in the family, and that's how many times they've done it. And that might even be questionable; maybe it was spontaneous conception, because surely *those* people did not do *that*.

"Squirt," older brother Nick laughed, "you're twenty three going on ten. Look at your wife. Can you imagine ever giving that up?"

That's different.

Okay, so I get it, I really do. But when I walked into the kitchen a few months before my dad's fiftieth birthday and saw my mother tracing...*stuff*...on his jeans—well, I couldn't just *unsee* it.

"Really," I told my siblings, "I just wanted to poke my eyes out with the blunt end of that giant weird wooden spoon mom keeps by the stove."

"What'd they say?" Eileen asked.

" *'Get out,'* " I growled, imitating Dad. "And you know he's probably pissed off at me, because Mom just laughed and followed me into the living room to see what I wanted in the first place."

"Scarred for life," Paul mused.

"Well, *yeah*. And it's not the first time, dammit. They're always...touching."

Eileen nodded. "You think we'd have learned to cough or something before entering a room they might be in."

We were sitting in wicker chairs on our parents' front lawn, watching Paul's eight year old daughter Nicole and her friends playing in the court. It was a mass of shrieking little girls playing an odd mix of Tag and Simon Says, and I gave up trying to figure out the rules ten minutes into it.

It was because of Nicole and my son Michael that the entire family, including Aunt Kris and Uncle Doug, was looking for some place we could share property lines but not houses. We wanted to be surrounded by family, to create a safe place for our kids to grow up. The original plan, to take over the houses on the street we'd grown up on, was shoved aside when our mother bemoaned the rising crime rate surrounding the neighborhood, and the too-often squeals of sirens slicing through the night.

Dad owned all but one house on the court; it would have been doable. He'd intended on gating off the street entry, making it a relatively safe place for kids to play, but Mom wanted a place for her grandkids away from being exposed to what she was sure was an increase in crime and the constant pestering from the professional panhandlers that were taking up residence on the corners.

We spent a huge chunk of our time together as it was; why not make it easier?

As it was, half of us were living with the parents anyway. Paul didn't have the heart to move Nicole away from her grandparents; she was dealing with her mother's death—those wounds barely over a year old—and struggling with the aloneness of not having her even within reach of the phone. He didn't want to compound her grief by tearing her away from her home, not yet.

Lydia and I were there with our son, still hanging out after our apartment had been torched. We held onto family after the turmoil of my former seminary roommate grabbing her and running to the coast, the aftermath of my brother Nick putting a bullet through Jake Catero's throat. We moved in because we had nowhere else to go, and by the time Michael was born the family was making these grand plans to find some place big enough for all of us; moving out didn't seem to make sense.

Our original plan to buy the house across the street fell through; at the last minute the seller's son stepped in, begging his parents not to let it go. It's the family home, he argued; it's my childhood.

So we were living with my parents, waiting to find the right property for six families to move onto.

Nicole was squealing with laughter and I heard Paul sigh. "Damn. It just hit me how big she's getting. Before I know it those eyes are going to be rolling at me every five minutes, just so I get the message that I'm the biggest moron in the world."

"It's nice that your daughter knows you so well," Nick said.

Paul lazily kicked out at Nick. "Someday it'll be you on the end of pre-pre-teen angst."

"Someday."

Eileen barged straight into the None-Of-Your-Business. "When are you going to give up and let Katie have what she wants?"

"You should talk. When are *you* going to spawn?"

"I don't know. I think about it once in a while but I'm still kind of ambivalent. I may be more suited to be the fun aunt instead of the mean mom."

"You wouldn't be mean," Nick said.

"Come on. You know I'll be the one doing most of the discipline and saying 'no' all the time."

Nick did not argue and Eileen turned her face away from him. She wasn't going to say it: Eileen would be the one getting up at night, every night. Eileen would be the one reacting to sibling squabbles and midnight earaches. Eileen would be the go-to parent for the first years of their children's lives.

It wouldn't be because Spider would drop the parental ball; he simply wouldn't be able to hear them and Eileen would suffer in intentional silence. She would rationalize everything: I'm already awake, why not let him sleep? Why bother him when I already heard the fighting and have a handle on it? Why not just let him be Fun Dad; he has enough crap to deal with.

And there was the big What If.

What if their kids were born as deaf as Spider?

"You can borrow my kid any time you want to indulge in baby barf and diapers," I offered.

She was supposed to turn and stick her tongue out at me. Instead she said, "Good. I'm borrowing him tonight."

"For?"

"You've got a play date with your wife to go drinking with Topher and Debby."

Nick chuckled.

"What? You're supposed to like Debby. She's *your* sister-in-law," I pointed out.

"It amuses me. Debby had major hots for you and Topher was Lydia's high school boyfriend. How'd you get from Debby freaking out about you getting married to being drinking buddies?"

"It helps that Debby's doing Topher," Paul grunted.

He had a point. "Debby seems to like being someone's center of attention, and Topher never intended to be with Lydia beyond high school, so it's all good."

"Sounds like a porn movie," Eileen said. "Debbie Does Topher."

"Why not?" Nick snorted. "Debby did half of Washington D.C. before she came back here."

"That's cold," I said, even though he wasn't far off the mark; Debby was no angel and had moved back to California to get away from her reputation and her father's stern disapproval of it. She had expected me to be here waiting for her, though I'd never given her any reason to. While she was sleeping her way through a long list of Washington interns, politicians, and soldiers, I was immersed in pre-theological studies in a seminary, with every intention of becoming a priest. It never occurred to me that offering a long distance shoulder to cry on could be mistaken for anything more than it was.

I left the seminary and by the time she moved back to California Lydia's name was indelibly written on my soul; Debby had been sure I'd be available and ready to receive her with open arms, clean sheets, and a jumbo pack of condoms.

"Does Lydia really like Debby or does she just put up with her?" Nick asked.

"Both, I think. I don't think they'd go shopping together but they get along really well when we're all out doing something."

"You all like Topher," Eileen pointed out.

"Aw, Kevin has a best friend," Paul teased.

"Jealous?"

"Maybe a little," he conceded.

I hadn't known Topher well in high school; he was just the guy who had snagged Lydia's attention; he was the safety net I both detested and appreciated. I hadn't wanted to get to know him because he was getting to know her all too well, and it hurt.

He was not the great love of her life and he knew it. When we graduated and he left for college, their relationship was over. When he came home three years later, a little bruised from a failed college football career, he wasn't looking to hook back up with her; he was only looking for a friend. I found him in the parking lot of her apartment building, staring in frustration, trying to decide which door he should knock on.

Lydia needed his reminders. She knew she wanted to marry me someday, but until she saw him and he reminded her of everything we'd said we wanted when we were too young to do anything about it, she didn't realize how badly she wanted to say yes to my frequent proposals. He gently mocked her for her resistance; he'd known he was a placeholder and was all right with it; everyone else had expected us to wind up together, so what was she waiting for?

She was hit with a flood of memories: all the times we played games of *what if*. What if Kevin wasn't going to be a priest, what then? We mapped out a future we were sure we'd never see, including the wedding she wanted, on a beach at sunset, surrounded by family. We planned and plotted all the things we could never have, because *someone* had a vocation.

She dated Topher because she couldn't have me. She slept with Topher because that was a line I refused to cross and curiosity wore her down. But it was me she had loved, and me she had wanted since our first terrifying date as awkward fourteen year old freshmen.

Topher sat in her living room and brought back all those memories in a heady rush so overwhelming that she asked me to propose to her again. Just ask one more time. Please.

Topher tossed a pillow from the sofa onto the floor and told her to say yes, because I was so cute that if she didn't, he would.

Topher, the ex I was supposed to hate, was half the reason that two weeks later we were standing barefoot on the beach, surrounded by our families, promising to do as many of the things we had teased each other with as kids for the rest of our lives.

I *had* to like the guy.

If he was falling in love with the girl I had started to think of as the Evil Blonde One, far be it for me to judge. Debby gave up on me and focused on him; I liked him, Lydia liked him, and once they became a package deal we made the effort to forget that she had been a royal pain in the ass and that he had seen my wife naked.

Only sort of, Lydia pointed out once. You don't see much when you're wiggling around the back of an unlit van at midnight.

Still.

We'd become friends; Topher and I were learning to golf, and we sometimes went out to dinner together. Someday Lydia and Debby might be the kind of friends who did lunch and went shopping, but they weren't there yet.

Paul glanced away from his daughter and her friends and asked, "Where's your much better half this afternoon anyway, Squirt?"

"She and her mom took Michael to the mall. I may see them again sometime this week."

"Just as soon as your checking account is drained," Nick offered.

"Nah. Lydia window shops. I don't know why and I don't get the thrill, but they go out for hours on end and she rarely buys anything."

"I do that with Mom," Eileen said. "It's not the shopping, it's having time with Mom away from you morons and away from Dad."

"We should take Dad shopping," I suggested to Paul and Nick. "Give him a rest from his little blonde hornball."

"How about we take him fishing instead?" Paul asked.

Nick and I both laughed; before we did that, Dad would have to get over his odd squeamishness about baiting a hook.

"I don't see Dad running from the house screaming," Eileen said.

"Poor guy is probably too tired to run," Nick snorted. "Right now he's probably curled up on the kitchen floor in one sweaty, sobbing lump."

"Let's take him camping," Paul said. "No fishing required. We can sit by the lake and drink beer, and he'll have a couple of days to catch his breath."

I wasn't sure we could get him to agree to it, but both Nick and Paul were certain that if we approached him when Mom was there, she'd make him go.

"Anything for father-son bonding," Nick said.

"You just want the beer," Eileen mumbled.

She might have been right, but none of us saw anything wrong with that.

~

Chip

Kevin stayed outside until his grandparents pulled into the driveway; he reluctantly followed his grandmother into the house, face beet red, and he made an effort to look anywhere except at his mother or at me. His discomfort was reason enough for me to plop down at the table across from him, where avoiding me would be so obvious that one of his grandparents would say something; I owed him for interrupting something that was definitely heading somewhere other than the kitchen.

As far as his mother and I had known, everyone was out of the house; we'd have heard Nicole banging through the front door if she ran back inside for something, and Paul had walked in on one thing too many to move around the house quietly. If we'd heard Kevin walking through the living room we could have darted down the hall behind the stairs and into the study, or at the very least warned him that he might not want to come into the kitchen.

My opportunities to make him squirm were limited by the presence of his grandparents and he knew it. He made small talk with them, updated them on his four month old son, his calm disposition and frequent giggles and smiles. Kevin knew that by talking about Michael I would get sucked into the conversation, and he'd be free from my deliberate picking on him.

My in-laws were there to discuss the possibility that they would move in with us; Terry and I wanted them to, either before or after we moved out of my father's oversized house, but they had been dragging their feet on making a decision. They argued that their age made a two story house too difficult; I countered with an offer to turn the study into an apartment for them and a promise that when we did move it would be to a single story house with plenty of room for their privacy. They agreed that they wanted to live closer to their grandkids and great grandkids, but they weren't sure that they wanted to be all that close.

"We have a compromise," my father-in-law announced that evening during dinner. "We'll move closer, but we won't move in with you."

"We have the space, Pop," I started, for the umpteenth time.

"It's not about space; it's about how we want to live. We found a very nice retirement community just fifteen miles from here, and it suits our needs just fine."

Terry was dubious. "Retirement home? Dad, that'll be full of old people."

Her mother cocked her head a touch and smiled. "Hon, what do you think *we* are? And it's not a home. It's a community with a recreation center and swimming pool. We'd have our own apartment and access to immediate help twenty four hours a day. We could even use the cafeteria if I didn't feel like cooking."

"And," the elder Paul added, "we'd be surrounded by people our own age. It's an active place, and I would have guys to go fishing with." He looked at me with an exaggerated eye roll. "Men that don't cry when they have to bait their own hooks."

"I don't cry."

"The point is that we'll have friends right there, but we'll also be close enough that we can see more of you and the grandkids."

Terry was gently gnawing on her lower lip, a sure sign that she was trying to choke back her disappointment. "Do you have a problem with Chip and I checking this place out before you commit to it?"

Translation: *I don't like it, but as long as it gets you close by, I'll accept it.*

"Not at all." Her mother seemed a bit relieved; there wasn't going to be an argument, and she understood her daughter's disappointment.

I nodded my agreement. "I wouldn't mind seeing what you old farts seem to think is fun. I bet you'll even have shuffleboard and a pinochle table."

Translation: *If I get to the paperwork before you do, I can pay for it.*

After they left and the kids were in the back yard, we went into the kitchen to finish cleaning up; Terry stared out into the back yard and said almost mournfully, "It really will be quiet once we've moved. I had really hoped they would move in with us."

"I did, too. I was counting on hearing the pitter patter of little feet again…very old little feet shuffling down the hall."

"Speaking of little feet, did I tell you I bought a pregnancy test kit this morning?"

"What?" I felt a surge of panic, and then tossed the dish towel at her when she started laughing. "That's not funny, Woman."

"Yes, it is. You went pale there for a second, Irish."

She dried her hands on the towel and reached for me, pulling me tight against her. "We'll get used to the quiet," she assured me. "We might even get to where we like it."

"And if we find the right property the kids will all be outside making noise anyway."

"We'll institute a rule that says they have to ring the bell before coming in. Just in case."

"You're still planning on grinding me into dust in our old age, aren't you?"

"It's a thought."

She was about to follow that thought with a kiss when the patio door slid open and Kevin stepped in. He sighed hard and muttered, "Do you two not know what your bedroom is for?" and then he turned around, heading back towards the pool.

"I'll miss that when we move," I told her.

"Being interrupted?"

"Embarrassing Kevin."

"Irish, I think you're going to find ways to embarrass him until the day you die. And even then I think you'll find a way to yank his chain from the grave."

"Probably."

She took a step back, looking into my eyes. "That was a quiet 'probably.' Something wrong?"

"I'd rather not contemplate my death. It's bad enough that I already have more years behind me than I have ahead of me. I'd rather not go there, if we can."

"All right."

She stretched up onto her toes for the kiss Kevin had interrupted, but the door slid open again and Paul walked in. Unlike his brother, he wasn't bothered by his parents being latched together at the lips, and he leaned against the breakfast to wait until she pulled away.

"What?" I growled at him.

"Nick and Kevin and I were talking earlier…"

"Good. Go back outside and talk some more."

"You free this weekend? We thought we'd take you camping and give you a break from the blonde with the wandering hands."

"What makes you think I want a break?"

Terry slipped her arms from around my neck and picked the dish rag back up. "Go, Irish. You'll have fun."

"Beer and a campfire," Paul said. "We can drag Uncle Doug and Grandpa along."

"No girls allowed?" Terry asked.

"Well. Nothing personal, Mom."

"He wants Doug because Doug has a garage full of beer. He wants his grandfather because he has a camper," I pointed out.

"We want Uncle Doug," Paul argued, "because he likes camping. And we want Grandpa so someone can bait your hook if you decide to fish."

"Very funny."

"He'll go," Terry said to Paul. Then to me, "You've been working a lot lately, Chip. You could use a weekend away from the phone and paperwork."

The Blonde One had spoken.

I was going camping with my boys.

~

Terry

"I keep thinking," Chip mumbled drowsily. "When you told me you'd bought a pregnancy test…"

"Forgot I'd had a tubal and got a little excited there?"

"Not in a good way."

"Done with babies, are you?"

"With raising them, yes. Grandbabies… I could hold Michael forever, I think. Or until the next dirty diaper, and then Kevin could have him back. I'd like a few more."

"Grandkids are nice," I agreed. "Those you can send home to someone else. Eventually."

"I'm feeling selfish in my old age."

"Stop it. You're not old."

"Old enough."

"For?"

He mumbled through his fatigue. "I want to be able to get up however late I want, I want to stay up at night as late as I want. I like that we can go anywhere we want without worrying about a babysitter. I like the idea of having dinner with you and no one whining about having to eat peas, other than me."

"And you like the idea of getting naked anywhere in the house you want."

"That too."

"Especially if you have company."

"If it's you."

"Kind of awkward with one of the kids right there."

"Funny," he exhaled.

I waited for the sound of his breathing to even out, hoping he was finally falling asleep. I could practically feel the fatigue seeping from his pores, but knew if I moved he would wake up.

I must have twitched, because a few minutes later he whispered, "My mother died when she was thirty eight, Terry. My father wasn't even sixty."

Going there, I sighed to myself. He was half asleep and going to the places he resisted when he was fully awake.

"You're in good shape, Irish. You watch what you eat, and you work out every day."

"But I can't ignore family history. I'm almost fifty. And I hate that it means I might only have a few years left with you."

"You might have thirty."

"That's not likely. And a few more isn't enough. I need more time with you. I want—"

I lifted up onto my elbow and tried to see his face in the dark. His eyes were only half open, but his lashes were wet and he was fighting tears along with fatigue.

"We all have an expiration date, Chip. I could get run over by a bus tomorrow."

"You're not allowed to die before I do."

"Oh, I get to be the one left behind?"

"I can't stand the idea that you'd go first."

"Well, it wouldn't be a thrill for me, either."

"You would be okay without me."

"No." I kissed him lightly. "I wouldn't."

"I think you would. I think that you would rally the kids around you, and you'd be profoundly sad for a while, but then you'd be okay. I wouldn't get past being profoundly sad."

"Chip…"

"Grant…my father never got over my mother's death. He sat in this house and mourned for years, as if living well would be some kind of betrayal. I didn't get it then. I get it now."

"Your kids will not let grief swallow you up, Irish."

"They can't stop it. I don't want to live without you."

"Not wanting to is different than not being able to."

"I know."

"And I wouldn't want you doing anything to follow me into that great beyond."

"I wouldn't."

"I'll do everything I can to keep you young and healthy until you get very, very old."

"Like groping me in the kitchen?"

"And everywhere else I can get away with it." I kissed him again and snuggled close. "Go to sleep, Chip. You're so tired."

His arms tightened around me and his breathing was starting to slow again, when he whispered, "I used to not be afraid of dying."

"I know."

"I want great grandkids," he breathed, voice trailing.

"I know."

He drifted off; his arms relaxed and I could hear his breathing slow, but he wasn't quite asleep and I was afraid to move.

Max jumped up on the bed; Chip startled, and blurted out, "Promise me we'll never spend another night apart again."

I wasn't sure where that came from, but I whispered, "I promise. Go to sleep, Chip. You're more than halfway there."

He turned just a touch, pulling me a little closer. "Don't die."

"All right."

Within a minute he was completely asleep, and I wasn't sure if I should laugh or I should cry.

2

Kevin

The house hunt was on.

"Topher found out about the development through some guy he works with," I told my dad. "It's an entire court, brand new construction, and it's the first new single family home construction in that town in a long time."

"It's new but priced out of range for most people," he said. "We don't need to jump unless the houses are exactly what we're all looking for."

"The only problem is that there are six houses on the court, not seven," Paul noted. "If Grandma and Grandpa change their minds…"

Dad shook his head. "They won't. I think the fact that they've settled on a retirement community seals it. They're pretty determined to live amongst their own kind."

"Their own kind?" Paul chuckled.

"The old and the extremely active. Your grandmother wants to be with people she can relate to, and your grandfather wants to be around people who actually like to go fishing. Apparently his only son-in-law is a failure."

I could see that. Dad wouldn't hesitate to shoot someone smack in the middle of his forehead if the situation called for it, but to skewer a worm on a hook? It wasn't happening.

Our guide through the row of model homes was a perky brunette who didn't seem to register the notion that the blonde with the death grip on my dad's hand might take offense to her overt flirting. I questioned her intelligence when she kept batting her eyes at him, ignoring that he'd been pretty open that the throng following him was his family, but Dad pretended to not notice her.

"Sales tactic," he said later. "She was after my wallet and nothing more."

We wandered from model to model, feigning disinterest—let's not give them any excitement to pounce upon—while trying to figure out which house fit whom, universally complaining about the size of the bedrooms but oddly thrilled with the three car garages.

When the brunette was done espousing the virtues of each house—"Sure the bedrooms are small but how much time does anyone really spend there? The masters are sizeable and the kids' rooms, well, kids don't take up much space…"—Dad nodded thoughtfully and asked to see the actual homes under construction.

She pointed to a map on the wall, and started to tell him about the neighborhood and its amenities; he stopped her and said firmly, "I won't even consider this if we can't see the actual houses, even if it's just from the outside. Today."

She sputtered. There are workers there right now. Hammers and saws and nail guns and all that. It's dangerous.

Dad didn't care. He thanked her for her time and gestured for us to leave in one happy Davis-Brennan-Stone mass. We turned and filed out the door, but I caught a glimpse of the small smile on his face when the brunette's boss rushed out of his office and stopped Dad before he could get to his car.

Of course we could see the houses. After all, the construction was nearly done. It's not like anyone would be in danger of being run over by a backhoe.

We walked around the corner, a bunch of over grown day care kids being lead on a field trip by the head teacher (minus the holding of hands, because that would have been awkward and weird) to the court where the houses were being built. The front lawns were nothing but dirt, the houses needed paint, but it was quiet and I didn't see any workers.

"All have four bedrooms and two baths," Contractor Guy told Dad.

I could have been insulted; after all he wasn't buying all six houses. We would pay for our own, but his reputation preceded him. Dad was known for buying up huge chunks of real estate, and in a market where houses seriously tipping over the half million mark weren't selling…well, you wanted Chip Davis and his giant wallet taking serious consideration of what you had to sell.

"Lot sizes?" Dad asked. I wanted to get inside and start looking, and he was intentionally making Contractor Guy wait.

"They run between seven thousand square feet, up to fourteen thousand. Enough for some nice sized yards, except for this one." He gestured to the house on the end of the court. "It's got a good sized lot, but it's awkward. It wouldn't be the best choice for someone with little kids."

"How big is that one?" Uncle Doug asked.

"A little over twelve hundred square feet."

"Big enough for us," Aunt Kris said. "Unless you plan on getting pregnant anytime soon."

Uncle Doug nodded thoughtfully. "I considered it. Could be fun."

"Doors open?" Dad asked.

He nodded.

"All right then." He turned to the rest of us. "The grownups will scope out the smaller houses, you breeders can look at the others. But the house with the best back yard is mine. I want a pool."

Translation: *Your mother wants me to have a pool, so I can wear tiny, tiny swimsuits for her amusement as I do laps every morning.*

As Nicole followed Paul into the house next to the one our parents were headed for, I heard her ask, "Daddy? Are we breeding?"

Nick must have heard her, too, because he shouted from across the street, "Sweetheart, Daddy needs to find a girlfriend first!"

Mentally, I'm pretty sure Paul flipped him off.

~

I had to admit, after nearly a lifetime of living in my parents' house, the one Lydia and I were looking at felt tiny, and I was embarrassed that the first thought that popped into my head was 'totally middle class.' But that was exactly what we were after; normal lives for our kids, in the relative safety of a small town.

Lydia seemed underwhelmed, but still interested. "The master bedroom is huge," she said, standing in the middle of the empty room. "The other bedrooms are small but they're big enough for kids. And there are three of them."

"One for Michael and two potential siblings?"

"Unless we get to having a third and I pop out twins like your mother did."

She didn't say it as if it were a horrible idea; she said it as if wondering what to do with four kids in three very small rooms.

"Well, if that happens then we eat up part of the garage and renovate. It's doable."

We revisited each room; the kitchen wasn't huge but it made my mom's current digs look old and worn. There was a formal dining room that opened to a small living room, and on the other side of the kitchen there was an oddly shaped family room with a gas fireplace and, inexplicably, a rack for holding firewood. The back patio was covered, and there was plenty of space for a sandbox and swing set later. The only thing I could see that would need to be changed was the six foot privacy fence between this house and the next.

Fences might make good neighbors, but they didn't make for lots of room for kids to run.

"Could you live here?" I asked as she headed for the front door.

She pointed to the cement under our feet. "As long as there's something on the floor and we can pick out the paint colors, sure. I'd be happier with bigger bedrooms for the kids, but it would work."

"Moving here means a longer drive to work."

"Ten minutes more. Normal people do that, you know. They get in the car and drive."

"Maybe I'll hire a driver."

"You will not! You're so spoiled."

Mom and Dad were already waiting outside with Uncle Doug and Aunt Kris; Contractor Guy looked like he was talking a mile a minute, and Dad was nodding soberly.

"So, "Aunt Kris asked us, "What'd you think?"

"Those bedrooms are tiny," I told her. "So's the living room. I can't imagine more than a couple of us in there at one time."

"That your only kid?" Contractor Guy asked.

"First," Lydia replied. "But we're planning on at least eight or nine more. Might be kind of hard to squeeze them in there."

He didn't miss a beat. "Bunkbeds," he said. "Kids love bunkbeds."

Before I could think of some smart ass thing to say, Nicole was running towards us. "Daddy *has* to get a girlfriend!" she squealed. "That's too big for us!"

"Maybe that dog he's been promising you can have its own room," I said.

She crinkled her nose. "I want cats. I don't have to walk those, and Daddy says I can have *two*."

"So?" Dad prompted Paul.

"Adequate," he said. "Not enough room for a pool, so we'll have to borrow yours."

"Do any of these have a back yard big enough?" Doug asked.

Dad nodded. "Big enough for a short lap pool and a hot tub. I'm not thrilled with the size of the master, though. No fireplace."

Mom patted his arm. "Poor baby. There's a fireplace in the family room."

"Yeah, but we—"

"Let's just leave it at that, all right?"

Spider and Eileen were there, and everyone was looking around for Nick and Katie. Contractor Guy suggested we all go in the house they'd been looking at but we declined in unison.

I'd already walked in on my parents doing nasty things to each other. I didn't need to walk in on my brother.

~

Nicole gave us an out; Contractor Guy wanted to "talk turkey" but Dad didn't want the rest of us to decide anything; no one seemed overjoyed and he wasn't about to debate the merits and drawbacks of the houses versus the location in from of the builder. Just as the guy was warming up, starting to espouse the virtues of the school system and the low, low crime rate—which we were keenly aware of and was the primary reason we were considering the area in the first place—Nicole announced to all that she was *starving* and if she didn't get dinner soon she was *going to die!*

Before Paul could say anything to her about her manners, Dad seized on it.

"My granddaughter says she's hungry, she's hungry," he said to Paul. "She doesn't typically interrupt like that unless she means it."

And she didn't. For the most part Nicole was a polite eight year old. But now she was tired, excited, and hungry on top of it, and it just slipped out.

Dad shook Contractor Guy's hand and said he'd let him know soon.

We headed for the nearest restaurant, a massive steakhouse that seemed out of place in the small town, but Dad swore we'd like it.

Nicole protested the dead things on the walls—a collection of deer heads and stuffed birds—but when her father offered me $50 to eat a two pound steak, she decided I was more amusing than the dead deer were gross.

"All right," Dad said after we'd all ordered, "and without talking all at once…what'd you think?"

"I think that everyone is right," Eileen said, "Those bedrooms are tiny, but the rest of the house was all right."

"Most kids don't have bedrooms as big as yours were," Mom pointed out. "And you wouldn't have if your grandfather had lived longer. You might have grown up in an apartment sharing one room."

Dad flinched at that, but I don't think Mom saw.

They had been separated for two years, and during that time when he had a small apartment, we did share one bedroom when we were with him. He hated it, but he never thought he'd be there that long.

She wasn't thinking in those terms; in her head Nick was the only one of us who had ever lived anywhere but Grandpa Davis's gigantic house.

"Nicole and I don't need that much space," Paul said.

"Until you get a girlfriend and get married and have more babies, and then we'll need a big house!" Nicole said.

He couldn't even reply, because Mom was laughing; there was no point in telling his daughter that was rude when Grandma was worse.

"Nick? Katie?" Dad asked.

"Better than where we're living now," Nick said.

Katie agreed. "One more bedroom than we currently have, and a formal dining room. What's not to like besides the neighbors?"

"Ha. Funny," Paul groused.

Dad looked at Lydia and me.

"Fertile Myrtle here had worried about what we'd do if we wound up with more kids than we'd intended, but it's a three car garage. One of them can live out there."

Michael picked then to let out a high pitched squeal. He was sitting in Lydia's lap, his little hands banging on the table top, and he broke out in a wide grin.

Nick leaned forward and smiled sweetly at his nephew. "We won't let him shove you out there, Mikey, I promise."

"Are you gonna have a baby Uncle Nick?" Nicole asked suddenly.

Quiet. No one knew what to say. Babies had been a sore spot with Nick and Katie, and no one was sure whether they had actually agreed on whether to have one or not.

"Darlin' if I ever have a baby, it'll be a miracle," Nick told her.

She giggled and rolled her eyes. "Not *you*, Uncle Nick."

"Someday, kiddo," Katie said.

"Well, I know how you get one started, if you need me to tell you."

Mom was trying to not laugh, her grin hidden behind clasped hands.

"Grandpa told me how a long time ago," Nick assured her. "And I'm pretty sure he knew what he was talking about."

"Well *yeah*," she said, rolling her eyes. "He did it *three* times. Look at you all!"

We were spared further explanation of our parents' reproductive record by the waitress bringing giant bowls of salad and baskets of warm bread.

"No one is bubbling over with excitement," Dad said after a while. "I think we should pass. The town is nice but I can't see my grandkids in those small bedrooms, and chances are Kevin's kids are going to be huge."

"There's always the garage," I reminded him.

"It's not quite the right place," Uncle Doug agreed. "For the price he wants we could do better."

I wasn't sure if I was disappointed or not; I liked the idea of buying a house for my wife and son, but they were right. It wasn't quite right, and everyone seemed to agree.

Keep looking.

Somewhere out there was The Place. That just wasn't it.

3

Terry

In the years following our reconciliation, Chip and I cultivated a habit of soaking in the bathtub together most nights; if we hadn't had a chance to talk during the day, that was where we did it. I filled the tub with water as hot as we could stand it while he lit candles, and under the watchful eye of Chip's cat, Max, we relaxed together and tried to connect.

Chip barely said a word after we left the restaurant and other than complaining about being too old to sit on the floor while he played with Michael before the grandkids went to bed, I wasn't sure I'd heard him say anything.

Without any prompting he followed me upstairs and took his clothes off while I filled the tub, and he sighed when we slid into the water together.

"You've been a little quiet tonight, Irish," I said, leaning my back against his chest.

"Digesting."

"The steak or something else?"

"This whole moving thing."

"Changed your mind?"

"I'm not sure I ever got to where I completely liked the idea to begin with."

"You want to stay here."

"Not necessarily. The house is too big for just us."

"If we don't move, chances are the kids won't either."

He was quiet for a moment. "Do you realize that we haven't ever been kid-less here? They've all left at some point, but there's always been one here and they keep coming back."

"If we move, we'll be living alone," I pointed out.

"I know. And it's not the where of it…I'm ready to find out what life without my offspring is like, I guess. Moving would get me that."

I turned to look at him.

"I'm not sure we're doing them any favors."

"By letting them live here, or by all of us moving to the same place?"

"Moving," he said. "If it wasn't for that I know Kevin and Lydia would be out already. And Paul would be gone soon."

"Then…?"

"Does the whole thing feel normal to you?"

"Does it matter?"

"I don't know. It just seems like they're supposed to grow up and move out, and not across the street from Mommy and Daddy. Are we stunting their growth by doing this?"

Parenting skills were the fat Chip constantly gnawed at. He worried about whether or not he'd been a good father, and whether or not we were to blame for the wrongs that filtered into our kids' lives. It was a conversation I knew almost by heart but tried hard to not belittle him for. I simply stated the same facts that I always did: Nick left home when he was eighteen and he'd done fine. Kevin left when he was seventeen to go to the seminary; it was just all that…stuff…that sent him home. Eileen did the smart thing and stayed until she was married. She could have moved out and into some sleazy apartment with Spider right after high school, but she knew better. Any one of them could have screwed up a dozen times, but they made good decisions. We did what we set out to do, we raised them to be adults by the time they were eighteen.

He always had something to counter with, and this night it was, "Yet Paul got his girlfriend pregnant when he was fifteen."

"And he didn't run away from it," I reminded him. "He stepped up when he needed to because he *wanted* to, and he's been a very good father."

"That he has."

"Then what?"

"I just want to be sure we're doing the right thing, that's all. It's not this house, Terry. I don't care where we live, just that we're not screwing them up by making this move."

"Up until a few decades ago, families living together were the norm, you know."

"Ever wonder what the fratricide and sororicide rates were?"

"Funny."

"I don't know from normal, Ter. I didn't grow up with it. I just want to be sure that my grandkids have normal, even if their parents aren't."

"Our kids are normal," I said lightly.

He kissed the top of my head. "Reasonably."

"Our kids are close. Isn't that what we wanted for them when they were growing up? Now they like each other well enough that they want to live close enough to be there for each other. And for their kids."

"I know. The whole creating a safe place thing."

"You don't buy that?"

"At some point we'll buy a court," he said. "We'll put fences behind each house and we'll put a gate up at the top of the street. It's a cage, Terry."

"And it's what you wanted to do when we moved into this house. Hell, we were going to do that here right after Michael was born."

"I know."

"Chip." I turned to face him completely, splashing water over the edge of the tub as I slid closer. "They want a better place to raise kids, where they know those kids can knock on any door at any time and someone will be there to protect them. They want their kids to grow up together and be friends. They want their kids' grandparents to live close by. They want *us*, and it's a compliment. How many people do you know whose families are so close they actually want to live next door to each other?"

"I'm not saying we aren't lucky."

"Then I don't get it."

"I think it's just not what I always imagined. I don't know. I just never pictured myself holding court, so to speak."

"King of your castle, you are."

"The King thought he would have abdicated by now and would be off doing kinky things to the Queen on some tropical island beach."

"The King can still do that," I assured him.

"The King would like to do that while he and the Queen are still a little bendy."

"The King is a dork," I snickered, pulling him toward me for a kiss. "And the Queen is still very bendy, if he would like a demonstration."

"He would, very much."

Later, when the cat was disgusted enough to stomp off and we were lying in a sweaty mess on top of the bed, he whispered near my ear, "Long live the Queen."

~

The next day I found him standing in the bedroom in his underwear; he had the waistband hooked under his fingers, and he was staring down, fixated so intently that he didn't look up when I walked into the room.

"Please tell me it didn't fall off," I said.

He didn't flinch. "No, it's still there."

"Good. Because that's my favorite toy, you know."

When he still didn't look up, I went over to him and peeked into his briefs. "Is it doing a trick?"

"You know, they tell a guy that he'll start losing hair as he gets older. They just don't say *where*."

"You won't miss it," I promised.

He finally looked up. "But if I lose all of it how are you going to floss?"

I snatched the waistband from his fingers and let it go with a stinging snap. "I *was* thinking about demonstrating my bendiness again."

"Woman, I haven't recovered from last night yet. Besides, I have to go snoop at the restaurant. Wanna come?"

"Who will we be snooping on?"

"Day bartender. Paul's not sure if the guy is a slacker or if he just doesn't like his personality."

"Does it matter? You can't have a jerk behind the bar."

"It matters if Paul is the only one put off by him. He might be smooth as silk with everyone else."

"Wouldn't he just turn on the charm for you?"

"I doubt he knows who I am. When I'm there during the day I stick to the office or the dining room."

"Ah. Out there flirting with the waitresses, are ya?"

"I like to terrorize the new ones before Paul lets them try a night shift."

"So today we're going to hit the bar and get drunk. Isn't it a little early?"

"You can get drunk. I'm just going to sit there and be a pain in the ass."

"And here I thought today might be different."

"Funny, woman. Just for that you can buy your own drinks."

I raised an eyebrow suggestively. "Wear those faded jeans that I like, and I might buy you lunch."

"You really are a hornball, aren't you?"

"No, if I were a hornball I'd have said 'wear those jeans and you'll *be* lunch.'"

He playfully pointed an accusing finger at me. "The fact that your mind went there, that's the proof. Deep down you're a thirteen year old boy just discovering porn."

"And when you were thirteen, what were you discovering?"

"Apparently that I needed to prepare for a lifetime of you."

"It took you an awful lot of preparation, mister."

He kissed the tip of my nose and headed for the closet. "I'll wear the jeans," he said, "and you can look, but no touching."

This felt backwards, but I wasn't complaining. I'd get to watch him torment some poor young bartender, we'd have lunch together, and I was pretty sure I'd have him out of those jeans by four o'clock.

~

The hiring and firing of bartenders usually fell to Will Parker, who was not only the bar's manager but Paul's assistant manager. Chip hired Will when he left the priesthood to pursue the woman who had captured his heart, when he was too confused about his next step to think about how he would pay the bills.

Will had a doctorate in psychology and had a dozen different avenues open to him, but he decided he liked working behind the bar, where he could still talk to any number of people, but not be responsible for their mental or spiritual health. He loved the job and didn't mind the late hours, but after eight years he finally agreed with Chip that it was time to take more than just two or three days off, and when Paul needed someone to make a final decision on the bartender he'd been struggling with, Will was in the last few days of a four week vacation and was likely being pulled by the hand around Disneyland by his eldest son.

We were greeted at the door of the restaurant by Sherry, the hostess Paul hired after Monica died; Sherry had needed any job she could get in order to face sudden expulsion from her parents' home—she turned twenty two and they shoved her out the door, not caring that she was less than two months from finishing her degree and still deeply wounded over losing her best friend. While Paul was slowly taking the reins from his father, Sherry began busing tables; she quickly worked her way through the kitchen, finally landing the position she had wanted from the beginning. She had a firm hand on the wait staff and the busboys and was the go-to person in Paul's and Will's absence.

If Will quit, Chip was certain Sherry could step into the assistant manager's shoes without a hiccup. And something he appreciated was that she seemed genuinely happy to see every person who came through the door; we stepped in and her smile lit up. While I'd normally chalk that up to it being Chip—smile for the boss—I knew that the panhandler who frequented the corner could come in asking to use the restroom and she'd smile just as brightly for him.

The fact that she was as friendly as she was made it easy for us to come in and not worry that any of the newer employees would be tipped off to who Chip was; she treated everyone as if they were important. Chip quietly asked her to seat us in the bar, and to not let on that he was not only the manager's father, but the owner as well.

She glanced at the bartender and knew what Chip was likely to do, but didn't let on as she sat us at the center stools that he was about to have his feet put to the proverbial fire.

James seemed friendly enough as he made his way from the end of the bar to get our orders; he smiled as he tossed down coasters, and grabbed a basket of popcorn before asking what we wanted.

"Diet Coke," I replied when he asked.

He tilted his head and with a boyish grin said, "Oh, come on. You seem like a mojito kind of girl to me. I can crush some mean mint, you know."

"Just the Diet," I said. "One of us has to drive."

"Point taken. And you, sir?"

Chip was eyeing the bottles on the top shelf. "Grey Goose, tall shot."

James looked up to the line of bottles, sucking in a deep breath. "The Stoli is just as good, and it'll save you a couple bucks."

Chip pretended to consider. "What's in the freezer?"

"Nothing right now. So, Stoli?"

"Shouldn't the good vodka be in the freezer?"

James lifted his shoulders lightly. "It's all out here. Stoli? Smirnoff? Both are really good."

"Grey Goose." When James blanched Chip added, "And put the bottle on the bar. I'd like to crack the seal."

"You seriously want me to get up there for a single shot?"

"I do."

James exhaled sharply and dragged the step stool from the far end of the bar, setting it down with a loud clunk. He had his hand around the bottle of Grey Goose when he said, "I've got some Belvidere up here and it's already open. How about that?"

Chip shook his head.

When the bottle was on the bar, Chip ran a finger from the neck down, pushing a thin layer of dust down to the label. He looked back up to the shelf, and said, "All right, now bring down the Wild Turkey."

"You really don't want to mix those."

"Just get the bottle."

James repeated the same annoyed moving of the step stool and agitated retrieving of the bottle. Chip ran his finger through more dust, shaking his head ever so slightly.

"So what's it going to be? Vodka or whiskey, or mix them for the hangover from hell?"

"When was the last time that shelf was cleaned?"

James' tight smile waned. "Hell if I know. That's not my job."

"You're the bartender, right?"

"What are you, the health inspector?"

"You're the bartender?" Chip pressed.

James leaned against the bar. "Look, I'm just the day guy. The bar manager is on vacation, and he usually deals with the pricier booze. I never get up there."

"Wouldn't his being on vacation make it part of your job?"

"They don't pay me enough. Now do you want a drink or not?"

Chip slid the bottle of whiskey towards him and said, "I would think you'd want to get that shelf cleaned. You know, just in case someone like a health inspector showed up."

"It's not my problem."

"I'd say it is now."

"Look, bud, you want to crack the seal on one of those, go right ahead. I'll even pour you a double if you aim your OCD at something else."

"My OCD is aimed at getting the bar cleaned up." He looked over to the front door, and gestured for Sherry to come over. "Would you get the manager for me?"

James watched her walk towards the office door and was shaking his head. "Oh, come on. He's not going to do anything. I doubt he even knows what the top shelf is."

"Really now."

"Not the brightest bulb in the bunch when it comes to the bar, you know. He's hardly ever in here."

"And yet he's your boss."

"The bar manager is my boss. This guy...Look, I'm just being level. It's not my job to get up there and clean that crap up. He'll just pacify you and tell you it'll get done to shut you up."

Before Paul could say anything, Chip held up the bottle of vodka and said, "You've got a bit of a dust issue. Sticky dust, even."

There was a flicker of annoyed embarrassment on Paul's face, there and gone quickly enough I hoped that Chip missed it. "Didn't

Will tell you to keep the entire bar area clean?"

"He said to keep the traps clean. He never said anything about cleaning off the shelves."

"He shouldn't have to," Chip said.

James spun on his heels and snapped, "Would you just leave already? I'm officially refusing to serve you. I have that right." He turned to Paul and added, "I think he came in drunk."

Paul looked at Chip and was about to say something, but Chip cut him off and said, "He's fired."

"What the hell?"

Chip was enjoying this just a little too much. "James, how long have you been here?"

"Eight months! And I'm damned *good* at it!"

Paul snorted. "So how could you be here than long and not have a clue who signs your paychecks?"

"You—"

"I just work here," Paul said. He turned to Sherry, gesturing towards Chip. "Who is this?"

"That would be Mister Davis, Mister Davis. The owner."

"Like hell," James stammered.

"Granted," Chip said, "we've only been in here a few dozen times since you started working here, but not knowing who we are is no excuse for your attitude. When I suggested you clean that shelf the correct response would have been, 'Yes sir, I think you're right. I'll get right on it.'"

"But that's not my *job*," James insisted.

"Apparently not anymore," Paul said. "Come back tomorrow before the lunch rush starts. I'll have your final check ready."

"You're serious."

"You're done here, James."

"Well," Chip said as James stomped off, "you were right. He's a jerk and not the person we want behind the bar."

"Yeah, but you fired him mid-shift."

"I should have waited?"

"That would have been nice. In about two hours people are going to start filtering in, and in two and a half I'll have a full bar and quite possibly no one to serve them."

"You're screwed, aren't you?" Chip asked lightly.

I patted him on the arm. "I think that you're tending bar until the next shift starts."

"Hey. You're supposed to be on my side. Besides, you promised me lunch, and I'm hungry."

"Surprise, Irish! You're in a restaurant."

He glared playfully. "You're no fun. All right, Paul, you've got a bartender until four o'clock."

"Until five," Paul said.

"Get on the phone, son. Get someone to come in early. Queen Gumby and I have plans."

"Who?"

"Oh my God, Chip! Paul, ignore him. He'll work"—I poked at Chip's side—"until someone else comes in."

"Great." Paul reached behind the bar for a wet towel, and dropped it in front of Chip. "The top shelf needs to be cleaned. Have fun."

~

I could have gone home while Chip tended bar, but it was quiet and I reasoned that I'd only have to turn around in two hours to pick him up. After an hour and only serving two customers he called Kris and Doug to come keep us company, and then called Kevin when the bar suddenly filled and the next shift's bartender clocked in sick.

"I am too freaking old for this," Chip grumbled during a lull. "I'm not meant to be on my feet for hours at a time. My feet hurt, my back hurts, and oddly my arms hurt."

"So go sit down, old man," Kevin kidded.

"Like I'll give you the satisfaction."

"You're not old," Kris told Chip. "It's just that young wife of yours is wearing you down. You're killing yourself trying to keep up with her."

"Oh, God," Kevin sighed.

Chip ignored him. "I really do need two or three nights of good sleep. That would make a huge difference."

"My ego is not so fragile that you can't beg off with a headache once in a while," I said.

Chip leaned across the bar, and with a sly grin said, "Lady, have you seen my wife? Trust me, she's hot enough that you'd take one look and suddenly want to switch teams. She bats those blue eyes at me and I just have to *do* things to her."

I started to tell him that was sweet, but Kevin groaned and told his father to stop already. "People can *hear* you."

Chip pushed a little further across the bar and kissed me, just long enough to make Kevin squirm.

"I am so not related to you two," he grumbled as he walked away.

Chip slowly backed away, reaching for his lower back. "Holy shit, I used to be able to do that without it hurting. When did I get this freaking old?"

4

Terry

The bedroom was dark when I woke up, but Chip was standing in front of the closet door mirror in his underwear, enough light bleeding from the bathroom that I could see him clearly. He was standing sideways, a hand on his stomach, and he was looking in the mirror with obvious distaste.

"While I like the view," I said sleepily, "aren't you supposed to be at the gym right now?"

"I'm leaving in a few minutes."

"Checking out what you want to work on?"

He sighed hard. "No. I just realized I'm getting fat. Look at this." He pinched at the skin on his waist, pulling up less than a quarter of an inch. "I don't get it. I haven't changed my diet and I work out just as much…"

"Water weight," I said.

"I don't think so."

"You're not fat."

"I got on the scale. I've gained fifteen pounds in the last month."

I sat up, pushing hair out of my eyes. He was honestly upset, looking at his tiny amount of body fat with more upset than he had upon his missing pubic hair. "You don't look like you've gained anything, Chip. If you hadn't weighed yourself, I never would have guessed."

"This sucks. It's like my body knows I'm turning fifty soon and it's rebelling."

"It's fine. And you either need to put some pants on and head to the gym, or come back to bed. Either way you'll get a work out."

The corners of his mouth turned up in a slight grin. "You have to wait a while, Woman. Parts of me still feel abused from your three-in-the-morning grab fest."

"That was several hours ago."

He sighed and reached for his jeans. "Yeah, but I'm old now. It takes me longer to bounce back than it does you. Just wait there, I'll be back in a few hours."

~

Doug

"Do you remember," Chip asked me when we were in the steam room, a towel held over his face, "a year or two ago when you warned me that once Terry hit menopause her libido might dwindle?"

"I do."

"Why didn't you tell me just the opposite could happen?"

"Are you complaining again?" I asked.

"Doug, I'm *tired*."

"Eh, you'll live. And she's not *in* menopause…just getting there."

"So I get to catch my breath, when?"

"Oh…in five to ten years."

He peeked over the edge of his towel. "You're freaking kidding me."

"Could be longer."

"Holy crap, I have to find something for her to do."

"Chip, she already did." I leaned back and chuckled. "You."

"That's not funny."

"Yes it is," I assured him. "And you've said before it doesn't really bother you and you wouldn't tell her no if it did."

"It doesn't bother me, exactly, but between her and getting woken up by the baby crying…I am so freaking tired. I need sleep."

"You need something."

"And now this camping trip with the boys…are you sure you and Spider can't come?"

"Wish I could," I said. "I have too many patients on the books for Friday and Saturday and Spider has parent teacher conferences."

"Somehow I doubt I'll get much sleep in Pop's camper."

"Make the kids sleep outside."

"The bed in that thing is hard as a rock," he said.

"You're tired," I agreed. "You're worried about your heart and your family history. You're achy and you've complained about some gained weight."

"I know. I'm a whiner."

"Let me ask you something. Not as your friend, but as your doctor."

"I'm all right, Doug."

I waited.

"Fine, ask."

"When did you start losing body hair?"

He lowered the hand towel. "What the hell? You were checking out my junk when I was getting undressed?"

"No, I meant leg hair and arm hair, but now that you mention it…"

"The suckitude of getting old, that's all."

"Chip, I'm ten years older than you and trust me, I still have it all."

"Terry assures me I won't miss it."

"That's not the point. Are you cold a lot? Dry skin? Brittle nails?"

"No. Why?"

"Just a hunch. I want you to let me draw blood."

"Exactly what do you think is wrong with me?"

"Thyroid," I said. "And if that's it, we get you on medication and you should perk back up."

"And I'll be able to keep up with Terry?"

"I don't think there are enough drugs in the world for that, but you'll be able to give her a run for her money."

"Fine." He got up and headed out into the locker room. "But I don't want you sticking me with anything. Let that cute blonde assistant do it."

~

"I agreed to bloodwork, Doug. Why do I need an EKG?"

I gestured for him to lie back on the exam table so that the nurse could hook him up. "I thought an entire physical was implied. You're overdue, anyway."

"You've never done this before."

"You've never been fifty before. And great news! Before you leave you can schedule your colonoscopy."

"Like hell."

"Welcome to middle age, Chip. It's full of fun things like tubes up your ass. And the prep...the prep is especially fun."

"You are not shoving a tube up my ass."

"Not personally," I agreed. "I won't even be in the room."

"I don't even want you in the room now," he grumbled. "How long until you get the blood test back?"

"By the time you get back from not sleeping in the wild, I should have it."

"And you think I'm sick?"

I was watching his heart rate on the monitor. "Well, your heart is certainly beating just fine. Pulse is in the fifties, nice strong rhythm. Your blood pressure is terrific."

"So?"

"So quit worrying about your heart."

"But you still think something is wrong."

"I think that your thyroid is a little out of kilter. It's not anything to worry about. If it's low, we'll put you on a replacement and you'll start to feel better."

"And if it's not?"

"Then we'll dig a little deeper. But I'll bet you a hundred bucks you're at least borderline hypothyroid."

"That was a lot of blood for a stupid thyroid test."

"Quit whining. And I'm looking at everything, not just your thyroid."

He looked up at the nurse. "He's lying. He had you take all the blood because he's mean and he's tired of losing to me at eight ball."

"Sure. Five tubes of blood makes up for over three decades of humiliation."

"Well, that and the tube up my ass..."

"I'm not kidding about that, Chip. Make the appointment."

He lifted an eyebrow, a definite *eh* response.

"Fine. I'll tell your wife it's time, and she'll make the appointment for you. And she'll drag your sorry ass in here kicking and screaming if she has to."

He sat up and pulled the EKG pads off. "You suck."

5

Kevin

Grandpa's reaction to the invitation to go camping was less enthusiasm and more like "Four days by the lake with you four? Two of you are two prissy to pee behind a tree, one of you is afraid of bugs, and my son-in-law folds up into a tight little ball if I whip out a fishing pole. You take the camper and leave me home with my air conditioning and big screen TV."

We borrowed two fishing poles along with the camper even though we all knew they'd remain in the rod rack bolted to the camper's ceiling. We had to at least make him think we'd give his favorite pastime a try.

The camper was battered and beaten and almost as old as Dad, who complained about all the bumps and jerks inflicted on his back as he drove. Paul managed to grab the front seat, leaving Nick and I to bounce along painfully in the back.

We spent most of the two hour ride to the lake picking on Paul, teasing him over his lack of a social life, smacking down any of his claims that he wasn't necessarily as socially backwards as we assumed. There were women he was interested in; just because he didn't talk endlessly about them didn't mean they didn't exist.

Nick explained, in terms meant for a small child, that the women we dream about don't count after we wake up. It was time for Paul to man up and start dating. "Girls over twenty one don't have cooties," he told Paul. "You can touch them and everything!"

"What makes you think I don't have someone I get all touchy with?"

"Alone time in the shower doesn't count," Dad pointed out.

"You can all just bite me."

From the back of the camper Nick snorted and said, "You'd enjoy it more coming from a woman."

"You'll have to take my word for it. There might be someone I'm interested in."

"Son, you'll have to take *my* word for it. Just being interested doesn't get you anything more than frustrated."

We were still giving Paul ten kinds of crap when we pulled into the campsite and set up lawn chairs just outside the camper. He heaped it right back at us, proclaiming his undying devotion to ten different women, and never seemed to get pissed off that we were aiming everything we had right at him.

As afternoon wore on, Dad went from active participant in the Let's Pick on Paul game to partly-interested observer; he laughed in all the right places but was obviously no longer into the game. When Paul brushed us off to take a phone call from Nicole, Dad excused himself, saying he wanted to take a short walk.

Nick and I surmised we'd finally worn his nerves to a frazzle and he would be back by the time Paul was done promising his daughter he wasn't having too much fun without her, but when he was still gone an hour later, I went looking for him.

I found him not far from where we'd set up camp, sitting under a tree. If he heard me approaching, he didn't show it, but he also didn't seem surprised to hear my voice.

"If this is as far as you got before running out of breath, I'm sticking you in a condition class and whipping your ass back into shape."

He didn't look up. "I can still run your sorry ass into the ground. You boys missed me so much you had to come find me?"

"You said short walk and I figured you'd be gone fifteen or twenty minutes, not an hour."

"Sorry about that. I wasn't paying attention to the time."

"No worries." I sat next to him, trying to see what he found so fascinating about the lake. "Fish jumping or something?"

"No, I was stopped by an odd sense of déjà vu. It took me a minute to figure it out, but this is where your Mom and I camped when Nick was just a baby."

"So you sat down to contemplate the memory of an overwhelming desire to toss Nick into the lake? I imagine he was a pain in the ass even then."

"Your mom left him with Doug and Kris. Coming out here was her idea."

"*Mom* wanted to camp?"

"She was pretty determined. Who was I to say no?"

"I can't picture her out here. She may be the only person who's more squeamish than you are about worms and bugs."

"And she hasn't been since."

He was fixated on the water, determined to not look anywhere else. His hands were on his knees, fingers clenching the fabric of his jeans.

"It wasn't a good trip?"

He wasn't seeing the water. His gaze was fixed on it, but he was seeing the twenty year old blonde wonder that had ripped his breath away.

"It became a good trip. But it was my fault she felt like she had to get me somewhere I couldn't run from, and if I'd refused...I don't think you'd be here."

He was not necessarily speaking to his youngest son; he needed someone to listen, and I was less likely to unintentionally make fun of him. Paul and Nick would mean well, but either one could miss the bigger picture and dismiss the fact that our father was sitting here in obvious pain.

Paul would turn it into something about sex; Nick would tell him to get the sand out of his vagina.

I had no problem with the depth my father's feelings ran.

"Why not, Dad?"

"My stupid temper," he said.

"What happened?"

He sucked in a deep breath, pausing to consider before he said anything.

I watched the water with him, waiting until he was ready.

"You know about my father, right?"

"You didn't know he was your father until just before he died,"

I said, thinking that was the nugget of family trivia he was chewing on.

"And when he did—I don't know what happened to me, but I damn near fell apart and instead of letting your mother hold me together, I kept pushing and pushing…It was all anger, all the time, and I took it out on her and on Nick."

"How?"

He glanced at me sideways. "No, don't even think that. I never hit either one of them. But I think she was afraid that might happen. I was right there with her but not *there*. Nick was just a baby and he was talking like a toddler and I barely noticed. He'd ask me to play with him and I'd shut him down…I couldn't have a normal conversation with your mom; I snapped at her all the time and just expected her to suck it up. I was so fucking mean, Kevin."

"Depressed?"

"Doug thought so."

"And he didn't treat it?"

"They didn't hand out Prozac like candy then. And Doug thought it was just a whole lot of sadness and anger I wasn't controlling. He told me to set a time frame and if I hadn't snapped out of it, he'd send me to a shrink."

"Nothing wrong with that. Did you?"

"I didn't have that kind of time."

"So you went…camping?"

"So she got Doug and Kris to watch Nick, they shoved me into the car, and she brought me here."

"It's an odd kind of marital therapy, but whatever works."

Bare nod of the head. "It was her last ditch effort. From here there was nowhere for me to run. Either I pulled my head out of my ass and reconnected with her, or she was leaving me."

My gut reaction was to tell him that she never would have done that, but we both knew better. "So you reconnected."

"She helped me figure out where my anger was coming from and let me know it was all right to be pissed off as long as I didn't take it out on her. So yes, we reconnected. If we hadn't…"

"Paul and Eileen and I wouldn't be here."

"Paul would be. I didn't know that she was pregnant… I don't doubt that she would have taken Nick and left if I'd made the wrong choice, and I may have never really known Paul at all."

"She wouldn't have cut you out of their lives."

"Then? I think she would have. She wouldn't have had much of a choice."

"Dad, when you guys separated a few years ago, she fought to make sure we had a relationship with you. There were weekends when we wanted to do other things but she wouldn't allow it. It was always 'he's your *father*, you owe him this.'"

"Gee, thanks."

"We were kids. We were entitled to be selfish and stupid."

"I know."

"The point is that she didn't cut you out of our lives. You would have known your kids."

"A few years ago I deserved to be your father. Back then, I didn't deserve to be much of anything for anyone."

"And both times, you got her back," I reminded him.

"I did, indeed."

"Then what? Why does being here make you so sad?"

"It doesn't. I like being out here with you kids."

"Then…?"

He bit his bottom lip as if he was considering whether he wanted to share any more of what was on his mind or not. "My mother died when she was thirty eight," he said. "And my father was somewhere in his fifties."

"Fifty four," I offered.

"Both had heart attacks. I don't know anything about their parents or siblings, but the fact that they both died young…"

"Doesn't mean that you will," I said.

"I've had this conversation with your mother. I know all the obvious things. I'm more active than either of them was. She's anal about my diet and Doug watches my health. I try to stay in shape. But sometimes you can't fight the inevitable and it pisses me off to no end that I may only have another five or six years."

"The idea doesn't thrill me, either."

"I can't stand that." He finally looked away from the water and at me. "How would you feel if you realized you might only have a few more years left with Lydia? As little as four or five?"

"Cheated, " I guessed.

"Exactly."

"So you can't stand the idea of not having enough time with Mom? I get it. I think it might drive me a little bit crazy."

"I'm pretty sure she thinks I am a little bit crazy."

"You didn't really want to come with us, did you? I won't be insulted if you didn't."

"I did want to come. I need to spend more time with my boys."

"But?"

"But I also hate the idea of losing even one night with my wife."

His wife, not our mother.

"We can go home," I said.

"No, we can't. My sudden separation anxiety isn't fair to any-one. And don't say anything to Nick or Paul, understand?"

"All right. But face it, if we'd brought another car, you'd make an excuse to go home, wouldn't you?"

He turned back to the lake. "I'm sorry."

"Don't be *sorry*, Dad. It's not personal. How can I take it personally when you're basically saying you love *my* mother so much that it hurts to be away from her?"

That made him smile, just a little.

"And no, I won't say anything to Nick or Paul, because I don't think they'd get it. Not completely."

"Nick might."

"I'm not sure he would. He's a lot like you sometimes, but I don't see him looking at Katie the way you look at Mom. He and Katie love each other, but I don't see either of them as being half of the other."

"And you have that," he said.

"I think I do."

"No, you *have* that, Kevin. But the difference between you and me is that I don't think you'll ever torture Lydia with emotional gymnastics."

"No, I won't, and you know why?"

"Enlighten me."

"Because I paid attention. I saw how much pain your separation caused you, and I was just smart enough to realize that most of it could have been avoided if you'd just talked to each other. And when you got back together, I realized that a whole lot of potential trouble was smoothed over every time you showed her you respected her and every time you asked her what she thought and what she wanted, and you did more than take her opinion at face value."

"You almost make it sound like our stupidities were a good thing."

"How you handled them when you were wading through all that muck, trying to get back together...and how you treat Mom as if she's the most important thing in the universe—it was a gift, Dad. Lydia and I have our issues—and I admit they're mostly mine—but we talk about them. And I will always try to treat her with the same respect you treat Mom. I see you treasure her every day. I can't offer my wife anything less."

"If that's the biggest thing you take from me, then I did something right with you."

"I think I turned out all right."

"That you did."

"You're a good father, Dad. Whatever mistakes you made with Mom, you've always been a really good dad."

He reached out and grabbed me by the neck, pulling me in so he could kiss me right at the temple.

"You're a good grandfather, too."

"There you go, trying to make me feel old."

"That's just it, you're not old. Not yet."

"Almost fifty."

"And fifty isn't fatal."

"So your mother tells me."

"And my mother happens to be one of the wisest women I know."

"Yes, she is."

"So listen to the wise woman and instead of freaking out about dying in five years, concentrate on all the days that you *do* have with her. And start planning the party for when you don't have any of us underfoot and you have an entire house to yourselves."

"I'm already planning that," he said.

"Do me a favor and lock your freaking door so I don't accidentally walk in on it," I said, getting up. "I haven't recovered from the last time."

I left him sitting there watching the water, but he laughed as I walked away.

When I made it back to the camper I pulled my cell phone out of my backpack, and without asking Nick or Paul what they thought, dialed home.

We were only two hours away, and she could easily make it before dark.

~

Nick was about to make a smart assed comment in reply to Paul's fumbling hint that he had a potential date when Dad wandered back from his spot under the tree. He glanced around the campsite, making a mental note of the stack of firewood Nick and Paul had gathered, and the number of beer cans already under Paul's and my lawn chairs.

He didn't say anything, but he sighed deeply before he sat down.

"Quit picking on your brother," was all he said.

Paul didn't mind; he could dish it out as well as he could take it, and was soaking it up so he'd have a reason to pick on Nick later.

"Too many women to chose from," he said to Nick, though his eyes were on Dad, who looked tired and had leaned forward, his elbows on his knees. "How can I just pick one of them?"

"One at a time is all you need," Nick pointed out.

"What, a rotating schedule? Mondays for blondes, Wednesdays for brunettes, Fridays for redheads?"

"What about Tuesdays and Thursdays and weekends?"

"A guy has to rest sometime."

I was curious. "Have you had a date at all?"

Dad looked up. "That's none of our business, Kevin."

"It's all right," Paul said. "And no, Kevin, I haven't."

"Still too soon?"

Paul's wife had been dead for a year and two months; while he had loved her his marriage was mostly turmoil, and no one expected his self imposed social exile to last this long.

"Seriously, son, don't answer that if you don't want to. How long you grieve isn't up for debate or even discussion."

"If I don't, they're just going to keep picking on me, and one of these days they'll do it in front of my daughter."

"No, Paul," Nick said. "I'm an ass and I'll torment you until you crack, but I wouldn't upset Nicole."

"Besides," I added, "she's checking out every available woman in the dojo, rating their worthiness and deciding who she's going to introduce to you."

"I know. I get a running commentary on all the moms she thinks are available, but she still has these major moments where the only thing she wants is her mother, and if she can't have that, she wants me. I'm not sure she's really ready to move past the idea of Daddy dating into the reality."

"So Nicole might not be ready for Daddy to have a social life, but Daddy is," Dad mused.

"Basically."

"Nicole may never be ready," I said.

"No, but there's going to come a day when I'll know she can adjust to someone else in my life."

"But if you're ready..." Dad started, letting the argument trail off.

"I miss Monica," Paul admitted. "But yeah, I've wanted to start dating for a while now."

"So ask someone out," I said, and before he could protest I added, "She doesn't have to know. You're not going to introduce her to anyone until you're at least halfway serious, right?"

"She should know, Kev."

"You should have a social life. And I'm a willing babysitter."

"So are your mother and I," Dad said.

"What, I lie to her and say I'm at work?"

"No," Nick said, "you tell her you're going to dinner with some friends. Or to a movie. She doesn't need to know it's a date. She *is* okay with you having friends, right?"

"Why is this so important to you?"

"Because we love you," Dad said.

Nick snorted. "Well, he does. The rest of us, we just need more ammo against you."

I was about to offer Paul a few introductions, single women from the dojo that Nicole knew nothing about or that she hadn't considered because they didn't come with instant siblings, but the thought was interrupted by the sound of tires crunching on gravel.

They all turned to see who it was; I watched Dad, waiting for the expression on his face to change.

He didn't disappoint. When he realized the blue sedan that had pulled in beside the camper was the same one he had washed and waxed just a few days before, the fatigue left his face and he fought back a smile.

In unison Nick and Paul wondered out loud, "Mom?" and they both got up to go over to her car.

Dad got up, too, gesturing for me to get out of my chair. "Thank you," he said, kissing me again.

"I still won't tell Paul and Nick. But you weren't going home and you needed her here."

"They'll want to know why."

"Yeah, I've thought of that. And I'll figure out something to tell them, but for now, just go rescue her from them."

~

"I don't buy that Mom just wanted to bring beer," Paul said later.

Dad had grabbed a blanket and led Mom down to the small beach. In the dimming light they were almost a silhouette against the sky; they sat on the blanket shoulder to shoulder, her head on his shoulder. They hadn't started groping each other yet, but I figured that would begin in less than half an hour, when the sun would be down enough that they could presume at least a little privacy.

"I called her," I admitted.

"Aw. Kevin missed his mommy," Nick chortled.

"Yes, I did. The idea of a couple nights out here with you made me I realize I needed my mommy."

Paul handed me a beer. "Dude. You're here to protect *us*. If you need Mom, we're all screwed."

"I'm pretty sure Mom can protect us. I hear she has a mean snap kick."

Nick waved off the bottle Paul held out to him. "Why is she really here?"

"Is it a problem?"

"No. Just curious. You're a bit of a pansy, but not *that* much."

The half-lie that slipped out surprised me. "When I went to look for Dad earlier I found him over there"—I pointed off to the left—"sitting under a tree. He'd just realized that this is the same spot he and mom camped when Nick was a baby, and he was wishing he could share it with her again. Apparently it was something special."

"But," Paul guessed, "he didn't think he could get her to come out here if he asked."

"I was surprised that she'd ever been camping to begin with. Mom is not the outdoorsy type."

"So you called her to surprise him?" Nick asked.

"I didn't think you'd mind," I said. "Dad only came in the first place to make us happy. He's not exactly the camping type, either. I figured with Mom here he'd at least have a good time."

"Well, she brought beer, and she brought Uncle Doug's best, so she's pretty much ensuring we all have a good time."

"Except for Nick, who is obviously not drinking," I pointed out.

"I figured if I did you'd beat the holy crap out of me," he said.

"You've got nothing to prove to me." A year and a half earlier, we wanted Nick to stop drinking. He was stressing out over quitting law school and accepting a position with the agency, and had started to drink far more than anyone was comfortable with, especially his wife.

For her sake, he stopped drinking. No one thought he was an alcoholic, but he stopped anyway.

Paul held out another bottle to him. "Only if you're sure you can stop at one or two," he said.

"You're in charge of the cooler, Paul. I don't get more than two tonight."

"I'm not your babysitter. Don't open that if you're not sure."

"I drink occasionally, Paul," Nick told him. "And Katie knows. She's fine with it now that I don't exist on beer and weed."

"And there they go," I muttered, watching Mom and Dad.

"So she kissed him, Squirt," Paul snorted. "So what?"

"So nothing. I just figured they'd wait until it was darker to start mauling each other."

"I'd hardly call that mauling. I've seen them do worse before breakfast."

Nick leaned over, rooting around in his backpack. "I hope I can get this without a flash."

"What?" I asked.

He pulled his camera out. "Look at them, Kevin. Them against the sky and the water…that's a beautiful picture."

I had to give him that. He quietly shot a series of photos, Mom with her head on Dad's shoulder, Dad sneaking a kiss; she jumped up as if she was about to run and he caught her within two steps, pulling her into his arms and up off her feet, I could hear her laughing, and reasoned that I could stand it if they started grabbing each other as long as clothing didn't go flying in all directions.

~

Chip

If Paul and Nick minded that their mother crashed what was supposed to be a No Girls Allowed camping trip, they hid it well. She was greeted with hugs, and when she opened the trunk and showed them the cooler of beer, with kisses as well.

"Your Uncle Doug's home brew," she told them. "He sent forty bottles and said if it's not enough to blame me because I wouldn't let him add a second cooler to the trunk."

"Well, you're mean," Kevin teased.

Later, when Nick had a campfire going and the sun was starting to slide from the horizon, I grabbed a blanket from the back of the camper, took Terry by the hand, and headed for the strip of sand near the water, the same spot we'd once spent more than half the night talking.

"This looks familiar," she said lightly.

"We did nasty things to each other right here over twenty five years ago, woman."

"And you were hoping to repeat them?"

"Sadly, we have an audience."

We sat on the blanket and watched the sun start to slide past the horizon. She inched as close as she could get, her cheek resting on my arm.

"I hope the boys don't mind that I showed up out of nowhere," she said.

"Kevin obviously doesn't."

"He told you he called me?"

"It wasn't hard to figure out. I'm glad he did. I was missing you and he knew it."

"Perceptive, isn't he?"

"Indeed." I was not telling her I'd whined to our youngest son; let him seem like a genius rather than me coming across as pitiable.

I'm not above using my kids.

She slipped her hand into mine. "I was missing you, too. We're kind of pathetic, aren't we? You'd been gone for all of three hours and I was thinking that it was going to be a long, lonely night. Your cat is not the best company."

"I did make you promise that we'd never spend another night apart."

"You remember that?" She lifted her head to look at me. "You were so out of it that night I figured you'd have no memory of anything we talked about."

"I was feeling very raw. I remember all of it and I thank you for not poking fun at me for it."

"Chip. It was funny but not *funny*. You don't get that emotional very often."

"No, but I've noticed it more often lately. I think I get a little mushy when I'm tired."

I was tired a lot, and she knew it; it was her fault I was tired a lot.

"I am flattered that you asked me to not die," she said.

"You would be doing me a big favor if you didn't."

"Well, it would make me happy if you returned the favor, you know."

"I'm going to try my damndest."

"Know what else would make me happy?" she asked.

"I'd like to make you ecstatic, but our kids are watching."

"Very funny. Just a kiss. If they can't stand that, then they can all crawl into the camper and go to bed."

"I suppose we could horrify Kevin again and start getting all grabby."

She kissed me, lips lingering just long enough to make me think she could be taking me seriously. "Kevin protests, but deep down he's happy we're still horny for each other. It gives him hope for himself in twenty years or so."

"I suspect Lydia will be trying to break him the same way you keep trying to break me."

"Poor baby."

"You know, sometimes I wish Mother Nature wasn't so mean. If you could be with my twenty year old self, you might be happier."

"I understand your twenty year old self was not the man I wanted to spend the next eighty years with. I'd much rather spend a little time waiting for you to catch your breath than live with him."

"All righty then, my twenty three year old self. You did quite a bit to him right here."

"Nibbled on his sense of humor, I did."

We both sighed.

"We should stop talking about that," she mused.

"Probably. You're giving me ideas I should not have with those yoyos sitting back there."

"You already had those ideas."

"Well, yeah. But now you're kind of making me wish we were alone."

"Just kind of?" Her hand slid across my thigh as she kissed me again. "I'm thinking more than kind of, mister."

"Jesus, Terry, don't."

"I can be discreet."

"No one is that discreet."

"Well, not if you start moaning *oh my god* at the top of your lungs."

"Don't make me pick you up and toss you into the lake."

"Fine." She moved her hand to my knee. "You owe me."

"It is seriously not fair that I'm on the downslide while you're peaking all over the place."

"I get one last hurrah before full on menopause hits," she said. "It's fair enough."

"One last hurrah? Doug did tell you this could go on for a good *ten* years?"

"You sound frightened."

"I think I should be."

"I'll be gentle," she promised.

"You need to distract me from your impure impulses. Who has my granddaughter while you're out here trying to get all grabby on me?"

"You're no fun," she sighed dramatically. "She's with Lydia and Michael."

"I called him Mickey the other day. Kevin got pissed."

"You can get away with calling him Mikey."

"It's more fun to annoy my son."

"What do you think you'd have gone by if your parents hadn't changed your name?"

"Chip."

"Funny."

"Grant would have called me Michael. He wasn't big on nicknames. I was Jeremy and my brother was David. Period. But he also didn't throw a fit when everyone else called me Chip or when I started calling my brother Dave."

"Still don't know where 'Chip' came from?"

"All the people who could tell me are dead. Kris says in all the time she was with Ron, he never mentioned it."

"I get the feeling Ron never told Kris much of anything while they were married."

Ron Gallery, Kris's first husband. I'd thought he was my father, and Ron never knew any different. He died thinking I was his son because no one wanted to break his heart with the truth.

"It sucked for Ron, but I'm glad she followed her heart and married Doug."

"Well, listen to you, Mister Romantic."

"I can be mushy sometimes."

"You're very good at it," she said. "My daughter-in-law tells me that your ability to wax poetic rubbed off on your youngest, and he's quite comfortable with being all drippy and mushy."

"Good for him. But it's not like I sat him down and gave him lessons."

"No, but I'm sure he's overheard some of the drippier things you've said to me over the years."

"It might not be that."

"Then what? He had to learn it somewhere."

"I think he learned what not to do, Terry. He's determined to never let himself drift so far from Lydia that he finds himself sitting on some random apartment balcony watching little kids play in the pool below."

"We certainly showed our kids the worst of what we could be, didn't we?"

She didn't apologize; typically any time I mentioned our separation she'd blanch and fall all over herself to say she was still sorry. That she didn't was forward motion, and it had only taken nine years to get there.

"I think," I told her, slipping my arm across her shoulders, "that we spared them from the worst of us. They didn't have to see us shouting and they didn't hear either of us verbally rip each other apart."

"Still. They went through two pretty horrible years."

"And they have the scars from it. But they healed up quite nicely."

"Kevin and Eileen did. Nick and Paul, I'm not as sure."

That surprised me. "Why not?"

"Nick takes Katie for granted. He just assumes that because they had this great teenage love and that they're still together that he doesn't have to work terribly hard to make her happy. Everything is on his timetable, too. And Paul…"

"Paul would probably not have Nicole if we hadn't temporarily derailed."

"I don't think he would. I think if you'd been home all along you might have nipped his hormonal impulses in the bud before they got out of control. I was too blind to realize what he was up to…then surprise, you're going to be a grandmother."

"Well," I ventured, "would you trade Nicole to get those two years back?"

"Chip, that's a horrible thought."

"But there it is. Paul had sex with any girl he could talk into it from the time he was fourteen right up to when he got Monica pregnant. He ran wild because I was off watching little kids play in the pool. It's fairly certain that we would not have our granddaughter if we hadn't split up."

"I can't imagine her not being here."

"Right there is reason enough to have no regrets."

"Paul's life would have been so much less painful, though."

"He would have had it much easier," I agreed. "I'm not sure that it would have been better for him in the long run. He really was a selfish horny little teenager. If fatherhood hadn't tripped him up I imagine he might have been a whole lot more like I was."

"That's a sad parallel," she said quietly.

"How so?"

"Paul worked hard at being a good father, but he cheated on Monica more than once and he was a little shit, right up until just before she got sick. And then a couple of months later she was gone…it took her dying for him to really grow up."

"And it took someone dying for me to get there, too."

Paul's dead someone was his wife; mine was a teenage hooker I'd promised to marry; instead I crushed her. Monica died from bone cancer; Brenda Webb killed herself in my apartment.

She looked up at me. "Do you ever visit her grave, Chip?"

"What? Where did that come from?"

"It's fine if you do. I know Kris visits Ron's grave and makes sure it always has flowers."

"I don't. Once, a long time ago, the thought ran through my head that she deserved a better headstone than she had, but I didn't do more than make sure that happened."

"I visit your parents' graves," she admitted.

That surprised me. She liked Grant but had never known my mother, and was not her biggest fan based on what she did know.

"Why?"

"Because they had you," she said simply. "I don't go often, but once in a while I go and sit there, and wonder if they know what you're up to and that they have grandkids. Sometimes I brag to them how wonderful you are to me."

Bragging to Grant, most likely; I doubted she cared what my mother might have thought.

"Thank you for that. It means a lot to me."

She snuck in another long kiss.

"It scares me sometimes, too, Chip. I sit there and realize that someday I'll be at my own parents' graves. Sooner than I'd like."

"Your mom is too stubborn to die. And your dad is healthier than I am."

"You're not even fifty and you already worry about dying, Irish. My dad is seventy three years old."

"And he's the youngest seventy three I've ever met. I'm pretty sure he's got another fifteen or twenty left in him."

"Then why can't you be that sure for yourself? And don't tell me it's because of family history. My grandfather died before I was born, so I don't think my dad has longevity on his side, yet here he still is."

"I don't know. Maybe it's just because I used to be so *not* afraid of dying and it hit me hard that when I do, I lose you."

"So think about the fact that we probably have at least another twenty or thirty years together. And that when one of us does die, we'll be together again sooner or later."

"Or not."

"Why would you doubt that?"

"There are some things you just can't be forgiven, and I've done most of them."

"You're not burning in hell, Chip."

"Third circle, at least."

"Maybe a time out in Purgatory. I think we both might get that...but then we'll wind up floating together on some cloud, watching over our kids and grandkids."

"And I'll probably be telling you to quit grabbing me even then."

"Now there's a thought," she said. "Celestial sex. Will Chip and Terry still be crawling all over each other, or will their wings and halos get in the way?"

"Ah, I get it. Purgatory is when I get to finally rest."

"Hush. You get to rest tonight, apparently."

"Saved by my boys."

She put a hand on my chest and gently pushed me backwards, until I was lying down on the blanket. "Your boys," she told me, face an inch or two above mine, "are going to have to accept the fact that their mother is at least going to get a few very long kisses out of their father."

"Just don't forget they're there."

"Fine. Damn kids. Why did we have so many, anyway?"

I didn't remind her that she wanted more. I just let her kiss me, and tried to make sure her hands didn't stray too far, lest we inflict permanent emotional scars on our youngest child.

~

Kevin

"Should we turn our chairs around and face the camper?" Paul asked of no one in particular.

Mom had shoved Dad onto his back and was half on top of him.

"Is this normal?" Nick asked.

"Probably not," Paul said. "But it is entertaining in a warped sort of way. It's like watching Animal Planet, but with horny parents instead of lions and tigers."

"I meant more that Mom's the aggressor and Dad is like 'Dude, what the fuck?'"

"Dad calls her 'Dude'?" I asked.

"All right," he conceded. "It's like 'Woman, what the fuck?'"

Paul laughed into his beer. "And Mom is all, 'Exactly. Exactly! Right *now*!' Maybe we *should* turn our chairs around."

"Or we could cheer them on," Nick suggested.

"Let's not encourage them," I said. "It's bad enough that they crawl all over each other when they think no one is looking. They could stand a lesson in self restraint right about now. It'll be good for them."

"The squirt doth protest too much," Paul said.

"Fine. But if they keep this up poor Dad is gonna be in a world of hurt later on."

"You presume that they won't wait for us to all fall asleep and finish what they started," Nick pointed out.

"I don't think either of them would actually have sex with us fifty feet away no matter how badly they wanted it," Paul said.

Nick shrugged. "No one says they have to go all the way. I'm pretty sure they could be creative and quiet and we'd never be the wiser."

"Thanks, Nick, like I really wanted the image of Mom giving Dad a hand job stuck in my head."

He smiled at me. "You're welcome. And don't tell me if it was you out there with Lydia you wouldn't be trying to do exactly what they are."

"That's different."

"How?" Paul asked, laughing.

"We're young, dammit. We're supposed to be all over each other."

"I'll remind you about that in twenty five years, Squirt," Paul said.

Nick started to say something else, but was interrupted by the sound of another car pulling up behind Mom's.

"So, what?" Paul asked. "Uncle Doug? Eileen? All of them?"

Nick sucked in a deep breath and muttered a few expletives under his breath, and got up. I didn't recognize the car, or the two men that got out, but Nick was walking over to them and his irritation was an express invitation to not follow.

In less than a minute Nick was in a heated, whispered argument with them. I was so intent on trying to figure out what was going on that I didn't notice Mom and Dad walk up, dragging their blanket along.

"Safe to say Nick's camping trip is over." Dad dropped the blanket next to the chair Nick had vacated.

Paul turned back towards them. "What? You know who that is?"

"Not specifically."

Mom slipped her hands around Dad's arm and leaned into him. "So much for the desk job?"

Dad nodded.

"What does that mean?" Paul asked.

"It means Nick is about to wander off to We Don't Know Where again," I mused.

"Why? Isn't he just a computer guy?" Paul wanted to know.

"Data analyst," Dad said.

"Same difference. Maybe the mainframe crashed and they need him to reboot it."

Dad looked at Paul and shook his head sadly. "It's not the same difference, Paul. Nick's job is a lot more complicated than that."

Paul was about to ask more, but Nick was stomping back towards us.

"Can you tell me where you're headed?" Dad asked him.

Nick shook his head.

"What's the weather like?"

Nick took the camera out of his backpack and handed it to Paul and said, "Print out the good ones and then give it to Katie."

"Nick?" Dad pressed.

"It's hot, Dad. Very hot."

"Sand? Mountains?"

"The former."

"In which global quarter?"

"Dad…"

"Accessible via water or not?"

"Yes. Dad, stop."

"Does Katie know?"

"She knows something is up because she told them where to find me, but I'm not going to have a chance to go home and tell her anything. I have to freaking piss her off with a damned text message from someone else's phone, and she won't even be able to reply."

"Just go," Dad said. "I'll tell Katie."

"Nick, wait." Mom let go of Dad and reached for Nick, holding on as tight as she could. "Don't be the hero, Nicky."

"I won't, Mom." He had to pry her away and step back, practically handing her to Dad. "I'm just the brains, not the brawn."

He started to walk back, but Dad asked, "Time frame, Nick?"

Nick glanced at the men waiting for him and shook his head, but as he turned to walk away he held up two fingers, and then four, behind his back.

No one said anything until the car had pulled away.

"Chip?"

Dad kissed the top of her head and said, "We have to go."

"You can't tell us anything?" Paul asked. "Do you know where he's going?"

"Let's go. I have to talk to Katie."

Mom started picking up beer bottles while Paul and I shoved the lawn chairs into the back of the camper. Dad watched the car Nick was in disappear down the road, arms folded against his stomach and his eyes rimmed with red.

The last time Nick went to We Don't Know Where he came back with a tan and souvenirs.

From the look on Dad's face, I was pretty sure no one was getting a t-shirt this time.

6

Chip

Terry and I left in her car while Kevin and Paul doused the fire and finished cleaning up the campsite. I didn't want to evade any more questions; Kevin could connect too many dots and didn't need any more information than Nick had already given us, and Paul didn't need to worry.

She waited until we were on the Interstate before asking anything, giving me time to go over it in my head.

After half an hour of silence she poked through my silence with, "Where's he going? I know you're not supposed to tell me, but you're not supposed to know, either."

No, I wasn't supposed to know. But I knew the political climate, and I knew where Nick's interests were; he never spoke about his work but he was too well versed in some geographical areas for it to be coincidence.

"Iraq," I said quietly.

"And the fingers behind his back? What did he mean?"

"He meant that it was supposed to take no less than two weeks, possibly four."

"But he could be gone longer."

"It's possible." I glanced at her sideways, trying to see her face but not lose sight of the road. "You don't look as upset as I thought you would."

"This was bound to happen sooner or later, but I hate having to tell Katie."

"She probably knows he's headed somewhere. And no, I am not

telling her where. He specifically did not say where, so we don't specifically know."

"I got it," she said. "But are you going to tell her how long he's supposed to be gone?"

"I don't know."

"Years ago," she said, "you told me you'd be gone for a couple of weeks, and you were gone for five months. And I started to believe the worst."

"What would you have wanted to hear, then?"

"Tell her as much of the truth as you can, Irish. It could be a long time. She doesn't need to be waiting and wondering if he's ever coming back."

"It'll be different for her, Terry. She'll have all of us to lean on."

"Having someone to lean on doesn't always help, and sometimes it can blow up in your face."

"We'll keep her away from Doug," I mumbled.

"Chip!"

"I'm sorry. That was low."

"A little low. If Nick is gone for a long time and we see her getting too close to Paul..."

"He wouldn't."

"When you and Kris left I'm pretty sure you never thought Doug and I would. Paul is already lonely as hell and might not think straight if he's the one helping Katie survive the emptiness. And it *is* emptiness, Chip. It's soul sucking loneliness and so, so empty... If Nick is gone as long as you were, and she gets scared...I got scared."

"You got drunk," I reminded her.

"I know. And I'm not bringing this up to hurt you, but I don't want my son to go through the pain his father did."

"Katie will have more than one person to count on, Terry. It's not the same. I left you here with no one *but* Doug. We didn't even tell your parents."

"Will Katie tell hers, you think?"

"I hope so. But if not, she has us, and she has both of Nick's brothers and his sister. She has *her* sister. She'll be fine."

She sighed, and was quiet for a long time. I drove at eighty five miles an hour towards home, still tired and wishing I'd had her drive so that I could just fall asleep, but half hoping she was taking a chance for an hour to snooze.

I sped down the Interstate, trying to figure out what I was going to say to my daughter-in-law, not knowing if she really had a clue that by sending Nick's associates to the camp site she was telling them where to pick him up.

Five miles from home Terry cut through the quiet and said, "You still owe me, Irish."

"Your baby boy is headed off to the great unknown and you're still a giant ball of hormones?"

"Nick's a big boy, and I've already done my worrying about someone being off in the great unknown. Only this time, I'm not pissed off about it. You're here, and I want things from you."

"You *have* been through this before," I reminded her. "I haven't."

She reached for my arm, her hand gently squeezing. "Chip, I'm sorry, I wasn't thinking."

"I don't know how to wait for someone. And I know too much to not worry."

"You trust in Nick. Trust in his common sense, and trust in his training. He *will* be all right."

Physically, I thought he probably would be. But Nick was not like I had been; Nick was going to see things that he probably wasn't ready to see, things that I hadn't cared about in the years before he was born, when working for the agency satisfied my warped death wish.

Nick didn't have a death wish; he had an overwhelming want of saving the world. That could make him too cautious. It could make him a target.

Nick was too compassionate to do some of the hard things he might need to do.

A mile from Nick and Katie's house I pulled off the road and into a parking lot, one last scramble to figure out what to say to her, hoping to hell she was expecting to hear that he had gone.

~

Terry

Chip pulled off into the first fast food parking lot he could find after leaving the Interstate; we were less than three minutes from Katie's house, but he wasn't ready to face her. He cut the engine and stared straight ahead, whispering, "I don't know what to tell her."

"If we make it seem like a big deal, it becomes one for her."

"It *is* a big deal."

"Chip, look at me." He swallowed hard, and when he did turn towards me, his eyes were filled with tears. "Oh, Chip, no. No, no, no; if you start crying, I will, and that won't do Katie any good."

He blinked, and sent tears spilling down his cheeks. "Just give me a minute."

I brushed my thumb across his cheek, trying to wipe the sadness away with the tears. "This has a lot less to do with telling Katie that Nick had an assignment dropped on him than it does the idea you can't protect him from it."

"Possibly. Maybe." He sighed hard, and nodded. "If it was Kevin, I'd worry, but not like this. Kevin is as skilled at defending himself as he is smart. Nick is just smart. I know what he's heading into and I'm not sure he's ready for it. He's still training, Terry."

"Think back to your own days with the agency, Irish. They taught you to fight, right? They trained you to defend yourself and how to walk away without much more than a scratch? Surely they trained Nick as well, if not better. He may be more deadly than Kevin is."

"But I know what Kevin knows. I taught him a large part of it. The things his sensei couldn't teach him, I did. I've never seen Nick fight. I need to *know*."

"He's never failed at anything he's set his mind to. You know *that*."

"I know the facts. But I can't help being very afraid for him."

"Trust a mother's instinct, then. I know Nick can take care of himself, and he'll be home sooner rather than later."

He wasn't done being afraid, not by a long shot, but he'd had enough time to blink back any more tears.

"Okay." He started the car and backed out of the parking space, and I hoped that by the time we got there the redness in his eyes would be gone.

~

Chip

An hour later we were home; Kevin was waiting in the living room with his son on his lap and Paul was upstairs checking on his sleeping daughter. I shoved aside the backpack that was on the floor in front of the sofa with my foot and dropped next to Kevin, trying not to jostle the baby. Michael's eyes were at half mast, his fist jammed awkwardly into his mouth, drool dipping from his chin.

"Katie okay?" Kevin asked.

"Appears to be."

Terry stood in the doorway, leaning against the wall. "Katie," she told Kevin, "was not surprised and seemed more in a hurry to leave than to ask any questions about anything Nick might have told us."

"So maybe Nick got hold of her," Kevin ventured.

"No, she hadn't spoken to him, but when we got there she was on her way out the door to meet her sister and seemed satisfied to know that he'd at least had the chance to ask your father to come see her."

Kevin looked from Terry to me. "Ticked off?"

"I'm just tired," I said. It was at least half the truth; I felt drained, but whatever else I was feeling wasn't anger aimed at my daughter in law.

Terry was less magnanimous. "Well, I'm not exactly thrilled with her right now. You think she'd at least wonder if he'd told us where he was going and for how long."

"She knows better, Terry," I said. "She's been expecting this as much as we have."

"And if she's going to get upset in front of anyone, it'll be her sister," Kevin pointed out. "Why else would she head out to meet Debby at midnight? Or maybe Nick has told her enough about what he's been working on that she doesn't think it's anything to worry about."

I doubted it. "I'm sorry about the camping trip, Kevin."

Kevin shrugged it off. "There are worse things than coming home and being able to give your son a bottle."

"He might appreciate it if you actually had a bottle to give him," I pointed out, reaching for my grandson.

Reluctantly, he allowed me to take the baby from him. "Mommy is in the kitchen warming it up. Someone is very particular about the temperature of his formula."

"You would be, too, if you were used to getting it on tap and suddenly someone was shoving a rubber nipple into your mouth and expecting you to like it."

"It's his own fault. The little shit sucked her dry."

For the first time in four hours, I smiled.

"Come on, Irish," Terry said. "Give your grandson a kiss and then come upstairs with me. You need to soak in the tub or something."

"Ah, is that what you're calling it now? 'Or something?'" Kevin chuckled.

"You be quiet," I growled, placing a kiss on Michael's head. "I'll be up in a minute, Ter. I'm not done being drooled on."

"I'll fill the tub for you," she said. "You'll need it if he drools much more."

Kevin waited until she was halfway up the stairs before he said, "Um, yeah, I think you're getting that 'or something' in the tub, old man. Hand over the kid, and go make your wife happy."

I wasn't ready to give up my grandson. "In a minute."

"Sitting here isn't going to make her happy."

"I know what makes her happy," I assured him.

"Spare me the details." He suddenly leaned forward and reached for the backpack on the floor. "Wait, I got something you'll want to see."

He pulled Nick's camera out and turned it on, looking at pictures on the view screen on the back.

"Look at this," he said, turning it to show me. "You and Mom by the lake."

We were a silhouette against the backdrop of the water; Nick had captured us in mid-embrace, when I'd lifted Terry off her feet, reveling in her laughter.

"Wow."

"Who knew Nick could take a decent picture?"

"Your brother can probably do quite a bit we don't know about," I said, trying to avoid letting Michael stick his wet fingers into my mouth. He was rubbing spit across my cheeks and my nose, but his ultimate goal lately was grabbing Grandpa's teeth, as if he might be able to pull them out.

"I know you can't tell me where Nick is headed," Kevin ventured, "but can you tell me what he really does?"

Michael had both hands on my face and was gently rubbing them on my cheeks. "Specifically, no. But in general…Nick takes bits and pieces of information from field reports and finds the common threads in them. It's like putting together a giant data puzzle. If he gets enough information he can piece it all together and give them a better picture of what they're looking for, or a broader idea of what they need to do."

"Don't they have computers for that?"

"They do," I said around Michael's fingers. "But there's nothing that can substitute for the human mind, someone who can make a logical connection between illogical things."

He reached over and pulled Michael's hands away from my face. "But Nick can do that from his office."

"Usually. Sometimes information in the field is too sensitive to send back through satellites or the phone, and when that happens a team leader can request an analyst to be sent to them in the field. If they don't have all the information he needs, he could be following them around until they do."

"So they essentially send a desk jockey into a combat position to observe and report?"

"More like sending a journalist in to cover combat stories. Like the reporters embedded with troops in Iraq and Afghanistan right now."

"And the troops protect the reporter."

"They have to. And at least with the agency, one team member will divert from the mission, and his sole job will be to protect the asset."

"The asset being Nick."

"Exactly."

"So Nick is being sent to We Don't Know Where, and he has a bodyguard."

Lydia came out of the kitchen with Michael's bottle, so I handed my grandson back to his father, who was not going to let me feed him.

"Nick has a bodyguard," I echoed. "I see what you did there."

"Yes, I figured it out because I'm *that smart*, so now you can go upstairs and make my mother happy with that bath or the 'or something' and quit worrying so much about Nick. He's probably excited getting his first real assignment and doesn't need you to sit here expecting the worst."

"Son, I'm already tired. You want me to go up there *now*?"

"Take it like a man."

I tilted my head back to look at Lydia, who was leaning against the back of the sofa, watching her son sucking on his bottle. "Won't you save me?"

"You're on your own, Chip. But I'm sure if you ask her nicely, she'll put the whips and chains away."

"You won't let me have your kid so I can distract her with him? Really, I'll finish feeding him, I'll read him a story, I'll change him, and I'll put him to bed."

"That'll distract her for half an hour," Kevin said. "Then she'll still want that 'or something' and you'll be half an hour more tired."

"Well, he could just say no," Lydia said.

I didn't appreciate the laughter, especially when it followed me up the stairs.

~

Terry had the tub filled and was lighting candles when I finally made it upstairs. Max was lounging under the sink, where he seemed to feel safe from the threat or water and fire. She was still dressed but I started taking my clothes off as soon as I was through the bedroom door, leaving them in a trail right up to the bathroom.

For all my protests, at that moment all I really wanted was to sink into the tub with her, no matter what else she might want from me.

"Relax, Irish," she said gently. "Just get in. I'll leave you alone."

"Like hell." She didn't seem to be in any hurry to take her clothes off, so I snagged her shirt at the hem and pulled it over her head. "I don't care what else we do, but you're getting in that tub with me."

"Am I now?"

Nick has a bodyguard. Nick is fine. Nick doesn't need you. But she's here and she wants a whole lot of things from you right now.

I was suddenly not as tired and not nearly as interested in getting into the tub as I was in picking up where we'd had to stop earlier. The fatigue flipped off like a light switch and all I could feel was the memory of her hands drifting across my skin, fingers brushing where I'd asked her not to because of the audience behind us.

I stood there and watched as her clothes came off piece by piece; she stripped slowly, being deliberate in how she dangled each piece from her finger tip and then dropped them.

"Breathing a little hard there, Irish," she teased when the last of her clothing hit the floor. She took a step closer, trailing a finger down my chest and stomach, teasing me. "That's pretty impressive for an old man, you know."

"This is going to be quick and dirty," I warned.

"Trust me, I'm more than halfway there already."

I had to pull her hand away. "Seriously. You keep doing that and I'm done."

"No nibbling on your sense of humor?"

I could hardly breathe and my heart felt like it was about to beat right out of my chest. Before she could touch me again, I picked her up and took her into the bedroom, dropping her not so gently onto the bed.

If she minded, she didn't say so. Her mouth was on mine and her legs wrapped around me before I could suck in a deep breath; she moved as frantically as I felt, straining against me, rolling until she was on top and in control.

Quick and dirty.

The bath water didn't even have time to cool off.

~

Kevin

We both looked up at the ceiling at the same time.

"Holy crap," I said. "I think she broke him."

"Jealous?"

"I think I might be." I patted Michael on his back, trying to get one more good burp out of him. "You. Little man. Go to sleep. We have things to do."

Lydia was still looking at the ceiling. "I'm sorry, but I don't think I can do *that*. I don't even know *how* they're doing that."

"I'm not even sure *what* they're doing."

"Whatever it is, your dad either really likes it, or he's seriously injured."

"If he yells for help, you get to go up there."

"They're your parents, Kevin."

"Yeah but I've seen enough of their horny little gymnastics to last me a while. It's someone else's turn to be mortified."

~

Chip

I woke to the sound of tiny feet thumping against the crib mattress in the next room; I opened one eye and grumbled under my breath because we'd forgotten to close the curtains and with the bright light cutting across the room I knew I'd never get back to sleep.

Seven o'clock.

Terry rolled over and was beginning to stir, no doubt woken by the same streak of sun that had me swearing under my breath. Before she could fully wake up, I slid out of bed and grabbed a pair of shorts, then went into my grandson's room; the pocket door that connected his room to Kevin and Lydia's was half open, but he wasn't crying and there was no sound of movement coming from their side of the wall.

Sometime during the night Michael had spit up and had dried formula stuck to his chin and cheeks; he'd soaked through his diaper and his clothes and sheets were cold and wet.

"'Morning, Big Guy," I whispered. "Why aren't you crying? I think I'd be crying right now if I were you."

He stuck his tongue out, blowing spit down his chin.

"We're gonna let Mommy and Daddy sleep, okay?" I told him, peeling his wet clothing off. "Can we be really quiet until we get your diaper off and get you into Grandpa's room?"

"I think Michael can, but I'm not sure about Grandpa," Terry whispered from the doorway.

"Did I wake you?"

"No, but I heard you and couldn't resist coming in here and seeing you with him."

I rolled up the diaper and tossed it in the trash can. "Can you go fill the bathtub? Big Guy here barfed all over himself and needs a bath."

"Sure. Leave the sheets, I'll get that in a little bit."

While she went to run the bath I grabbed a clean diaper and clothes for him, then carefully lifted him from the crib. "No peeing on Grandpa, got it? We have to get all the way to the bathroom naked, and peeing on Grandpa is rude. So is anything else you might be inclined to do on me."

Terry had the tub half filled and was reaching for a towel when we came into the bathroom. "I assumed Grandpa was going to bathe his grandson the same way he did his kids."

"Damn straight."

She took his clothes from me and tossed a washrag into the tub. "Did you leave his pajamas in the crib?"

"I figured they belonged with the sheets. Do me a favor and yank my shorts off so I don't drop him."

"Did you close their bedroom door?" she asked as the shorts came off.

"Now see this?" I asked Michael. "This is called Grandma distracting herself. She's only asking because she doesn't want to think about getting Grandpa naked when it has nothing to do with her."

"Chip, you're horrible."

"I may be horrible, but I'm safely in the bathtub without getting groped."

"There's always later."

I sat Michael against my bent legs, his feet on my chest, and began washing the dried spit up off his face. "Remember, no peeing on me."

Terry sat on the edge of the tub and leaned over to kiss me. "I promise, I won't pee on you."

"Oh, she says that now," I told Michael, "but just wait. In forty years she'll be sitting on my lap and next thing I know…"

"I'll hold you to that," she said.

"What, you're making an appointment to demonstrate your future incontinence?"

She scooped up a handful of warm water and dribbled it across the baby's chest. "If it'll get you to believe you'll still be here in forty years, you bet."

"In forty years he could have a grandson of his own."

"Reason enough for you to stick around."

"I can't even imagine him and Nicole our ages, with kids and grandkids of their own. Hell, I can't even imagine our kids being our age."

"I have to admit, when you used to bathe the kids this way, I never pictured you sitting in a bathtub with your four month old grandson. I just thought when Kevin and Eileen got too big for this, that was the end of your splashing in the tub with babies."

I started to tell her that this might be the last time; it wasn't like I was going to schedule bath time with my grandkids and once they moved out it would fall into the realm of Too Weird. She turned away when she heard Kevin step into our bedroom and went out to tell him where Michael was.

He knocked on the door jamb before coming in. "I know you're not decent," he said. "Can I come in anyway?"

"Since I have your kid, I suppose so."

"Did he wake you up?"

"No, I just went to check on him and he was awake. And someone," I said, washing tiny toes, "was wet and covered in barf this morning."

"Then you should probably not wet the bed anymore, Dad."

"Funny. Why are you up? Take the chance to sleep in while you can."

He sat on the edge of the tub where his mother had been. "He's usually got me up by six thirty. I did sleep in."

"Well, I'm not giving him back for a while, so you might as well go back to bed."

"I'm awake now. No point."

"Your daddy is kind of thick," I informed Michael. "Did I tell him to go back to sleep? No, I told him to go back to bed. Where I'm sure Mommy still is."

"Mommy is awake, too."

"But still in bed."

"I was going to bring him in so we could cuddle together before breakfast."

"God, that's too cute, son. Seriously, too cute for this early in the morning. And I'm still not giving him back. I can get him dressed, and I can feed him. You're not working today, so you don't have to be up. Go back to bed."

"Not sleepy, Dad."

"Oh my God. Michael, he really is dense."

"I'm not dense."

"Then go. Let me have my grandson for a while."

He didn't get up. Instead he bit his lower lip, all the while his eyes fixated on his son.

"He's nearly four months old, Kevin. You're past the point of having to wait."

"I know."

"So what, then? Forgot how?"

He almost smiled. "Doesn't mean she's ready."

All right, he had me there. By the time Nick was six weeks old Terry was practically frothing at the mouth and when Doug said it was all right, she was all over me. But with Paul it took longer, and with Kevin and Eileen it was over six months. Between nights lost to pacing the floor with crying babies and dealing with two overly active boys, she didn't even think about it, not until I finally said something.

"Are *you* ready?" I asked.

He snorted.

"Then push a little, son. It might not be on her radar until you do."

"That's not exactly sensitive."

"You're going to have to trust me on this. She might not realize just how ready she really is until you let her know what you want. And then you might wish you'd hadn't said anything."

"The voice of experience?"

"Been there, done that. Just go back in there and tell her you're not getting possession of your son until at least noon. Crawl back in bed and talk. It doesn't have to be sex yet."

He sighed hard. "He gets thin rice cereal for breakfast. And he's not really great with a spoon yet, just sit him in his bouncy seat—"

"I can feed a baby, Kevin."

"But—"

"You're still alive, aren't you? I actually fed you a few times, you know. Half a packet of the cereal, mixed with a little warm formula. If he's still hungry, then he gets however much of a bottle he wants. I'll even remember to burp him."

"Dad."

"Seriously, Kevin, go."

"No…I was just going to warn you…he's peeing on you."

~

After he'd been fed and burped and changed again, Terry demanded equal grandparental rights and took the baby from me, reasoning that I needed breakfast, too, and it wouldn't be easy to eat while holding him. He sat in her lap, gnawing on her fingers, and occasionally he tilted to the left.

"Still haven't mastered the whole sitting up thing, have we?" I asked him when she propped him up for the third time. "I bet you're not even trying to crawl yet, either."

"We'll be happy when he starts rolling over."

"At least that's some sort of mobility. Just don't be in too much of a hurry, mister."

"They always are," she sighed.

"I'm not sure they're in so much of a hurry as we're just trying to slow time down so we can soak more of it all up."

"That's why we get grandkids, Irish, so we can pick up on all the little things we missed the first time around."

Michael reared his head back, smacking Terry in the chest. "I bet you don't miss that," I mused.

"His father did that so many times I'm surprised my boobs didn't invert."

"I'm not so sure that your right one didn't just now."

She might have let me check, but Nicole wandered in, blinking a sleepy fog out of her eyes. "'Morning," she muttered.

"You don't look like you're quite awake, sweetheart," Terry said.

"I'm not." She pulled a chair from the table and sat down, resting her chin on her hands. "This is Saturday, right? No school?"

"No school," I agreed.

"Well, this sucks."

Terry got up and handed Michael to me. "Hungry?" she asked Nicole. "I can make you some eggs or pancakes."

"Eggs," Nicole sighed. "Uncle Kevin says I need more protein before karate class and that I shouldn't eat cereal or syrupy stuff."

"Uncle Kevin," I told her, "used to ask for chocolate cake for breakfast."

"Ugh. Too sweet." She yawned and set her head on the table.

"Nicole, you can go back to bed," Terry said. "You were up late last night and Uncle Kevin isn't even going to teach class today."

"I would but Uncle Kevin and Aunt Lydia are...noisy."

I had to clench my teeth together to keep from laughing, and Terry turned quickly so that Nicole wouldn't see her trying to hold it back.

"Must be rearranging the furniture," I mumbled.

"I don't think so," Nicole sighed. "But you might wanna check later because I think one of them kicked a hole in the wall."

I turned to look at Terry; she was still facing the other way, obviously laughing under her breath. "You want to go check on them?" I asked her.

All she could do was shake her head.

"One of them might be hurt," I pushed. "You know, when a boy gets hurt, he usually wants his mommy."

"Stop it," she snickered.

Paul shuffled into the kitchen, looking as tired as Nicole; he was dressed and had clothes for her in one hand and her sneakers in other.

"Hi, Daddy," she groaned. "Did they wake you up, too?"

He looked at me, eyes widened as if asking 'what the hell?' "Sweetheart, why don't you and I go out to breakfast, just the two of us?"

"Grandma's making eggs."

"It's all right. I haven't started them yet," Terry said.

"There we go." He handed Nicole the clothes he'd brought for her. "Just change in the bathroom down here. You can pick your pajamas up later."

She slid from the chair and walked slowly towards the hallway, and Paul watched until she had closed the bathroom door.

"Oh. My. God. You should hear them up there!"

"Blame your father," Terry said.

"I don't even want to know," Paul said as he sat at the table.

"Hey, I didn't tell them to bounce off the walls. I just told Kevin to get his ass back to bed and take advantage of the fact I wasn't letting either of them near my grandson for a while."

"Yeah, but sheesh…"

"They knew we'd be down here with the baby," Terry said. "They probably forgot Nicole was right across the hall."

"And *when* are we all moving?" Paul asked.

"Like you've never," I chuckled.

"Not like that, I don't think." He waggled a finger at both of us. "You're all just trying to make me feel bad, right? Last night it was you two, now I wake up to a freaking mixed martial arts match going on across the hall."

"Whatever do you mean?" I asked innocently.

"You know damn well what I mean."

"Dad," Nicole sighed hard from behind him, "just get a girlfriend already. Then maybe *she* can put your foot through a wall."

That's when Terry lost it, standing in the kitchen with eggs still in hand. She started laughing and as Nicole turned to head for the front door she added, "Oh yeah, I said it. *Someone* had to."

7

Chip

Doug kept me waiting for half an hour, long enough to make me think there were better things I could be doing than sitting in his office waiting to hear that all he really needed to do for me was call in a prescription, things like scooping cat poop out of the litter box or poking hot matches into my eyes.

If not for plans to go look at a new housing development after the appointment, I might have gotten up and left. Sure, he would have called Terry and tattled, but her disappointment in me would have waned with a kiss or two.

When he finally walked in, he tossed his stethoscope onto his desk and apologized. "Six year old kid with gummi bears shoved up his nose," he explained. "Getting that last one was a bitch."

"Did he say why he shoved gummi bears up his nose?"

"They were green like boogers," he chuckled, "and they fit."

He sat at his desk and started poking at keys on his computer. Ten years earlier he would have strolled in with a file folder in hand, and would have spent fifteen minutes trying to decipher his own hand-writing.

He squinted at the monitor. "Your thyroid is actually in the nor-mal range. Barely. It's in the low normal range, but still normal."

"Good. You owe me a hundred bucks."

"I'll take it off your bill." He was still looking at the screen. "All right, so you're tired, you've gained fifteen pounds, and you're los-ing body hair. Have you noticed any changes in the amount of weight you're lifting in the gym? Any weakness along with the fatigue?"

I paused to consider it. I didn't feel weak, but I had been struggling with the bench press and with bicep curls. "Upper body," I said. "I haven't dropped the amount of weight I'm lifting, but I'm fighting it."

"Lower body?"

"No problems on the leg press or with squats."

"Any muscle pain?"

"Vague achiness sometimes."

"All over?"

I nodded.

"Issues with impotence?"

"God, hell no. Terry wouldn't permit that."

He tried to not smile. "You've hinted at not being able to keep up with her. That could imply difficulty on your end."

"My only difficulty," I said, really wishing we were talking about something else, "is that she's still got the hormones of a twenty year old, and I don't. If she wants sex more than once in a night, she sometimes has to wait a while."

"That's normal at your age," he said. "How long does she have to wait?"

"Doug, holy shit, you're nosy."

"A few hours? A day? Longer?"

"A few hours. But not always. Why?"

He turned the monitor so that I could see it. "Your thyroid is almost normal," he said again, "but some of your other hormones are off. Your testosterone is a little low, you have slightly elevated estrogens and an elevated prolactin level, something I'd normally expect to see in a pregnant woman."

"As opposed to a pregnant man."

He ignored me. "The lower testosterone can account for some of the tiredness, and the estrogen for loss of body hair. You also have no discernable growth hormone."

"I think I'm done growing, Doug."

"Everyone has some growth hormone," he explained. "Your brain typically produces it at night while you sleep to help repair muscle fiber. Without it, you lose muscle mass, can feel weak, tired, and achy."

"You're basically telling me my brain and my balls are broken."

He didn't laugh; I expected at least a chuckle. "I would expect your growth hormone levels to be lower at your age. And it's not uncommon for your testosterone to drop off after fifty. But yours is lower than it should be, and you should be making *some* growth hormone."

"And?"

"Do you feel thirstier than usual? Notice a significant increase in urination?"

"No. Well… No."

"Breast tenderness?"

"I don't have man boobs."

"Breast tenderness?" he repeated.

"No."

"Dizziness? Like you might feel if you stood up too quickly after being crouched down?"

"No. Where are you going with this, Doug?"

"You may just have low hormone levels and we'll get you on a replacement for them."

"But?"

"But first I want to see if we can figure out why they're low, and why your prolactin levels are elevated."

"I'm not pregnant. Terry had her tubes tied, remember?"

Again, no grin.

"You could be in andropause," he said carefully; he seemed like he doubted it, so I waited. "In a nutshell, menopause for men. I wouldn't expect it until your mid-to-late fifties, but it's not unheard of in your forties."

"I'm a couple months from fifty," I reminded him.

"I know. But I'm not convinced that's the problem." He turned the monitor back around, and flicked it off. "I want an MRI of your brain, Chip. I think you might have a tumor."

8

Chip

Instead of scoping out real estate, Doug went home with me, and sat at our kitchen table as he tried to explain to Terry what he suspected was wrong.

The moment the word "brain" was out of his mouth, she started crying.

"If you're going to have a brain tumor," he said carefully, making sure she heard him, "this is the kind you want. Probably as much as twenty five per cent of the population is walking around with one and they never know about it. It's not even discovered until autopsy."

She was listening but not really hearing him.

"Pituitary cancer is extremely rare, so rare that I'm confident enough to tell you that if he does have a tumor it's not going to be cancerous."

"I might not have one," I added. "All of this might be unrelated, and all I need is a few hormone replacements."

"You wouldn't be telling me any of this if you didn't think he had a tumor," she said to Doug.

"I want a peek at his brain, just to see."

"And cancer might be rare, but it does happen, right?"

He nodded soberly.

"So you can't promise me that he doesn't have cancer."

"I can tell you it's so rare that I'm sure he doesn't."

"And if he has a tumor, what's next?"

"I'll send him to a specialist who can determine what type it is and whether or not it can be treated with medication, or if it has to come out."

"What do you mean, what type? You just said you thought he had a pituitary tumor!"

"There's more than one category. It could be a granuloma, which is basically a grain of irritant. It could be a prolactinoma, which accounts for that elevated hormone and what I suspect he has. It could be a craniopharengioma."

She looked up sharply. "And why is that the only one you're not explaining?"

"It would require more than medication, most likely. And you don't need to worry until we know if he has a tumor at all."

"It's cancer," she said flatly.

"No. That one is more like pre-cancer. And it's treatable."

She wiped the tears away with her thumb, swallowing hard. "You swear to me you won't let him die."

"Terry, he's too stubborn to die and we both know it."

Normally that would have made her smile; this time it made her angry. "Doug, he's *obsessed* with the idea that he'll be dead within five years."

"He was worried about his heart," Doug said gently, "and now he knows it's in very good condition. Let's just get from this to getting the MRI done and see if he even has one, and we can move on from there. I'll put him in the best hands I can, I swear."

"How long before he can get the MRI?" Terry asked.

"He scheduled me for next week in Sacramento," I told her. "It was the first opening he could find."

"And how long until you get the results after that?"

"A day or two," Doug said.

"You can tell Kris," I told him, "but I don't want the kids to know anything just yet. Not until we do. There's no point in worrying them over what could turn out to be nothing."

Terry nodded, a bare tilt of her head.

"Are you going to be all right?" I asked her.

"I feel like you two just kicked me in the stomach."

Doug stood up, patting me on the shoulder. "I'm sorry, I really am. But it'll be all right."

"Is that coming from our doctor or our friend?" she asked.

"It's coming from someone who loves you both very much, and

will turn inside out to make sure the closest thing he has to a brother will be just fine."

When the front door clicked shut, her eyes filled with tears again. "You have to get me out of here. The kids will be home soon, and if we're not telling them… Just take me to the park. We'll walk around the pond until I can get it together."

The drive to the park was quiet, punctuated by an occasional sniffle. She stared out the window as I drove, her hands clenched around the seatbelt. After I pulled into the parking lot she was out of the car before I could cut the engine, and she stood there leaning against the door; when I got out and around to her side, she fell against me, sobbing hard.

"I can't lose you," she cried. "Nick is gone and I can't lose both of you. I can't lose *you*."

"Nick is coming back," I said gently. "And I'm not dying."

"I wish you could promise me that. All of it."

"Doug wouldn't say he was sure I'd be all right if he didn't mean it. He doesn't hand out fluff. He would warn me up front if it was going to be hard."

"Going to be? It already *is* hard."

"Look at me."

"Chip…"

"Look at me," I insisted. And when she lifted her head from my shoulder I looked into her eyes and said, "This could be a good thing. It accounts for how off I've felt lately, how tired, and it's *not* my heart. You know I've been terrified there was something wrong with my heart. This sounds a whole lot better than dropping dead from a massive coronary."

"But it's your *brain*."

"Just under my brain. A tiny little gland hanging there like a punching bag. And I can take a hard punch, Terry."

She rested her head against my chest again, her arms tightening around my waist as if she never intended to let go.

~

By the time we went home it was late; none of the kids would blink twice if we walked in and headed upstairs without saying any more than "We're home," as we zipped past the living room. Paul was on the sofa, the TV a quiet buzz in the background, but he was alone and I assumed that Nicole was already in bed.

Kevin and Lydia's bedroom door was closed, light bleeding under it into the dark hallway.

We undressed quietly and dropped into bed in an exhausted heap; Terry stared at the ceiling and I rolled onto my side, watching for but hoping I wouldn't see any more tears.

After a while I whispered, "Are you okay?"

"I should be asking you that," she said, just as quietly. "This is about you, and you've spent the entire evening trying to make me feel better."

"I think it's about us."

She rolled onto her side, reaching out to place a hand on my hip; she wanted contact, any kind of touch to assure her that I was right there. "Do you believe Doug?"

"I think if he knew that it was really bad he would say so, just to give us time to prepare for the worst."

Her hand slid from my hip to my chest, settling there as if she was making sure my heart was still beating. "You're the little brother he never had, Chip. I don't think he can break your heart twice in a lifetime."

"He would if it meant getting me to take this seriously enough to fight for my life. If Doug says I have practically zero chance of this being cancer, then I'm going to believe him."

"I am terrified out of my mind, Irish."

"Just because I believe that it's not going to kill me, that doesn't mean I'm not worried."

"How are we going to get through this week?"

"We're going to look for land we can build on, or another neighborhood that has a court with six good houses on it. We're going to take long walks at the park, and we're going to have wild monkey sex as many times as we can, wherever we think we can get away with it."

"I'm not sure how wild I'll be getting this week."

"That's all right. We can be quiet in how bendy we get. But

don't avoid being with me because you're afraid of losing me."

"Just hold me tonight, all right? By morning I'll have had time for it to sink in. I'll be okay if you will."

"I'll be fine," I promised.

She slid as close to me as she could get, her breath as warm against my chest as were her tears.

"I won't die," I whispered against her hair. "I promise."

~

Kevin

Three o'clock in the morning; I woke up hard and fast to the gut punch of my name being roared in utter panic. Lydia sat up, but I scrambled out of bed and through Michael's room to my parents', where my father was sitting up in bed, his eyes wide open, breath coming in ragged gasps.

Mom was shaking him gently, tying to wake him up, but he was staring straight ahead, and called out my name again, an agonizing wail of grief and fear.

I sat beside him on the bed, reaching for his shoulder. "I'm right here, Dad."

"Kevin, no. No, no, no. Please, no…"

"Dad." I turned his head so that he was looking right at me. "I'm right here."

He grabbed my wrists, holding my hands to his face. "You can't go. You have to stay here."

"I'm not going anywhere."

Michael started to cry in the next room and from the corner of my eye I could see Mom twitch, the impulse to go get him there and gone in less time than it took her to blink.

"I need you to stay here," Dad pleaded. "Please don't go."

I could hear Lydia shuffle into the baby's room, her soft murmur soothing him as she picked him up.

"I won't go anywhere," I promised.

"Please."

"Go back to sleep. I'll stay here."

"You can't go after Nick. Please don't go."

"I won't. Nick can take care of himself. He has a bodyguard, remember?"

"You have to take care of your mother."

Mom slid her arms around him, burying her face against his shoulder. "Chip," she breathed, voice choking on his name.

"Promise me, Kevin. Stay here and take care of her. You can't go after Nick."

"I swear. I'll take care of Mom. Nick can take care of himself."

"I need…"

"What? What do you need?"

His eyes fluttered, and he let go of my wrists. "Paul needs a bartender," he murmured.

"Chip," Mom whispered, "lie down. It's all right now."

She urged him back, curling next to him on her side, propped up on her elbow.

"He's more worried about Nick than I figured," I said quietly, watching as he closed his eyes.

"It would help if Nick could come home," she agreed.

"Are you okay?"

"I'm fine. Thank you, Kevin. I'm not sure I could have talked him back to sleep."

"He wasn't ever awake. Just a really bad dream."

"You need to go back to bed, too."

I leaned across Dad and kissed her. "He's asleep, Mom. Don't lie here staring at him all night. Turn the light out and go back to sleep yourself."

"I will."

The light clicked off as I went into Michael's room, but I was fairly sure that she'd be awake the rest of the night.

~

Lydia was sitting in the rocking chair in the corner of our bedroom, rubbing Michael's back, when I crawled back into bed.

"Everything all right?"

"My parents sleep naked," I muttered into my pillow. "I totally did not need to know that."

~

"He just wasn't there," I said. "I'm not even sure if it registered with him that I was there or if he was talking to some random Kevin inside his head. But damn, he was freaked out."

This was a rare night out; except for Nick, we were all available for a family dinner. Paul was technically working, but the perks of being the boss include being able to take a break for dinner with the parents and siblings.

Paul, Spider, and Eileen were sitting across from Lydia, Katie and me. Michael was in Lydia's lap, having already been passed around the table by aunts and uncles eager to hold him. Nicole was spending the night with a friend; she'd been offered the chance to come with us, but she rolled her eyes and declared, "That would be *boring*."

Mom and Dad were wrapped around each other on the dance floor, loosened up and relaxed by a couple of margaritas and a strong Irish whiskey; her arms were looped around his neck and she practically melted into him, both of them barely moving with the music.

"Why should you be the one to stay home and take care of Mom?" Paul huffed pretentiously. "I can take care of her. Cripes."

"Well, why would I go chasing after Nick? I don't know where the hell he is."

"It's your ninja skills," Spider signed. "The rest of us are worthless and weak."

Earlier in the day, before Dad declared that he wanted to spend an evening with his kids, I walked past the study and there they were, holding onto each other like two people who had to say goodbye but couldn't let go long enough for the words to come out.

The rest of us were certain Nick was coming home; I couldn't fathom why they didn't seem to believe it.

"Should I talk to them?" Katie asked. "Nick was pretty clear on the fact that the only way he'll ever be in danger with this job is if he does something stupid."

Normally I would latch onto that and make some snotty comment about my brother's intelligence, but this time I was grateful that he was outright smart.

Paul didn't think she should. "Intellectually," he said, "they know the facts. They know Nick is probably safe, but it's a whole other thing to *know* it. I get it…it doesn't matter if your kids grow up; you worry whether they're twenty seven or eight or four months old. It's one of Mother Nature's dirty little secrets. Raise them, shove them out the door, and then worry about them until the day you die."

"They still haven't figured out that whole shoving them out the door thing," I said.

"I'd have moved last year," Paul said, "but…"

"But Mom would have grabbed you by the hair and dragged you back," Eileen said. "It wasn't just Nicole who needed family around after Monica died."

"And we'd probably still be there if Topher hadn't needed someone to take over his apartment," Spider added. "I think your Mom would be happy if we all moved into one giant house together on the far side of the county."

"Dad would choke," Paul chuckled. "He wants us out."

"He does and he doesn't," Lydia said. "I think he'll be seriously upset the first morning he walks into the dining room and doesn't see one of his grandkids there."

"He's willing to take that chance," Paul said.

"And he'll love it when we're all in the same neighborhood and he can sit on the front lawn and watch his grandkids play," Katie pointed out.

Paul leaned forward, looking at her. "And when are you planning on adding to his collection of munchkins?"

She leaned forward to match him. "When are you planning on finding a woman?"

"By the time you spawn, I'm sure my daughter will be ready to let me date."

Katie sat back and snickered, "I'd like to have a child long before then, Paul."

"It's not like I can't *find* a date," he protested.

"I'm pretty sure she means one not of the blow up variety," Eileen said.

He looked past Spider and stuck his tongue out at her. "Bite me."

"Come over to the dojo," I told him. "Seriously, there are several young—"

Lydia poked me in the ribs. "If you say 'hot' you're sleeping alone tonight."

"—*available* female students I could introduce you to," I finished. And to her I said, "I don't notice hot young women anymore."

"Liar," she laughed. "But you should introduce him to Sam. She's actually mentioned she'd like to meet someone nice."

"And she's not a student," I mused. "She's one of the instructors. About your age, too, Paul."

"Really, guys, I don't need help."

"Paul." Lydia raised one eyebrow. "She's *hot.*"

"And she likes Nicole."

"There you go!" Eileen squealed. "A hot date that can beat the crap out of him!"

"You can really be quiet now," Paul told her.

"Meet her," Katie urged. "It wouldn't kill you, and plus, maybe you can seal the deal before I actually do have a baby."

"Seal the deal as in just have sex with the woman, or do I have to marry her?"

"We'd all settle for you getting laid," Eileen assured him.

"He could pay someone for that," Lydia pointed out.

Katie nodded. "This is true. No money should change hands, Paul. That only seems fair."

"Oh, God, you guys are gross. If I was going to do *that*, I would have already."

"You considered it?" Spider asked.

"Oh, hell. Fine, I'll meet Sam. But—" he pointed at Katie "—it's not going to take me nine plus months, presuming she and I hit it off."

"It doesn't even have to be Sam," Katie said. "But whoever it is, it has to be because you're really into her, not because you want to win."

"Wanna bet on it?"

"Well, aren't you just Mister Romantic. All right, what are you offering?"

"Just the honor and glory of victory."

Katie shook her head. "I want something tangible."

"Fine. You have a kid before I have sex, and I'll buy you a freaking minivan so you can cart the kid and all his crap around."

"All right," she laughed. "And if you have sex first?"

"Then I win!"

She reached across the table to shake hands to seal the deal, but before he could pull his hand away she added, "And Paul? You only have six months."

9

Chip

Just before 8:30, Paul apologized and told us that we had to vacate the table for a large group that actually intended to pay for their meals. The kids said they would head for home and meet us there, but I wasn't quite ready to leave, so Terry and I moved to the bar, where we could pick on Will and make him wish he was still on vacation.

From where we sat, the far side of a booth towards the middle, we could see most of the dining room. More than half the tables were vacant; it was walk in service, no reservation required. I counted only four servers, with Paul filling in spots where help was needed, and three busboys with one drink runner. The bar was doing decent business, but it wasn't the shoulder to shoulder mass that it used to be.

I opened the restaurant when I was nineteen years old; at the time it was the only fine dining restaurant in a three county area; if you wanted an expensive night out and didn't want to drive to San Francisco, the Charybdis was where you went. Considering its age it still looked decent, but the area surrounding it was in decline and people were going elsewhere.

It wasn't a relic, but it was headed in that direction.

We watched as Paul tried to appease an obviously angry couple; they got up, he threw his napkin down, and they stormed out. I caught Paul's attention and waved for him over.

"Just tonight's Gimme A Free Meal couple," he explained before I could ask. "She supposedly found a blonde hair in her food; I offered to comp her dinner…"

"But they wanted the whole meal for free," Mom guessed.

"It was cheese. It was a long string of cheese, and oddly, she didn't note this wayward hair until she'd eaten almost all of it."

"So technically this was a dine-and-dash," I pointed out.

"Technically. It's not worth calling the cops over."

"You got a minute to sit?" I asked him.

He slid onto the booth seat across from us.

I gestured towards the dining room. "Is it like this every night now?"

"Tonight's a little slow. But for the most part, yes, business is down by about twenty per cent."

"It's not going to get any better, Paul. People just don't want to come into this part of town anymore."

"I know, but what are we supposed to do? Pick the place up and move it?"

"That's exactly what I'm thinking. I don't want to close the restaurant down, but moving to a better location…if we don't, eventually we'll lose it."

"Are you sure you want to take this on right now?" Terry asked.

"What's wrong with now?" Paul asked.

"We're trying to find a place for us all to *live*," she reminded him. "He has a dozen other business ventures to take care of. Is he supposed to drop everything else and find a place for this on top of everything?"

"Mom…"

"It was my idea," I said, slipping her hand in mine. "And it's not a new one. It's been brewing in the back of my head for a long time. It's just done percolating now."

She gripped my hand, holding on a little too tightly for a little too long. "It can wait, Chip."

"Maybe. I've had my eye on a fairly large vacant lot in Vacaville, and it would be a prime location for this place."

"Going out there means going from fine dining to straight family style menus, Dad. We may get more foot traffic, but it's not exactly where you take a date to impress her."

"It could be."

"And you two can work out the particulars later," Terry said.

"Tonight we were just going to spend time with the kids, and most of them have gone back to the house."

"And some of us are stuck at work," Paul sighed.

"You'll survive," I told him. "And I want dessert. Seat us at the server's table who got shafted with the dine-and-dash. She should get a shot at making up the tip."

~

Paul

"Your grandpa left a hundred dollar tip on a fifteen dollar tab," I told Michael, holding him in my lap, "and yet he didn't pay me for the dessert. What's up with that? It's like Grandpa thinks he owns the place."

"I bet Grandpa didn't pay for dinner, either," Kevin guessed.

By the time I got home, Mom and Dad were already upstairs, Kevin and Lydia were wrapped around each other on the sofa, and Spider and Eileen were sitting on the floor, debating whether or not they wanted to go home or stay the night.

Eileen latched onto the nonmonetary slice of news. "Mom let Dad have dessert?"

"Grandma," I said, still speaking to my nephew, "shared a slice of triple chocolate mousse cheesecake with Grandpa. No, Grandpa's not allowed to have a whole slice to himself. Grandpa isn't even allowed to have Twinkies or Ding Dongs and he only gets cake if it's someone's birthday."

"That's because Grandma wants Grandpa to have a hot body until he's ninety," Eileen offered.

"Don't listen to her. Grandma wants Grandpa to have a healthy heart, so she gives him lots and lots of chicken for dinner and tons of organic vegetables and organic fruit for dessert. Grandma worships the organic. We're not supposed to tell her that he sometimes sneaks into the restaurant and has ice cream."

"I'm telling you, Michael, it's all about the hot body."

Kevin kicked a lazy foot at his twin. "My son does not need to hear that his aunt thinks her own father is hot."

"Your dad *is* hot," Lydia confirmed. "So is your mother. So are you. So get used to the idea that once you hit thirty, I'm not letting you have cake anymore, either."

"This is why we need our own house. Otherwise you're going to learn about the evils of high fructose corn syrup and I'll never enjoy food again."

Michael's eyes started to flutter; I could have handed him back to his mother, but I lifted him up and held him against my chest, rubbing his back as he drooled on my shoulder. "Speaking of hot. When are you going to introduce me to Sam?"

"Heh," Kevin snorted. "Someone wants to win that bet."

"It sucks that we can't say anything in front of Mom and Dad," Eileen said.

Spider shrugged. "Not ours to tell. She wants to be able to tell them with Nick."

"I hope Nick is going to be half as happy as Mom and Dad will be," Eileen said.

"He wants kids," Kevin said.

"In a future thinking sort of way, sure. Katie never pictured being married to him this long and not having started a family already."

"Let Nick hold Michael when he's like this," I suggested. "There's nothing like a sleeping baby to make the urge to procreate rear its head. I really miss this."

"You think you want more eventually?" Lydia asked.

"Whoever I wind up with has to want at least one. I'd like to do things in the right order next time."

"Should I ask Sam if she wants kids before I introduce you?" Kevin said with a little bit of a chuckle.

"Just let me meet her. We'll see what happens from there."

I wouldn't admit it, but Sam would merely be a distraction for my siblings; I certainly had no intention of sleeping with her. If they knew where my heart was headed, they'd get nosy and involved, and I wasn't ready to share anything about the woman I had been interested in and flirting with for nearly a year.

"So what if she wants kids," Spider asked, "and you really hit it off, but she's the type that plans on holding out for the gold ring?"

"Then I guess I'm buying Katie a minivan."

~

Chip

"Four in the morning, Irish," Terry said quietly. "If we were smart we'd be asleep."

I had been asleep; we dropped into bed at midnight and I was asleep within five minutes. Sometime around three she rolled over and inched closer to me, sliding an arm across my chest and a leg over mine as she buried her head against my neck. I woke to the feeling of her fingers tracing over the scar across my chest, slow and deliberate, as if she was burning the thin white line into memory.

Still half asleep, I reached for her hand and kissed the tips of her fingers. "I'm still here," I whispered. "I'm not going anywhere."

"I didn't mean to wake you up."

"I don't mind."

"But I know you're tired. You practically fell asleep before your head hit the pillow. I really didn't mean to wake you up. I just wanted…"   •

"To connect," I finished when her voice trailed off. "You can wake me for that, woman. Whether you just want to be held or kissed…any reason."

"I just don't want to let go."

"You don't have to."

"What if we don't have any choice? I can't get it out of my head—"

"I know." I couldn't get it out of mine either; the odds were in my favor even if there was a tumor latched on to the lower part of my brain. But that slim chance—that was the ugly little Maybe that we were both fighting against.

All the what-ifs.

What if it's big enough that it's seeping higher into my brain than Doug seems to think?

What if it's big enough that it has to come out?

What if it's cancer?

She was quiet long enough that I thought she'd drifted off, but then she lifted her head and kissed me. "I just want to be with you."

I did say she could wake me for anything she wanted.

What she wanted was slow and sweet and quiet; long, soft kisses and hands gliding gently over skin. My lips barely left hers, lingering there until she was too breathless to kiss me back.

We were still curled around each other an hour later, too spent to move, neither of us willing to let go.

"No place we have to be in the morning," I said when she noted the time. "No reason to get up before noon. We don't have to go back to sleep."

"But you're halfway there."

"The other half wants to stay awake and make out with Queen Gumby."

She kissed the tip of my nose. "The Queen is content enough that the King didn't mind waking up in the middle of the night to make love to her. He can go back to sleep. She won't be offended."

"The King wants a kiss." She obliged, and against her lips I said, "He would also like to do it again, but he's gotten too old and has to make her majesty wait until around eight or so."

"The King is incredibly obliging, but he's also very sleepy. Just hold me, Irish."

"Not if you're going to lay there awake, counting my heart beats."

"I won't."

"And not if you're so wide awake that you're going to think yourself into tears."

"I'll go back to sleep," she promised. "I might have done that if you hadn't woken up, but I think I'm tired enough to sleep again."

She did fall asleep, but when I woke up at nine, she was sleeping with her head on my chest, ear to my heart, as if she was listening.

It's beating, I thought, pushing hair from her face. *I'm not going anywhere yet.*

~

Terry

Chip was in the shower when the phone rang; Kevin knocked on our bedroom door at ten, making sure it was all right before he came in.

"Uncle Doug," he said, holding the phone out to me.

I waited until he left the room before answering, and then sat on the edge of the bed until I heard the water cut off. I was in the bathroom before he could step out of the shower stall, handing him his towel before he could reach for it.

"You missed the eight o'clock window, Queen Gumby. I just showered and you want me to get all sweaty now?"

I held the phone up. "If we can get to Sacramento by one this afternoon, you can get your MRI today. Doug will meet us there."

I think he wanted to turn around and barricade himself in the shower; his face paled and he swallowed hard, but after a moment he started to dress. He threw on sweatpants and a t-shirt, and rolled up a pair of jeans that he tucked under his arm.

"Nothing metal in the MRI," he explained to answer the question I was about to ask. "I can change after."

"Are you all right?"

"This is good. We'll get this over with, and we'll know in a couple of days."

That was the problem.

We'd have an answer in a couple of days, and I wasn't sure I wanted to know.

~

On any given day Chip drives at least ten miles an hour over the posted speed limit on the Interstate. He gets into the fast lane, accelerates until he's blowing by other traffic, and doesn't care if he's pulled over for speeding. It used to bother me, until Kris pointed out that he'd been taught to drive insane speeds with lethal objects flying at him; wayward SUVs on a California freeway were tame by comparison.

He did agree to not drive like he was trying to get to hell so quickly with any of the kids in the car, and most of the time I could talk him into taking slow surface streets; this time, there was no getting there in time on city streets or back roads. He was in no hurry, either; Chip drove in the middle lane, the cruise control set at sixty five, and he never complained about the cars that were zooming around us, or about the number of trucks that pulled up within a foot of the back bumper, trying to force him to speed up.

He wanted to get there in time to get the MRI done nearly a week ahead of time, but he wasn't going to get there any quicker than he had to.

We took my car, a sedate blue sedan, rather than his gas-guzzling two-seater sports car, the one I'd mocked when he brought it home, anointing it the Bluebird of Happiness. I pointed out that whether he realized it or not, he'd bought himself a car that people would notice. Female people. He was headed into middle age with a midlife crisis car, yet he swore he bought it because Nick and Paul liked it.

This wasn't a ride he wanted to make in his now fourteen year old convertible. He wanted quiet; he wanted tame. Neither of us knew what to talk about anyway; he kept his eyes on the road and I stared out the side window, watching the mile markers, anxiety building with each one we passed.

We were an hour early in spite of the speed Chip drove to get there. He found the right building and parked, and both of us hesitated getting out of the car at all until he spotted Doug's blood red Cadillac convertible just a few spaces away.

Doug and Kris were waiting for us in the lobby, taking away one of Chip's excuses to slow down. He wanted to wander aimlessly for a few minutes, to be able to honestly say he didn't know exactly where to go, but Doug led us there and had Chip checked in within five minutes.

"They had another cancellation," Doug told him. "If you're ready, they'll take you back in about ten minutes."

Chip wasn't, but he wouldn't be any more ready in an hour.

"You didn't have to be here," Chip said. "How many patients did you blow off to come here and hold my hand?"

"I had a clear schedule this afternoon. It's my golf day, you know."

"Yeah, and when did you take up golf?"

"When I realized it would get me an afternoon off. One of these days I'll even go buy some clubs and give it a try. Besides, we came here for Terry, so she wouldn't have to wait alone."

For that, Chip was thankful.

"And," Doug reached into his pocket, fishing out a medicine bottle, "I brought valium. An hour stuck in that machine without really being able to move can be stressful."

"I'm not claustrophobic."

"Chip…it's over an hour of lying still, with nothing but the banging of that machine and the voices in your head to keep you company."

He didn't want Chip in there stewing over the worst possible outcome; we all knew it, and after a moment of consideration, Chip stuck his hand out. Doug dropped two pills into it, and pointed towards the water fountain.

"You'll start to feel it in a few minutes. By the time they call you back, you won't give a damn."

"You should have drugged Terry instead."

"I'll be fine." I patted the chair next to me. "Sit down, Irish. Pacing won't help."

The waiting room was lined with hard plastic chairs padded by thin cushions; whoever chose the décor likely never envisioned having to sit there bathed in stress for more than a few minutes while waiting for someone they loved to be photographed from the inside out. Kris took the chair on my other side, and Doug eased into one across from us.

"Your ring," he said, pointing to Chip's hand. "You can't wear it and if you give it to the technician…"

Chip nodded and struggled to get his wedding ring off his finger. He took a look at it before handing it to me, and then said, "I don't think that's been off since we got married. It doesn't feel right."

"Just for an hour," I said.

"Crucifix, too." Doug pointed to the chain barely peeking from the collar of Chip's t-shirt.

I slipped his ring onto my middle finger and reached up to unclasp the chain for him. When I started to slip it into my pocket he grunted "Nope," and took it from me, hanging it around my neck.

"That means as much to me as the ring does, woman. Let Jesus nestle between your boobs for a while."

When the technician came out, Chip stood and swayed horribly. Doug got up and took him by the elbow, steering him towards the hall. "See? You don't give a damn, do you?"

"No, right now I don't give a flying fuck." He turned back around and bent over to give me one more kiss. "Except for you. I give a flying fuck about you."

We watched Doug lead him down the hall and around the corner.

"Doug should have brought along enough for all of us," Kris muttered.

"He can keep some in reserve in case this goes badly," I said, only half kidding.

I waited for her to spout off the usual platitudes, about how this was Chip, of course he would be okay; Chip was one wayward molecule away from being Superman. He had survived being shot at, being sliced open by a butcher knife, he had maimed and killed and had been the target of people bent on turning him into a memory long before I met him; surely this was just a small bump in the road.

Instead, she asked gently, "How are you holding up?"

The first thing that came to mind was that concern about me wasn't fair to Chip; he was so busy making sure I wasn't freaking out that no one was finding out how he was. But Doug had shown up; Doug made sure he didn't get shoved into that machine alone.

"I feel like I'm stuck in the middle of someone else's really bad dream, or a childish prank that's gone way too far to be even remotely funny."

"Yet you want it to be, so that it will be over and you'll have someone you can yell at."

"I want someone I can beat the hell out of. And I keep thinking of how obsessed he's been lately with the idea that he might be dead in five years. What if that's been some weird cosmic warning?"

She didn't brush that aside, either. "When you first start out, twenty eight years seems like forever. Then you get there and it's not nearly long enough. You want to get to thirty. And then you want to see thirty five. Then forty."

"And I screwed up two of them. Hell, more than two years when you consider how much strain I put on us when Nick and Paul were just babies."

Kris didn't need me to spell it out; there was no getting around that ugly factoid of our lives. When she and Chip were off saving the world, I slept with her husband.

"That's been long forgiven and forgotten," Kris said, very quietly.

"But I hurt you all so terribly, and Chip never deserved that."

"It wasn't as painful as you think. From where I stood, it was better you than some random trash Doug could have picked up to take care of any horny impulses he might have had. It didn't happen because he didn't care enough about his marriage to stop himself. If happened because you were both tired and terrified, and you caved in to the complete hopelessness that Chip and I thrust on you."

"Kris..."

"I mean it, Terry. We were every bit as much to blame. And you know I was never angry or even really hurt. It happened. It wasn't anything personal against me or against Chip. I know that. I knew then."

"But Chip *was* hurt. It nearly broke him, Kris. It wasn't even the idea that I'd had sex with someone else, it was the promise. When we got married, he meant it. No one else, ever. The whole time we were separated he could have slept with a dozen different women and I know he had a trail of them sniffing him out, but he wouldn't even consider it. What hurt him was that shattered promise. He was supposed to be the only one, ever. And it wasn't just a promise to him, it was a promise to myself, and it was obliterated with five minutes of drunken fear and curiosity."

Tears were streaming down my face and I couldn't stop them.

"And yet," Kris said, "everyone has forgiven you for it. It never bothered me, and Chip forgave you over two decades ago. The only one who hasn't forgiven you is you."

I knew that; I had trained myself to stop apologizing to Chip any time the subject came up in even the most remote of ways. He was tired of hearing me say it because he didn't need to hear it again. It was fractured minutes of our past. But to me, it exacerbated the sorrow I felt over having kicked him out of his own house a little over ten years later, when he ran off to complete an assignment for the agency.

I couldn't justify those two lost years; I wanted them back as badly as I wanted to have never hurt him in the first place.

And now I was staring down at the idea that I could lose him for good.

Kris reached over and took my hand, holding it between hers gently. "I love you like a sister. Like a best friend and a daughter all in one. So listen to me when I say that you need to get over it already. You don't need to make it up to anyone anymore, not even Chip. All you need to do is be there for him, no matter what the outcome of this test is."

I couldn't stop crying, not even when Doug sat back down across from us. To his credit he said nothing about my tears and didn't try to make me feel better about anything.

"They've started. It should take about an hour, give or take a few minutes when they have to stop to run dye into the IV."

"Chip hates needles," I said absently, sniffing back more tears.

"That explains the whining. I told him he was being a big baby, and he agreed."

"He's entitled right now," I said.

Chip could whine all he wanted, as long as he got through this.

~

Chip

In theory, I knew what to expect—a room with a giant machine in the middle, a large tube with a hole in the center and a table that slid in and out of it. I'd seen pictures; those apparently had been taken in bright rooms with brand new equipment. This was dim and nearly dingy, clean but not exactly appealing, and that hole didn't look big enough to accommodate more than the slimmest of pre-teens.

I was suddenly grateful for the valium.

"Anything metal on you?" the technician asked. "Jewelry, zippers, surgical staples?"

I shook my head.

"Any piercings I can't see? Nipples, genital?"

"Oh, hell no."

Doug grinned. "She has to ask. You might be sporting a giant PA for all she knows."

"A what?"

The tech was trying not to smile, too.

"I'll explain later."

She handed me two yellow wads of foam and gestured towards my ears. "You'll need these. The machine is louder than loud." She patted the table. "Hop on up. We'll get you comfy and start the IV."

"What IV? No one said anything about an IV."

"It's for contrast dye," Doug explained as I inched onto the table. Slowly. Hoping for someone to say I didn't have to go through with it after all. "Halfway through they'll stop and inject a dye into the IV line so that we can get images with contrast."

"You should have told me this beforehand."

"Eh, you're just being a big baby."

"So? Let's see you do this."

"Will it make you feel better if she stabs me first?"

"Yes. Definitely."

"Too late." Doug put his hand on my shoulder, and gave it a light squeeze. "While you were whining, she got the IV in, and you didn't even cry."

I looked at my arm. "I'll be damned."

"All right," the tech said. "Get comfortable. Once I slide you in, don't move, but if you have to, wait until you don't hear the machine banging. There will be stretches where it won't be imaging, and will be quiet then. Ready?"

"I'll see you when it's done," Doug said.

He started to walk out the room. "Hey. Keep Terry's mind off this if you can."

He nodded and left, and the table jerked as I was moved slowly inside, grateful again that Doug had thought to drug me up.

When the banging started, I closed my eyes, hoping I could drift off and sleep through most of it. I didn't want to lay there and stew over the possibilities, what we would do if the worst happened. I didn't want to lay there and ponder getting my will updated; I didn't want to think about scrambling to buy enough land for my family to build homes on or the start restaurant construction. I didn't want to dwell on my grandkids and whether or not I'd done everything I needed to make sure they'd be taken care of, if their trust funds were performing well enough, and if I'd ever set anything in motion for future grandkids, because surely at some point my kids would start popping them out right and left. I didn't want to contemplate whether or not Terry would be all right, how she would handle the stress of getting me from "oh yeah, it's brain cancer" to me dying.

I didn't want to think about any of that, but I did.

It was all I thought about.

~

An hour later when the tech let me out of the tube from hell, the valium was beginning to wear off and my head was pounding from the noise that had thundered at me in ten minute spurts. By the time she pulled the IV out, I gave a damn, and all I wanted was to get out to the waiting room, get my jeans, and get out of there.

I came around the corner and Terry was laughing, her hand over her mouth the way she did when Nicole said something inappropriately funny, when she couldn't help but laugh even though she knew she shouldn't.

I saw the smile dancing at the corners of her eyes, and was very grateful to Doug and Kris for making the drive to be there.

"What'd I miss?"

Terry was still smiling when she jumped up, grabbing the front of my t-shirt to pull me in for a kiss. "Remind me later to get you online so you can see for yourself what a PA is."

"Do I really want to know?"

"Probably not." She was still holding onto my t-shirt, folds of red cotton clenched between her fingers. "You don't look any worse for the wear."

"I wouldn't want to do it every week, but it wasn't too bad. The valium helped."

"Then my work here is done," Doug declared, pushing up on his legs as he stood.

"Not so fast," I said. "I'm starving. You called before I had a chance to get breakfast, and we left the house right after that. You people are going to feed me."

"I called after ten," Doug said. "How lazy are you that you weren't up early enough to eat before that?"

Terry had let go of my shirt, but she was still leaning against me, so I put my arms around her. "Blame this one. She woke me up in the middle of the night with these wanton ideas in her head."

She tried to shove me back but I had too good of a hold on her. "Chip, you're horrible."

"I'm guessing that's not what you said to him in the middle of the night," Kris teased.

"No, but I may have a whole lot to say to him later."

"Oh, she's all flustered now, but I guarantee what she has to say will be x—"

She pointed a warning finger at me. "Watch it, buddy."

I was grinning stupidly and about to say something that probably would have really made her mad, but Kris steered her towards the door and they walked out, presuming, I suppose, that we would follow.

"Blame it on the valium," Doug chuckled.

"She's not really mad. I think. She's not really mad, right?"

"Definitely the valium."

"I've told you how bendy she is."

"Yes, but not right in front of her. And not in front of Kris."

"But she is bendy."

"And insatiable. I got that memo a while back, Chip. Focus. We are taking our wives out to lunch, and we will not discuss how bendy they may or may not be, nor will we talk about what *they* talk about in the middle of the night. Let's not embarrass them."

"Well, you know they talk about us."

"As well they should. We're gods in bed, and deserve the praise."

"Of course." I slowed, wanting to let Kris and Terry get well ahead of us. "Help me out at lunch, Doug. Keep the conversation off the topic of my brain. She's freaking out enough as it is."

"And you're not?"

"I'm trying to internalize my freaking out. I just want to spare her from worrying for a little while. You know as soon as we get home she'll start chewing on it, waiting until you get the results."

"We can try. I'm not sure any of us has much else to think about right now, though."

"House hunting," I suggested. "The kids. Wanting a mutual grandchild. Anything else."

"Just don't get upset if she needs to talk about it."

"Fine." Kris and Terry were at the door; Terry looked back to see where we were and smiled before following Kris out. "There. See? She's not pissed off."

"You amuse her," he said.

"Doug, seriously. Before we get out there and have to start squirting sunshine out our asses. What's your best guess?"

"Bearing in mind I'm not a neurologist or an endocrinologist, and based on lab results...I still think you have a prolactinoma. And as long as it's not bigger than a pea, we can treat it with medication."

"Drugs."

"Bromocriptine. Possibly a steroid. It wouldn't be my call, Chip. If you have a tumor, I'm handing you over to someone else."

"Steroids. Prednisone? I won't take it if I can avoid it."

"Wait. No, probably not. But why wouldn't you take it?"

"Doug, I'm stressing over gaining fifteen pounds. Put me on that and I'll probably gain fifty or sixty if not more. No thanks."

"I didn't realize you were so vain."

"Well, I am," I admitted. We stopped at the door; Kris and Terry were already by our car, waiting. "Look, I know she loves me no matter what. That wouldn't change."

"Exactly. She loves *you*."

"Yeah, she loves me. But she seriously likes the package. I've killed myself in the gym for nearly thirty years, and I let her feed me the most boring food on the planet to keep it this way. If there's a drug that won't turn me into a mass of quivering flesh, I'll take it, but—"

"—but you really are a vain little ass. Who knew?"

"I'm sure you all suspected."

"Eh, a little," he admitted. "Don't start worrying about the treatment until you know what the problem is. Chances are we'll get the images of the inside of your head, and we won't see a damn thing."

~

"Fish. Green stuff. More green stuff." Doug looked at the food on my plate with measured disgust. "Fry that fish and then pour a little melted imitation cheese over everything, and that might look edible."

"What, and chug a pint of melted lard to wash it all down?"

"Or beer. Beer would be good."

"If we let you drink beer this early, you'd be puking that cheese covered fish all over the inside of your tuna boat of a Cadillac. Freaking lightweight."

"Bite me. I'll have you know, I can now drink *two* beers without getting tipsy."

"And if you ate more like Chip does," Kris added, "you wouldn't have heartburn half the time. Vegetables won't kill you, you know."

"Apparently peas will," Terry said. "You should hear the whining that goes on when I make peas."

"Sooner or later Nicole will outgrow that," Kris said.

Terry snickered, "I'm not talking about Nicole. He's also fairly sure that if I feed him any more chicken he's going to sprout feathers."

"I like broccoli," I said absently. "Why don't we have more broccoli?"

"Because broccoli doesn't like *you*."

"Spare us the details," Doug said. "And here's your argument against peas. They're not really a vegetable. They're a starch. You might as well scarf down a potato in their place."

"Stop helping," Terry warned him.

"No, really. Same thing with corn. All starch. Good in small amounts, but he'd be better off if you gave him the broccoli and a few simethicone pills."

"Doug, I am going to stab you with my fork in a minute."

"She's annoyed," he said. "It only took me six minutes to get her to threaten me."

"Good job. Since you're so useful, tomorrow I'll let you go scope out some property that might work for all of us."

"I have patients in the morning, but I'm free after twelve thirty. Where are we looking?"

On the other side of the county, near the outskirts of Vacaville, there was a new housing development under construction. On paper it seemed to be a better fit than the last property we'd looked at; the kids wouldn't be settling for massive master suites offsetting tiny bedrooms for their future offspring, and construction was still at a point where they could add their own vision of what the ideal home was; they could still pick out the colors and flooring, they could trade bedrooms for more garage space if they wanted.

And there was the restaurant. I knew where it was going; I wanted Doug's opinion, an affirmation that I wasn't over thinking the concept of moving it. If I'd blundered, he'd say so.

Terry wanted to know how long I'd had the notion brewing in the back of my head. I might be prone to whims, but not where our investments were concerned, and especially not with the one that Paul was pinning his future on.

"I've been thinking about it for a couple of years," I told her. "All those same reasons you want to move…the entire area around the Charybdis is transitioning, and not in a good way for an expensive restaurant. People aren't going to keep coming there to drop over a hundred bucks on dinner for two."

"So it's time for a change," Doug mused.

"I think it's time to not only move, but become a little more family friendly. People want something affordable, and somewhere they feel like their kids will be welcome."

"Not another chain clone," Terry groaned.

"No, we're not going to imitate any of the chains. For the most part we'll keep the same menu, but we have to lower prices and we have to bring new customers in or there won't be a Charybdis in ten years."

"It'll be sad to see it go," Terry said. "The sheer electricity in it.

Face it, a guy takes a date there and he can be pretty sure he'll be getting lucky later."

"That doesn't have to change. We do most of that with lighting and music anyway. During the day we keep it bright and pipe in satellite radio, and around seven o'clock the lights go down and the music goes live. We keep the bar, and we keep the dance floor. We have the menu loaded with kid friendly food during the day, and impress your date food at night."

"Your chef is going to have a cow if you tell him to expand the menu."

"If you want to bring in new people," Doug offered, "you're going to have to start frying a few things and take the green crap off the plates."

"He can have the junk people like," Terry countered, "but still expand to offer more heart healthy things. Whole wheat pasta. Advertise that you have organic fruits and vegetables and free range chicken. Your red meat from cows that graze, not cows force fed corn."

"See, you knew corn wasn't great," Doug chuckled.

"And it's not great advertising fodder," I said. "They're great, and I'll look into the costs, but I'm not sure how well saying we have free range chicken will look in an ad."

"If you have a healthier menu maybe Terry will even let your grandkids through the front door more often," Kris said.

"If I ever get more grandkids to worry about, maybe so," Terry agreed.

"It would be nice if one of those grandkids happened to also be ours," Kris mused.

Doug nodded. "Even if Spider and Eileen aren't ready, we are."

"I'd like to have a grandchild or two while I'm still young enough to enjoy them."

We weren't sure Spider and Eileen would be ready anytime in the near future. It seemed more likely that Kevin and Lydia would have two more before Eileen decided to give up being the fun aunt in favor of being someone's mother. There was no telling when Nick would cave in to Katie's want of a baby, and Paul...it would help if he would just start dating.

"He says he's ready," I said. "He doesn't think Nicole is ready for the whole concept of him spending that much time with anyone else."

"Isn't she shopping her friends' mothers, trying to get him to ask one out?" Kris asked.

"She likes the idea. He doesn't think the reality would go over well."

Terry agreed, but thought Paul needed to push the idea a little. "Otherwise Nicole with be eighteen and he'll still be alone. At some point he has to accept that kids don't get to make those decisions for their parents."

"He's trying to be sensitive about it," I said. "Just because we're ready to see him happy doesn't mean Nicole is ready to share him."

As soon as that was out of my mouth, I regretted it. The next thing Terry would be chewing on was why Paul was alone; he'd had a horrible marriage, yet when it seemed like they were working it out and were determined to get back together, Monica was sick, and a few months later she was dead.

I didn't want Terry's mind going there; I didn't want her to start thinking about death, especially with most of her brain occupied with the idea that I might be headed in that direction.

I looked at Doug, hoping he could find some way to change the direction the conversation was going, but Kris suddenly smiled and said, "Oh! You know, we're really close to that Galleria mall in Roseville, and they have a new baby clothes store. Tons of cute things for your new grandson."

"Oh, hell," Doug moaned. "They're going to drag us around a mall."

"Fine," Kris said. "If you're too lazy to walk the mall, there are two cars. You and Chip can head home instead." She turned to Terry and added, "We should call your Mom and see if she wants to get out of the house for a while."

After lunch we stood in the parking lot and watched them leave in Terry's car. "I owe you," I told Doug as we got into his. "If anything will keep her occupied, a little retail therapy with Kris will do the job."

"And might cost you a ton of money. You know they're not just going to shop for baby clothes."

"Maybe she'll buy me new toys," I said. "Something kinky."

"I thought she was kinky enough all on her own."

"She's bendy," I reminded him. "But kinky enough."

We waited for them at our house; we played pool, beating Spider at nine ball, and I watched Lydia mop up the floor with Doug in eight ball. I played with my grandson and reluctantly allowed Doug to hold him; we chewed off time until our wives came home, managing to avoid talking about anything remotely related to my brain. But before Doug could leave I pulled him aside, wanting to talk to him while everyone else was occupied.

"Realistically, when will you get the results?"

"A couple of days, Chip. Once a radiologist has gone over them, they'll courier the film over to my office."

A couple of days.

Surely I could distract Terry that long.

~

We hadn't been in the first of the model homes for more than three minutes when Doug said, "We have got to get the kids over here. Holy crap."

I had to agree. The court itself was huge; there were three houses on each side, and at the end of the court there was a large gap between them, big enough for a small playground. We could put up a swing set and a sandbox or anything else Nicole and Michael and any future grandkids might want. The smallest of the lots was at least twelve thousand square feet; they were all big enough for pools, hot tubs, or anything else we wanted. With no fences between the houses, there was plenty of room for kids to run, and enough street surface for bicycles and skateboards.

"All of them are single story," I mentioned in an offhand sort of way. "Since I don't want to be dealing with stairs when I'm as old as you, that's good."

The model home we were in had two master suites, and a smaller third bedroom. If Terry's parents ever agreed to move in, we'd be set. The third room could be set up for any overnight babysitting we might do.

"Or a den for yourself," Doug pointed out. "You can think beyond the scope of short people."

"Aren't they why we're doing this?"

"I'm not sure why I'm doing this. I just got one house paid off, for Christ's sake."

"That explains the car," I mused. "Terry thought mine was over the top, but cripes, Doug. You paid a hundred grand for that thing."

"I'll let you drive it. You'll see."

The second model home was a four bedroom monstrosity; there was the option, the builder's agent told us, to turn the fourth bedroom into a den with built in bookcases or an entertainment center. It was well over twenty five hundred square feet; even if Kevin and Lydia slipped up and had more than the three kids they were planning on, or they were all as tall as he turned out, it was big enough.

"Any chance I can make an appointment with the builder?" I asked her. "I'd like to bring my family by within the next week or so."

"Not a problem." She had her Blackberry out and was glancing over a calendar. "Which house should I tell him you're interested in?"

I gestured towards the court across the street. "All of them."

"All of them."

"I'd also like to know what the requirements would be to have the court gated off at the point of entry, and fenced off at the back of each property line. No fences in between the houses. Whether you can do that or if I have to get permits from the city."

She was tapping away furiously. "Can you bring your family by on Thursday?" she asked, still looking at her cell phone. "He'll make time if you're serious."

"I can, and yes, I'm serious."

On the way out, Doug tossed me the keys to his car and said, "I think you made the woman wet herself, Chip. And I'm not sure she believes you really are interested in them all."

It was only a five mile ride to the lot where I wanted to build a new Charybdis, but it was long enough for me to develop a major case of the Wants for Doug's car.

"Told you so," he said when I handed the keys back. "Worth

every penny."

"Does Kris know how much you paid for that?"

"Hell, no."

"Didn't think so. Terry would beat me with her giant spoon if I bought that car."

"Trust me, it would be worth it. And once you took her for a long ride…consider her bendiness in that back seat."

I had to look back at the car.

She would only be upset for a little while.

And I wouldn't have to tell her what it cost.

"This," I told him, gesturing to the empty lot, "is where the new Charybdis will go. It's just off the Interstate but not so close that traffic noise will be a problem, the outlet stores are nearby, and a higher end retail strip is going up on the other side of the freeway."

"Lots of potential traffic going by," Doug guessed. "One to two hundred thousand cars a day easily if you count both flow from the retail arenas and Interstate off ramps. There's very good investment potential here."

"Good. Because I already bought it. And no, Terry does not know yet."

"Wait. You'll spend, what, a million bucks on land, but you won't buy an expensive car without her permission? That might not be the best idea you've ever had."

I shrugged. "She's never been interested in my business deal-ings. She doesn't know half of what we own. Besides, if we buy those houses, she'll like the idea of the restaurant being so close."

"Great for Paul. What about the rest of your business holdings? How far from those will you be?"

"No worse getting to those that I am now. Things are scattered around a three county area."

He started to say something but was cut off by his ringing cell phone. He had to take it, and walked a few steps ahead as he talked.

If we all made the move, Doug wouldn't be much farther from his practice than he already was, and he had been talking about cutting back his hours, anticipating retirement in a few years. Nick wouldn't be more than a mile or two more from the agency and Katie had started teaching in Vacaville anyway. The only ones facing a commute were Kevin,

Eileen, and Spider, but it wasn't so far to be considered unreasonable.

It was what they said they wanted, anyway. They could suck it up and drive.

I walked back to Doug's car, thinking it would wind up being a sweet deal as long as the kids liked the houses, and I didn't see any reason why they wouldn't. He hung up and leaned against the car, but before I could reach for the door handle he said, "We need to go, and you need to call Terry. Your MRI results are in."

~

I'd spent enough time over the years in Doug's office to know that most patients never set foot in it. Good news or bad was usually delivered in an exam room, with the patient and a family member seated in chairs against the wall while he perched on a little round stool. He used his office for research, spending long lunches pouring over medical journals and textbooks as he looked for answers to the problems dropped at his feet every day.

Aside from his desk and the bookcases that lined the walls, he had three chairs; two were comfortable and intended for people who were waiting for him, usually his wife or his friends. The third was a metal folding chair that had last seen a good day in the late eighties.

Terry and I waited in the comfy chairs; normally we had no trouble filling up the wait with small talk, poking fun at Doug in his absence, all the magazines he had piled and shoved behind stacks of books like he was trying to hide porn. This time neither of us felt like talking, and we waited in silence until Terry murmured, "I feel like I'm going to throw up."

I could feel the anxiety drip from my fingertips in static pulses; we'd been waiting for twenty minute while Doug went into the next office to get and read the MRI. At first we could hear him speaking to people who wandered in and out of the room, and then nothing for a long time.

"If he took the time to go to the bathroom it can't be all bad news."

She didn't laugh.

When he finally came back, he had the oversized film in hand along with the envelope it had arrived in; the tension in his face, the lines at his eyes and the tight set of his jaw screamed that he was struggling to make the switch from the man we had chosen to be our children's only uncle to the doctor who treated us all.

Terry took one look at him and started to cry.

He tossed the envelope on his desk and reached for the metal chair, folding it open without letting go of the film. He sat close enough to be able to reach out and touch either of us, and when he did he came out with it, no beating around the medical bush.

"You have a two centimeter pituitary adenoma. Most of it is seated towards the anterior side of the pituitary, and there's a slight thickening of the gland itself."

I glanced at Terry; tears were sliding down her face, but she looked at him with hopeful expectation.

I wanted to know what it meant.

"It means you need to see a neurologist, specifically one who specializes in the pituitary. And you need to see an endocrinologist. There are also a few tests we might as well go ahead and run so that you have those results to show them…there's no point in delaying anything longer than we have to. I want to get an ACTH stimulation test in the morning, and I'll schedule a visual acuity test with an ophthalmologist as soon as I can."

"For?"

"The optic nerves run very close to the pituitary gland," he explained. "We need to know if the tumor is touching it at all and if you have any blind spots in your visual field that you just don't realize are there. The stim test will tell us about your stress response and let us know if that part of the pituitary is compromised at all."

I didn't ask if he was in a hurry because he needed to be, or because he was my friend. I wasn't sure I wanted to know.

Terry sniffed and asked what I couldn't. "Is it cancer?"

"I don't know. I can't tell from these images, but the neurologist sees these routinely and will have a much better idea. I can tell you this much, and I want you to know this right up front. This is a large adenoma; under one centimeter it's a microadenoma. At this size it's a macroadenoma."

"Which means it probably has to come out," I said.

Doug nodded.

"How?" Terry wanted to know, anger painting rough lines over the fear. "How the hell are they going to get it out? It's on the underside of his brain. Are they going to cut his skull open and lift his brain out, then scoop it up like ice cream? And what happens if they can't get his brain back in? What then?"

"That won't happen," he replied gently. "Typically the way pituitary tumors are removed is by either going through the nose or under the upper lip. The surgeon drills through the back of the sinus cavity, and the pituitary is right there."

"Sounds simple enough," I said.

"I'm not going to minimize it for either of you. This is major surgery, and it's not risk free."

That made Terry cry even more, silent tears that streamed down her face and dripped from her jaw.

"How soon can I get in to see the other docs?" I asked him.

"I already made you an appointment with the endocrinologist for next Tuesday, and I'm waiting on a call from the neurosurgeon I'd like you to see. Can you be here first thing in the morning for the stim test?"

"Define first thing."

"He'll be here," Terry said. "What time?"

"As close to seven as you can make it. And don't eat anything for at least eight hours before."

"Should he do anything else to get ready for it?"

"No. When you get here, we'll draw blood to have a baseline, and then you'll be injected with cortisone. After that you sit for an hour in the waiting room, we draw more blood, and you're done."

Done.

Like hell.

It was a freaking medical merry go round and someone bought me a fist full of tickets without bothering to ask me if I even wanted to ride.

10

Kevin

I didn't think twice when I walked past my parents' bedroom and from the corner of my eye saw my mother sitting on the edge of her bed, tying her shoes. I barely registered that she was there until I was in Michael's room and realized that as I'd walked by, she was crying.

Dad was downstairs feeding his grandson, otherwise I would have gone down and told him that he might want to head up and see what was wrong, but it also occurred to me that he might be the problem.

Nick would barge in there and try to solve her problems by telling her what to do. I leaned toward the belief that my parents' issues were none of my business and typically left things alone, but after I'd grabbed a fresh diaper and was headed back down the hall, it hit me that she wasn't angry; she looked sad.

I didn't knock; the door was wide open so I went in and sat down beside her. When she didn't look up I asked, "You okay?"

She had to swallow past the tears before she could choke out, "I'm fine, Kevin. Just tired."

"Isn't that Dad's line?"

She patted me on the leg but still wouldn't look at me. "I actually let him sleep last night, so he should be perky today."

"I can go get him if you want me to."

"It's all right. I'll be down in a minute anyway."

"Did he say something to upset you? I can beat him up for you, you know."

She leaned into me, setting her head on my shoulder for just a moment. "You know your father. He can't stand to see me upset. He'll walk away before he'll fight."

"Yeah, but if he did fight back it would upset you," I ventured. "Really, I can take him."

"Kevin, please. He didn't do anything."

"Nick?" She was up and crying a couple hours before she would normally roll out of bed, and the thought that my brother was still We Don't Know Where and vulnerable stabbed at me. "Did something happen to Nick?"

"No. Kevin, no. We haven't heard anything about Nicky."

"Then it's just one of those mornings?" She'd had a lot of those mornings in the past, but that was when Dad was across town in a tiny apartment she'd never seen, and she hadn't spoken to him for months.

She nodded. "It'll pass. Now take that down to Michael. I'm betting he needs that more than I need to sit here feeling like I'm worrying my son."

"I'm not worried. I was just hoping I could make you feel a little better."

She got up, heading for her closet. "You do make me feel better. And I'll be downstairs in a few minutes."

I was dismissed, and she couldn't bring herself to look at me.

When I got back to the dining room Dad was wiping cereal from Michael's face, and it hit me: his face was drawn in the same tired lines as Mom's. For all his protests of fatigue over the last few weeks, now he looked it. He was taking care of his grandson, but he wasn't making the same faces he normally did, trying to get Michael to smile. He was talking to Michael, but it wasn't with the same patter of joy that seemed to leech from him every time he held my son.

I went into the kitchen where Lydia was mixing a bottle, and leaned against the breakfast bar, my back turned towards my dad. She started to say something to me, but I put my finger over my lips, and signed instead of speaking.

"Can you take Michael into the living room to finish feeding him?"

She nodded.

"I need to talk to my dad," I explained.

She set the bottle on the counter. "He's a little off today. I thought it was just me."

"Something's wrong. It might be nothing, but—"

"Don't stick your nose where it isn't welcome," she warned.

Dad came into the kitchen then, Michael in his arms. "What are you being nosy about?" he asked.

Lydia reached for the baby and snatched the bottle off the counter before he had a chance to protest. I watched her leave, and part of me wanted to walk out of the kitchen with her, but by then Dad had blocked the way.

"What's up?"

"Mom's upstairs crying."

His eyes closed briefly as he exhaled, and when he opened them he looked up to where he knew she still was.

"She says it's just one of those days, but..."

He turned and leaned against the counter next to me. "She's all right, Kevin."

"So you already knew she was upset?"

"I am aware, yes."

I could see him reflected in the glass door of the double oven across the kitchen. He had his arms folded and resting across his chest, and he was looking down at the floor.

"I don't think you're fighting," I ventured.

"No, we're not."

"And you look as tired and anxious as she does."

He didn't answer, but he uncrossed his arms and stuck his hands in his pockets. I kept watching his reflection, waiting for him to look up.

He wasn't moving; I could hear him swallow hard, and his breath quickened, but he wasn't trying to leave; he damn near took root right there, determined to not even twitch.

No, they weren't fighting. This wasn't how they were when they were ticked; if they were angry with each other they'd sit in the same room and glare, or Dad would suck it up and apologize whether he thought he was in the wrong or not. He wouldn't leave her crying in their bedroom. And if it was just Mom having a bad day, feeling a little weepy, he'd be the one trying to soothe her feelings.

This wasn't just sadness.

This was fear.

Fear wrapped around sadness, wrapped in a neat little bow of anxiety, and it had nothing to do with my absent older brother.

"Which one of you is sick, and how bad is it?"

At this he looked up. "No one said anything about being sick."

And yet, he didn't deny it.

"You know, I haven't seen you two do anything remotely inappropriate this week," I said. "No wayward groping when you think no one else is looking. No kisses that make me wonder if you both end it with tonsils intact. Yet more than once I've seen you holding on to each other like you were trying to keep each other from falling apart."

"We hug, son."

"Yeah, but it's always with a lot of lightness. It didn't click with me until just a few minutes ago when I came back here and saw you washing off Michael's face. Mom's upstairs crying, and you just look sad."

"Tired," he grunted.

"You've *been* tired. A lot."

"I've also got a lot on my plate right now."

"And you would drop everything on that plate to make goofy faces and rude noises at your grandson. You'd also be upstairs with Mom at the first hint that she was in tears, unless you'd been trying all night to make her feel better and knew it wasn't going to happen. You sure as hell wouldn't be standing in the kitchen with me, staring at the freaking oven."

"Kev—"

"I'm not letting this go, Dad. It's six-thirty in the freaking morning and you don't *do* morning anymore. You're up for a reason, and whatever it is you're both miserable. What else am I supposed to think?"

I turned to look at him; he was biting his bottom lip, considering, thinking hard and fast and probably looking for something to say that would make me give up and go away.

After several starts and stops, he came out with it, choking on every word.

"I have a brain tumor."

He might as well have sucker punched me in the gut.

I would have preferred a sucker punch; that I could do something about. This…Dad was supposed to whine about getting older and falling apart. He wasn't supposed to actually have something go wrong.

"How bad is it?" I asked when I could get a coherent word out of my mouth.

"We don't know yet."

I didn't ask who 'we' was. 'We' was always him and Mom; it was in his head but it was their tumor.

"Where?" I was looking at his reflection again, and he was still staring at his feet. "In your brain, I mean. Where?"

"Just under it, pressed against my pituitary." He drew in a long, slow breath, and exhaled sharply. "Doug can't tell exactly what it is from the MRI…"

He had more to say, but trailed off, I suppose considering the possibilities. I needed to hear more, but I suddenly felt like a five year old who had face-planted into the sidewalk and all I wanted was my dad.

I slid my arm around him and pulled him into a hug, and he slumped against me, face buried against my shoulder.

He let me hold him until Mom shuffled into the kitchen, her eyes red and face flushed. She fell against him, one hand resting on my arm.

"It's not cancer," she sobbed. "It's not."

Dad had both arms around her, holding her tight, and he whispered against her hair, "It's all right. It will be all right," but I wasn't sure if that was for her as much as it was for himself.

"What did Uncle Doug tell you?" I asked once Mom's hand had relaxed and she was no longer digging into my arm with tense fingers.

"That it's big, and he has to hand me off to other doctors," Dad murmured.

Mom let my arm go, and slipped hers around Dad's waist. "It's a two centimeter pituitary macroadenoma," she said as if reciting from a report. "It's why he's been so tired lately, and Doug can't treat him, and he has to see a neurosurgeon and an endocrinologist…"

"And we have to go," Dad sighed. "Kevin, I'm sorry, but I have to be at Doug's office in about twenty minutes. I'll tell you everything I can when we get back."

"That's all right. It'll give me time to get online and start reading up on pituitary tumors."

Dad smiled weakly. "I'm not surprised."

"Google is my friend," I informed them.

He managed to disentangle himself from Mom, and leaned over to kiss me. "We haven't told anyone else, son. I'm not sure when—"

"I won't say anything," I promised. "Except to Lydia."

I watched them as they walked out of the house, noting that Mom's hand never left him; she was either touching his arm or the small of his back, but she wasn't letting go, not unless she had to.

~

While Lydia made breakfast for Nicole, I sat on the couch with my laptop and surfed the Internet for anything I could find on pituitary tumors. Michael was on his back in his playpen, smacking himself in the face with his own hand; I watched him out of the corner of my eye, trying not to smile at his complete surprise every time his fist made contact with his nose. I resisted the urge to turn him onto his stomach to spare him the self-pummeling; he wasn't crying and didn't seem to mind that something he couldn't quite pinpoint was smacking him over and over.

"The good news," I told Lydia when she came back into the living room, but quietly so that Nicole wouldn't hear, "is that malignant pituitary cancer is so rare that there's virtually no chance he has it. There have only been around a hundred cases reported, ever."

She dropped onto the sofa, leaning against me so that she could see the computer screen. "What about benign cancer? Even that could be seriously problematic."

I was focused on finding out about the possibility of malignancy and hadn't specifically looked for anything on benign pituitary cancer. "All I know right now is that it's not likely he has a malignancy, but if he does, it's really bad news. Seriously bad."

"So we focus on the good."

"He's going to have to have surgery, with a tumor that size. The question is whether or not they take any of the pituitary out, or even all of it."

She looked up at me. "Can he survive without it?"

"He'd be on a lot of medication for the rest of his life, but I think so."

"How much is a lot?"

I scrolled the page down and showed her a diagram of the brain and where his tumor likely was. "This thing is your body's master gland. It creates and controls most of the major hormones. If they remove it, he'd have to have at least six of them replaced. I know it creates that many but I'm not sure how that works, if they then go on to create other hormones."

"Then if he gets it removed, it's that simple? He just takes drugs for the rest of his life?"

I didn't think it was quite that simple. "It might be tricky. Like cortisol. If his is messed up it affects his blood pressure, blood glucose, insulin release, immune response...it does a lot in the body and I'm not sure how easy not having it is to manage."

"So he can wind up being all right, but not all right."

"Lots of things could go wrong."

"And yet," she said, closing the laptop, likely in deference to the sound of Paul's footsteps on the stairs, "you seem rather calm, considering."

"I'm scared out of my freaking mind."

"Is that because he's your dad, or because you understand more of the biology behind this than you're willing to admit right now and what he might be facing is bigger than you want to tell me?"

"He's my dad," I breathed out.

I don't think she believed me, but Paul walked through on his way into the kitchen, and neither of us was willing to let him think anything more than we were sitting there watching our baby boy commit random acts of self battery.

~

When they came home three hours later, Dad was wearing a long sleeve t-shirt; it was ninety degrees out and he was sweating, but I didn't have to ask why. He had new puncture wounds in the crooks of each of his elbows, and he didn't want Paul or Nicole asking why. He couldn't hide the sheer fatigue that was etched into his face, though; he and Mom both looked like they needed to sleep for a week.

He claimed he needed food more than anything, but before he could take a step into the kitchen Mom guided him toward the sofa and told him to go sit down. She would fix him some breakfast, and then he would—not could—go lie down for a while.

There was no arguing with her; he sank into the far end of the sofa, his head leaned back against the cushion. "I am now ten years old," he grumbled. "I'm not capable of feeding myself, or getting blood sucked out of me by myself."

"She just needs to take care of you," I said.

He knew that; he didn't mind her hovering, or even that she stared down the medical technician who was supposed to take Dad's blood and inject him with the cortisol when it was suggested that she stay in the waiting room. It didn't matter that Uncle Doug was also there; they weren't touching Dad unless she was right there with him.

"Think how fun she'll be if you need surgery. Some guy is going to have his fingers in your brain and she'll be right there at his elbow, threatening to rip his balls off if he dares to even think about sneezing."

He managed a wan smile at the image.

"Supposedly after I eat, I'm taking a nap. I might not want one, but dammit I'm going to take one."

"Nothing personal, Dad, but you look like you could use one. You're not sleeping worth shit, are you?"

"Doug offered sleeping pills…"

"But you don't want them?"

"No."

"It might not be a bad idea."

"If I start taking something to sleep, I might sleep a little too deeply."

"Uncle Doug wouldn't give you anything that would kill you," I said.

He shook his head. "That's not it. I need to be able to wake up and be clear headed, even if it's the middle of the night."

"In case Mom needs you."

"I don't want her curled up in bed crying while I'm effectively unavailable."

"She'll adjust. Give her a few days, and she'll adjust to everything that's going to happen over the next few weeks. She's a lot stronger than she seems sometimes."

"She also breaks easily," he said softly.

"She melts a little, for about thirty seconds. If she's already threatening people and telling you what you're going to do, she's starting to dig her heels in. That's a good thing. You can worry about Mom a little, but Dad, this has to be about you."

"We're a package deal, Kevin."

"And part of the package is that once Mom has time to catch her breath, she'll kick into overdrive and fight like hell to take care of you, and to let you feel whatever you're feeling without it being mostly worry about her."

"Until I know for sure what the outcome of this is going to be, I'm going to worry about her. There's no way around it."

He wanted to make sure he had all the legal bases covered, that Mom would have someone who could handle all of his investments. He wanted to make sure she was on the titles and deeds to everything, just to make things easier. He wanted her safe and comfortable, and he wanted the family to find a place to live as soon as possible, so that he would know she would be surrounded by the people she would need most.

"You can handle that stuff later," I told him. "You're not going anywhere right now, except into the kitchen for breakfast, and then you're going to go upstairs and lie down with your wife, curl around each other, and just *be* for a while."

Two hours later I walked by their bedroom; the door was open just far enough, and I could see them tangled around each other in the middle of the bed, sound asleep. Their foreheads were pressed together, and Mom's hand was on his ass.

Perfectly ordinary, like nothing was really wrong.

~

Mom still looked tired when she came downstairs later, but it was mixed with determination; she was definitely digging her heels in.

Dad was still asleep and she was taking her chance to corner me while she could.

"I need a huge favor from you, and you have the right to say no without disappointing me."

I'd thought that cleaning the kitchen would be a big enough favor; I was practically domestic all afternoon, doing dishes and scrubbing the annoying gunk that always seemed to accumulate around the oven burners. I tossed the wet paper towels I had in hand aside and leaned against the counter. "All right."

"I shouldn't ask you," she started.

"But you're going to anyway."

"Your father has this idea that he can get through the next week without saying anything to Paul or Eileen."

"No way in hell," I said. "They're going to know something is wrong."

"Exactly."

"But you don't think he *can* tell them."

"I think he's going to obsess over saying anything to them, and it's just going to make him crazy."

"So you want me to."

"He needed to tell you, Kevin. But telling them...Paul will get angry and he can't take seeing Eileen cry. I have no idea how Katie will take it with Nick not here."

If I delivered the news, Paul would still get angry, but he would be more willing to ask questions, find out how Dad was doing and what he could do to help rather than spout out streams of moral indignation on our father's behalf. Eileen would cry, but I'd made her cry enough over the years that I was almost immune; she would tumble into Spider's arms instead of leaping for Dad, who was trying to hold Mom together and might not be able to make her feel any better.

There was no one here for Katie, though, and she loved him as much as we did.

"Dad is going to be ticked," I warned her.

"Oh, he's going to be furious. He'll be as angry with me as he's ever been, but that's all right. I think in this case it's better that I wind up asking his forgiveness later than asking his permission first."

"I don't envy you that conversation."

"Mine will be a lot easier than yours. I just have to let him vent. He doesn't do it often, but when he does…"

"You have ways of distracting him," I assured her. "He won't stay mad long."

She managed a small smile. "And here I thought contemplating that embarrassed you."

"I'm just embracing my inner fourteen year old, Mom. I don't exactly want to walk in on it again, but I do appreciate what you have."

"The fourteen year old you never thought we would have that again."

"But I did. I prayed for it, Mom, and that's one prayer I was sure wouldn't get a no answer. I just didn't know how long it would take."

"Sometimes," she said, wrapping her arms around my waist, "your faith amazes me."

I hugged her back, as tightly as she seemed to want me to. "I have to have faith. Right now we all do."

I hoped faith was enough.

~

Terry

I waited in the living room for Chip to wake up, silence cracking all around me. Kevin and Lydia dropped Nicole off at her karate class and then headed for Eileen's, where they were going to meet with Paul and Katie. I wasn't sure how Kevin would break the news to the rest of his family, but I overheard him telling Lydia he just hoped that Paul would be able to suck it up and clear his head before he had to pick Nicole up.

They were wise enough to leave the house in case Chip had a meltdown when I told him that I'd asked Kevin to be the bearer of bad news to his siblings. Chip's reaction could be anywhere between a shrug of the shoulders to anger so explosive that he would walk out the door.

I was banking on some middle ground, where he would fume and vent all over me, until he had nothing left to say. I could take that; I could sit quietly and let him get from a simmer to a full on boil, and then wait for him to cool off. If he got physical at all, it would be a fist through the wall, and thanks to a few wayward feet thundering through drywall when Kevin practiced his side kicks in his bedroom, Chip had gotten fairly good at patching holes.

I knew this wasn't fair, but all I wanted was to protect Chip where I could, and this was something I could do.

After Kevin and Lydia had been gone for almost an hour, I heard Chip moving around upstairs, the soft shuffle of his feet across the floor, the sound of water rushing through pipes as the toilet flushed. I could picture him in my head, washing his hands and then running a comb through his hair, grabbing the jeans he'd left on the floor and slipping them on. Looking for the t-shirt he had absently tossed across the room as soon as he'd gotten through the bedroom door earlier. His socks, his shoes.

When I heard him on the top stair, I was struck with the sudden wish that I hadn't asked Kevin to do this; the last time I'd made Chip as angry as he was sure to be was a good nine years earlier, just before we reconciled. He stood in the kitchen, supposedly upset with Nick, when two years of frustration erupted and he turned his ire onto me, a loud and unforgettable venting that he was instantly sorry for. I'd deserved it then; I deserved it now.

Then, I had managed to remain calm, letting him seethe until he was done; surely I could still handle that much.

He was still covered in sleep when he sat next to me on the sofa, but he leaned over to kiss me and I made sure it was a good one, lips lingering long enough to hopefully make him want more, even though I knew as soon as I told him where Kevin was and why that he wouldn't want to be within five feet of me.

He stole a few more kisses, completely turning the tables on me; the want of pinning him down on the sofa and putting off saying anything plucked at me, but the guilt was worse.

"I slept half the day away," he sighed when we pulled apart. "Sorry about that."

I ran a finger across his cheek, wanting to touch him. "You needed it. Though I was only going to give you another half hour or so before I woke you up, so you can sleep tonight."

"And how," he asked, pulling me onto his lap and burying his face against my neck, "were you going to wake me?"

"Just like this had occurred to me. But I settled on ice water."

"Gah. You're mean." He slipped a hand under my shirt, teasing.

This was what I had wanted; he was groggy enough that he wasn't thinking about anything else, and I could have easily gone with it, at least for a while.

"The house is awfully quiet," he said. "Are we actually alone?"

"For now," I said against his lips.

"How long? Long enough?"

I grabbed at his wrist and pulled his hand way. "Chip, you have to let me up."

He sucked in a sharp, disappointed breath, and let me slide off his lap. "Sorry. I misread the cues."

"No. You didn't." I almost reached for his hand but thought better of it. "Trust me, I want to…but I have to tell you something, and once I do chances are you're going to want to blow, and not in a happy ending sort of way."

"Come on. There's not a whole lot you could do that would upset me that much."

"The house is so quiet," I said as evenly as I could, "because Kevin and Lydia took Michael over to Eileen's. I asked them to. They're meeting Paul and Katie, too."

"For?"

"I asked Kevin to tell them, Chip."

It took a moment for his brain to register what I wanted Kevin to do. His eyes went dark and he twitched away from me."Well, that's one thing you could do that would piss me off beyond belief. What the hell, Terry? How could you put that on him? It's not fair to anyone, especially not to Kevin."

"None of this is fair."

"No shit! We don't have all the information yet. What's he supposed to tell them? The only thing he knows is one simple fact that might break their hearts. I didn't want to worry our kids until we had something tangible to tell them, there's no *reason* to worry them before we know what this is."

I sat back, ready to let him hit his stride. He wasn't half way done working up to the boiling point, and I didn't have a reason for sending Kevin to do this, other than it seemed to me to be for the best, whether Chip liked it or not.

He was up off the sofa, running his hands through his hair, and I'm sure I was about to get hit with something a decibel or two above his usual I'm-so-damned-annoyed-with-you register, but the doorbell rang and he stomped off to answer it, yanking the door open and snapping, "What?" before he had it open far enough to see who it was.

Doug pushed past him and walked in before Chip could tell him to get the hell out. Kris followed; neither of them said hello, but Doug said, "Yep, he's pissed."

Chip stood at the door and grunted, "This isn't a good time."

Doug shrugged it off. "I don't care. Get your wallet. We're going to the restaurant so we can sit in the bar and pester Will while he works."

"Not right now."

"Yeah. Right now."

Kris sat next to me on the sofa, where Chip had just been. "Chip, just go."

"This is not a good time," he hissed.

"I know what time it is," Doug said. "It's time to get you out of here before you say something you can't take back."

"Kevin called you?" I asked.

Doug nodded and then said to Chip, "One way or the other you're leaving this house until you don't feel like breaking things."

"Do you know what she did? Do you know how fucking unfair it is to Kevin?"

"Get your panties out of a wad and just get your wallet."

"Kiss my ass, Doug."

Doug sighed and held up his keys. "Come on. I'll let you captain the tuna boat."

Chip snatched the keys from Doug's hand, but started back towards the sofa; Doug made a grab for his arm but he shook it off.

"I'll go with you, dammit, but I don't care how pissed off I am. I'm getting a kiss before I go."

He slammed the door behind him, one last You Suck aimed right at me. I had to laugh, because as mad as he was, his kiss was a little more than 'I'll see you later.'

"You know he's going to come home drunk," Kris said. "If he's not over being mad, you'll have to deal with a drunk *and* angry Chip."

I knew that, but I figured that by the time he came stumbling home the kids would be back, and he'd keep it to a quiet boil until he fell asleep, and by morning he'd be over it.

~

Kevin

Paul wanted the world to share in his minivan misery; he'd bought one when Nicole was a baby—because that's what parents do—and as much as he hated it he inexplicably bought another one five years later, and was still bitching about it. Just before Michael was born he tried to convince Lydia she wanted to trade the minivan for her pickup truck, reasoning that we needed it more than he did, what with all the baby crap we'd need to haul around.

She smiled sweetly at him, told him there was no way in hell, and promptly sold the truck and bought a PT Cruiser. All the space to haul the baby stuff around, she gloated to Paul, and it's *not* a minivan.

I drove her car to Eileen's while she sat in the back seat with Michael, and I almost wished she had traded with him. The Cruiser was perfect for her, but I was cramped behind the wheel, driving with my legs pressed against the underside of the dash board. Normally I'd let her drive to spare myself the discomfort, but this time I wanted the distraction; I had no idea exactly what I was going to tell everyone, and I didn't want to dwell on it until I had to.

All they knew was that I needed to talk to them, and it couldn't wait. Eileen and Paul tried to press the matter over the phone; Eileen was simply curious but Paul didn't want to leave work at the start of the dinner rush and thought whatever it was would be fine to just tell him on the phone. Katie just agreed to be at Eileen's at six o'clock; whatever it was, at least she was getting out of the house and spending some time with family.

We arrived before Paul or Katie, and Eileen didn't waste any time. I was setting up the playpen in her living room while Lydia got Michael out of his car seat, and she grabbed the other side to help me push the side brackets into place. "Spill it," she said before I could completely unfold it. "This has to be important if you're calling this meeting away from Mom and Dad's."

"We don't have to include Mom and Dad in everything."

"I've been a nervous wreck since you called, Kevin."

The playpen was open, support brackets locked, and Lydia had Michael out of his car seat. I took a rag out of his diaper bag and wiped the pad off before she could put him down; I wasn't going to tell Eileen to not be worried or afraid, that what I had to say was happy crap radiating with Care Bears and rainbows. I also wasn't going to tell her anything until Paul and Katie were there.

She stomped off into the kitchen when I told her she'd find out with everyone else; Lydia handed the baby to me and said she would try to calm my sister down.

Spider and I were left standing in the living room; Michael started to fuss and I didn't want to put him down, but there was no way to talk to Spider with him in my arms. Spider could lip read, but it wasn't always reliable, and I didn't want Eileen to overhear anything, especially a one sided conversation.

I set Michael in the play pen and rubbed his belly until he relaxed and focused on a rattle that I held a few inches from his face. He wasn't reaching for many things on his own, but if I wrapped his fingers around it, he would hold it and flail it back and forth, squealing as he played.

"This is big, isn't it?" Spider asked after I sat in a chair close to the playpen.

"It is, and you'll need to stick right by Eileen when I say it," I signed.

He gave a slight nod. "I walked in on Mom and Dad talking a couple days ago. They shut up as soon as they saw me there but I caught enough of it to get an idea."

That was one of Spider's stealth talents; he had great eyesight and could read lips across a room, allowing him to overhear snippets of things people didn't necessarily want him to know.

"I know there's something wrong with Uncle Chip," he went on, "but I haven't said anything to Eileen in case I misunderstood."

I wanted to ask him how much he knew, but the doorbell rang and Eileen stomped out of the kitchen to answer the door. Paul came in grumbling about having to leave just as the restaurant was filling up; Eileen told him to quit whining and to just enjoy having dinner with his wonderful sister.

"Someone else cooking?" he asked brightly, dodging her poking finger.

She barely had the door closed when the bell rang again. "If I didn't have to answer this I'd be throwing things at you," she shot back.

Katie was there, and I realized with a sick sense of dread that everyone I needed to tell was in the room. Everyone except for Nick, and a small part of me was glad he wasn't there; Dad only told me because I was right there and had pressed him to admit there was something wrong, but Nick's feelings would be a little hurt that it was me in whom Dad confided, and me that Mom wanted passing the news on to the rest of their kids.

"All right, Squirt," Paul said as he dropped onto Eileen's over-sized sofa. "We're here. What was so earth shatteringly important that it couldn't wait?"

All eyes were on me; I was sitting in a chair that put them in front of me like expectant college students. Share the wisdom, dude. Spill it. Paul and Katie were on the sofa, Eileen and Spider were on a loveseat angled next to it, and Lydia was sitting on the floor next to the playpen.

"Come on," Paul urged. "What's up?"

I took a deep breath. "This may sound worse than it is," I started, "and I don't want anyone to get too upset or go nuts or anything because I don't have all the details yet."

"I was right, wasn't I?" Eileen interrupted. "Is there something wrong with you, Kevin? You wanted to tell us before telling Mom and Dad?"

I wished it was that simple.

I looked at Lydia, who nodded slightly, urging me to go on.

"There is no nice way to tell you this, and I am really sorry that I'm going to suck at it. But Dad has a brain tumor."

Eileen erupted. "I *knew* it was something bad. I knew—"

Spider put his hand over hers; interrupt her signing, and interrupt her train of thought. But Paul was starting to sputter, and it wasn't as easy as grabbing his hands to distract him. The anger was bubbling just under the surface, and I could see it in his face: he'd shot back to a cold day a year and a half ago, when he sat in a hospital room with Monica, having to hear that his wife was so riddled with cancer that it was too late. There was really nothing that could be done other than prolong the two months she likely had left into four, something she refused to consider.

He was hearing that death sentence in his head and he shot off the sofa, hands clenched into fists. "What the hell, Kevin? What the hell!"

Before he could take more than half a step towards me, Katie was up, urging him back. "He's just the messenger, Paul," she said quietly.

Eileen was crying; Spider had his arms wrapped around her and she was sobbing against him. Katie managed to get Paul to sit back down and she slid closer to him, holding his hand, as much for herself as for him. I looked at Lydia, and her eyes flooded with tears.

It was out there; they knew, and it was breaking my heart.

"How bad is it, Kev?" Katie asked. "Did they catch it early?"

I told them the little I knew: There was a large mass on the underside of Dad's brain, pressing on or wrapped around his pituitary gland, and the chances of it being malignant were slim. That alone didn't mean there was nothing to worry about; a dozen different things could go wrong, but we needed to latch onto the idea that Dad didn't have some malignant bearer of doom invading his brain.

"It's going to be a roller coaster of doctor's appointments and medications, and he's going to have to have surgery to remove it," I said. "For once we need to be Dad's support system, not the other way around. Whatever they'll let us do for them, we do. No questions asked and no excuses about work. We can find people to cover classes or the dinner rush."

A few tense moments of silence blanketed the room, punctuated only by the sound of a baby rattle being smacked against the side of the playpen.

"Squirt," Paul said, cutting through the quiet, "why are you the one telling us? This smacks of something Dad would want to do himself."

"He doesn't know that I am. Mom asked me to, so she could spare Dad the pain of seeing his girls cry and his boys looking like they feel powerless."

"Dad is going to be so pissed," Eileen whispered.

"Mom understands that," I said. "She doesn't have a problem with it…but I called Uncle Doug to head over there and rescue her from the worst of it. He said he'd drag Dad out of the house long enough for him to calm down."

The dinner Eileen made went mostly untouched; we tried to eat and tried to find things to talk about other than Dad, but the best we could manage was noncreative pushing of food around plates, and stretches of quiet interrupted long enough for someone to ask a question about the baby, or about Nicole. At seven Paul realized he needed to pick Nicole up, and wasn't sure what to do with her; he didn't think it would be a good idea to take her home, just in case Uncle Doug hadn't been able to get Dad out of the house.

"Take her to the restaurant with you," Lydia suggested. "She likes to pretend that she's helping out."

"Or just plop her down in the office for a little bit," Eileen said, "and I'll come get her in a little while. I think it's a good night for Nicole to spend with her aunt and uncle. Tell her we're going to stay up late and we'll play games and watch a DVD, and if she wants to, make cookies or brownies. I just need a little time to regroup."

Normally Paul would have thanked her; tonight all he could do was nod and push away from the table. He waited a beat before he stood up, and then gestured for me to go to the door with him.

"This is why Mom wanted you to do this," he said when we

were away from everyone else. "If Dad had been here we'd have been tripping all over ourselves trying to make him feel better and it would have been too much for him. And it would have been like some warped competition, even though we wouldn't have meant for it to be. Dad doesn't have that much attention to be able to divide."

"Mom is looking for anything she can do for him."

"You did good, Kev. I'm sorry you had to be the one to do this, but you did good."

I tried to thank him, but he brushed it off.

"I will never tell Nick this, because he's got this image in his head that he's Dad's second, but the truth is, if it's any of us, it's you. And like it or not Dad's going to need you to lean on, because the rest of the time he'll be too busy holding Mom together and trying to make the rest of us feel better."

"I'm scared, too, Paul."

"God. I didn't mean... I know you are, and I didn't mean to infer that you weren't. But the thing is, you're the strongest, the smartest, and you're the one we *all* confide in. Nick stepped into Dad's shoes when he needed to and he did a damn good job of it, but you were always the one we went to, even Nick. And that's what Dad is going to need. He'll need the son who is most like him on his best days, and most unlike him on his worst. I know it's not fair to ask you to be that, but..."

"Dad's going to need all of us, Paul."

"But it's you he's going to admit his fears to, and it's you he's going to tell the things he can't tell Mom."

I didn't know if I wanted to be that person.

He left, and when I got back to the table Eileen was asking Katie, "Is there any chance that you've heard from Nick and just can't tell us?"

"Well, you get bonus points for intelligence," I said to her. "That's kind of an oxymoronical question."

"Bite me."

"I swear," Katie said, "I haven't heard from him, but I hope he gets back soon, especially now."

While I wanted my brother home and safe, especially safe, the thought occurred to me that Nick being gone a little bit longer wasn't a bad thing. Let Dad get through all the doctor visits, at least to the point where he was surer of what was going to happen and when, without Nick's particular brand of help.

Nick was going to come home to a double whammy; news that he was going to be a father, and news that his own father was facing some pretty serious crap.

I didn't envy that. The joy of finding out you're going to have a baby—presuming Nick was indeed happy about it—shouldn't be clouded with the notion that the man you practically worship might not be around to meet your first born.

After Katie left, we moved back into the living room, and I admitted to Eileen and Spider that a small part of me was relieved that Nick wasn't there. While he always had the best at heart, this was one thing no one needed him trying to fix.

Eileen was curled up on the sofa, her feet tangled up with Spider's. "Be honest with me, Kevin. If it's not malignant, what are the worst of the things that can happen to him?"

"I honestly don't know. I've been trying to research these tumors online, but there are so many of them, and half the stuff I find is total garbage, mostly people who want to sound smart spouting off presumptions that have no basis in biology. I know what the pituitary does to a certain extent, and that it controls so many hormones...I need more time and better literature to study."

"No one expects you to become his doctor, Rabbit," Lydia said.

"Just our translator," Eileen said. "Sucks to be you, but you were born with the brains in this family. If anyone can pore over the medical speak and understand it, it's going to be you."

"Uncle Doug," I reminded her.

"My father can only tell you so much," Spider said. "He's got that whole doctor-patient thing going on. If Uncle Chip doesn't want us to know something, Dad's not going to tell us."

Eileen didn't think that would be an issue. "Dad's not going to shut us out of this."

"Not unless he thinks he's protecting us," Lydia said.

"I want to know how close that tumor is to his optic nerves," Spider said.

"All I know is that those nerves run uncomfortably close to the pituitary," I told him. "Why?"

"It's selfish. If the tumor compromises his optic nerves, he could go blind. And if he goes blind, I have no way of talking to him, not without someone else to speak for me. I love you all, but there are times when I want to talk to him alone."

Spider confided in Dad as much as the rest of us did, and I was a little bit ashamed that it hadn't occurred to me.

"You know I'm close to him," Spider went on. "Just the idea that could be taken away hurts. But...if it meant the difference between him living and dying, I'd never speak to him again."

I sat there soaking in the sight of my sister wrapped around her husband. Dad loved Spider before he loved me; he loved Spider before he loved Paul. And truthfully, if not for Spider, we might not have a relationship with Uncle Doug and Aunt Kris at all. Spider was the glue that held the most tenuous strands of Dad's friendship with Uncle Doug together, during the searing agony of Dad being told that his wife and his best friend had slept together, during the months it took for those wounds to scab over.

If not for the fact of Spider's existence and Dad's love for his godson, there might have never been any reason for Dad to do anything but walk away.

With no Spider in the picture, who would Eileen be wrapped around right now? Who else would have been so respectful of her while she was just a teenager, refusing to take one step further than he knew would be appropriate? Who would be the one who would be holding her all night long while she cried it out?

Eileen was curled up with someone who would, no matter how badly it hurt, give up being able to communicate with the man who was as much his father as his own, if only it meant he would live.

Spider was the reason I had my only aunt and uncle.

Spider was my brother by choice.

Spider would expand his envelope of silence if it meant my father would be all right.

It hit me all at once; my father had something growing in his head and we had no idea what it was. He was absolutely terrified and my mother was going along for the ride; he wanted to spare his kids the worst of the fear, the not knowing, but I'd just picked them up and thrown them on the ride with him.

We didn't know what it was.

We had no clue what it was.

That he could go blind never crossed my mind.

He could die.

My dad could die.

I crumpled there in the chair, my son sleeping in his playpen and my sister resting against her husband; Lydia saw it coming and was already moving towards me when I buried my face against my arms folded in my lap, and I started to cry.

~

Doug

I wasn't sure if Chip was trying to calm down before we got to the restaurant or if he just liked driving my car that much, but we took the long way around; a five minute drive took us twenty, and it was in complete silence. There wasn't much I wanted to say to him anyway; Kevin called and needed help, and Kris was willing to drop the plans that we had in order to go sit with Terry. As long as he was out of shouting distance to his wife, I couldn't have cared less if he didn't say a word until I was sure he was safe to go home.

The bar was busy for as early as it was. At seven o'clock it was the dining room that was usually full, but tonight all the bar tables were taken, so we wound up on stools at the middle of the bar. Will was behind it mixing drinks, but as soon as he saw Chip he handed them off to someone else and came over to see what his boss and friend wanted.

"Bourbon," Chip grunted.

"You might as well bring the bottle," I added, "otherwise you'll give yourself a nasty case of tendonitis with all the pouring you'll do."

He pulled a step stool over and grabbed a bottle from the top shelf, carefully wiping it down before setting it and two glasses in front of us. I shook my head and said, "Someone has to drive him home."

Chip slapped at the bar and said he'd be right back. "Gotta make room for how much I'm going to drink."

"That bad?" Will asked.

"Oh, yeah."

"Then go ahead and drink with him if you want. I'll make sure you both get home all right, even if I have to drive you myself."

"Hell, you might want to join us."

Will looked at me for a moment, then at the other bartender, and then went over to one of the booths. He bent over to whisper to one of the customers there, and when they got up he beckoned me to bring the bottle over.

While I waited for Chip, Will got a third glass, and said as he sat, "I can manage a short drink."

When Chip came back he slid miserably onto the seat across from us and reached for the bottle. He filled his glass and then mine, and started to fill Will's, but Will grabbed the bottle and only poured out a splash for himself.

"What are we drinking to?" Will asked.

"Not what we're drinking to," Chip replied. "More what the doc here is trying to keep me from doing."

"And that would be yelling at his wife," I said.

Will was intrigued but didn't ask. While I had known Chip longer and knew him better, Will knew more about the private workings of Chip and Terry's marriage; he had counseled them through their split and was their confessor even after he left the priesthood. I was familiar, too familiar, with Chip's temper and had been on the receiving end when he let it loose; Will understood how it affected Terry, when it scared her and when it made her angry right back at him. He was probably the better person to listen to Chip; they were friends but Will knew how and when to disconnect, and I wasn't sure I could.

"Terry," Chip said after quickly slugging back a shot, "used Kevin in one of the worst ways...like I don't have the balls to do my own dirty work. It's not fair to make Kevin give any bad news to *my* kids. I could have done it myself, I *should* have done it myself...goddammit she had no right to even *think* of asking Kevin to call them all up and then let him stand there saying anything at all."

Will didn't say anything; he didn't try to defend Terry or even ask what Chip was talking about. He simply let Chip wind up so that he could get it out, and waited for him to wind down.

"Holy hell. Hasn't that kid been through enough already? He's been screwed over more ways than one and putting any kind of burden on him is short sighted and selfish…what if Kevin can't handle it? What if just knowing what he knows is enough to break him? What if adding on top of it having to tell his brothers and his sisters because dammit, Spider is just as much his brother as Nick and Paul and he loves Katie like a sister, what if that puts him back in that same dark place he fell into when he came home from the seminary? Why would Terry risk that? What the *hell* is going on in her bubble blond head?"

"Stop it." Now Will leaned forward, slapping his glass on the table. "I don't care what you're angry about. You don't have the right to disrespect your wife by insulting her, whether she's here or not."

"Ah, but Will…"

"No. I don't care what the problem is. Be angry with her, yes, but there will be no insulting, no disrespect, or I'll toss you out of here on your ass myself."

Chip slumped against the back of the seat and nodded. I was impressed; if I'd said that, he would have argued with me, dared me to even try to get him out of the booth and out the door. It wouldn't matter what position I took; he would argue just to argue and he wouldn't worry about taking a swing at me. But a small part of him still thought of Will as Father Parker and kept in him a position of authority.

Once it seemed as if Chip had run out of steam, Will asked, "All right, what's the problem, if it's not too personal to ask?"

I was sure he'd asked Chip far more personal questions.

Chip poured another shot, and stared at the glass. He started to speak and then stopped, took a deep breath and looked at me. Pleading.

"This," I said pointedly, "is why Terry asked Kevin to tell them. Because you can't. It doesn't matter how much you think you should be the one, you can't do it."

"Hell. You two aren't splitting up again, are you?" Will asked.

Chip shook his head.

"Do I have your permission to tell him?" I asked.

I took the small movement of his head as he looked back into his bourbon as permission.

"Chip has a two centimeter mass on his pituitary gland. And we're not yet sure what it is."

Will sat back, a stunned scowl crossing his face. He poured a bit more of the bourbon into his glass and asked, "What exactly does that mean?"

"It means he has a brain tumor, and Terry thought the kids needed to know now, but that Chip didn't need to be the one to tell them.

"I was going to wait until I had more that I *could* tell them," Chip argued.

"Your kids aren't exactly kids anymore," Will pointed out. "You don't need the stress of hiding something like this from them, and they're sharp enough they'd know something wasn't right. You have to give the people who care about you—"

I wasn't sure where he was going with that, but Paul slid into the booth beside Chip and Will stopped in mid-sentence.

"I have Nicole with me," Paul said. "She's in the office, but I wanted to make sure you're not too drunk before I go in there and let it slip that Grandpa is here."

"I'm getting a buzz but I'm not drunk yet."

"Eileen is going to be here in a few minutes to get her. Do you even want to see her right now? It's all right if you don't."

"Of course I want to see my granddaughter," Chip said. "Go get her."

"In a minute." He slid his arm behind Chip and pulled him close, pressing a kiss into his father's head the same way Chip frequently kissed his sons, just at the temple. "I am so, so sorry, Dad."

Chip let Paul hold him for a moment; there were a dozen people watching but he didn't care. I doubted that he even considered that his openness of affection with his kids was somewhat unusual.

"Nicole doesn't know, does she?" he asked.

Paul's arm stayed around his father's shoulders. "No, and I don't think she should, not until we know what the tumor is doing to you."

"Even when you have surgery," I told Chip, "she doesn't have to be told exactly why. You can honestly tell her you're getting a deviated septum fixed, because if it's off even a little bit, it'll be taken care of during the surgery. It'll be a couple of weeks until there's a pathology report, so until then you can spare her any real worry."

It was also a ready excuse for Chip's fatigue. Grandpa just isn't sleeping well. That damned deviated septum, makes it hard to breathe at night. He might not be able to spare his kids, but he could shield his granddaughter as long as possible.

Before Paul could get up and get Nicole from his office, Chip put his hand on his arm and asked, "What about you? Are you all right?"

"I'm a little numb," he admitted, "but I resisted the urge to put my fist through anything in Eileen's apartment, so I guess I'm okay. But damn, don't worry about us, we'll be all right and we're here for whatever you need."

"What I need most is for you to be there for your mother. I don't care what she shows you; inside she's falling apart."

"Trust me, Dad, I know. I've been on her side of this. I understand the not knowing and the hoping and the inner terror. All of you got me through it; we'll get you and Mom through this."

"What helped?"

Paul stopped to consider. "What made me feel best were those moments when everything felt ordinary, when everyone wasn't thinking about the fact that Monica was definitely going to die, and they were just themselves. Like when we were all at the beach for Kevin and Lydia's wedding…there were so many punctuated moments of perfect normal that both Monica and I were able to relax and have a good time."

"That's not a bad idea," Will said. "Grab as many of your kids as you can and head for the beach. Put everything else in a holding pattern and go off and have a good time with your family."

I could see it spinning in Chip's head: get through the first doctor appointments, get the kids over to see those houses, get everything in motion to move the Charybdis…how many things could he possibly get done in a week or two, and how much time did he have before some hot shot neurosurgeon would be probing into his brain?

Nicole ran through the bar and practically leaped up at him; he caught her in a hug and she sat on the booth seat on her knees facing him, both hands clutching his arm.

"Grandpa, guess what? I got to spar a brown belt today and I kicked him in the face and he didn't even get mad! And it was really cool because he said I did it really good and that I can kick pretty hard, and he let me try to get him again!"

"Very cool," Chip agreed. "What kind of kick did you nail him with?"

"I got him with a crescent kick and I've never done that in sparring before, and it was awesome!"

"You're getting very good, you know. I bet Uncle Kevin lets you test for your next belt pretty soon."

She scrunched her nose. "I don't know my kata very good yet. He's really mean about those."

"I know, sweetheart. He won't let me test for my next belt until I learn a new one, too."

"He can do that? You're his dad!"

"But Uncle Kevin is Grandpa's boss in the dojo," Paul laughed. "Come, on, let's get your stuff. Aunt Eileen just walked in."

Paul met his sister at the door and pointed towards the bar; Chip slugged back what was left in his glass, but he didn't pour another one.

Eileen leaned over and kissed him on the lips, and kept him wrapped in a hug until he gently pulled her arms away, making her sit down beside him.

"I swear, I'm not going to cry right now," she said, "but I'm reserving a few minutes alone with you in a day or two so I can be five years old again. I swear, I won't be a whiny little pest, but I want a few minutes with my daddy."

"I think I can arrange that."

"I know you didn't want Kevin to tell us, but Dad…it really was the right way to do it. Sometimes brothers and sisters need to get a little sobby with each other. And then we're okay."

"What about Kevin? Is he all right?"

She hesitated for a fraction of a second, long enough for us both to know that she was going to lie, and lie well. "Kevin handled it just fine. He and Lydia are taking advantage of free babysitting tonight and they're at a movie right now."

"You left Spider alone with a baby?" I asked, slightly amused.

"He's sitting on the sofa staring at Michael sleeping in the play-pen, and I'm pretty sure by now Spider's panicking at the idea he'll wake up and need something."

Spider was staring, I was sure, because he was afraid if he went into another room, Michael would wake up and he wouldn't know.

"See," I said to Chip once Eileen had left to get Nicole. "Except for Nick, all your kids know, and they're fine. And you didn't have to go through the pain of telling them."

"Except Kevin."

"And you were able to tell Kevin because whether you realize it or not, you needed him for this."

He poured another drink. "I'm still getting drunk."

~

Terry

We heard the car doors slam from the living room, and we both got up; I assumed Doug would be dragging Chip through the door, but it was Will who coaxed him up the front steps, half dragging, half pushing.

"Yours is in the car," he told Kris. "You can have him after you take me back to the restaurant."

"They're both toasted?" she asked, amused.

"I think they invented a new level of drunk."

Chip stumbled through the doorway, grinning. "I'm not that drunk," he said. "I'm just twelve kinds of buzzed."

"Like I said," Will chortled. "Have fun."

I steered Chip towards the stairs, and he grabbed hold of the banister tightly, taking the stairs slowly, determined to not be that drunk.

"Into the bedroom, Captain Morgan," I said when he was at the top of the stairs, looking confused about where he should go next.

"I don't drink rum," he informed me. "It tastes like plastic."

"I'll remember that."

He started peeling his t-shirt off, but lost his footing and fell backwards onto the bed, his arms tangled above his head, the shirt wrapped around his neck.

"Need a little help there, Irish?"

He pulled at the shirt but it only twisted more. "I can't see anything."

I leaned over him and pulled the shirt the rest of the way off. "Better?"

"Yes, thank you."

He lay there quietly while I pulled his shoes and socks off, but when I started to unzip his jeans he lifted his head to look at me and said, "You can nibble on my sense of humor if you want."

"Can I, now?" I slid the jeans off his legs, and then grabbed the waistband of his underwear.

"You have the King's permission," he said. "If you want. No pressure."

I stretched out on the bed next to him. "The King is very considerate."

"Hey. This isn't fair. I'm all naked and you're not. Even if all you're gonna do is nibble, I'd still like the Queen to be in her birthday suit."

I kicked off my shoes and then stripped while he watched, and when my clothes were in a pile next to his, I straddled him on the bed.

"Better?"

"Much. I'm drunk, you know."

"I was pretty sure about that."

"You don't have to do this if you don't want to."

I moved until my face was over his, my hair falling around his head. "I want to, Irish."

"Is the booze breath gonna bother you?"

"The only thing bothering me right now is the fact that you have two good hands and you aren't using either one of them."

He grinned, sliding his hands up my sides, teasing me with his thumbs. "You might be a little bothered with the bourbon boner," he said as he lifted his head for a kiss. "Half mast at best right now."

"I can work with that," I assured him. "Just give me a few minutes."

Later, after we'd turned the lights out, he rolled onto his side and lifted up onto an elbow. "I'm still mad at you."

"I know."

"But I love you."

"I know that, too."

"I won't be mad in the morning. I promise."

"You can be mad for as long as you need to be, Chip. It's all right."

He fell asleep with his head buried against my neck and he held me close all night; and true to his word when he woke up late the next morning, the last of his anger was gone.

11

Kevin

"It was like the world's lamest video game," Dad told Uncle Doug. "See a spot of light, press the magic button. When it was over and the kid told me I'd missed one freaking spot, I was actually disappointed, like I wasn't going to win the prize."

"Well, you were going to get a balloon and a lollipop, but you blew it."

We were standing outside the office of the home builder Dad was supposed to meet; we'd already taken a look at the outside of the houses under construction, and were underwhelmed. They looked like any other cookie-cutter suburban homes on any other suburban street, but with brand new sod and freshly laid driveways.

Mom and Aunt Kris were sitting in Uncle Doug's air conditioned car, and everyone else was packed into Paul's minivan. Builder Guy was late, and not racking up the brownie points with the guy who was set to drop a whole lot of cash into his lap.

Dad had gotten through his first two appointments; he saw the endocrinologist on Tuesday, who seemed sufficiently impressed with his lab results, but wasn't sure she agreed with Uncle Doug on his thought that the tumor was a prolactinoma. It was positioned well enough for that, but his prolactin levels weren't that high.

On Wednesday he had a visual acuity test, looking for dead spots in his vision. He thought it was a wasted hour, time he could have spent getting some work done, or just time he could have spent with Mom, but Uncle Doug assured him it was important.

The one missed spot, I wanted to know. What did it mean?

"It means your Dad blinked. He passed the test with flying colors."

"Colors, my ass," Dad grumbled. "It was a mass of boring light gray."

"Well, you're just never happy with anything, are you?" Uncle Doug snorted.

"So it means the tumor isn't on his optic nerve?" I asked.

"Apparently so," Dad replied.

"Spider will be relieved."

He paused to consider that; the far reaching implications if it had been affecting his vision hadn't occurred to him either. Neither did what that meant for his godson.

Uncle Doug may have, but he wasn't saying so.

Dad was about to give up and call it a lost cause when Builder Guy came screaming up in his pickup truck. He had pink streamers tried to the antennae, and the cab was filled with pink and silver Mylar balloons. I watched the irritation drain from Dad's face as the guy jumped out of his truck, his hand already extended, apologies spilling out.

Dad shook the guy's hand and said, "Let me guess. It's a girl?"

Builder Guy damn near exploded with pride out in front of his construction trailer. "She's five hours old, and looks just like her mother."

"First?" Dad asked.

"Sixth, but it never gets old."

Dad agreed, and gestured for everyone to get out of the car and the minivan. There were three model homes open, but Dad only wanted us to see two of them; he sent Mom and Aunt Kris into the third, assuming that none of us would want a three bedroom house with two master suites.

"The court you're looking at has two of each model," Builder Guy said as he let us into the first. "This one and the next that you'll see have four bedrooms, or three with a den."

"What defines the den?" Paul asked.

"Closet space. You want a bedroom, we'll put in a closet. You want a den, we'll put in built in shelving or an entertainment center. With the exception of the floor plan, you can pick out any specifics and any options you want."

Compared to the last set of houses we'd looked at, this was

massive. Off to the left of the doorway was a smallish living room, but around the corner was a family room big enough for all my siblings if they were hanging out, or for a decent sized family with more than two kids. The floors were hard wood polished so brightly they looked wet, and the walls were painted a light brown.

We split; Paul and Nicole headed down the hallway to check out the bedrooms, Lydia and Katie went for the kitchen; I stood in the living room, trying to soak it all in.

Dad was in the family room with Spider; they seemed rooted there, not really looking at anything.

"I will always find a way to hear you," Dad signed.

I turned around and headed down the hall, not wanting to intrude any more than that.

"You are not going to believe those rooms, Squirt," Paul said as he came out of the master bedroom. "You wondered what you'd do with an oops baby? They're big enough your kids could share. No converting the garage. You could stick three to a room and have nine kids, easy."

"Three's enough," I assured him.

Nicole grabbed my hand and pulled me towards one of the bedrooms. "Look! This one is going to be mine!"

"What if Daddy wants this one?"

She put her hands on her hips and rolled her eyes. "Uncle *Kevin*. Daddy wants the big room."

"Well, that's kind of selfish of him, don't you think?"

"No. He's going to need a bigger room."

"How's that, short stuff?" Paul asked.

"For when you get *married*," she said as if it was a done deal.

"Sweetheart, I don't even have a girlfriend."

"Well then don't you think you better get one?"

I almost laughed, but Paul wasn't smiling. "How are you going to feel if I start dating, Nicole? Because you know I probably won't marry the first woman I meet."

"I know that. You have to test them out first."

"And if I do start dating, I'm not going to let you meet most of them. I don't want you to get attached to anyone until I know if there's a relationship there."

She shrugged. "I don't care. I just think you should have a girl-friend."

Paul leaned against the doorjamb, carefully considering his young daughter. "That might mean that I'll go fun places without you, and that sometimes I won't be home for dinner or to tuck you into bed."

"Daaaad. I'm not a baby anymore." Nicole looked up at me. "Tell him, Uncle Kevin. He needs a girlfriend! And Grandma or Grandpa will watch me while he's on dates."

"Or I will," I offered.

"See, Daddy?"

"Uncle Kevin did offer to introduce me to someone," Paul said, watching Nicole carefully, weighing her reaction.

"He knows lots of girls!"

"Don't tell Aunt Lydia that," Paul chuckled.

"Don't show him to Sensei Sam," Nicole told me.

Hot Sam, the one he'd been counting on introducing me to. "Why not? I thought you liked her."

"She's nice. But I think she likes girls."

"Well, that would complicate things," Paul said, looking at me like *how the hell could YOU not know this?*

I had no clue. All I knew was that she'd said she wanted to meet someone. "What makes you think she likes girls?" I asked.

"I saw her kissing a girl in her car," Nicole said simply. "Maybe she likes boys, too."

Nicole ran off to tell her aunts that Daddy wanted to get a girl-friend; she skipped down the hallway, yelling out, "Guess what?!"

"Really, Paul, I had no clue."

"*You* had no clue? I had no clue that my daughter even under-stood that sometimes grownup girls don't like grownup boys."

Nicole was practically giddy while we poked through the rest of the house, and while we went through the next one. Mom joined us at the second house, declaring the model she and Aunt Kris went through to be "just about perfect."

Somewhere between house one and house two, Builder Guy left discreetly to open his office, giving Dad a chance to ask us how we felt about living there.

"If we're really interested," he said as we all stood in the kitchen, "we need to jump on it. I don't think these will last long, and we're headed into a serious seller's market."

"Which means massive price jumps," Mom mused.

"He's asking six hundred twenty thousand for this house; figure in another twenty to thirty for upgrades. In six months, the same house will cost close to eight. We either need to buy now, or wait three or four years for home prices to drop again."

"If they do," Doug offered.

It didn't matter that Dad could afford any or all of those houses at higher prices; he wasn't paying more than they were worth, on principle alone.

"I like them," Paul said. "I think Nicole does, too. I wouldn't have a problem buying either one."

Spider and Eileen agreed, and Lydia was nodding.

"What about you, Katie," Dad asked. "Do you feel comfortable making this decision without Nick here?"

"The only thing Nick wants is a cook's kitchen, and I think this one will blow his socks off. He won't mind at all if I say yes."

"All right. You kids can keep looking around, and your Mom and I will go start the ball rolling."

~

Later that night I sat in the darkened kitchen at the table, looking out into the back yard. It was almost midnight but I couldn't sleep and had gotten out of bed to make sure that my tossing and turning wouldn't wake Lydia; I headed downstairs thinking I'd self medicate with a beer and then watch TV until I felt sleepy.

Just before I flipped the kitchen light on I heard splashing in the pool, and looked outside; my parents were out there, illuminated by the underwater light and a few random solar torches that Dad had put around the deck.

I knew I was eavesdropping but they weren't doing anything I shouldn't see; Mom was stretched out on her stomach on the diving board and Dad was treading water. So I watched. They were talking, but I could hear Mom's laughter every now and then so I was sure it wasn't serious; they weren't out there dwelling on the thing inside

Dad's head.

Was that a deliberate decision, I wondered. Did they sit down and purposely decide to not talk about it, give each other a break from the worry over What Might Happen? Or did this just happen, this slice of everyday, Mom and Dad playing in the pool like nothing was wrong and everything was just how it was supposed to be?

Either way, I wondered how they accomplished that.

How could they not be worrying?

Footsteps on the stairs; Paul was still at work and Nicole was long asleep. I listened as she walked through the living room, and when she entered the kitchen I said, "Don't turn the light on. I don't want them to know I'm up here."

Lydia bent over and kissed the side of my neck. "I wondered where you were."

"Did Michael wake you up?"

She pulled one of the chairs closer to me and sat down, running her hand along my arm until she could weave her fingers through mine. "No. I think he's good until around six or seven. We may be getting lucky. I think he's sleeping through the night now."

"I'm sorry if I woke you. I got up so that I wouldn't."

"Ah, so you didn't specifically come down here to spy on your parents?"

"I could have spied on them from the bedroom window."

"They look happy." She squeezed my hand lightly. "You needed to see that."

"This is normal for them; I think that's what I needed to see. This"—I nodded towards the pool—"this used to happen a couple of times a week when I was a teenager. Once they were sure Eileen and I were in bed they'd sneak out here and fool around by the pool. In the water or out...damn, my Dad can make her laugh."

He reached for the end of the diving board and pulled himself half out of the water, stretching up to kiss her. Mom leaned over to make it easier for him; he held himself up for a long time, the kiss slow and deep enough that by the time he dropped back into the water, Lydia sighed.

"Well, I'll kiss you like that you give me half a chance," I teased.

"I just like how he is with her, Rabbit, that's all. He's very..."

"Gentle?"

"Tender," she decided.

Mom slid off the diving board and into the pool, and swam to where Dad was at in the shallow end. I half expected their swimsuits to come flying out of the water, but he only reached out for her, and her hands went to his face, fingers tracing lightly over his whiskers.

"Your parents are now officially making out," Lydia said with a little bit of a laugh. "Shouldn't we leave them to it without an audience?"

"They're not naked yet."

"I'm not sticking around until they are, Rabbit." She tugged at my hand, urging me to get up. "Let's go in the living room. We can hear Michael from there, and we can give them privacy in case they really do want to get naked in the pool."

We turned the television on for light—and to let my parents know that there was someone in the living room, lest they come back inside with swimsuits in hand—and I stretched out on the sofa, pulling Lydia on top of me. I was under no illusions: there wouldn't be anything more going on in that living room than cuddling, not with the very real chance that my mother and father could walk by at any moment.

"I hope we're like that in thirty years," she whispered.

"Minus the massive stupidities," I agreed.

"Everyone gets stupid."

"All right. As long as you don't sleep with my best friend, we're probably good to go."

She placed a long kiss on my chest. "About that."

"I wouldn't believe it if you said you did."

"Topher is pretty much your best friend," she reminded me. "I never thought I'd see that happen, but here we are."

"Ah." I kissed the top of her head and amended the statement. "Okay, as long as you don't sleep with him again, we're good to go."

"I couldn't imagine ever wanting to." She shifted until her face was above mine. "What you were watching in the pool...you're that way with me, Kevin. I don't think you know how badly I sometimes want to find my seventeen year old self and tell her to just be patient for a few more years."

That made two of us; I wanted that so badly that it sometimes hurt. I couldn't tell her that, not now. Instead what I said was well rehearsed, the line I kept practicing in my head, hoping that someday I would believe it.

"The seventeen year old you had to figure things out for herself. And even if I knew then what I know now, I'd have still headed for the seminary. I still would have gone."

"I know. But I would have been waiting."

"If it hadn't been Topher it might have been some jerk who didn't understand you half as well as he did. At least Topher knew who you really loved, and in his own warped way respected that."

"How come you've never asked about anyone else? You realize there was a good three year gap between Topher and when you came home."

"I haven't asked because it doesn't matter. It's not a contest. It doesn't matter who did what first or with whom or even how many times. If I asked, I wouldn't expect to hear that you never dated."

"I dated, but that's it," she said, pressing her lips into mine. "No one serious, and nothing beyond a kiss or two goodnight."

"It's none of my business."

"That doesn't mean I don't want you to know."

"And if I spent my off time chasing the girls in town near the seminary, would you want to know that?"

That made her laugh. "If you got lucky with any of them, sure."

Any time I went into town, I was in a giant seminary-boy mass, and she knew that. "Sadly, the only one I ever got lucky with was myself."

"Oh God, Rabbit," she snickered. "I don't need that image in my head."

"What, me going out to dinner with my friends?"

"No, you getting busy with yourself in a seminary. Weren't you supposed to be beyond that, all chaste and pure?"

"I was human. Hell, I was still a teenager. Would you like to burn into your brain the current image of me getting busy with my-self?"

Her smile waned. "I thought that was on your list of things you didn't want to do with me."

The sad thing was that I did have a list; it was a mental list but she'd been made all too aware of it, things that should have been a matter of course but I wasn't willing to even try.

"Therapy is helping," I admitted.

Therapy my family knew nothing about. Therapy she insisted on to get me through a fresh onslaught of guilt after Nick shot Jake Catero through the throat. Therapy that was making me feel a little too uptight about the things I should be wanting.

"Honestly, Kevin, I would just be happy if I could get my lips below your navel for more than a few seconds without it freaking you out."

"I've—"

"You try. You really do. But the only time I've been able to get you to hold still from start to finish was on our wedding night. I've never been able to figure out why."

"All right."

"All right?"

I shrugged lightly. "You wanna blow me, then blow me."

And that's when I heard footsteps coming out of the kitchen. "At least wait until we're upstairs," Dad sighed.

Lydia buried her laughter against my chest.

I could hear the sting of Mom's hand on Dad's ass, chastising, yet she was snickering, too.

"Wonderful," I muttered.

"Come on, that was funny," she said, lifting her head again. "And I will, you know."

"Great, and then Paul will walk through the front door, and come in here to see why the TV got left on."

Her fingers were at the waistband of my shorts, teasing and nearly threatening. "I'll take that chance. Or we have a perfectly good bedroom upstairs. Either way…"

I wanted what my parents had, and it was obvious I was getting it. I wanted that spark, the connection and the laughter. Along with it I was getting something else my Dad had: a horny, pushy wife who wasn't going to take no for an answer.

~

Once we were inside the bedroom, she stopped in the middle of the floor and turned to me, her hands on my chest.

"Change your mind?" I asked.

She tilted her head a little bit. "I think I have. This shouldn't be such an issue, Kevin. It shouldn't be something I have to hold you down for and force you to like. I just want to know why it's so difficult."

It. The code word for everything I was squeamish about. Things anyone else would probably be begging for. Normally she'd shrug it off and move onto something else. Kevin doesn't want a blow job? Fine, lick a nipple, whatever. Kevin freezes if his lips make it past a belly button, fine, grab him by the ears and pull him up and kiss him.

I had issues. Tons of issues. I was fully aware of them, and struggled with each one.

"My therapist thinks it's just a matter of being a little too catholic," I told her, "and I don't know how I get over that."

Her hands dropped from my chest, and she went across the room to sit in the rocking chair where she usually held Michael in the middle of the night. I sat on the edge of the bed as close to her as I could, but I couldn't reach out and touch her, and at that point I was pretty sure she didn't want me to.

"I don't think that's it," she said after a moment. "Not that I'm some psych whiz. But I really don't think so."

I waited; she didn't want to hear another excuse from me, or for me to try to validate my therapist's notions about why I had as many hang-ups as I did.

"If it were a matter of religion…Kevin, think back to when we were teenagers. You wouldn't have done half of what we did. Do you remember when we were sixteen and went out to the lake? We realized it was deserted and that we could get away with pretty much anything we wanted."

"I remember."

"Your hands were everywhere and you weren't all that shy about what you were touching and how. And when I slipped my hand into your shorts you didn't pull away and you didn't try to stop me. You only moaned that you wished you had a condom. If not for that, we would have had sex then, and you know it. And if I had even thought about blowing you, you wouldn't have stopped me."

"And it would have been a mistake…"

"Maybe. But the fact is that back then, if we'd thought of it, you wouldn't have had a problem with it. You'd have gone to confession, tossed out a few Hail Marys, and started over again. Kevin, if you were *that* catholic you'd have issues with everything we did when we were teenagers, and you wouldn't be so willing to use condoms now. And you sure as hell wouldn't have been a closet masturbator in the seminary."

She didn't ask what had happened between then and now. Everyone knew what had happened to me between then and now. But I didn't think that what Jake had done to me had anything to do with this.

I didn't realize how important it was to her.

On our wedding night she asked me to trust her.

Do you trust me? Just let go…trust me.

"So how do we get past this? Because we have to. If we don't, it's going to get bigger and uglier until you're so pissed off that you can't touch me at all."

"That will never happen." She slid out of the chair and onto the bed next to me. "I can't decide for you, Kevin. Pick something. We'll try it. If you get uncomfortable we'll keep trying until we know if it's just a hang-up or something you truly dislike."

"Except…"

"I know. We're not dogs," she said lightly. "I don't expect you to start swinging on chandeliers, Rabbit. All I want is for you to relax sometimes and let things happen."

I didn't think I could do both, but I wasn't going to admit that right then.

"We should get some sleep," she said, rolling onto the other side of the bed. "Michael will probably be awake in about six hours and it might be nice if his parents could peel themselves up, too."

I laid back and rolled towards her, stealing a kiss.

And oddly, I felt disappointed.

~

Chip

Terry pulled me into the bathroom and closed the door softly, sighing, "I really wish we hadn't heard that."

"I don't think they realized both doors to the baby's room were mostly open. I thought about closing one, but…"

"But then they might have gotten embarrassed and stopped talking." She started to fill the bathtub; I'd been headed for the shower but that wasn't the point. If they heard us bumping around in the bedroom, they'd clam up.

I dug the lighter out of the vanity drawer and lit a few candles.

"At least they're talking," I pointed out.

"And at least she seems understanding."

"She knew before they got married that he was going to come with some baggage, Terry. I'd be disappointed if she wasn't extremely understanding."

"He's loved her since he was a little boy. I don't know, I guess I just assumed they were always on the same page now. I don't think I wanted to know this much about their sex life, but it's kind of heartbreaking, you know?"

I stepped into the tub, sliding down into the water. "Come on." I held out my hand to her. "It would be heartbreaking if they weren't talking about it or if Kevin was ignoring what Lydia wants."

"And it seems like such a simple thing to want." She sat in the tub facing me, her feet resting on my thighs. "I could see it if it was reversed, if Kevin wanted—"

"I suspect he does."

"Then why?"

"Think back to when we first started sleeping together and I was trying to draw you out of that shyness. You finally realized you weren't going to break anything on me, and I started pushing…"

"You never pushed."

"I likely pushed a little. And I did make it clear what I wanted and I probably wasn't as nice about it as my daughter-in-law seems to be."

She grabbed my hands and pulled me towards her, sliding to meet me halfway. Her legs slipped around my waist, and she ran wet fingers across my chest. "You were very understanding."

"And when I asked why you didn't want to at least try it, you told me what?"

"That I didn't know how," she said, laughing at herself. "Come on, that was a very long time ago and a whole world away from the things kids grow up knowing now."

"Most kids. But Kevin was never like most kids. He only crossed his self imposed lines with Lydia, and I'm betting he wasn't the type to boast about it in the locker room, or even in general trash talk with the guys. That kid has probably never even seen thirty seconds of porn."

"Well, neither have I, mister, and I figured it all out."

"You figured it out because you knew what the problem was and you asked me what I wanted you to do. And like it or not, I had definite ideas about what I wanted and I wasn't shy about getting it."

"But he doesn't have to do anything, Chip, just lay back and take it."

"And after that, what? Roll over and go to sleep? At some point the expectation will be for him to return the favor. And if that's in the back of his head and he's not especially clear on the concept, then yeah, he's going to be a little gun shy about any of it."

"If he were gun shy, I would think sex in general would be a problem for him, and we've all heard just now much it's not. I think Nicole was right, you better check their room for drywall damage."

"Sex in general is probably easy for him. He loves Lydia, he wants Lydia…but all of this is something he never expected to be doing, and when he was very young he started stuffing all those curiosities into the back of his brain as something he shouldn't even think about. What he said about this therapist, that might not be too far off the mark."

"He's too catholic."

"He's too caught up in the forbidden. He can have sex with his wife because that's what he's supposed to do. He can use birth control because that's what we taught our kids. But there's that image in his head that sex is *always* making love, and it's always warm and wonderful, and even when it's really good…there's something proper about it. He may be able to get Lydia to sink her nails into him and draw blood, but there's always that line he's not allowed to cross because he was going to be a priest, and he's not supposed to be doing this."

"And you don't think it's always making love."

"I think," I said carefully, stealing a kiss, "that Kevin needs to understand that sometimes it's messy and it's dirty, and sometimes you just want to get…"

She cocked her head to one side, slight grin playing at her lips. "Say it."

"Fucked."

"Charming."

"But I am right. Stop laughing. He needs to know that it's all right. It's not like every single time there's going to be some angelic chorus in the background and the swelling of symphony music at just the right moment. Sometimes the woman who has been driving you crazy all day is going to shove you onto the bed at night and ride you like a pony."

"And sometimes the woman who has been nibbling on your sense of humor might want a nibble back."

"Exactly."

"It could take him years to figure that out, Irish. And longer to work up the nerve."

"It could. Or it could take half an hour in the back yard with his old man, who has no problem sitting the boy down and talking with him the same way I did his brothers."

"You're going to teach him about oral sex?"

"Well…tell him. If he doesn't know how, I'll tell him how."

"You're kidding me. You told Nick and Paul—?"

"No, but those two never needed anything beyond what goes where, and respect her or I'll rip your balls off."

"And thusly was our granddaughter born."

"I'm just going to talk to him, Terry. If it feels like I'm headed into completely unwelcome territory I'll back off, but I'm willing to bet he'll listen to me."

"Chip, I'm really not sure you should even let him know you overheard that conversation."

"I can be tactful. And I will tread lightly, I promise."

She sighed, still not sure. "All right. Just keep in mind he *can* hurt you. And last I saw, he has a wicked side kick."

~

Terry

Chip didn't waste any time. He rolled out of bed at nine and threw on shorts and a t-shirt, and then headed downstairs for break-fast, but when he found Kevin sitting at the table holding Michael, he shifted plans before I could barely blink.

"Good. You're here. You can help me clean the pool."

Before Kevin could protest that he'd cleaned the pool just a few days before and he was slightly busy spending some quality time with his son while his wife took the chance for a long hot shower, Chip reached for the baby, kissed him on his forehead, and handed him to me.

"Don't worry," Chip said as he ushered his son through the door, "she knows what she's doing. She only dropped you twice."

If Kevin had a clue what his father really wanted, I doubt he'd have taken a playful swipe at him. I doubt he'd have given up his son so easily; instead he would have used him as a tiny human shield to get his dad to back off.

Michael watched his own father walk out the door, and started to fuss, his forehead furrowed in frustration. I patted his back, hop-ing to calm him down before he erupted; Lydia was upstairs with her head under water, but she already had Mommy Ears and would come running if he began to wail.

"It's all right," I whispered against his head. "Grandpa just wants to embarrass Daddy, that's all. He'll be back."

He set his head on my shoulder and relaxed while I paced the floor, rubbing his back while I spied on my husband and son. Kevin had the pool squeegee in hand and was attaching the long handle to it while Chip slowly lowered the vacuum into the water.

"Pay attention, Michael. Someday Grandpa is going to make you do this, too."

I wanted to know what Chip was saying; Kevin was laughing while he scraped the squeegee down the sides of the pool, so I didn't think Chip had gotten to the point yet, but it was coming and Kevin effectively had a weapon in his hands.

This was definitely Chip's territory. He had no problem discussing sex with his kids and there hadn't been anything they'd thrown at him that he found embarrassing. They asked questions; he answered them. If Nick or Paul had asked him anything beyond the basics, I'm sure he didn't think twice before answering. Even Eileen, who hit puberty with a vengeance while her father and I were separated, went to him.

Kevin, though; I don't think Chip had ever done more than made sure that Kevin was aware he could ask his father anything. We took it on face value that his vocation was real, that his decision to draw lines he wouldn't step over was firm, and we let it go.

Why talk about sex with someone determined to never have it?

He dated constantly in high school, and we knew he was in love with Lydia through all of it. We had no doubt that there was more than casual making out in the back seat of his car with her going on, but we were sure they weren't doing *that*, so why bother?

But for the want of a condom when he was sixteen, they would have.

A small part of me wished they had; maybe that would have spared him the pain of ending his third year in a seminary tied to a cement bench at the mercy of a deranged roommate who intended to show him none.

Kevin tossed the squeegee into the water and stood there with his hands on his hips. Angry.

Chip was on the other side of the pool, his back to me, but I knew his expression: *So what? You'll talk to me one way or the other*.

Michael went slack in my arms, falling asleep with his head on my shoulder. I could have taken him into the living room and put him in the playpen to sleep, but he was my excuse for pacing by the kitchen table. I wanted to see how Kevin was reacting, but it felt intrusive to just stand there and watch.

Paul stumbled into the kitchen while I walked the length of it with my grandson; he was dressed in jeans and a torn t-shirt, and he hadn't shaved.

"He's asleep, Mom," he said. "You can probably put him down."

"I could, but I don't get to do this as often as I'd like."

He grinned. "He has selfish parents, always wanting to hold him themselves. You'd think they never had a kid before."

"Oh, like you were any better, mister. You spent the first six months of Nicole's life walking around with her in your arms, looking like you couldn't believe what you'd done."

"No one could believe it."

"I meant in a good way. You were so in love with that baby…"

"Nothing's changed there," he said as he reached into the refrigerator for the orange juice. "She's still Daddy's little girl."

Kevin's face was beet red and he hadn't moved from his spot at the side of the pool; his hands were still on his hips, defiant, and his jaw was set and tense.

Paul noticed, too. "Is this something I need to break up? Kevin looks like he wants to take Dad's head off. And he probably could."

"Trust me, you don't want to get involved."

Kevin stomped around the back side of the pool, determined to get into the house and away from his father; Chip grabbed his arm and pulled him back, refusing to let go when Kevin tried to shrug him off.

"Man, I've never seen Kevin so…red."

You would be, too, I thought, if you were as absolutely mortified as he was.

"Don't worry about them." I gestured to his hole-riddled t-shirt. "Where are you off to dressed so formally?"

"Helping someone move. Remember Sherry Armstrong, Monica's friend?"

She was the head hostess at the restaurant, of course I remembered her.

"Her roommate bailed on her, so she's moving to an apartment in Vacaville. She's not happy about it, but she can't afford to rent a house by herself."

"That's kind of a drive from work."

He shrugged. "I told her Dad was thinking about moving the restaurant, I guess she figured she might as well go now and save herself the commute later."

Chip was holding on to both of Kevin's arms, and Kevin's head was thrown back, like he was looking up for divine intervention.

"Oh, just so you know, Nicole gets out of school at noon today, but Katie's picking her up and I don't think they'll be back until after dinner. I didn't want you worrying when three o'clock rolled around and she didn't get off the bus."

He rinsed his glass out and set it in the sink. "All right," he said, kissing me on the cheek as he went past, "I'll probably be back by six, but I don't know how much crap she has, so don't count on it. And call me if either of those two needs medical help. I'll come back and laugh while the paramedics treat them."

Surely it wouldn't come to blows. If Kevin was that upset, Chip would let him walk away.

They sat down together at the edge of the pool, feet dangling in the water, shoulders nearly touching. I couldn't see their faces, but if Chip had gotten him to sit, then Kevin was at least listening.

We did this to you, Kevin, I thought. *We assumed. You're lucky you're not totally screwed up, all that time we spent apart, not talking to each other when we should have been showing you a picture of another future you could have.*

Kevin turned to look at Chip; his face was still flushed, but he no longer looked angry.

Listen to him. He's not just trying to talk to you about sex. You have to hear that, too.

They sat there together for the longest time; I had baby drool dripping down my arm, and tiny fingers poking into my neck. Michael was fourteen pounds of dead weight with a drum beating in his chest and he was getting heavier with each step I took.

Kevin was staring into the water, but he didn't look as tense.

Chip put his arm around him, and Kevin didn't shrug it off.

Lydia was coming down the stairs; I was going to have to hand Michael over, retreat from my excuse for watching Chip as he tried to get Kevin to hear him.

Kevin buried his face in his hands, but Chip kissed him, got up, and was laughing.

He opened the back door at the same time I was handing my grandson to his mother. Kevin was still sitting by the pool, staring at the water; Lydia looked confused, but didn't ask.

Chip kissed his grandson's cheek, then Lydia's, and reached for my hand.

"Come on, woman," he said, pulling me away. "You and I are going to find something to do today."

~

Kevin

I sat by the pool, my feet in the water, until long after I heard the doors slam shut on Dad's car, long after he backed out of the driveway and took off down the street. I sat there knowing that Lydia was probably alone in the house with our son, and that she wasn't going to bring him out there with the sun beating down, she wasn't going to expose his tender skin to a burn.

She was probably sitting in the kitchen, watching me the same way I had watched my parents the night before. Waiting for something. Wanting something.

I watched the vacuum crawl across the bottom of the pool and told myself I was sitting there making sure it didn't get caught up in the hose, that it sucked up every last particle of dirt, the same way I had just a few days before.

He played the brain tumor card.

He freaking played the brain tumor card.

You have to talk to me. I have a brain tumor. That trumps you being embarrassed.

I offered to rip the damn thing out through his nose, and he just smiled.

Yeah, we heard Kevin. We didn't mean to, but damn, the doors were open and if I'd closed them…

I threw the squeegee into the pool and was ready to bolt; I didn't owe him that discussion, not one bit. It was none of his business and I said so, but he didn't care. He watched me turn ten different shades of embarrassed, but kept on talking, as if this were a subject we discussed every day.

'How's your sex life, Dad?'

'Awesome, son. She blew me in the shallow end and we did it in the kitchen. Might wanna watch where you step in there.'

I didn't want to hear about his sex life; why would he think I was open to dissecting mine?

He blamed himself. Whatever issues I had, he thought it was his fault. No one ever thought I'd ever do anything but avoid sex anyway, so it was easy to not talk about.

It was easy to not stop to think that maybe Kevin needed to know more, just in case.

It was easy to not let Kevin really understand that sometimes it's nasty and kinky. And sometimes nasty and kinky is fun. Just let Kevin believe in puffy pink clouds and sunshine pouring over the marital bed like a symphony of sedate and simple sex.

I know what she wants.

Yes, I know how, goddammit.

You won't throw up.

Get out of my head, Dad.

The only way to get over it is to do it. And spare her thinking it's because you owe her. Gentlemen go first, kiddo.

He wasn't going away, wasn't going to stop talking.

And he knew. He wasn't laughing at me, wasn't pointing fingers at the odd little man who had too many hang-ups to count.

Nick would laugh.

Paul would laugh.

I could have gone to Eileen, but I didn't want her pity.

You can live your life doing exactly what you're doing and you'll be perfectly happy. But at some point she's going to resent it, Kevin. She'll love you like crazy and melt against you and adore you forever. She'll never say so, but she's going to resent it.

Lydia was right; at sixteen I would have done almost anything she wanted. If she'd said she didn't care that we were there completely unprepared—forget having a condom, let's do it anyway—I would have.

We all have things we resent, I tried to tell my dad.

I resented that moment that I couldn't have back, the moment when I didn't have the nerve to cave into risk, the moment that would have made me first.

I could protest it all I wanted; Topher was my best friend, there was no doubt about that, but I resented the hell out of the idea that he was first.

She loved me, not him.

Even then, she wanted it to be me.

She would have said yes.

There's the beauty of life. You get a lot of firsts, and you only really missed out on one, right?

It was one that mattered to me. And I can't ever tell her that, because I've sworn that it doesn't.

I'll tell you what, I was nowhere near innocent before I met your mom, but she showed me in vivid color that anything I'd done before wasn't out of love. When you love someone that much...it is a first. She had sex with him, Kevin. She made love with you. Big, big difference. And the gift you give—she gets all your firsts. So trust her with them.

She asked me to trust her, and I said I did.

"Sometimes," I told him as he was getting up, "I fucking hate you."

"Yeah, but you're gonna get the house to yourselves for the rest of the day. Hate me all you want."

"If you think I'll be able to get freaky in every room of the house now, think again."

"Just talk to her, and be honest. You're allowed your regrets, son, and you're allowed to get past them."

Just like that.

~

Terry

"I don't know if he'll actually sit down and talk to her or not, but he's at least thinking about being completely honest with her."

We didn't know where else to go, so we headed to the park and walked around the pond, the same pond we'd been lapping for thirty years. The park was shabbier, the ducks looked underfed, but it still felt like our place. We went there to be closer, we went there when we needed to talk but couldn't stand to be locked in the same room together, and we worried endlessly about our kids as we circled the track.

"Surely he understands she was just a teenager doing what teenagers do. And he was intentionally making himself unavailable; it's not as if she could have known they'd wind up together. I'm not sure why it matters."

He got that. But that didn't mean he liked it or that it didn't tug at his heart every once in a while.

"Does my past ever bother you?" Chip asked.

"Me? No. I knew right from the start that you had a sordid little history, you and your four thousand women."

"Four hundred."

"Four thousand, four hundred, whatever. Anything over fifteen and there's just no point in keeping track. The point is that I was fully aware of what a little man slut you were. I admit, once in a while I wonder if you don't have a bastard child or two or ten running around out there, but the fact that you'd slept around didn't bother me."

He flinched at the idea he might have unknown children. "I was always careful. Very careful. Hell, the only one I wasn't careful with was you."

"Ah, yes, you of the 'I don't want to be a father yet so I hope I didn't just knock you up, but hey! Let's get married!' proposal."

"Hey. You said yes."

"And just a few months later, surprise. You're going to be a daddy after all."

"That was good news, woman. And beside the point. You didn't care and still don't that you weren't my first. Kevin doesn't want to care, but he does. I don't think it's a guy thing, because it wouldn't have mattered to me if you'd given it up to some horny fourteen year old in high school."

"If you had loved me from the time you were just a boy, it might matter."

"All right, it might," he agreed. "And that's only a small part of Kevin's problem, and he knows it. He's still tangled up in old expectations and is having a hard time getting those unwound without losing his faith."

"And without faith…"

"Kevin wouldn't be Kevin," Chip said. "If he can combine the ideas of piety and sex…yeah, we're definitely going to want to move just to get away from the bouncy springs and *Oh My Gods!*"

"Somehow I don't think a blow job is going to bring him any closer to God."

He pretended to consider it. "You might be surprised. And I'm not sure I've ever heard you actually say 'blow job' before."

He had, but I let it go. "Well, there you are. One of my firsts."

He stopped walking and pulled me up against him. "I might like it if you talk a little dirty, you know."

"You might also like it if I pulled you under some of that playground equipment and did things to you right there, but it's not going to happen."

"Killjoy." He let me go and started walking again, holding my hand tightly. "What else do we want to do today if we can't go home and you won't violate me under the slide?"

"That depends. Are we avoiding going home because there may be some fighting and-or loud kinky sex going on, are we avoiding thinking about your brain, or are you just really in the mood to just go hang out somewhere?"

"All of the above?"

This time I stopped. "You're allowed to obsess about your brain, Chip. You don't have to invent things to do. I'm past the crying stage, so if you need to talk…"

He shook his head. "I have a few days until I see the neurosurgeon. I *need* to pretend everything is fine until then. I think you do, too. Paul called it 'punctuated moments of perfect normal,' and it's what got him through some of the worst of it with Monica. That's what I want. I want to embarrass my kids by making them have talks with me they'd rather not, I want to grope you inappropriately in odd places, and I want to just go hang out with the most beautiful woman in the world. Because that's normal."

I stretched up on my toes to kiss him. "Normal it is. And let me call Katie to see if she can keep Nicole until Paul gets home. We can go anywhere you want and stay as long as you want."

"Anywhere with no kids."

"If you're hoping to get lucky, no kids around would be a bonus."

"Then let's go to the beach. I know a cheap place we can stay. It's got a great view of the ocean, and I once even took this really hot blonde there and did unspeakable things to her."

"With her," I corrected.

"Well, to her until she decided it was okay to peek."

"We'd have to sneak home to get clothes."

He shook his head. "Not a chance. There's a mall along the way. I have a credit card and I'm not afraid to use it."

"I'm still not talking dirty."

~

Kevin

We had the house to ourselves but we didn't exactly have the time Dad presumed we would; I had to get the dojo open and ready for the first class, and Lydia needed to get the front office open and get messages off the answering machine. While she returned phone calls and fielded questions from parents too lazy to check the schedule to know whether or not their kids needed to bring sparring gear, I was in my office with Michael, going over instructors' notes from the previous night's classes. I needed to know who had shown up, who was ready for the next testing cycle, who needed extra help, and who just needed a kick out the door. I had a hundred things I needed to get done, but only one thing on my mind.

I let Michael cry in his portable crib while I stared numbly at the notes in front of me.

Everyone has hang-ups, Kevin. Everyone has something they just won't do. But if it matters that much to the person they love...

Don't you have enough to worry about without sticking your nose into my love life?

Dad was trying to not think about the things he could be worrying about; instead he was going to butt in where he wasn't wanted and hadn't been asked to be. Why the hell did it matter to him? Most of the time Lydia and I were fine, and when we weren't we talked about it.

Talking is wonderful...if you're honest.

And hurting her feelings? Where does that fall in the realm of Let's Be Honest? It's not like she can go back and change anything.

I can suck it up, I really can. She doesn't need to know.

Lydia knocked on the office door; it was open but she followed the same rules I required of my students: knock first in case I'm on the phone or talking to another student. Michael was crying in earnest, gut wrenching baby sobs heard clear across the dojo, and I was just sitting there staring at paper.

She closed the door behind her; the question in her eyes was *what's wrong?* but she didn't ask. I'd been distracted since my parents left the house, and she wasn't sure she should ask.

"There was a message from Brandon," she said as she picked Michael up. "He's not feeling well and needs you to take his class."

"You mean he's still hung over from whatever and whoever he was doing last night and woke up at two this afternoon, realizing he would never get through a class of loud little kids."

"If it helps, there are a couple of adults waiting for the class, too."

I reached over and locked the door so that I could change into my uniform without being barged in on by a not-quite-thinking student. I peeled off my clothes and was standing there in my underwear, gi pants in hand, but hesitated putting them on.

"Rabbit, I can call Sam. She might be able to get here in time for the class."

You can swallow it whole, but someday you'll explode and likely beat the snot out of Topher.

I stepped into the pants and then reached for my red school shirt. "I can teach. Sparring today, right? Is there a brown belt on the floor that can help?"

"Vince is here. I think he's hoping you'll let him take over part of the class today."

"Good." I tugged at my belt, making sure it was going to stay tied. "He can take the kids, I'll take the adults."

"There are only two," she pointed out.

"Male or female?"

"Male. Why?"

"Beginners?"

She shifted Michael to her other hip. "Red belt and blue belt. Scott Turner and Pedro Angeles. They should be fairly evenly matched."

They should be, but I wasn't planning on letting them spar with each other.

They took turns on the floor, three and five minute rounds, where they mostly ran for their lives, wondering why in the hell Mr. Brennan was trying to kick the crap out of them. I allowed in the occasional kick and jab, but I mostly kept them running.

Pedro left the floor just before the class was over, preferring to throw up in the locker room instead of in front of everyone else.

I sparred through the next class, rotating four brown belt students who were a little more confident and willing to at least try to score points on their instructor.

I sparred through the class after that, taking a few good hits from a student who had just promoted to black belt, someone who seemed genuinely happy to spend half the class trying to take my head off even though he didn't stand a chance.

I was ready to teach the fourth class; Sam was there and had two advanced students to help her, but I wasn't quite done, not until Lydia gestured for me to get off the floor and follow her into my office.

"Enough," she said once I was through the door. She closed it and leaned against it after she locked it. "Tell me what your dad said to you earlier, Kevin. Because if you don't, by the time the last class is over you'll have broken someone's nose."

"I'm not hitting hard. For the most part I'm making them run."

Michael was in the crib, kicking hard against the slats. I leaned over to look at him, and was rewarded with a wide, gummy grin.

"I'd pick you up, Big Guy, but I'm all sweaty."

"Take your shirt off," Lydia said, reaching into the closet for another one. "You are gross, if nothing else."

I peeled off my wet shirt and tossed it over by my desk, but didn't put the clean one on. Instead I sat on the love seat that faced the desk, stretching my legs out. "You don't want me teaching another class."

"I don't want you taking whatever's bugging you out on any more of those students."

"I just wanted to spar today, Lydia. And it's good for them to see how far they need to go and how hard they need to push."

She sat down beside me, her hand on my leg. "What did your dad say?"

Getting out of this wasn't going to be as easy as bolting to teach the next class; I could hear Sam starting the warm up, and if I left now, Lydia would probably chase after me, dragging me by the belt back into the office.

I knew who was in charge here; I didn't need my students to know.

"My parents overheard us talking last night," I said after a while. "Oh. *Oh!*"

"Yeah. And my dad is a nosy son of a bitch and didn't think twice about butting in."

She turned on the love seat to look at me; I could feel my face burn and really just wanted her to look anywhere else but at me. I could hear what she wasn't saying—*please tell me*—but I focused on our son, watching him until she leaned forward and turned my head so that I was looking at her.

"All right. You win. Put the clean shirt on and go stand on the sidelines in class and scare the hell out of the poor kids who think they have to fight you."

"They do."

"Don't be mean. You have a bunch of little ones out there." She grabbed the end of my belt and pulled me towards her, demanding a kiss before I joined the class. "Spar with Sam. Let those kids see that girls can be just as tough as boys."

"Sam might hurt me."

"Good."

~

After the last student was out the door, I locked it, and while Lydia turned the answering machine back on and shut down the computer, I made one last sweep through the locker rooms to make sure there were no stragglers. I turned lights off as I went along, a stream of darkness flowing behind me.

She'd already turned off most of the lights in the parents' waiting area, leaving only one dim one by the front door, and the lights in my office on.

I peeled my shirt off as I walked into the office, looking for the street clothes I'd left in a heap behind the desk. Michael was asleep, pacifier stuck in his mouth, one arm jutting between the crib slats.

"Shame to make him move," I said absently, wondering where my socks were.

"We're not going to." She sat on the loveseat and patted it. "You're going to sit down and talk to me."

I was untying my belt, still not sure where my socks were. "We can talk at home, can't we?"

"If we wait until we get home, Nicole will be there wanting to see you. And Paul will be there wanting to hold his nephew. And in between that I'll be fixing dinner for you and me, your son will need to be fed, and then he'll need a bath…"

I folded my belt and set it on the desk, then reached for my jeans. I nodded, just slightly, so she'd know I'd heard her, but changed out of the gi pants before I sat down.

"All right," I finally said as I dropped onto the love seat. "We'll talk."

She waited, but I had no idea exactly what she wanted me to say.

Um, hey, my dad offered to tell me how to perform oral sex on a woman. How's that for father-son bonding?

I didn't think so.

"So your parents overheard," she said when it was clear that I wasn't going to start. "I know you're embarrassed, but come on. I've never seen you push your students that hard before. Never to the point where you have students throwing up because they just can't keep up with how intense you are."

"I was intense?"

"You were overly aggressive. It might be all right once in a while, but not four classes in a row. So what did your dad say that made you so upset?"

Gentlemen go first.

"He told me to be honest with you."

"Kevin, you've always been honest."

Mostly, I had, but I'd never seen the point in being completely honest with anything that was going to hurt her feelings for no good reason. Things that couldn't be changed; things I wish we'd done differently.

So what do I start with? The idea that yeah, maybe the therapist was right, I'm just a little too catholic to get past the idea that there's nothing wrong with getting a little freaky? Or hey, I really wish we'd risked putting ourselves in Paul's position when we were just sixteen. Because it wouldn't have been the one time, it would have been the start of something that would have ended in broken hearts, or a forever we were too young to grab on to.

I reached up and turned the floor lamp off, leaving only the dim glow of a desk lamp on the other side of the room; she wanted to talk, we'd talk, but not where she could see me turn five different shades of red.

And not where I could see her disappointment in me.

"Topher," I finally said. "It bugs the shit out of me."

"What did he—?"

I didn't have to say anything more; she rested her forehead on my shoulder, and I could feel her breath brush across my skin. Her hand slipped around my arm and she pulled herself tight against me.

"Kevin, I am so sorry."

"It's not your fault. It's just how I feel. I don't want it to matter, but sometimes...yeah, it does. You don't know how badly I want to go back to that one moment by the lake, because if I could..."

"You said it would have been a mistake."

"I wouldn't have even had to ask, would I? If I hadn't had that one hiccup of worry, we would have kept right on going, and you would have let me."

"I wouldn't have been letting you," she said in a near whisper. "We would have done it together."

"I hate that it wasn't me, Lydia."

She lifted her head and pressed a warm kiss just under my ear. "So do I."

It didn't have to make sense. It was no one's fault; not mine, not hers, and not Topher's. And I knew the litany: if we had caved in to ourselves at sixteen, if I hadn't gone on to the seminary, if there had been no Topher and no bloody night tied to a bench, we might not have been sitting on that loveseat, listening to our baby boy suck on his pacifier.

I watched him pull his arm back into the crib, watched him stretch and slap his feet against the mattress, watched him turn his head so that his face was away from us, watched the gentle ride and fall of his chest with each breath.

My reason for doing.

It shouldn't matter to me.

I felt the loveseat give way as she got up, and cold skipped across my skin where she'd been touching me. She reached over the desk and turned the lamp so that it was facing away from us; the room wasn't dark, but it was safe. When she came back she straddled my lap, holding my face in her hands.

"I never loved Topher," she breathed.

"I know."

"And I never wanted Topher."

I tried to kiss her, but she wouldn't let me.

"All those things you're hung up on, I never did any of them with him, Kevin. I never even considered it."

"I don't need to know…"

"I think you do. It was just the one thing, Rabbit. And it was rushed, horrible, one sided teenage sex. I never even had—"

Her hands slid from my face to my neck, her thumbs slowly tracing my jaw line. I had a dozen things to say, but waited, because she wasn't done and was struggling to get there.

If I could have seen her face more clearly, I think she would have been as red as I'd been standing across the pool from my dad.

"Our first night together," she said. "You wanted to know if you sucked at it, and I told you that you were the polar opposite of suck, that you weren't in a hurry and that you made me feel completely loved. And I meant it, Kevin, I meant every word. Because I'd never realized what it was supposed to be like and before then I'd never…"

What, I wondered. Seen a man completely naked? I knew that

already. Done it with someone dorky enough to leave his socks on? I knew that, too.

"How graphic do you want me to be?" she asked, exasperated with herself.

"My dad offered to teach me all about oral sex today. Does that make you feel better?"

She finally kissed me. "This can't be as embarrassing as that."

"Then tell me."

"What I was expecting was for us to fumble around like teenagers and for it to be over before I had a chance to blink twice. But you took so much time and were so gentle and considerate, and not all grabby and self involved—it felt like you were there for *me*, not for yourself, and by the time you finally slipped inside me…I was ready for it for the first time, Kevin. And you sent me right over the edge, held me there, and brought me back and you waited until you were sure I'd gotten there before you finally jumped over the edge with me."

She touched her forehead to mine. "Rabbit, the only name I've ever cried out is yours, and if we never get around to any of those other things, we'll be fine. But if we do…they're all firsts for me, too. Even our wedding night was."

I didn't know what she needed to hear and I didn't want to say the wrong thing, so I kissed her.

She reached for my hand and pressed it to herself, just under her left breast. "I've told you before, you got *here* first. You've always been there, even when I didn't think I'd ever see you again."

She blinked, sending a tear down her cheek.

I brushed it away with my thumb and whispered, "I love you, Mrs. Brennan. Don't ever doubt that."

"I don't, and I hope that Mr. Brennan understands that he's not just the other half of my heart. He's my soul mate."

"We did get that, didn't we?"

Lydia leaned in for one more long kiss, and then she slid off my lap, reaching for my hand. "Take me home, Rabbit. Let's play with our niece and let Michael's uncle hold him for a while, and after he's been fed we can give him a bath together. If you want to talk about anything else after he's in bed, we can talk all night long if we need to."

~

Terry

The beach house had been locked up for almost a year, and when Chip opened the front door we were hit with the smell of air so stale that it had weight and taste to it. He grimaced and took a step back before he went in, and once inside he started opening windows.

I dropped the bags filled with clothes and food onto the table, and helped him pull the two by four from the beach side door. It had been a quick fix to remedy a broken door; it closed but didn't always stay latched, something we weren't aware of until a neighbor called Chip to let him know the door kept swinging open.

The door had been kicked in a year ago; Chip didn't want to hang around and wait for someone to do the job right, so he bolted brackets to wall and slid a two by four into place. It was the best he could do at the time, wanting nothing more than to get away from the house.

I saw him glance at the blood stains on the couch, but he didn't say anything about them, didn't offer an explanation. Instead, he reached for my hand and said, "Come on. Let's take a walk and give this place a chance to air out."

Where I inhaled stale air, Chip inhaled fear and surprise, and I wondered if we'd be better off getting in the car and going home.

We headed towards the jetty, and halfway between it and the house I could feel his grip on my hand get tighter and his pace slowed, until he stopped and turned towards the house.

"Right here," he said quietly. "The freak that kidnapped Lydia..."

He rarely spoke about that day; I knew the basics: Kevin had almost caught up to them and would have tackled Jake Catero and pummeled him into the sand, but was stopped by the sight of a knife poised at Lydia's ribs. Kevin was armed with a blank-loaded revolver, all for show because he had never fired one and Doug didn't trust him to not shoot someone accidentally, yet somehow Kevin turned the gun on himself and nearly split his skull in half.

And there was Nick, standing behind Chip and Kevin; no one

knew he was there, no one knew he had followed them to the beach, but when Jake lifted the knife to Lydia's neck, Nick fired his gun once, nearly severing Jake's head from his body.

He saved his brother's wife, and broke his father's heart.

"Kevin and I made it this far," Chip went on. "If we'd had another second, he could have overtaken them, but Jake heard us running up behind them…Kevin pleaded with him, Terry, he was begging, but that little tool just kept going on about Kevin needing to go back to the seminary so he could find his own salvation. No worries about Kevin's, just his own."

I didn't think Jake cared about Kevin one bit; if he had he never would have tied my son to a cement bench by the seminary's pond and raped him in a drunken fit of rage.

"And Kevin… Doug gave him that damned gun and you'd think someone as sharp as Kevin would understand how blanks work. But goddammit, he pointed the gun at his own head, as if Jake would care enough to just let Lydia go on that threat.

"And then the shots—one right after the other. Kevin hit the ground and I thought Doug had shot Jake but he was standing behind them and hadn't even drawn his gun. He was staring right behind me"—he turned back towards the jetty—"and there was Nick, standing with a gun in his hand looking like he couldn't believe what he'd just done."

And in that instant, Chip knew that our son had defied us on the one thing we begged from our children: if the agency ever came with an offer, slam the door and never look back.

"And what would have happened to Lydia if he hadn't?" I asked gently. "If Jake had the knife at her neck…"

"I don't know. I don't think I could have crossed the distance in time if he'd really wanted to hurt her. He'd be dead either way, but Lydia—?"

I tugged on his hand and led him back toward the house. "We don't have to stay here, Chip. This was supposed to be a distraction but if it's giving you something else to chew on, we'll go home."

He was a half step behind me and in no hurry to catch up, so I turned and walked backwards through the sand, watching his face, trying to figure out what he was thinking. What he might be seeing in his mind: Kevin shooting part of his scalp off, Lydia lunging for him as he hit the ground, the spray of blood as Nick's bullet tore through Jake's neck?

We were halfway back to the house when he said, "We have to stay here sooner or later. Someone does."

"No, someone doesn't. Kevin and Lydia don't want to come back here, and the rest of the kids don't care. We don't need this house, Chip."

He stopped on the sand in front of the house, and looked up at it. "Sell it?"

The pain in his eyes when he said that slapped at me and I instantly regretted even hinting at the idea. This was his mother's getaway, the place his father had chosen in hopes that it would give her distance when she needed it and space from the man they all thought was Chip's real father. It was where he ran to when life pushed back at him too hard, countless teenaged weekends spent on the porch staring out at the ocean while his parents scoured northern California looking for him.

"I didn't mean that," I said, even though it was exactly what I had meant. "I just meant that we don't have to come here, not for a long time. We don't have to count on this as a place for the family to go. We can find somewhere else."

"If the family gets much bigger we won't be able to all be here at once," he said absently. "Even if Kevin wanted to come back he'd have to give up that upstairs bedroom. They can't take Michael up there."

"I'm not sure they'll ever come back, Chip. Lydia—I don't know what Jake did to her but Kevin has made it clear this is the last place she wants to be."

"She says he didn't do anything but torment her with threats of what he was going to do with the knife if Kevin didn't do what he wanted." He tore his gaze from the house and looked at me. "She spent most of her time trying to figure out if she could get it from him and cut herself loose. Or kill him with it."

He started walking again, making his way to the porch. But instead of going inside, he rested against the railing, looking in through the bay window.

"I can't sell this place, Terry."

"Then we won't." I leaned on the railing next to him, and would have reached for his hand, but he shoved them both into his pockets. "We'll just avoid it for a while."

He was still staring through the window. "This is where I told you I loved you for the first time. The first time we made love was here. Kevin took his first steps here and where Eileen said her first words…Nick and Paul taught them to read sitting on the floor in front of the fireplace."

"Lots of wonderful memories here, Irish."

"Once you set foot in here it became a happy place. Right up until last year. And I think it being here saved Lydia's life."

"How?"

"Once Jake grabbed her he headed for the coast and she was able to steer him to it. She knew Kevin would be able to find her here. If not for this house, who knows? He could have taken her somewhere else and gotten so frustrated with Kevin not finding them that he would have hurt her. Or worse."

"You need to tell them that, Chip."

He nodded, and pushed off the railing, reaching for my hand as he headed inside. Once we were in the middle of the living room he stopped and turned to face me.

"Our family started right here, Terry, in this spot. Right at the moment I told you I loved you, when I was absolutely terrified that you wouldn't love me back…"

"And you didn't exactly give me a chance to say that I did. You kissed me to shut me up."

"If you were going to tell me it was too soon…I wanted one really good kiss before that happened."

"When did I say it, mister memory chip? I would have said it back right then if not for the extra tongue in my mouth."

He grinned, and gestured toward the bedroom with a slight nod. "In there. After."

I reached out for him, snagging belt loops on his shorts, pulling him toward me. "So take me back in there, Irish. Let's reclaim the house as our place."

"Think that'll chase any demons away?"

"I think," I said, stretching up on my toes to kiss him, "that it would be awfully difficult for the hate to stay in here when there's this much love being made."

He couldn't argue with that.

~

Kevin

Nicole sat at the table while Lydia fed Michael; she was bubbling over with excitement over her afternoon with Aunt Katie, and aimed her post-shopping glee at the only available female in the house.

Paul and I were sent to the living room with an all knowing, "You're boys. You wouldn't like it."

Paul dropped into a chair in the living room and huffed, "I might not enjoy it but I'd still like to hear about my daughter's day out with her aunt."

"She'll tell you. When you go to tuck her in tonight, she'll spill it all."

"I hope so. I figure I'm four years away from being too stupid to understand anything. I'll listen to pedicure stories if it'll keep her talking."

"Think that's how Dad did it with Eileen? I know he got sucked into playing with dolls and having tea parties with her."

"Dad just doesn't take no for an answer."

"Tell me about it."

"What the hell did he say to you this morning? You looked like you wanted to shove the pool vacuum up his ass."

I wish I'd thought of that.

I was spared having to cough up and answer for him by his daughter, who bounded into the living room and bounced on the sofa next to me.

"Guess what! Aunt Lydia says I can read a story to Michael tonight before he goes to sleep."

"Well, then you need to go upstairs and pick out a book," Paul said.

"Make it your best one," I added. "Michael needs an awesome story."

"Know what you need Uncle Kevin?"

"Hm?"

She jumped up and headed for the stairs. "A bath!"

"Nicole!" Paul shot off the chair and went after her.

I don't know what he was upset about; she was right. I'd soaked through two t-shirts and my gi pants during classes. While he chased her down I went into the kitchen to tell Lydia I was headed upstairs and would give Michael his bath after I'd scraped my own grime off.

Maybe the hot water would help clear my head.

What else could she want to talk about?

I took my frustrations out on my students; if she asked I would admit that. I was embarrassed and angry and they were there; they needed to spar, I needed to sweat. They needed to test their tolerances, I needed to hit, even if it was with as much control as I could measure.

It was a win-win, as far as I could see.

I didn't know what else we could say.

I stuck my face under the hard spray of water, hoping that the sensation of pins and needles would numb the near feeling of dread that was starting to envelope me. She wanted to talk; I'd already said what I thought I needed to. I told her the truth, but there was nothing either of us could do about it, other than sucking it up and moving on.

I heard the bathroom door open; she was grabbing a towel and a washcloth, probably tired of waiting for me to get out and dry off. Someone needed to bathe the baby and if I was going to hide, she'd suck it up and do it.

I started to slap the water off; I was an idiot but not a coward. My hand was on the faucet when I felt her hands go around my waist and her body slide against mine.

"Paul is giving Michael a bath," she explained, "and he'll put him to bed when Nicole is done reading to him."

I turned around and her arms slid up around my neck. "Did Paul volunteer or did you ask?"

"Paul asked," she said, pulling my head down so that I would kiss her, "and told me it would be a good time to be checking for ticks, and who knows how long that will take?"

"I'm still a little grimy. You might want to be careful how you pull those ticks off."

She reached past me for my wash cloth and the shower gel. "So we'll rub the grime off each other first. I might be a little on the sweaty side, too."

"And then what? We're clean and tickless—?"

"We'll figure it out."

We stayed in the shower until the hot water started to run out and dried off quickly, practically dancing towards the bed, locked at the lips and hands.

She stopped just short of the bed, her lips still on mine, and said, "Don't over think it, Rabbit. I just want to make love with you."

I wasn't thinking at all at that point.

She pulled me down on top of her, and threads broke loose, one last thing to stop being hung up on.

Gentlemen go first.

~

Lydia put her finger across my lips, and gestured towards the baby monitor. We'd made sure the door was closed, just in case Nicole helped Paul put Michael to bed so that she wouldn't wind up seeing something her father would need to explain, but the monitor was on and we could hear every movement coming from Michael's bedroom.

I glanced at the clock; Paul had taken over an hour to bathe him and for Nicole to read to him, either giving us time in case the door wasn't closed, or more likely, stealing time alone with his nephew while he could.

He still had his best baby-soothing voice, speaking in hushed tones designed to lull an infant to sleep. It didn't matter what he said as long as he spoke gently; Michael would either fall asleep or try to play with him.

"All right, short stuff. Let's see if I remember how to do this. Nicole was very picky about bedtime when she was your age. I had to walk the floor with her until it felt like my arms were going to fall off before I could put her down. But you're a good sleeper, right? Mommy and Daddy put you down and you don't shriek like someone poked you with a straight pin."

The squeak of the crib mattress, Michael's feet slapping against it. Paul opened drawers, and after a moment asked Michael, "Ok, I know you sleep with a plug. Any idea where you last put it? Ah…here's one."

Michael was cooing and babbling, and we could hear him kicking at the crib slats, the way he did when he was just happy to have someone talking to him.

"Here you go. You're a back sleeper, right? And I remember Daddy telling me that you love to have your tummy rubbed. Nicole liked that sometimes, but mostly she cried. I think she was afraid she was going to miss something if she just let herself fall asleep. But you know what? She didn't. I'd put her to bed and then her Mommy and I would go to sleep, too, because she wasn't sleeping all night long the way you do. I knew I was going to have to get back up in two hours and that made me a grumpy daddy."

Michael must have spit the pacifier out, because he rewarded Paul with a long squeal.

"I really wish you could have met Nicole's Mommy. She would have loved you to pieces, just like everyone else does. Or maybe you did meet her before you were born. Your daddy thinks she counted all your fingers and toes before you got here, and that makes me smile a lot.

"But you know what, Big Guy? Even though I really miss her I think I'm ready to move on. And your daddy wants me to meet someone he knows, but I haven't told anyone that there's already someone else I like, and she likes me, too. I'm just not sure about it. Maybe I should let him help me meet a few new people first. But I really do like her and I've known her for a very long time. I even helped her move into a new apartment today and after she kicked her brothers out we sat and talked for a long, long time. She even cooked dinner for me, that means something, right?

"So whatcha think? Should I play the field just in case, or should I just trust my gut and go for the girl I know I really want? I mean, I *really* want her. It could get very nasty if it didn't work out because she works for me and I don't want to make her uncomfortable at work, but she's very nice and sweet and funny, and she thinks Nicole is adorable and loves her already. And she would be a very good aunt to you, too, you know.

"Oh that's nice. Fall asleep instead of helping me sort out the love life I don't have. I'll remind you of this in fourteen years when you want to talk to someone who isn't your own father about girls. Oh, yeah, I'll remember."

I slid out of bed and reached for the first pair of shorts I could find, and slowly slid open the door that connected our room to Michael's. Paul was still leaned over the crib, very gently rubbing Michael's belly.

"Go with your gut, wonderdork," I whispered. "You've been half in love with her for a long time."

He stopped rubbing Michael, but left his hand resting on my son's chest. "She was Monica's best friend, Kevin. I'm not sure that's a place I should go."

"Risk it and ask her out, Paul."

He slowly lifted his hand and stood up. "I never should have asked you to set me up with someone. I thought it was a good idea, but I just..."

"Ever stop to think that Sherry's been right there for a reason?"

"Go back to bed," he sighed, pushing past me. "I'm pretty sure you still have a tick or two."

~

Terry

"If that didn't chase the demons away," Chip said sleepily, "then at least they got a good show."

"Think you want to stay, then?"

"At least until morning." He sighed hard and sat up, swinging his legs over the edge of the bed. "Crap. I hate getting old. Be right back."

"Remind me to be grateful I don't have a prostate," I teased as he went into the bathroom.

"You can just bite me."

"Is that a request?"

"Maybe. If you're gentle."

"Third time tonight," I reminded him when he crawled back into bed. "I'm surprised your kidneys haven't shriveled up."

"I'm an idiot and drank half a gallon of water tonight."

"That'll do it."

"If someone would stop making me sweat, I wouldn't be so thirsty."

"Get used to the thirst, mister. If my libido is going to dry up at menopause, then I'm going to use you while I can."

12

Terry

We stayed the weekend at the beach house; on Saturday morning Chip decided there was no reason to go home, and giving Kevin more time to be less annoyed with him seemed like a better idea than going home to be glared at. He spent his time on the porch watching the waves lap the sand and we dove headfirst into memories of all the times we'd been there alone and the chaos of weeks spent there with the kids when they were all young enough to need constant supervision.

I wasn't sure which had been more fun: long weekends lost with each other, or too-short weeks spent trying to keep the kids from killing each other.

"They both had merits," Chip decided. "I think even now I'd give up a little horny fun to sneak up on the boys standing on the porch railing trying to see who could pee the farthest."

"Really, I'm just glad you didn't join them."

Monday morning he decided it was time to head home; he had an appointment with a neurosurgeon on Tuesday and as much as he wanted to drag his feet, he didn't want to have to get up early on Tuesday and then scramble to get to Sacramento for it.

He wasn't quite ready to go home, though, so we stopped at the restaurant for lunch. He had the joy of tormenting a new waitress and Paul had the headache of trying to explain to her that his father wasn't always an ass and wouldn't quiz her on ten different menu items and wouldn't change his mind every fifteen seconds about his order on future visits.

He gets the grilled chicken with broccoli and green beans every freaking time. And he wants his salad dressing on the side, always. Don't take any crap from him.

I don't think she believed him, but she was as good as Chip could have hoped for and earned every penny of the giant tip I made him leave on the table.

We'd been there for half an hour when Kevin wandered out of the bar and spotted us. Chip half held his breath as our youngest child walked across the dining room, but managed a smile when Kevin grabbed a chair from the table next to us and sat down.

Somewhere between leaving Kevin sitting by the pool and Kevin walking across the restaurant, Chip realized he had crossed the line with his son and was ready to apologize for the intrusion and the embarrassment, but Kevin gestured towards the bar and said, "Will says you fired James while he was gone on vacation."

"I did," Chip admitted as he reached for the pitcher of ice water the waitress had brought him after he'd asked for a third refill.

"Why? He was really good at it, and the customers loved him."

"Could have fooled me," Chip said, and went on to explain his encounter with the former bartender.

Before Chip could finish, Kevin was shaking his head. "Why didn't you just wait for Will to get back so he could talk to James? Why ambush the poor kid when his defenses weren't just down, but on vacation?"

"That 'poor kid' acted like an ass, Kevin."

"And you didn't? Dad, if he copped an attitude with you it's because he just didn't get it. He doesn't get a lot, which is why he *always* worked with Will and only with Will. He had no way of knowing he should have picked up the slack because Will didn't tell him to. If he thought for even half a second you were backing him up against the wall, he was going to panic, and for him that means an attitude."

"I don't want someone who can't take a little pressure behind the bar."

"But with Will supervising him, he's good, Dad. He can make any drink you can throw at him, and as long as Will is there to get to stuff off the damned top shelf, he's fine. James was terrified of that step stool. And by the way, you don't have to actually put the top shelf stuff on a freaking top shelf, you know."

"It looks better that way," Chip said off handedly.

"What is it about James that we're missing?" I asked Kevin. "Why would he be so good at the job yet piss us off so unbelievably?"

Kevin's head cocked to the side just a little, and he considered his father. "You really don't know? James is mildly autistic. He misses social cues all the time and tries to cover that up...so yeah, if you don't know and he doesn't have someone there to buffer for him, he can come off as a real ass. He took ten kinds of shit for it in school, but thought he finally found a niche here."

"I really didn't know, Kevin, and I don't think Paul did, either."

"You used to get to know your employees. You didn't used to count on Paul to know the things you're supposed to. Hell, he should have known, but you own the place, and I'd think you'd protect the people who deserve it."

I waited for Chip to snap back at Kevin; while our son manned the bar on occasion and had worked in the restaurant off and on from the time he was fifteen, I doubted Chip would allow him to criticize how he handled his employees, but he drained his glass for a fifth time and said, "You're right. I don't know these kids as well as I should, and I should have waited to talk to Will about him. And I will, I promise you that."

He tossed his napkin down and excused himself, saying he would be right back.

Kevin watched his father walk away, and looked surprised when he didn't head straight for the bar.

"You try drinking that much and then avoid going to the men's room," I said lightly.

He nodded towards the nearly empty pitcher. "How much of that did he drink?"

"All of it."

"Is he peeing a lot?"

"It's the joys of getting older, Kevin. Something you can look forward to."

"I don't think so. When did you notice him drinking more and peeing more?"

"He's been thirsty all weekend," I said, though I wasn't sure when I noticed that Chip was inhaling water like air. "He chalked up the peeing to his prostate."

Kevin was digging his cell phone out of his pocket before I got the whole sentence out. I knew who he was calling and why, and didn't try to stop him.

Chip got back to the table just as Kevin flipped the phone closed, and before his father could sit down he said, "You have an appointment with Uncle Doug at three o'clock."

"And why do I have this appointment?"

Kevin gestured to the glass Chip was once again filling. "It's not your prostate, Dad. It's the tumor."

~

Chip

Before Terry could work herself into a panic, Kevin calmly added, "It really isn't a big deal in the grand scheme of things. The tumor just knocked out another hormone, and Uncle Doug can give you something to replace it. You'll probably be in and out of his office in ten minutes."

What Kevin couldn't do was assure his mother that the tumor had not grown already, and she teetered on the edge of nausea until we were in the waiting room of Doug's office.

Out of at least thirty chairs in the waiting room, only four were vacant. We dropped into the only two available that were side by side, and I was grateful that it was in a corner, away from all the crying and coughing kids and their stressed out parents.

We'd been there only a couple of minutes when an older man dropped into the chair across from us, looking at me expectantly. It took a moment for me to recognize him, his dark hair having gone completely gray, but when I did I whispered in Terry's ear, "I hate to have to ask you this, but can you go sit over in the cootie section while I talk to this guy?"

She didn't ask questions, she simply nodded and got up, crossing the room to the only other chair available.

When she was seated and smiling at a toothless baby, I looked at him and grunted, "Barron."

"Call me George," he said with a friendly air I had never before sensed from the agency's Secretary General.

"All right, George. What brings you here?"

"Ostensibly, sudden back pain. Doctor Stone is my personal physician, too."

Goody for you, I thought, but I asked, "What do you want?"

"It's more like what you probably want. Word on your son."

I knew better than to ask. So I waited.

"He's a kick ass kind of kid, Chip. If I had a dozen more of him, I'd be a happy SG."

"Stay away from my other kids," I warned.

He waved it off. "I'm contractually obligated to pretend they don't exist. But Nick officially exists, and Nick is fine. I thought you'd want to know that."

I glanced at Terry. She was holding someone's toddler, and laughing with the little boy's mother.

"Is my kid really just a desk jockey?"

"Ideally," he replied. "But this is a fringe agency, Chip. In the best of times we don't get the funding we'd like and now…we're only getting about a third of what we need. Everyone is doing jobs they initially were told they wouldn't be doing."

"So Nick is essentially a field agent," I sighed.

It was the worst case scenario for him; behind a desk, he was relatively safe. As a field agent, he was a six foot tall brain with a target on his back.

"He's still an asset," Barron said, "and we protect our assets, even when they are as highly skilled at field work as he is."

"Is he? Is Nick that good, good enough I can assume the best?"

I wanted to know when he was coming home. I wanted to know if he would be coming home in one piece, both mentally and physically, but I knew I'd never get an answer.

And I did want to know just how good Nick was at this game.

"He's as good as you ever were, but he doesn't seem to have your death wish."

"And that could make him sloppy."

"I think," Barron said, "that knowing he has a family to come home to makes him very careful in the things he does. And he's never alone."

We protect our assets.

They would protect his brain at all costs; Nick's intelligence was the asset.

"Do you want him to be made aware of your current medical situation?" Barron asked.

I didn't need to ask him how he knew; my life had not been private since birth, and it never would be.

"He doesn't need the distraction."

Barron stood up when the nurse called out for Jeffery Dobson.

"Even if I die," I added. "Don't tell him a thing until he's on the plane home."

He nodded, and then turned to head through the door that led to the exam rooms.

Terry continued to play with the little boy, but watched me carefully until my name was called. She didn't ask anything until we were alone in the exam room, and when I explained who he was and that he only wanted to let me know that Nick was safe and doing just fine, she accepted it without any more questions.

But when Doug entered the room, she didn't bother so much as saying hello; she asked before he could get the door closed, "Does this mean his tumor is getting bigger?"

He didn't miss a beat. "All it means is that it knocked out his pituitary's ability to make Vasopressin, and we can replace that with a nasal spray."

"I got that much from Kevin," she said. "I want to know what it means."

Apparently, I was not needed for this.

"It means that his kidneys don't have the hormone they need that tells them when to hold onto water, so they let it all go. Thusly does he pee like a maniac, and thusly does he drink like a fish."

"If the tumor's not getting bigger, then why is this suddenly happening?"

He looked at me. "I don't think it's sudden. I think someone held out on me when I asked if he was urinating more than usual."

"I didn't think it was unusual for someone my age," I said.

"And the thirst?"

"When you pee a lot, you get thirsty. Right?"

He sat on the little round stool and scooted close to me. "You didn't graduate from medical school, Chip. No more self diagnosing. I don't care how out there or embarrassing it is; if I ask something, you have to tell me the truth, even if you don't think it's related to anything else."

"That could be as insignificant as a freaky looking hangnail," I said.

"Then you tell me if you're not sure. And I mean about anything."

"Fine. I think my balls are shrinking."

That made him scoot back a little, and he glanced at Terry for a fraction of a second, the look asking 'is he pulling my leg?' but he didn't otherwise react. "How much are we talking here? A little or a lot?"

"Minutely, and no, I'm not letting you check."

He stood and shoved the stool aside with his leg. "I think you are. Get up and drop 'em."

"Like hell."

My wife was a touch too amused. "He's seen you naked, Chip, and if it'll help I'll wait out in the hall."

Doug was snapping gloves onto his hands; I sighed hard—I should have kept my mouth shut because Dr. Doug doesn't take a smart assed comment the way Mr. Doug does—and got up.

"You can stay," I told Terry. "Make sure he doesn't enjoy this."

Doug managed to maintain an air of professionalism as he checked; Terry worked hard at not smirking, and I just wanted to get it the hell over with. When he was done he peeled the gloves off and told me I could pull the pants up if I wanted. Or not. Whatever made me happy.

"You're an ass, Doug," I said as I zipped my jeans.

"So I've been told." He looked at Terry. "Was he telling me the truth when he said he wasn't impotent?"

"He whines a lot about being used and abused, but he's not impotent."

"Anything different that you've noticed?"

Suddenly, I understood *exactly* how Kevin felt.

I owed the boy a deep apology.

And it bothered me that Terry didn't say no right away.

She looked at me as if asking permission to go on; I was already mortified, so I nodded. Why the hell not?

"Let's just say that things aren't as...firm."

"Spongy?"

"Cripes," I breathed out.

"In between spongy and as hard as he used to get."

"It's the marathon peeing," I told her. "I'm saturated."

Truthfully, that was something else I'd chalked up to getting older.

"You can maintain an erection?" he asked me.

"Jesus, Doug."

He looked to Terry, and she nodded.

"And you can finish?"

"Can I go now?" I asked. "I'd really like to go now."

"He gets there," she said simply, not at all flustered and looking more and more amused with my embarrassment.

"You do have some mild testicular atrophy; that could be entirely age related, but your testosterone was low, so none of this is exactly a surprise. When do you see the neurosurgeon?"

"Tomorrow."

"All right. I'll consult with your endocrinologist about putting you on testosterone. And I'm going to give you a prescription for a nasal spray that will replace the hormone that's making you urinate so much. Use it once in one nostril just before you go to bed, and that should get you through the night. If you notice the thirst returning early in the day, start taking it in the morning, too."

"And if it comes back, say, at four o'clock?"

"Then let your endocrinologist know. There are pills you can use when you get breakthrough. Honestly, you can live without treating it, but it's not a comfortable way to live. You have to drink to keep up with the thirst, and it can get pretty painful."

"What exactly is 'it'?" Terry asked.

"Diabetes insipidus. Not to be confused with diabetes mellitus."

"I'm a diabetic?" I asked.

"No." He sat back on the stool. "What you commonly think of as diabetes is diabetes mellitus. Think of that as sugar diabetes. What you have is diabetes insipidus, or water diabetes. Where a diabetic's body doesn't process sugar correctly, yours no longer processes water correctly. As long as you stay properly hydrated and your electrolytes don't get out of whack, this isn't that big of a deal."

Easy for him to say.

I was thirsty and I had to pee, and unless the dojo schedule had changed, I had a class of little kids to teach.

~

Lydia was in the front office on the phone—"Yes, the under-ten class is at four today. No, he doesn't need to bring his sparring gear"—so I waved at her as I walked past, and headed straight for Kevin's office. He was sitting on the loveseat giving Michael a bottle; when I knocked and went in I saw a dark scowl cross his face, but he recovered quickly and without saying hello asked, "What'd Uncle Doug say?"

"He said you were right. Your mother is getting my prescription filled while I run the little rugrats ragged."

"Was he able to assure her it's not the end of the world?"

"For the most part. Mind if I change in here? I don't particularly enjoy getting stuck in the locker room in my underwear with ten little boys staring at me."

He shrugged. "Look in the closet. We got new school shirts in. Wear one and make the little shits pester their parents to start buying them."

I grabbed one from the stack he had on the shelf and shrugged into it. "How does Master Timm feel about you letting the kids wear t-shirts in class? Has he said anything?"

Master Timm, the hard core military-style instructor who had taught both Kevin and me, was adamant about uniforms; they were always bleach-bright white, ironed crisp, and worn in their entirety in each and every class. No exceptions.

When Kevin bought the school he added red uniforms to the

mix, made black an option for advanced students, and he did away with mandatory gi tops. They were too hot, he said, and made the kids fidget too much. Attentive kids learn more.

He had learned just fine and adjusted to the requirement when he was only seven years old, but he hated it and I wasn't surprised that it was one of the first things he changed.

"He bought one of the first shirts," Kevin said with a grin. "And the first time he saw me playing Simon Says using kicks and punches with the kids, he thought it was—in his words—a hoot. He doesn't seem to mind the changes we've made."

"I suppose he accepts that change is inevitable."

"He asks about you," Kevin said, lifting Michael to his shoulder to burp him. "He thinks you should be ready for your second degree by now."

I should be; I probably was, except for the kata I never worked on.

Rank seemed pointless to me, and if I went for it, it would only be for Kevin's credit in advancing a student another degree.

"By Thanksgiving," Kevin added. "I want you to test by then."

"We'll see what kind of shape I'm in then."

"Just presume you'll be fine. Sam and I will work on the kata with you if you can drag yourself out of bed a couple of days a week to come here and work out."

"Talk to your mother. If I sleep late, it's her fault."

He grunted and looked down at his son, who was more interested in slobbering on his shoulder than burping.

I sat against the edge of the desk. "I owe you an apology, Kevin."

"Yeah, I think you do."

"I don't always stop to think that you're not a kid anymore and you don't need me to give you personal advice. I dropped the ball when you were a teenager but that's no excuse for embarrassing you. I am sorry for that."

"Dad, I didn't ask the questions back then because I got it all from Nick and Paul. You might not have thought I was ever going to have sex but they were hoping I would…and any problems I have now, I take those to Lydia. Not you. I'm sorry, but she's the one I talk to. She's the one I *should* talk to, and if we can't figure it out…we'll decide together if I need to talk to someone else."

They'd decided he needed to see a therapist; I was glad he'd done it, but I wished he didn't feel like he needed to keep it a secret.

"If it makes you feel any better," I ventured, "I got a real good taste this afternoon of how embarrassed I must have made you. I might be comfortable talking about sex with my kids, but I am definitely not comfortable being caught in the middle of Doug and your mother discussing my gonads with me standing right there."

"You went in there to get a prescription and your junk wound up as the topic of conversation?"

"Don't ever try to joke with Doctor Doug about the possibility that your testicles are shrinking. He'll demand proof, and then it all goes downhill from there."

The smirk that crossed his face reminded me of the amused look his mother had in the exam room. "So...you had to stand there and let Uncle Doug grope the goods with Mom watching? That's rich."

"It got worse. They then launched into a discussion of my potency and the quality of my erections. So yeah, I have a better idea of how mortified you were. And I swear, I'll never go there with you again unless you ask."

He got up and put Michael in the crib, and reached into the desk for a diaper. "I may ask," he said, looking at his son and not at me. "Not about sex exactly, but maybe your opinions on where my stupid hang-ups come from. I could understand it if I'd grown up in a completely uptight family, but you and Mom never hid the fact that you wanted time alone, and why you wanted it. That seems entirely normal to me, even if I do complain about your lack of boundaries."

"There's probably more to it than living with horny parents, kiddo. We split at a pretty bad time for you. You hit puberty right when your family exploded, and that's about the same time you began thinking you had a vocation. I can see it getting all mixed up in your head."

"My therapist," he said, picking up his freshly diapered son, "thinks it's all a catholic thing. I think that's too easy and doesn't explain more than a fraction of it."

He sat back on the loveseat, holding Michael close, and he left room for me to sit next to him. I got the message: talk to me, but please don't look at me. I focused on Michael instead, offering him my finger to pull on.

"For the most part I think Eileen hit the nail on the head when she told me that I'd been given two paths I could take, and neither one was the wrong one."

I knew Eileen believed deeply that God intended for Kevin to wind up right where he was; she claimed that God had been shoving Lydia in his face for too long, long enough that it had to be what Kevin was supposed to do. He'd fallen in love with her before he even liked girls, before he could work up the nerve to say more than one or two words at a time to her.

"You seemed pretty sure about the priesthood when you were just fifteen," I reminded him. "I think we should have followed Will's lead and tried to persuade you to wait for a while after high school to head off in that direction."

"Hindsight is wonderful," he sighed.

"Be honest. If you knew then that you would only stay for three years, regardless of why you left, and knowing you'd wind up married to Lydia, would you have gone anyway?"

"I would have."

"Then why—?"

"I would have gone because what I learned there was invaluable. It changed the way I saw a lot of things and how I embraced faith. But there are things I would have done very differently if I had known."

"Differently with Lydia," I presumed.

He nodded. "Take Topher out of the equation. He left after high school, anyway. She dated a little, but she never let herself get even remotely serious with anyone else. She was waiting and she didn't even know it. She was lonely, and she waited, without knowing if the person she was waiting for would ever come back for her."

"So at least then she would have known what she was waiting for."

"Maybe."

"The more likely scenario… You would have caved in, if not when you were sixteen, then when you were seventeen. You would have capped off a very real emotional connection to her with a physical one, and you wouldn't have been able to leave. You would have been Nick, Kevin. He couldn't let go when he needed to, and I think a few years would have made a huge difference for him and for Katie."

"You don't think they'll make it?"

"I think they will, but I also don't think they'll ever have what you do. I think they'll be struggling against it for the rest of their lives, that little voice in the back of their heads whispering 'what if' all the time."

I had no doubt that someday my oldest son would be celebrating his fiftieth wedding anniversary with Katie; I had serious doubts that he would always put her first.

"You think they were too young?"

"I think they were too serious too young. Nick pretty much made up his mind that Katie was it when he was fifteen. If he'd met her at eighteen and married her two or three years later…"

"When Nick was seventeen he thought he was thirty," Kevin reminded me. "You couldn't have convinced him that he was too young for anything. There wasn't anything he didn't know and he wasn't shy about sticking his nose into things. Kind of like someone else I know."

"And if you and Lydia had become more intimate than you did when you were that age—"

"I know, Dad. That doesn't mean I don't have some regrets, even if things did turn out exactly how they were supposed to."

"We all have those. Some of mine are huge."

"I can imagine. And I'd bet your biggest involve Mom."

"That they do. And still, I doubt I'd change a thing. We are who we are because of our own bone headedness, and I think she and I are terrific together."

"But if you could have back those two years?"

"We've actually talked about that. I doubt we would have Nicole, so no. I'll give up those two years and wallow in the misery if it means having my granddaughter." I slipped my finger out of Michael's grasp. He was half asleep and more interested in sucking on his fist than pulling on my finger. "If not for all the torment you two put yourselves through in high school, and the three years you were gone, you might not have this little guy, either."

"I've considered that. And I'll suffer all the hang-ups I have to if it means having him."

"Just do yourself a favor and take some time to enjoy him before you have the next one. That is the one thing I would change if I could, not having all of you so close together."

"You wouldn't think twice about it if Mom hadn't gotten so sick with Eileen and me."

"Maybe not. And true, too, chances are pretty high you wouldn't be the youngest. She wanted to fill every single one of those bedrooms."

"So why didn't you adopt?"

"We left that particular door open as an option."

He glanced sideways at me.

"I closed it after Nicole was born. I didn't want to start another family, Kevin."

"And she was okay with that?"

"I gave her a lot of years to decide. Once Paul had Nicole…I just wanted to be a grandfather. She understood."

"And now," he said, holding Michael close, "you're still stuck with kids in the house."

"Not stuck. We could kick you out anytime."

"When are we moving? Nothing personal, but I really would like to get my family into their own home."

"Offer was made and accepted, we just have to wait for construction to be completed."

"Great. That could take months."

"No. I gave them an incentive clause. We should be in by the end of August. By my birthday at the latest. It's worth an extra hundred grand for us to close before the last business day in August."

"Awesome." He got up and gently lowered Michael into the crib, cringing when there was a knock on the door. "What?" he hissed.

Lydia opened the door and stepped halfway in. "You might have a problem," she said to me. "There are at least thirty five kids here for your class. I don't think there's enough room on the floor for all of them."

Kevin flicked the baby monitor on and motioned for us to step outside the office. "Do you want to split them up and each teach half?" he asked me. "I can take some onto the practice floor. Or we can just warm them up and sit them on the sidelines and demo self defense techniques."

"Make this a class they can ask us questions?"

He nodded. "Find out what they want to see the most."

She glanced at Kevin with worry. "They'll want to see you two spar and I'm not sure that's the greatest idea."

"I won't take his head off."

"You won't hit or kick him in the head at all," she said firmly. "You don't know—"

"Hey, he might knock the tumor right out through my nose and save me the hassle of surgery. It'll be fine, Lydia. I doubt he can make contact with my head anyway. Every time he tries I'll dump him on his ass."

"Oh, it's *on*, old man," Kevin laughed. "You're going down."

~

"He handed my ass to me," I told Terry later while we soaked my aches away in a tub filled with water as hot as we could stand. "When the hell did he get so fast?"

"When he kept taking classes after you quit?"

"And holy shit…hitting him is like hitting a brick wall. He looks skinny, but damn he's all muscle."

She dipped a washrag into the water and began sliding it across my chest. "Same can be said for you, mister. I suspect if I tried to hit you I'd break a nail on your buns of steel."

"A year ago, maybe. I have body fat now."

"Oh my God." She draped the wash rag over my shoulder and pinched at my waist. "Instead of five percent body fat, now you might have eight. I've gained a hell of a lot more weight over the last few years than you have."

"Bullshit. Where?"

"All over," she said, sliding closer, until her face was just in front of mine. "But it doesn't matter, Irish. At our age we shouldn't have to beat ourselves up to look perfect. If gravity is going to settle in, don't fight it."

She grabbed both my hands, setting them on her ribs, encouraging me to slip them higher. "If my sagging boobs don't bother you," she leaned in for a kiss, "then what makes you think a microscopic layer of fat stretched out over all six feet three inches of you is going to matter to me at all?"

"Your boobs don't sag," I assured her.

"You're a wonderful liar. And don't stop that, not now."

"You're just trying to distract me," I whispered against her lips. "We can do this, but I'll still be whining about how much my body hurts, and I'll still be dwelling on that appointment tomorrow."

"That's fine." Her hand slipped lower and she added, "They don't feel any smaller to me."

"I was just trying to throw Doug off his game. But yeah, they are. Just a little. I'm not worried because as long as everything else works, I don't really need them."

"Oh sure," she snickered. "You might not miss the hair, but these you would miss."

I sucked in a sharp breath. "Maybe. Firm enough for you?"

She pushed my arms down, until they completely encircled her waist, and she arched back, grabbing my head and guiding it to her. "Maybe."

"The Queen would probably prefer this if we moved it to the other room. She rarely cares for riding the pony under water."

"We wouldn't want the pony to drown," she agreed. "I understand parts of him are already saturated."

13

Chip

Kevin greeted me the next morning with "You look like shit," and from the look on his face I knew he thought Terry didn't look any better. He sat at the table with the newspaper, distracted by the business section, when he realized what day it was. "Let me drive you. You didn't sleep at all last night, did you?"

I tried to wave him off, mumbling that we'd be fine, but he was on his feet and digging in his pocket for his cell phone. "Dad, if either of you drive it'll be as bad as if you were driving drunk. Let me call Sam to make sure she can teach the first class today, and I'll take you."

I couldn't argue. I knew I hadn't slept at all and I was sure that Terry didn't do much more than drift off every now and then, waking up every time she turned over and every time I fidgeted. Now I was tired and nauseated, fighting to keep from dry heaving over the trash can. He was right; I had no business behind the wheel of a car.

Terry tried to get me to eat something, even toast, but I knew I'd be bringing it up within five minutes.

It's just the initial consult, he's not going to jam an ice pick up your nose and fish the damn thing out right there.

No, but he could take one look at the MRI and tell me that I only have a few months to live.

My mind was not going to shut up.

Terry and I sat in the back seat of her sedan on the ride to Sacramento; I kept my eyes closed and she held onto my hand, her grip tightening when Kevin drove onto the off ramp and we were less than a mile from the hospital.

If either of them had wanted to talk during the hour it took to get there, they respected my obvious wish to just be quiet. No one said a word once we were out of the driveway, and Kevin turned the radio off when he realized it was grating on my nerves.

"I just want to pretend this isn't happening," I told Terry at two in the morning. "I know it's supposed to be all right and that everything is stacked in my favor..."

"But if everything was stacked in your favor, you wouldn't have the tumor at all."

When we got to the office I just wanted to sit quietly and wait; Terry checked me in at the front desk and Kevin took a chair across from me, deliberately waiting for me to be the one to break the silence.

I didn't have anything I wanted to say, and kept quiet until Terry handed me a clipboard and said I needed to look everything over and then sign it.

I scribbled my name without so much as glancing at the paperwork she'd already filled out.

Congratulations! You just donated both kidneys and your liver to science!

The waiting room was only half full; a few of the people waiting looked as terrified as I felt, but most seemed absurdly relaxed, as if sitting in the department of neurosurgery was a regular occurrence, like they'd been there so many times that the familiarity overrode the fear.

I didn't want to be there so often that it felt comfortable.

I didn't want to be there at all.

There was a little boy sitting not ten feet from me, his misshapen head shaved bald, a raw and angry stitch-riddled incision running from his hairline to the back of his head, arching across his scalp and over his left ear.

He was laughing.

His mother was smiling.

I wanted to throw up.

Terry touched my arm gently and stood; I hadn't heard my name called. She took my hand and guided me through the door into a long hallway, leading the way as she followed the nurse who was showing us the way to the exam room. I tried to concentrate on Terry, but in my peripheral vision I caught glimpses of people waiting in other rooms, and could smell their fear as much as I felt my own.

The fear of the unknown smells a lot like rubbing alcohol and sweat.

"Are you all right?" Terry asked as soon as we were alone; the nurse left the door open several inches, enough for other tormented souls to catch a glimpse of the terrified old guy being comforted by the cute blonde as they walked past.

"I just want this over with," I groaned.

She reached for my hand again. "I know. But this is where the real wait starts. We'll be lucky if we see the doctor within the next half hour."

I had visions of sitting there all day, the forgotten patient, locked in a room while the staff went home. I had to pull my hand away from hers so that I could lean forward and bury my head in my own hands.

If I could squeeze it tight enough, maybe the background buzz that was starting to invade my brain would quiet.

She reached for my back instead, her fingers rubbing lightly as she tried to make me feel better.

It was a distraction, but not enough to keep me from feeling like I was on the verge of passing out right there in the chair.

I was close to caving into the dry heave I'd been fighting along with the pins and needles of panic when the door swung open all the way. Dr. Mark Harris, neurosurgeon, pituitary specialist, was as tall as Kevin, and didn't look much older; he wore jeans that were too short and a baby blue shirt with a dark blue tie that stopped an inch before his beltline, and his dark hair was spiky and dyed blond at the tips. All I could think when he was extending his hand towards me was that I didn't want a teenager probing my brain.

He had the MRI in hand and shoved it onto a light box, and as he flipped the switch on it he leaned forward, squinting at the images the way an eight year old would look at a bug he'd just stomped on. Gross, but fascinating.

"Oh yeah. Dude, that totally has to come out."

I looked at Terry. *Did he just call me 'dude'?*

He was pointing at a specific picture of my brain, his finger running along the outside edge of the tumor. "Right here. See how it's got this little point? It's starting to creep up the pituitary stalk and is headed straight for the hypothalamus. You want it out before it gets there, for sure."

Yeah, dude. For sure.

"How long before it gets there?" Terry asked.

He looked at her, and considered it. "These are typically slow growing and it's not impinging on his optic nerve, so there's time."

"Can you tell us what it is?" she asked.

He peered at it again, and sniffed. "Well, we know it's not a prolactinoma. Your prolactin levels," he looked at me, "are up but they're not astronomical. It doesn't have the oily appearance I might expect from a craniopharyngioma, but I can't rule that out. Honestly, the only way we'll know for sure is to remove it and send it to pathology."

"When?" I croaked.

"End of August at the latest. I'll check my schedule before you leave today and we'll set appointments for a pre-op physical and the surgery."

End of August. We'd be moving then. If I delayed closing I'd have to drop a hundred thousand dollars on the incentive clause for no good reason.

Numbly I said, "If I'm not available at the end of August to close a business deal, I lose a huge chunk of cash."

He considered it for a moment, then got up and grabbed a pen and a note pad off his desk. "All right. Sit tight and I'll go see what's open."

"You can delay whatever business you have, Chip," Terry said.

"I dangled a hundred grand in front of the builder to get those houses finished by then. He'll get it done, and then if I delay the closing, it'll be money we might as well have flushed down the toilet."

"Then you lose some money. You'll get over it."

"What? You're angry?"

She turned in her chair to look at me; if she wasn't angry, she was definitely annoyed. "You are *not* putting this off because of bad timing on what really is just a business deal. If all he has available is the end of August, you're taking it even if it costs you a small fortune. We can move whenever. Or not move. Who cares at this point?"

I knew better than to argue; if I tried to push back the surgery even a day she would probably staple me to a gurney and wheel me into an OR by herself. I simply nodded, and she leaned back in her chair.

We waited in silence, five minutes of *I won't cry if you won't throw up*, and it ended with the crack of the door being pushed open by a size 14 sneaker.

"You're in luck," he said, waving his notepad. "I had a cancellation and I scheduled you in that slot."

Who cancels brain surgery?

"When?" Terry asked.

Unless they died.

"Friday morning. First case of the day."

He's a pituitary specialist, and someone died.

I had to swallow hard to keep the nausea from winning.

This is not happening.

Terry was looking at the MRI. "Tell me what you're going to do to him."

Surfer Doc came to life; he was so excited about describing the surgery to her that he damn near glowed.

"Transphenoidal resection," he said. "Basically, that means we go through the sphenoid sinus cavity to get to the pituitary gland. We can get there two ways; go through the nose and drill at the back of the sinus cavity, or go in under the upper lip and through the sinus cavity. I prefer going in under the upper lip because it gives me a little more room to maneuver, but either way is acceptable."

"Is one better than the other?"

"The patient doesn't need post op nasal packing if we go through the nose, and there may be a slight decrease in pain."

"But you prefer the other way."

He nodded. "Like I said, more room that way."

"How do your fingers fit either way?"

"Microsurgery," he explained.

He went on, but their voices were dulled by the increased buzzing in my head. I had three days before he was going to lift my face half off my skull, take a drill and bore a hole in it, and then dig out a tumor of unknown type.

I just wanted to go home.

Terry's hand sliding across my arm brought me back into the room.

"Thursday you'll come back for your pre-op workup. We'll get blood, a chest x-ray, and an EKG—"

"I just had one," I interrupted.

"That's cool. But we'll need an official one for the records, just to prove we made sure your heart was ticking the way it's supposed to before we knock you out." He was flipping through a file folder, his finger tracing over lines rapidly. "Doctor Stone put you on DDAVP just yesterday? Were the symptoms sudden?"

I shook my head but Terry said, "He decided they didn't matter. He may not be your most cooperative patient."

"That's fine. Most of my patients don't want to be here. I don't take it personally." He looked away from her and at me. "Any questions?"

I couldn't think of a thing I wanted to ask him.

"All right then. I will see you on Thursday, and if you think of anything between now and then, feel free to ask. In fact, if you think of anything, write it down. It helps."

He got up, and Terry followed suit. I struggled, my legs suddenly feeling like rubberized sludge.

When we got back to the front desk, she gave me a gentle shove and said "Go on, go outside and get some air. I'll set the appointment for you."

Kevin unfolded himself from the chair he'd been waiting in and followed me outside. I leaned against a bike rack bolted to the sidewalk, and inhaled deeply and rapidly.

He wanted to ask, but waited until I could breathe normally.

"He can't tell what it is from the MRI," I told him "It could be anything, and he says it has to come out."

"When?"

"Friday."

Panic etched his face in fast, thin lines. "This Friday? It's that bad that it has to come out *this* Friday?"

"No. No, I didn't mean that, Kevin. He was going to wait until the end of summer, but he has an opening this Friday and your Mom jumped on it. She's not giving me a chance to chicken out."

"Wow," he breathed, without adding the trailing thought, *this is really happening, isn't it?*

When Terry came out she walked straight to me and put her arms around me, hugging tight. "All right, Irish. You need to eat something. If you don't, you really will start dry heaving."

"Not yet. Give me an hour, I'll keep lunch down."

"You want to hang around here?" Kevin asked.

"God, no. Take me home, kiddo."

We headed for the car, but Terry stopped short of the rear bumper. "I have a better idea," she said, fishing in her purse for her cell phone. "Kevin, do have time to waste? Or do you have to get back for a class?"

"I can take the entire freaking day if you need me to."

"Good." She flipped the phone open and started dialing. "Going home is the last thing he needs."

~

Kevin

I hauled blocks of wood away from my grandfather's back door to a metal rack near the back fence while he and Dad sat on the patio. I'd moved the wood in November and stacked it neatly next to the back door to save him from having to carry it across the yard; now it had to go back because, according to my dad, wood stacked that close to the house invites termites.

I grumbled, but I didn't mind.

That back yard was why Mom thought Dad shouldn't go home; he was always able to relax on the back porch, sipping beer with Grandpa. Watching me sweat was just a bonus.

Mom was inside with Grandma, making lunch for everyone. I watched her look at Dad as he headed outside and knew she wanted to follow him, but with her he would stay wound up, torn between trying to figure out how to make her feel better while dealing with his own rising panic. She knew that once he was sitting there with his father-in-law he would start to relax; Grandpa had that effect on him. If he was scared out of his mind for Dad, we'd never see it. He'd simply cover it with the consumption of a cold beer or two, and by watching his grandson labor on his behalf.

I wondered, when I was halfway across the back yard with my arms loaded with wood, if Mom knew how many times Dad had taken us there when they were separated. I couldn't count the number of times they sat on the porch and watched Paul and Nick toss a football back and forth, or how many times Eileen and I worked on Grandpa's truck with them.

I don't think they talked about Mom very often; it was a place Dad could let down his guard, where the company wasn't wondering what the hell his problem was and why wasn't he doing back flips to make that beautiful blonde take him back. Grandpa would listen if Dad wanted, or just drink beer if all he wanted to do was sit and watch his kids. And in it all was Grandma baking cookies or cupcakes, determined to not make anyone think she was taking sides.

We knew where they stood; where they didn't push Dad, they had no problem telling Mom she was a complete idiot. She never argued the point; she agreed with them but had no idea to get from the place where she locked Dad out of the house to the place where she could say she was sorry.

I dumped the wood in the pile and headed back for more. Whatever Grandpa had just said had Dad chuckling, and when I turned and looked, he no longer looked like he was about to crawl out of his own skin.

So maybe it wasn't only the back yard. Maybe it was Grandpa.

"You're doing a bang up job, son," Grandpa said when I went back for the last of the firewood. "I think you even deserve some cookies for your effort."

"Only if he finishes his lunch," Dad said, taking a sip from his bottle of beer.

Complaining on my part was a requirement. "That's not fair. I earned the damned cookies."

"Not yet you haven't. There's still some wood waiting for you."

"Fine." I snatched up the last of it and stomped off pretentiously. "I'm telling Mom you're being mean," I called out.

He had a bottle of beer waiting for me when I was done.

"Just one," he said. "Someone has to drive me home and I suspect your mother is getting buzzed on white wine right about now."

I brushed pieces of bark off my shirt and then grabbed another lawn chair, parking it next to Dad. "A little early for drinking, isn't it?"

"Any other day, maybe. Today, I intend to get buzzed and stay that way."

"No, you won't," Grandpa told him. "You'll drink a few here but when you leave, that's it. You're going to go home and have dinner with your grandkids, and you don't want to be drunk for that."

"Buzzed," Dad corrected.

"Either way. Buzzed, you don't get to hold the baby, and buzzed, you don't talk to your granddaughter about what you're going to be doing on Friday."

Dad sighed hard, and slid in the chair a little. I could practically hear Nicole's name shoot through his head. *What the hell do I tell Nicole?*

"You can't hide it from her, Chip."

"I know, Pop."

"She'll know if you lie to her, too."

"I can't tell her I have a tumor. If I say that, the only thing she'll think is that I have cancer, and for her that doesn't turn out well."

"Maybe Paul should tell her," I said.

"Paul should be there, but no. I should tell her."

Grandpa agreed. "And none of this bullshit Doug came up with. Tell her the truth. She doesn't need to think you're getting your nose realigned and then find out later that you had a tumor. All that will do is make her not trust you."

"How do I do that?"

"By telling her it's there but her Uncle Doug doesn't think that it's cancer. Be honest, tell her there's a tiny, tiny chance that it is, but even so, it's a small tumor and Doug found it early."

Dad sat up straighter and then leaned over, running his hands through his hair. "Maybe she should talk to her great grandfather. He's probably better at this than I am."

I touched the cold beer bottle to his arm. "Hey, if you can talk to me about the things I would clearly prefer to never discuss with you, you can do this with Nicole. This has to be easier than…that."

"Ha!" Grandpa snorted. "Did you finally get the talk, son?"

Dad started to grin. "I thought he might want a clue where that baby came from."

"I *know* where he came from. How he got there in the first place…? That really should be a subject in junior high."

"Did you ever have that talk with your daughter, Pop?" Dad asked.

"I certainly can, if you think it will help you."

I got up and went to the back door, sliding it open just enough that I could call out, "Mom? Grandpa wants to talk to you!"

A minute later she came out, worry furrowed across her brow; she glanced at Dad, who was staring down at his beer bottle, and then sat in the chair I'd been in. "Dad?"

Grandpa inhaled deeply, deliberately, and looked at her with an intensity that for just a half second made me think he was entirely serious. "Terry," he started, pausing to look at Dad.

Dad wasn't giving an inch. He stared into that bottle as if his life depended on it.

"I have been seriously remiss," he went on. "There are things I should have told you a long time ago."

She gripped at the arms of the chair.

"Sweetheart…when a boy likes a girl, well, sometimes he—"

"Oh my God." She stood up and swatted at Dad's head. "Lunch is ready, you morons."

"Wait. They thought you needed to know where babies come from."

"All of mine came from North Bay Hospital," she sighed. "Now get inside and eat, or I'll feed it to the dog."

Grandpa got up and as he went inside he asked, "When did we get a dog?"

~

Terry

Doug was there to answer any questions that Chip simply couldn't, and to help Nicole understand better he drew a picture for her, a side view of a brain, sliced right down the middle.

Paul sat on the other side of the table, his jaw clenched, determined to let his father handle this, but inside all he wanted to do was pick Nicole up and run out of the room with her. Kevin and Lydia were outside, sitting beside the pool with Michael in his playpen; he wanted to help talk to Nicole, but he knew it would be better with fewer grownups trying to soothe her worries.

"The more people telling her to not be afraid, the more afraid she'll be," he reasoned.

"This," Doug told her as he drew in a small punching bag, "is the pituitary. And this," he added a tiny circle, "is where your Grandpa's tumor is."

"That's pretty small," she said, not looking up.

"Yep, it's about the size of a big pea. It also has a little finger on it"—he drew a spike on the tip of the tumor—"and that's kind of the problem. Right above this little finger is a part of the brain called the hypothalamus. If the finger gets long enough to poke that, then Grandpa will start having very bad headaches. So we want to take the tumor out before it does that to him."

She glanced up from the paper Doug was drawing on and looked at Chip. "It doesn't hurt right now?"

"Nope. Right now all it does is make me pee a lot."

"Will it hurt when they take it out?"

"I think it might hurt a little bit, sweetheart," he told her, "but the doctor will give me medicine for that."

"Like the medicine Mommy had to take to make her cancer not hurt?"

"Like that."

She glared at Doug. "That didn't help Mommy very much. You have to make sure Grandpa gets better medicine."

Paul gripped at the edge of the table, his fingernails turning white.

"Grandpa won't be in as much pain as your mom was," Doug tried to assure her. "After the operation his head will hurt for a while and he'll have to stay in the hospital for a few days, but by the time he comes home it will only hurt a little, and he'll be very tired, but that's it. I swear, he won't hurt as much as your mom did."

Nicole stared at the picture for a moment, tracing her finger over the places Doug had told her were the problem. When she looked back up she asked, "Do you promise that Grandpa doesn't have cancer?"

Doug looked at Chip, and then at me.

"Uncle Doug can't promise that," Chip answered. He held out his arms to Nicole, and she slid off her chair, very slowly leaning in to let him hold her. "But you know what? You know how many pennies there are in a million dollars?"

"A lot," she sniffed, burying her face against his chest.

"The chance that I have cancer is the same as one penny in all of a million dollars. If you filled the pool up with pennies, in all those pennies only one of them would be cancer."

"And then no one could swim."

Paul managed a tight grin, and he relaxed his death grip on the table.

Chip managed a half smile. "That's right. No one could swim, and then I'd have to make Kevin clean out the pool."

Nicole took a half step back, but didn't allow Chip to let go of her. "Are you scared?"

"A little bit," he admitted. "Even though I know I'll be asleep and won't feel the operation, it kind of scares me that it's going to hurt a little."

"You can't die from the operation?"

I saw Chip stiffen, and Paul paled again.

"Nicole," Doug said, getting her to turn around, "I know for a fact that the doctor who is taking the tumor out has never lost a patient during the operation, not someone who has a tumor in the same place as your Grandpa. And he's done this operation thousands of times."

"Okay." She looked over at Paul. "Can I visit Grandpa when he's in the hospital?"

"I don't know," he answered carefully. "We'll have to see how Grandpa feels after the surgery. He might not want anyone to see him, except for Grandma."

"He's going to sleep a lot for a couple of days," Doug added. "So don't be too upset if no one knows when you can see him, okay?"

"Okay," she sighed. "Can I go now? We had to run a lot in karate today and I'm tired."

"Take a bath first," Paul said. "I'll come up in a little bit to tuck you in."

"I'm a little old for that, Daddy."

"Well, I'm not. So you just have to suffer."

"Fine." She sighed dramatically and stomped off.

"Did that goes as well as I hope it did?" Chip asked of no one in particular.

"Better than I hoped," Paul said. "She'll think of a dozen more questions while she's in the bath tub, but I'm pretty sure I can answer them."

"If you need specifics, call me," Doug said as he got up. "I'll be up for a few more hours."

After he left and Paul was upstairs with Nicole, we grabbed soft drinks out of the refrigerator and went outside to sit with Kevin and Lydia.

A snap of warmth hit us when we opened the door, but once we were down by the pool we could feel the cool breeze, and Chip settled into his chair with a sigh. Michael was in the playpen on his back, his head turned towards a rattle that he had fixated on and was struggling to reach. Kevin wanted to get up and hand it to him, but Lydia told him to wait and see if Michael even got frustrated.

He was focused and intent, but he didn't look like he wanted to cry yet.

"Are we interrupting?" I asked when I sat down.

"We were just comparing notes," Kevin said. "Lydia talked to Debby today and I talked to Topher last night…we've decided they're morons."

I still wasn't sure when Kevin had decided Debby was worth his effort and his time, and it amazed me that Lydia was willing to give her more than a cursory thought, but their unlikely friendship seemed to be genuine.

"Topher," Lydia said, "wants to get married. Debby does not.

But they haven't told each other this."

"We can't decide if we should stick our noses into it or not," Kevin said.

"Why would Debby not want to get married?" I asked. "Isn't she crazy about him?"

Lydia nodded. "She says she wants to wait until she's got a better job and can contribute more."

I only wanted to be sure she wasn't waiting out of some dim hope that she could still sink her hooks into Kevin. He waved it off, and Lydia said, "Now she honestly believes that whatever itch she had for Kevin was just some cosmic way to get her back to California so that she would meet Topher. I don't understand why she feels like she needs a better job…Topher has a great one and it's not like she would need a huge paycheck—"

Kevin snorted into his beer.

"What?"

"Listen to yourself. How long did it take you to say yes to me? And remember your reasons for waiting?"

"Oh, hush. You're not supposed to remember things like that."

"Maybe someone needs to remind her that Topher is the prize at the bottom of the cereal box. She chewed through a lot of crap to get to him." He turned his head and grinned at her. "That is not a conversation I should have with her, by the way. It definitely sounds like girl talk."

"Don't think I won't. I may have seriously disliked her at first, but she's obviously good for him. And he's even better for her."

Michael grunted, throwing his left arm over his body in a desperate attempt to get to the rattle that was just outside the reach of his right arm. When that didn't work, he tried again, throwing his left leg into it, and rolled over onto his stomach, squealing with delight when he had the rattle in hand.

"I'll be damned," Chip whispered, the first words I'd heard from him since we left the house.

Kevin started to get up, but Lydia put her hand on his arm. "Let him play," she said quietly, awed by seeing him roll over for the first time. "I know you want to scoop him up, but he earned that toy. Let him play."

Michael stuck his arms and legs straight out, the rattle clenched in his tiny fist, and he let out a high pitched *eeeeee*, complete with toothless grin.

"That's right, Big Guy," Chip murmured. "You did good. And now we have to put gates up all over the house, because that's mobility."

"Are you kidding?" Kevin said. "I may never let him out of my sight now."

"Well, that could be awkward," Lydia snickered.

Chip was still watching our grandson wiggle. "I think I'll be relieved when you have him in a single story house. He could be crawling in a month or two, and I hated those damned stairs when you were a baby."

"Even after he was a baby," I reminded Chip. "It didn't do my heart any good when he was hanging from the banister near the top of the stairs. If he'd fallen…"

"Let's not go there," Chip murmured. He looked over at Kevin and said, "Nicole says she had to run a lot in class tonight. She wasn't complaining about it but she admitted she was tired. I'm guessing Sam taught?"

"Probably. I've gotten to where I'm surprised when Brandon shows up for his classes."

Brandon Atwood, who started training at the same school two or three years after Kevin did; he was a second degree black belt with, as Kevin sometimes put it, "ten times as much talent as common sense." When he taught, he taught well and the students liked him, but as the months wore on after Kevin took over the school, Brandon became unreliable and was hung over half the time when he did show up.

Kevin chalked it up to the freedom of finally being out from under his parents' oppressive thumb and a girlfriend who liked to party, but Chip didn't think it was a reason to put up with his behavior.

"You have to cut him loose sooner or later, Kevin. Hire one of the other black belts to take his place."

"I'm not sure I have one who has the ability to teach," he said. "Lots of raw ability, but that doesn't mean they can convey the material."

"So you teach them to be a teacher."

"Or," Kevin said, pointing his beer bottle at his father, "you start teaching a few more classes. That's all we'd need. Sam and I can handle the bulk of them, we just need someone for a class a night."

"After everything is settled," Chip said, surely thinking of the surgery and the move, "I can. But you need to start grooming a few of your advanced students as teachers. Sam might not be there forever. Look into the under belts, Kevin. You have a few red and brown belt students who really stand out. You may have a handful of future instructors there."

I waited for Kevin to brush his father off; it was his school and he was handling it well, having grown the student base by at least three hundred students since he had rebuilt the dojo, and he didn't have to take business advice from Chip.

Instead, Kevin nodded thoughtfully, and agreed. "If I ever want to expand, I'll have to," he said.

"Considering another school?" I asked.

"One of my teenaged students needed a project for a computer class and asked if he could map the dojo's demographics. What I learned…I have a huge chunk of the student population driving in from as far away as Dixon, but most coming from that direction live in Vacaville. It makes sense to open a second school out there."

"And you're moving to Vacaville, anyway," Chip ventured. "What about the current school?"

"Sam. I'm fairly sure that if she was in charge, she'd stay there long term. I know she's had the impulse to open her own school."

"What's stopping her?" Lydia asked.

"Gender bias," he sighed. "She would need Master Timm to be on board with the idea because she needs him for instruction and to test and advance black belt candidates. But he's got just enough of a stick up his ass to be wary of female instructors. He'll teach her and support her as my employee, but he would never be there for her if she tried to open a school of her own."

"Old school." Chip shook his head. "So you in essence become the man she hides behind."

"Until I've advanced enough to be able to do all those things in his stead…yes. I don't like it, but there it is. Sam has the talent and the drive, but she doesn't have the support of her own mentor."

"And you don't need the competition," Chip pointed out.

"I don't think she'd open a school anywhere near mine," Kevin said. "But who knows? Ten years from now if I've got another school and it's doing as well, I might consider selling the dojo to her. We could become cooperative schools."

"If you're serious about it, you need to start looking for the right location. Soon."

"Why soon?"

"We're on the precipice of a huge jump in the price of real estate, and if you don't buy soon you'll be paying half to seventy five percent more, and it'll take a good four to six years for a market correction."

"Is that why you dangled so much cash in front of the builder to get those houses finished?" I asked.

"It's exactly why. In seven or eight months he'll be able to get far more than that hundred grand for all them, and that kind of money makes a person look for legal ways out of a contract. He'd stall and try to force us out of the sale, being so generous about letting us out of the agreement—and all because he'd be able to turn around and sell each of those houses for a good two to three hundred thousand more than we're paying. It's an investment to get in before the prices shoot up."

"And you're certain they will?" Kevin asked.

"Certain enough," he said, casting a wary eye at me, "that I already bought land for the Charybdis to move onto. And I'm taking bids for construction."

"Why do you look like you expect me to hit you?" I asked. "It's not like I don't know that by the time you tell me you're thinking of some particular business venture that you've already decided."

"Doug seemed think the expenditure of that much money required discussion. Though, I don't know why, considering he's never told Kris how much he spent on his tuna boat."

"Sheesh, that thing has to be ninety grand at least," Kevin said.

"Hundred and sixteen," Chip said.

"Ah, she wouldn't care," I said. "And he's an idiot if he thinks she doesn't know. Surely she noticed that much money suddenly missing from their bank account."

"You didn't say anything to me when there was several hundred thousand suddenly missing from ours," Chip pointed out. "I did have to put money down."

"You have expensive business deals all the time," I said. "If I tried to keep track of what you take out versus what you put in, my head would explode. As long as you keep enough in my checking account, I'm happy."

"You need to know where everything is," he said, suddenly very serious. "I told Doug I didn't think you knew half of what I had going on, but I really didn't think it was an issue. But you need to know, Terry. And you need to know what to do with it all if—"

"Don't," I said. "There's no 'if' here. You're going to be fine."

"'We all have expiration dates,'" he quoted. "Someone very wise once said that to me."

"You have accountants and lawyers who know where it all is, right?"

"Yes, but—"

"But nothing. I don't want to talk about this, Chip, I really don't."

"Ter—"

I got up. "No. We're not doing this."

I could feel his eyes on me as I went back into the house, but I couldn't make myself turn around and ask him to come with me.

~

Kevin

A minute or so after Mom stomped back into the house Michael broke the uncomfortable silence; he began to whimper, and within seconds was up to a full blown cry. Lydia quietly said he was hungry and she would take him inside, leaving me beside the pool with my flabbergasted father.

"I didn't mean she had to know right now," he said after Lydia was inside. "I just meant…"

"You meant that she needs to start finding out what you own and where, and what to do with it eventually. I got that, Dad. But she hears 'I've got a brain tumor and I might be dead by Friday afternoon, so here's what I want you to do.' Honestly, that's what I was hearing, too."

"Yeah, well, maybe a part of me did mean that."

"Brad will make sure she figures it out," I told him.

Brad Colt, the lawyer she had worked with for at least half my life; he'd loved her, at least a little more than friends, and would still move the world if it meant making sure she was all right.

"He will," Dad agreed. And then with a deep breath added, "And if something does happen to me Friday, he'll be helping you, too."

I leaned forward and set my beer bottle on the deck. "How so?"

"I had to set things in motion, Kevin, just in case. If I die"—he held his hand up to stop my impending protest—"Doug is the executor of my estate, and essentially your mother gets everything, but there are some lengthy instructions for you. I'm trusting you—no, I need you—to handle the bulk of my business deals."

"Me? Why not Paul? Or Nick or Eileen?"

"Paul understands the restaurant, and it's his. Eileen doesn't have the slightest bit of interest or inclination to stick her fingers into anything I have going on, and I'm not sure she'd understand how I've structured it all. And Nick... God, I love him, Kevin, but I don't think he can see far enough ahead to keep everything going."

"I doubt I can, either, Dad."

"Yes, you can. Brad would hand you the paperwork and all the instructions I've left, and within a day you'd understand exactly what I was doing and why. You'd see far enough ahead to know when to let something go and when to invest heavily. But mostly...you'd make sure your mother was well taken care of the rest of her life."

"We all would."

He hesitated; I could see how hard he was thinking, trying to say what he wanted without it coming out wrong.

"Someday," he said carefully, "I would full expect your mother to move on."

"Like hell."

"I'd want her to, Kevin. I don't want her to be alone for the rest of her life. But neither would I want whoever she wound up with to get his fingers into what he shouldn't. I want our assets protected. She can spend what she wants on whatever she wants, and even whomever, but I don't what some theoretical *him* to be able to get his hands on any of it."

"So I'm the brick wall between some imaginary future boyfriend and your wallet."

"Essentially. And I'm counting on you to keep the assets growing so that my grandkids will step into trusts of value equal to what their parents did."

"Adjusting for inflation," I guessed.

"If possible."

"Isn't this all theoretical? This is a community property state. Mom gets it all by default, doesn't she?"

"She'll abide by my wishes, son."

"Cripes, that sounds so formal and fifties."

"You know what I mean. If I say I want you handling everything, she'll agree and she'll understand why."

"Then you need to tell her this *now*," I said. "Pin her down and make her listen."

"I know how to get her to listen to me. I just need to make sure you're on board before I do. If you're completely against it, I'll call Brad tomorrow and find another way."

"Tomorrow," I sighed, "you're going to spend the day with my mother, doing everything you can to make her laugh. You won't have time on Thursday…I'll be your brick wall, but you have to promise me that tomorrow it's all about her, because you know it doesn't matter what Doug says. She has her own giant What If hanging over her, and she's scared to death."

"I know."

"So go inside and talk to her. And tomorrow, forget you have kids and grandkids."

"Now wait…I want a family dinner tomorrow. At least give me that."

"Fine. I'll make sure everyone is here by seven o'clock. But from the time you get up until then…a part of her is afraid she's going to lose you, Dad. Give her something to remember, just in case."

He got up and handed me his soda can. "Toss that out for me."

"Will do." Before he could open the door I called after him. "Dad?"

He turned. "What?"

"Just remember. Gentlemen go first."

I held onto the sound of his laughing even as the door closed. Just in case.

~

Chip

"You have to understand," Terry whispered at three thirty in the morning, "some of the time I still feel like I'm dragging around guilt like two tons of dirty cat litter. And I will always carry that, no matter how upset you get with me that I still have it. It doesn't matter how many times you tell me I'm forgiven. I carry it and I always will."

I wasn't sure what I was supposed to say or even how that related to what we'd been talking about; I only wanted to be sure she was all right with everything I'd talked to Kevin about, that she grasped it was a What If thing and not Yes I Will.

She was laying flat on her back, staring up through the darkness at the ceiling; I rolled over and slid closer, until it was my face she was seeing instead of the shadows cast by the ceiling fan. "I thought we agreed that whatever mistakes either one of us made got us to here, and here is a pretty terrific place."

"That doesn't mean I don't have regrets, Irish." She put her hand on my cheek, fingers gently caressing. "I'd give anything to have never hurt you. And now this…"

She choked on the words and couldn't finish.

"Listen to me. We've both done some pretty stupid stuff, but I am grateful for every day I've loved you, and I've loved you every single day since long before I was able to say it to you. No matter what happens, I want you to remember that…at our worst, I still loved you."

She kissed me then, long and slow and sweet, and for the rest of the night I stayed there with my arms around her, hoping that if the worst did happen, she would cling to that.

I was truly grateful for every moment I'd had with her, even the days when I was alone and too angry with her to think straight.

I fell asleep with her head crooked beneath my chin and her hand on my chest, wondering how, even in her sleep, she managed to trace her finger over the shamrock tattoo that was just above my heart.

14

Chip

My cell phone chirped about two seconds after Terry's did. We looked at each other with slight confusion, and then worry; what else could concurrent text messages be but bad news?

Nick.

We lunged for our phones; hers was in her purse on the dresser and mine was in the jeans I'd left in a heap on the floor. She had her phone flipped open and was reading the message, looking confused, while I was still trying to figure out how the hell to open it.

Dude, I have a weird little tattoo on my ass. Totally rethinking mojitos and long islands with horny blondes.

"What the hell?"

"It's from Topher," Terry snickered. "Somehow I don't think this was meant for either of us."

"What, did he send this to everyone in his phone's address book?"

The laughter that erupted from Kevin and Lydia's room suggested that was exactly what he'd done.

"So Topher is probably toasted at eight in the morning on a workday. Very classy of him."

She shoved her phone back into her purse and bounced back onto the bed, pulling me with her. "He was probably toasted last night and just wanted to brag the horny details to his friends."

"And we're in his contact list, why?"

"Because he's Kevin's Doug, and he keeps track of everyone that would want to know if Kevin needed help and he was the only one around to get it for him."

"So we're liable to get drunk dialed on occasion. Wonderful."

"It's a small price to pay for Kevin to have a friend like that."

"I suppose it could be educational. Can I reply to him and tell him to rub a little Ben Gay on it?"

"You're evil."

"Thank you. Now, what do you want to do today? We have the entire day free, right up to seven o'clock, when I've issued an order for my offspring to come over to feed and amuse me."

"A command performance? I hope they can all make it. And that I'm not expected to cook."

I was sure they would all be there, except for Nick, and I didn't expect to see him anytime soon.

She wanted to spend the day doing ordinary things, go places we routinely went just to get out of the house. We took lunch to the park and sat under the same tree where we used to watch the ducks when we were dating; even after all this time I knew she was looking for signs of Quackers, the horny little duck that used to follow her around. Realistically she knew that he was long gone, but she'd also made it a point to find out that he theoretically could have lived to thirty, and might be waddling around the pond very slowly.

After the park we went for a ride in my car with the top down, and took the back roads to Napa. On the Interstate it was a twenty minute drive; taking the back way it took us over an hour to get there. We took winding roads that cut through thick strands of trees, and when the road straightened out enough that I could take my eyes off of it, I turned my head to look at her, to watch her hair flowing in the rush of air that zipped over the windshield. She had sunglasses on, but I knew that those blue eyes were twinkling and creased from the wide smile that was on her face.

We took the Interstate back and stopped at the restaurant for a drink and to see if Will had found a new bartender. I asked him if he would hire James back if he could and he didn't hesitate to say, "In a heartbeat."

Before we left he'd called James and arranged for him to come back the following week, and I swore I wouldn't again interfere in how he ran the bar.

Two minutes after we were back in the car and headed for home, my cell phone chirped again. I dug it out and handed it to Terry so that she could check the text message that had come in.

"Topher again." She laughed through her nose and read, "'Dude, help. She read the Kama Sutra. Tied herself into a knot.'"

"*This* is Kevin's best friend?"

She flipped the phone shut, and it chirped again almost instantly. "'Couldn't find the G Spot. F spot will have to do.'"

Two minutes later, "'Dude I shaved 'em. You were right. Ow.'"

I took the next exit and pulled into a grocery store parking lot. "We're being played with," I guessed. "Give me the phone."

Toothpaste takes the razor burn away.

"Chip, you didn't!" She laughed as she took my cell phone from me.

"I hope he really shaved and takes that seriously…"

Chirp.

"'Well that's just wrong.' I think you won, Irish."

"As well I should."

We were almost home when another message came in, and Terry was laughing before she even looked at the phone.

"It's Kevin," she said. "'Minty fresh is not a total-body experience. Don't ask me how I know.'"

"I'll ask Lydia instead," I said, cutting the engine.

Kevin's car was still parked out in front of the house but Lydia's and Paul's were gone. I knew Paul was at work, and guessed that Kevin and Lydia had taken Nicole to the dojo with them. The house was eerily quiet, and I wasn't sure I wanted that.

We had at least two hours to kill before anyone else would be home.

"Sure there's nothing else you want to do today? We have a couple of hours…"

She dropped onto the sofa and reached for my hand, pulling me to sit with her. "Just this. You've got to be tired, Chip. I know I am. Neither of us slept very well last night."

"You just want to sit here for two hours?"

She shook her head and got up, gesturing for me to lie down, and when I did she stretched out on top of me. "Just hold me for a while."

"I can do that."

I don't know which one of us fell asleep first, but I woke up an hour and a half later to Paul standing near the doorway with Katie, saying, "Well, at least they have clothes on."

~

Kevin

Sam didn't protest when I called her and asked her to come to the dojo early, but when she walked through the door it was clear she wasn't happy about it. Tension rippled through the muscles in her forearms, fists clenched; she was 120 pounds of pissed off brunette, and she didn't even look at Lydia when she came in. She went straight to my office with a glance at me that threatened *this had better be good.* Sam wasn't much taller than my mother, but an irritated Sam is almost frightening; she could hurt me if she wanted to, probably the only person in the dojo who could.

What would hurt the most was if she was angry enough to quit because I was dumping too much of the workload on her.

Lydia kept Michael at the front desk with her while she returned phone calls. He was perched in her lap with a plastic ring clenched in his fist, and from the office I could hear him slam it into the desk every few seconds, and his squeals of pure delight every time he generated a loud pop.

The moment I was in the office Sam started, "I can take your classes tonight, Kevin, but—"

"I know I've asked you to cover for me a lot lately, and I'm going to ask you to take on a huge chunk for the next week."

She sat on the loveseat and crossed her legs, one foot bouncing angrily. She was ready to say no before I could even ask.

There was no tap dancing around why I needed her, so I dumped it all out at once.

"My dad has a brain tumor."

The foot bouncing stopped, and she sat up straight.

"He's having surgery the day after tomorrow, and I need to be there to help my mom with everything until he's home and settled."

"Oh, shit. Of course you do. Look, I'm sorry. I—"

"I know. And I know we can't count on Brandon to take up any extra slack. In fact, if he doesn't show up for his next class, he's done here. I like him and I know the kids like him, but I need someone I can count on."

"Screw Brandon. How bad is this thing for Chip?"

"We don't know yet. He saw a neurosurgeon yesterday and the guy couldn't even tell him exactly what kind of tumor it is, just how he's going to remove it."

"Major," she exhaled.

"I don't think he wants the whole world to know, either."

She waved it off. "I won't say anything to the students."

"I'm not sure what they should be told. My absence will surely be noticed."

"I'll just tell them that you're taking some family time."

"Some vacation," I sighed. "Another thing I'd like you to do tonight is to start considering which of the black belts you think are ready to teach, and which of the advanced students have what it takes to be groomed for instructing. If you think any of them are remotely ready, this is the weekend to test them out. Give one of the beginner classes to a brown belt and see how it goes."

I could see her going through a mental list of students, ticking them off one by one as she quickly decided who she wanted.

"Seth," she said. "He's ready to test for black and he's good with kids. In time he'll be an awesome instructor."

Seth Bradshaw was seventeen and talented, but I wasn't sure how well the over-35 students would accept him. Some of them barely tolerated the idea that they weren't on a first name basis with me, and chafed at being required to address me as "mister." Stick a teenager in front of them and enforce the same rules, and the grumbling would be palpable.

"Anyone else?"

"Mitch Lambert. He's not the best in terms of sparring, but he's articulate and can make other people understand what he's trying to convey."

"All right. I'll call them both and see if they're interested in taking over a couple of the classes this weekend. But pay close attention to other students, too, and don't be afraid to ask them to lead a class. I may be looking for four or five more instructors. Six if Brandon doesn't pull his head out of his ass."

"Why so many? Even if it's just the two of us with occasional help from your dad, we have it covered."

"At some point we're going to want to take vacations, and we're always adding students…and I'm seriously considering opening another school in Vacaville."

She sat back, not quite sure what that meant for her. "Close this one and move, or start a second dojo?"

"A second dojo," I replied. "Presuming you want to run this one."

"I can't afford to. And Master Timm…"

"I'm not selling it, Sam, just offering the management. Master Timm might not like it, but he won't walk away, either. With any luck I'll make rank high enough to promote other black belts before he's done with karate altogether, or we'll associate with someone else."

"It all sounds great, but I work a full time job, Kevin. I do have a life outside this school."

It was retail hell, and I knew it; Sam hated her job more than Lydia had hated working at the bank before Michael was born. "Take this and I'll pay you enough that you won't have to work anywhere else. You'll have more time for a life than you do now. Hell, time to meet someone—"

"I met someone. You don't need to keep an eye out for the perfect date for Sam."

"Nicole did tell me she saw you smooching someone in the parking lot. She wanted to make sure I wasn't going to try to hook you up with her father."

"That would have been awkward," she said.

"What, dating my brother while working with me?"

"Dating your brother, period. I don't exactly bat for that team, Kevin."

"Ah. Well, I honestly wasn't sure whether you batted from one position or were a switch hitter. But I did consider introducing you two."

"Did it bother Nicole to find me kissing a girl?"

"She didn't seem fazed by it at all."

"And you? Is it a problem?"

"Some of the more conservative parents might have a problem with it if they find out, but they can suck it. You don't have to hide your social life any more than I hide my wife and son."

"Great." She got up and headed for the door. "I better get ready for the first class. After you call Seth and Mark, call my sister. She can handle the front and the phones this weekend."

Something I hadn't considered.

"Thank you, Sam. I appreciate this."

"I just hope your father is all right, Kevin. Take the time you need. I won't run the school into the ground."

"And if Brandon bails on you this weekend, can his ass if you want. If not, call me, and I'll do it."

"I'm not calling you unless it's an emergency."

I followed her out into the lobby. Lydia was off the phone and was cuddling with Michael, the plastic ring he'd been playing with abandoned in favor of gumming Mommy's cheeks with spit-laden kisses.

"Just let me make a few calls and then we can go," I said to her. "She has a couple of students she thinks will be able to teach."

"What about the front?"

"We're covered through the weekend, I think. At least until Dad gets home."

"Your parents don't know you're taking all this time off, do they?"

"Paul can't take that much time off. Eileen might, but Dad won't allow her to help with anything physical. Nick's not home…someone needs to give Mom breaks at the hospital because you know otherwise she'll hover, and someone needs to be able to watch Nicole."

"You know everyone is going to do as much as they can."

"I know, but I can make myself the most available. Face it, if Sam couldn't do this, I could easily close for a week."

"I can watch Nicole," she said. "And I'm sure Katie will want to help where she can, too."

"I know she will, but she's puking her guts out half the time right now and she doesn't want them to know she's pregnant."

She pulled Michael a little closer. "I wish she would tell your Dad."

So did I. It was the Just In Case I wanted him to have more than anything, but Katie was firm in wanting to wait. Nick didn't even know yet.

Nick didn't know a lot, and he was going to be super pissed when he came home. If anything happened to Dad, I wasn't sure he'd forgive himself for not being there.

~

"He wanted his family here," Eileen said, her voice twinkling with laughter as she looked out the patio door, "but he's going to spend the whole evening out there wrapped around Mom."

To be fair, we had all been out in the backyard until after the pool light kicked on and Dad started lighting the torches. We'd had dinner on the deck, played with Nicole in the pool, and then sat in lawn chairs talking, avoiding any mention of Dad's looming surgery, until Nicole pointed out that it was almost her bedtime and she still had two more days of school to suffer through.

Katie took her inside so that she could change into something dry; Paul wandered away when his cell phone rang; Uncle Doug and Aunt Kris left early because he had patients to see early in the morning; Eileen and Spider were cold, and Lydia needed to put Michael to bed.

I had other things to do and followed her into the house.

Mom and Dad stayed on the deck; he turned music on and held out his arms to her to dance with him, but they were barely moving.

Hanging on.

Surely they knew they had an audience. We were sitting at the kitchen table but the light over it was turned off; Spider left the sink light on so that he could see us, but it was dim light and not enough to be especially intrusive.

"He knows who the most important person in his life is," Paul said quietly.

"I wonder why he wanted everyone here tonight and not tomorrow night," Katie said, her voice as soft as Paul's.

"Because tomorrow," Spider signed, "he's going to be nauseous as hell and won't feel like seeing any of us. At least tonight isn't really any different than other family dinners."

"With the exception of Katie running off to hurl," Eileen pointed out.

"Three times," Paul added.

Katie pretended offense. "No fair picking on me. This part was supposed to be over by now."

"I was well into my fourth month before I stopped feeling like crap," Lydia told her. "But it got better fast, like one day a switch flipped."

Katie let out a long, sad sigh. "I told Chip to stay away from me so he wouldn't catch whatever I'm coming down with. I hate lying to them."

"He hugged you anyway," Eileen said. "And I wish you would tell them."

"I think Nick will want to."

Eileen was staring out the back door, her gaze fixed on our parents. Mom had a hand against his chest like she was pushing him back, and they were both laughing. "I just have a feeling something is going to happen. And if something does…"

"Is this an Eileen Proclamation?" Paul asked.

"I don't know."

Eileen had, from time to time, demonstrated an uncanny ability to know things before they happened. Long before she and I were teenagers we'd learned that if she said something with certainty that we'd better listen to her. But this time, she wasn't sure. This time the feeling was vague.

"I think the only thing that's going to happen is gross groping on the pool deck," I said, not wanting to back Katie into a corner, making her feel like she was obligated to share a secret she wasn't ready to share. I turned to Lydia and asked, "You want to go finish that thing upstairs while I go get them?"

She answered with a kiss, and headed upstairs.

"The rest of you…go hide in the den and play pool or something. Unless you want to be exposed to all the parental groping when they come inside."

"What did you do?" Paul asked suspiciously.

"Nothing to you or for you," I answered as I headed for the patio door.

I felt like I was intruding; they didn't seem to mind that I was outside, interrupting whatever it was they had started, but I could feel the want shooting between them in bursts of static.

"Where did everyone go?" Dad asked.

"Playing pool," I answered, reaching for the torch snuff. "Just so you know, I'll be driving you to your appointment tomorrow, and Lydia will be here when Nicole gets home from school."

"Stop that. You'll leave us in the freaking dark. And I can drive myself."

"You could drive," I surmised, "but I'm guessing you won't get much sleep tonight, so I'm driving. And Friday morning Uncle Doug is your chauffer. He thought you might prefer being in the back seat of his car, where you can stretch out a little and try to sleep on the way up."

The torches were out, and I reached for the stereo.

"What the hell, Kevin."

Mom was snickering, her face buried against his chest, so I signed. "Take her inside, Dad." When he looked like he wasn't sure what I was saying I added, "You don't want to be with your kids right now. Take her upstairs."

He smiled and nodded, and they headed into the house, holding hands like a couple of teenagers. When the door slid shut I dug my cell phone out of my pocket and dialed Lydia's, just to give her the minute she'd need to get out of their room.

~

Chip

The bed was turned back and the room was washed in candle light; there were wine glasses on the night stand and a small ice-filled bucket on the dresser with two splits of white wine and four bottles of water. Next to it was a tray covered with fruit; strawberries and mango, and a small bowl with melted chocolate.

Terry's favorites.

She picked up a box left by the wine glasses and held it up, grinning in spite of herself. "Condoms," she snickered. "I thought they realized this was not an issue for us."

"I hate condoms," I said absently.

"Really now. And when was the last time you used one? It wasn't with me."

"Then it's been thirty years." I took the box from her and peered closely. "Besides, these are for you, woman. They're flavored. You have your choice of strawberry, pineapple, or cherry. I might try one, if you're so inclined."

"Surely they've improved since your man slut days."

"One would hope."

Soft music filtered out of the bathroom; the tub was lined with more candles and there was another split chilling in the sink, with two glasses set on the vanity beside it.

Terry dipped her fingers into the water. "Still hot."

"Yes, you are."

That smile was brighter than all the flame heating up the room. "Did they do this together, or do you think it was just one of them?"

"Kevin, with a little help from his much better half."

She grabbed my shirt and started pulling it over my head. "If he's willing to do this for you, then all must be forgiven."

"This isn't for me. He did this for you."

"Me?"

"Your favorite wine, favorite fruit, favorite music. Not to mention a choice selection of latex for your licking pleasure."

She tossed my shirt aside, laughing, as she started to take off her own. "Oh my God, Chip, that sounds gross."

"I was under orders today to do everything I could to make you laugh. And I think he supposed I might not be able to do that, what with being so old and out of it...I'm guessing that's what the odd text messages were about. Making you laugh. And this"—I kicked the rest of my clothes off—"is to make you happy. I just reap the benefits."

Her hands slid across my chest, over my ribs, until she had pulled me close. "I think he wants his father to be happy, too."

"He gets it. If you're happy, I'm happy."

After opening the wine and pouring it into the glasses, we slid into the water and she relaxed against my chest, pulling my arms around her tightly. "I hope Kevin does this for Lydia once in a while," she whispered.

"When they're in their own place, you know he will."

She leaned her head back and placed a kiss on my chin. "I hope you know I don't take it for granted when you do things like this for me."

"And I hope you know I don't take it for granted when you don't seem to mind when I want to skip all the stuff like this and just…"

"Quick and dirty," she snickered. "Sometimes that's all I want, too."

"And tonight? What do you want tonight?"

"Tonight, I just want to soak for a while. Hold me until the water starts to get cold, Irish. And then take me into the other room and warm me up."

"I can do that."

"And talk to me, mister. I know you've been trying hard to make everything seem like normal but it's not."

"This," I buried my face against her neck, "is normal. This is us, doing what we normally do, except with alcohol and prodding from our usually embarrassed youngest child. Remind me to thank him."

"I thought you wanted to spend tonight with the kids."

"I do. And I did. They gave me what I wanted, a couple of hours of watching them be with each other, and seeing them play with Nicole and Michael. It would have only been better if Nick was here."

"He needs to get home," she murmured.

"Yes, he does. And soon. Katie needs him."

"So does his father."

"Not half as much as his wife does. She needs him here to be sympathetic while she pukes her toenails up, and he's going to miss all of that if he doesn't get home soon."

"You've noticed that, too?"

"She can claim she's sick all she wants, but in between bouts of throwing up she's just fine. She and the other kids whisper back and forth like we don't notice, and she looks happy as hell. Apparently we're supposed to be the last to know."

"I wonder why."

"I'm guessing Nick doesn't know yet. Or he wants to be the one to tell us."

"So...do we pretend to not notice when she obviously starts to show?"

"I think at that point we're within our rights to say something."

She turned so that she was facing me. "We might want to ask her, anyway. She might need all the support she can get."

"She has the rest of the family..."

"No, I mean when it comes time to tell Nick. He might not be as happy as everyone else."

That thought had crossed my mind, too. Nick talked about wanting kids someday, and he had agreed that as soon as his training was complete they could start trying. But technically his training wouldn't be officially complete for a few more months, and there was no guarantee he wouldn't find another excuse to wait.

Katie had been waiting for nearly ten years.

Nick would step up, he would smile graciously and would try to be a good father, but if his heart wasn't in it, he could easily plunge himself into his work, and lose his soul to the agency.

"I think," I said, scooting a little closer to her, "that I don't want to talk about the kids anymore. My job today is to make you laugh, and I'm failing miserably. If I can't make you laugh, then at least let me make you happy."

"You do make me happy," she assured me. "And the water is starting to cool off."

"We can't have the queen getting chilled." I stepped out of the tub and held my hand out to her. "And since her majesty wants to be warmed up, she needs to tell the king just how he should go about that."

She reached for a towel and wrapped it around my shoulders, using it to pull me closer. "In spite of what the prince might have intended, the queen doesn't want anything between her and the king. Since he's getting so old, she might only have one shot at him tonight, and would like it to be very slow and last as long as possible."

"That might get better after the surgery."

"I'm not complaining, Irish."

"I know you're not. But still...I do miss my body not being where my brain and my wife would like it to be."

"You just need a more patient wife. Come on, you promised to warm me up."

"That I did."

Before we tumbled into bed she took a strawberry off the tray and popped it into my mouth. "For energy," she said. "You're going to need it."

~

"Really, if I'd known how gross that was going to feel, I wouldn't have woken you up."

"So take it off."

"Much better. And it still tastes like cherries."

~

"It's five in the morning, Irish. You should be getting some sleep."

"I did sleep," I mumbled against her shoulder. "A couple of hours before you woke me because you wanted to sample the fruit box, and I got an hour before you decided you wanted to go for a ride."

"So go back to sleep. I'll leave you alone for a while."

"Define a while."

"The alarm won't go off for four more hours."

"So...I get to sleep for three?"

"Morning wood is a wonderful thing. It rarely fails me."

"Seriously, darlin'...I think within the next fifteen hours it's more likely that Christmas will come before I do."

"You might be surprised."

"Damn good thing Kevin is driving today."

"I think he planned it that way."

"Remind me again to thank him."

~

Kevin took one look at me and laughed, a deep, almost evil chuckle.

"Shut up. This is your fault."

"Did you sleep at all?"

"Here and there. Dammit, son, I think I'm too old for a night like that."

"Apparently Mom's not. She looks fine, yet you're the one walking funny."

"Right now, I think I hate you."

"Heh."

"And thank you."

15

Chip

Surfer Doc read the cover sheet clipped to the front of the file he'd dropped onto his desk, and then flipped through a few pages before looking up. Instead of an exam room, we'd been taken into an office; Terry and I were in chairs just in front of the desk, and Kevin was perched painfully on a small chair near the door, his legs nearly folded into his chest.

"We'll get a fresh blood test today but I imagine nothing has changed much. Your thyroid levels are near normal; TSH is a little high but your T-three and T-four are just within the normal range. Which means the pituitary is working overtime trying to achieve normal levels. You have diabetes insipidus. Testosterone is low, prolactin and estrogen are a little elevated."

He glanced at Kevin.

"He can hear it all," I said.

Dr. Harris nodded, and went on. "You have slight testicular atrophy with a report of marginally spongy erectile tissue and a prolonged post-coital recovery rate. It is certainly possible for most of those things to return to normal once the tumor is out, but I suspect you'll be on the DDAVP for the rest of your life."

"Is that a bad thing?" Terry asked.

"No. It does mean you'll be seeing your endocrinologist every year, but as long as you can maintain your electrolytes, you can live with it just fine. If the rest of the hormones don't recover you'll have to add a urologist to the mix and perhaps be on a testosterone replacement, but that will likely be a personal choice rather than an imperative."

"Imperative?" Terry wondered.

"Dad doesn't *have* to go on testosterone replacement," Kevin said. "But I'm guessing you'll want him to."

"You," I said without looking at him. "Be quiet."

"Like I'm wrong."

Terry hid her smile behind a hand; I reached behind the chair and flipped him off.

"Any questions?" the doctor asked.

I still hadn't thought of any, but Kevin leaned forward, his chair creaking under his weight, and he said, "Yes."

We turned to look at him.

"How long will this surgery take?"

"Roughly five hours."

"And given the size of the tumor and the proximity to his optic nerve, what are the chances that his vision will be compromised by the surgery?"

"I've never nicked the optic nerve, if that's your question."

"My question wasn't theoretical, Doctor Harris. I understand that he has a macroadenoma that with time would compromise both his hypothalamus and his optic nerve, and I want to know the odds that removing this tumor will cause him difficulties with his vision. This might be an insignificant consideration to you, but his son-in-law is deaf and their communication is entirely visual."

Kevin was flopping his brain out in a mini-display for the neurosurgeon; in terms of intelligence it was nearly an even playing field and he wanted the doctor to understand that he wouldn't be able to talk over his head.

"Infinitesimal," Doctor Harris replied. "The tumor is large, but I'll have plenty of room to maneuver."

"If this was a microadenoma, would you be removing it now?"

"I would, simply because I don't know what it is."

"And your best guess; is he looking at a craniopharygioma, a granuloma, prolactinoma…?"

"We've ruled out a prolactinoma based on blood tests. Beyond that I can't honestly say because it isn't presenting as a typical macroadenoma."

"I asked for your best guess, not even a hypothetical diagnosis."

"What the fuck is a granuloma?" I asked.

"Forms from a grain of irritant," Kevin said. "It could indicate future growths in other areas of the body. Commonly, the lungs."

Well, hell.

"Craniopharyngioma," the doc reluctantly said. "And truthfully, until we have a pathology report, I won't be able to tell you anything more than that is my best guess. I won't issue a diagnosis based on the appearance alone, unless in resection it presents obvious markers."

"Fair enough. Based on that best guess, though, are you going to initiate post-surgical treatment?"

"Regardless of what I see, I think there's plenty of time to wait for the pathology report before beginning further treatment."

"Is there anything we need to watch him for once he's out of the hospital?"

"He needs to be aware of his fluid intake and output, which is something his endocrinologist will address further. The rest of your family should look for episodes of cortisol deficiency, skin turgor, whether he's flushed or pale."

I wanted to ask what the hell that meant, but decided Kevin could explain it later.

"And when he's in the hospital, where will he recover? Critical care or neurology?"

"We have an excellent neurosurgical floor with a reasonable nurse to patient ratio. Other hospitals do send these cases to critical care, but I don't think it's necessary."

"And what should he expect immediately after the surgery? Besides pain?"

"Fatigue. Nausea." He looked at me. "You'll be bleeding and will swallow a quite a bit of blood. Expect to throw up within twenty four hours, and don't be alarmed at how much of it is blood."

"Wonderful," I muttered.

"If this is a craniopharygioma, what's the morbidity rate?"

Terry jerked in her seat, spinning to look at Kevin. "Wait. It could kill him?"

"No, Mom. Morbidity means recurrence. What are the odds it will grow back?"

"Fifty percent," Surfer Doc said. "But I suspect you knew that."

"Don't irritate the guy who's going to be digging around in my brain," I said to Kevin.

"I'm not irritated," Dr. Harris said. "Truthfully, once a patient hears bad news he only hears ten per cent of anything that follows. It's good to have someone alert and intelligent asking the questions and absorbing the information of the patient's behalf." He looked at Kevin again. "Medical school?"

"Karate instructor."

"Really now. I would have pegged you as an eager medical school student."

"He has the intelligence," I said, "but seems to prefer sweating and yelling at people."

"Only at you, old man."

"All right then." The doctor stood up and held out a slip of paper to me. "From here you go to the lab for a blood test, then to radiology for a chest x-ray, and finally an EKG. Tomorrow morning be at admissions at five thirty, and we'll start at seven."

"Five thirty in the morning?"

"Look at it this way: first case of the day and you get it out of the way. You can sleep while I work."

~

"They took him back for the EKG and forgot him," Kevin told Paul. "We waited for thirty minutes when it was supposed to take less than five. Mom finally had to go ask if they'd lost her husband."

By the time we left the building that housed the neurology clinic and all the pre-op annoyances, we were hungry. I told Kevin to head for the restaurant, and sat in the back seat with Terry, fending off her wandering hands. Kevin glanced in the rear view mirror once and reminded her that he was *right there*, and to please not forget that.

Paul took a break to sit with us, in spite of the dining room being busier than usual.

"So you're all set then?" he asked me. "Getting nervous?"

I'd been nervous; up until that morning, I'd been a jumble of nerves. But when Terry woke me up an hour before the alarm was supposed to go off, it occurred to me that I was calm for the first time since Nick had been dragged off from the camp site.

"Today," I said, "I am not. Tonight…I may be barfing like my daughter-in-law. Anyone talked to Katie today?"

"Not today," Paul said.

"It's amazing how someone can throw up that much and still be in such a good mood," I ventured, hoping one of them would crack.

They both looked away.

"The first one who looks at me confirms my suspicions," I said.

Paul got up without even glancing at me and grumbled that he'd be back in a minute, leaving Kevin swearing under his breath.

"You don't have to say anything, Kevin," Terry said. "But if Katie is pregnant, we want to know. Either look at your father, or shake your head no."

With a deep sigh, he caved. "This isn't my news to tell, Dad."

"And you didn't."

"Does Nicky know?" Terry asked.

"That would be in the realm of me not saying anything I'm not supposed to."

"Nick doesn't know," I said, carefully weighing Kevin's reaction.

"Dad."

"I needed to know, Kevin. Really. I needed to."

He dug his cell phone out of his pocket. "She might be relieved. We'll find out."

Terry reached across the table to stop him. "She doesn't have to know."

"I'm just going to text her, and ask what happens if the elder degenerates guess."

Paul dropped back into the seat he'd been in a hurry to vacate. "Business called."

"Business, my ass."

"Fine, so something that was none of my business called. Besides, I needed to double check with Sherry to make sure she was still available to be there when Nicole gets off the bus tomorrow."

"You don't have to be at the hospital," I said. "It's not like you get to actually stand in the OR and cheer the surgeon on."

He waved me off. "We're all going to be there and you know it. It makes us feel useful, in a useless kind of way."

Kevin flipped his phone shut. "Ok, now we wait."

"You need to tell Topher to develop better texting skills," Terry told Kevin. "Really. He got a tattoo while he was drunk?"

"He's mortified," Kevin chuckled. "Even his mom got that one."

"And the others?" I prompted.

Kevin shrugged, grinning slyly.

"And here I was hoping that he'd actually shaved the goods and then slathered them with toothpaste."

"And how," Terry added, "do you know that minty fresh is not a total body experience?"

"Did I not also say to not ask me that?" Kevin poked back.

"You *shaved*?" Paul asked.

"Trim the bush to make the tree stand tall," Kevin said with mock authority.

"Oh my God." Terry closed her eyes. "Please don't put that in my head."

"Fine. But no, I haven't been playing with the toothpaste. It's just a guess."

"Don't try it, son," I warned.

"On anyone," Terry blurted out, wishing instantly that she could take it back.

"Truly, not something all women want to experience," I said, wincing at the sudden elbow in my ribs.

"All right." Paul pushed himself up. "I think I'll go back to work with the somewhat sane and the non-perverted. Have fun driving them home, Squirt."

If Kevin was embarrassed, for once he didn't show it. We went home and spent the afternoon playing with our grandson and watching Nicole while she splashed in the pool. It wasn't until dinner time that the nerves kicked in; while Terry and Lydia finished cooking, I tossed the salad, and realized then that I wanted to toss my cookies instead.

Terry realized it, too; I leaned against the counter, willing my appetite to over ride the urge to throw up what was left from lunch, and she took the salad bowl from me, handing it to Kevin. With a kiss on my cheek she sent me into the living room to sit down and wait for dinner to be ready.

I picked at my food, cutting the chicken into small pieces that I shoved around my plate, hoping that Nicole wouldn't notice that Grandpa wasn't eating; if Grandpa didn't eat, there must be something to worry about.

As soon as Nicole was finished Terry told her she could go into the living room and watch TV for a while, and Kevin ushered Terry and I away from the table and out the back door.

We curled up on a chaise lounge together and I worked at willing the nerves to subside. We sat there quietly, until Kevin strolled out forty five minutes later to say that Katie had texted him back; if we honestly guessed, she would be fine with it. And she wanted him to tell me she'd be at the hospital tomorrow, and that she loved me.

I renewed my protest; there wasn't a damn thing any of them could do other than sit and wait, and it was going to take a good five hours from start to finish. After that, it wasn't likely that I would want to see anyone, anyway.

"We're going to all be there, Dad," Kevin said as he made his way back to the house. "Like it or not."

"They love you, Chip," Terry whispered, her lips pressed against my temple. "That they'd be there is a given."

I buried my face against her shoulder and held her a little tighter. "Not a given," I sighed. "A gift."

~

I woke to soft lips on mine, and cool fingers brushing across my cheek. The room was still dark, but I blinked against the light filtering in from the hallway, wishing she would turn it off and let me go back to sleep.

"Come on, Irish," she whispered. "Time to get up."

"Please tell me you're waking me early because you want to do things to me."

"Doug and Kris are already here."

I forced my eyes open. "What time is it?"

"Four-fifteen. I turned the alarm off. You were actually

sleeping…I didn't think it mattered if you had time to shower and shave."

Throw me in the car and go, don't leave me any time to think too hard about where we were headed. She had clothes laid out for me, and as I headed for the bathroom she said, "Remember, don't drink anything."

No food or water after midnight; I'd gotten that memo. By midnight I was in bed and asleep, no small wonder considering the horde of people tap dancing in my stomach. I had no idea if she'd been able to sleep or not, though I suspected she'd been awake all night watching me.

I brushed my teeth and slowly got dressed, fighting the urge to crawl back in bed.

Surely if I hid under the blankets, no one would find me.

They were all waiting by the front door, looking far more awake than I felt. Kris greeted me with a kiss on the cheek and Doug went straight for the door knob.

"Don't you have a job to go to?" I grunted at him.

"You are my job today," he grunted back.

So fine; neither of us wanted to be awake at four in the morning, but at least he didn't look like he was about to pass out.

Doug would, he said on the ride to Sacramento, be able to poke his head into the OR and then the recovery room every now and then to keep Terry and the kids updated. He estimated that the surgery would be over by one o'clock—reasoning that it would not begin at seven exactly—and that I would spend another two to three hours in recovery.

"But," he added, "it'll seem like no time at all to you. One minute you'll be wondering why you're starting to feel so loopy, and the next you'll be wondering why the hell your head hurts so much."

"Thanks. Something to look forward to."

He stopped the car by the curb near a hospital entrance, and asked Kris to park while he steered us towards admissions. After he got us where we needed to be, he would meet her by the front entrance where they would wait for the kids, and then go en masse to the waiting area.

He guided us through the maze of hospital corridors and then stopped just outside the admissions office door. "It'll be fine," he said, though I wasn't sure if that was meant for me or for Terry. "You'll get through this. You've been through worse."

I probably had, but back then I didn't have a short blonde and assorted offspring and their spouses to worry about.

Terry hugged him, something I'd had the urge but not the wherewithal to do.

"By the time you're ready, I'll have the kids in the waiting area and I'll come up to the OR desk to get you," he told her. "Just wait for me there. Don't try to find your way alone."

He walked off, and I wanted to go with him.

Instead, Terry opened the door and with a hand on my arm, urged me to go inside.

~

Forty five minutes later I was standing in a multi-bed room wearing nothing but a flimsy hospital gown and white support hose, waiting for an OR escort. Terry tied the back of the gown for me, but there was no getting around the fact that if I turned just right—or wrong—I would moon anyone who happened to walk by.

"Why," I asked when the nurse handed me the hose, "do I have to wear these?"

"They'll accent your stunning legs," she said with a smile. "And they'll help prevent blood clots from forming."

Terry tried to not laugh when I put them on.

"There's no escape now," I said after she finished tying the gown for me. "They have my clothes and my shoes, and probably blocked all the exits. I'm doomed."

She reached for my left hand. "And I hate to do this, but I need to take your wedding ring. And your crucifix."

I slid the ring off and put it on her middle finger, and then slipped the chain from my crucifix around her neck. After I had it clasped, she fell against me, burying her head against my chest.

Trembling.

"This sucks, but you know I'm going to be fine," I said, kissing the top of her head. "Doug wouldn't send me to someone who was going to do a half assed job and screw me up. You know that."

"Intellectually." I could feel her breath, warm and moist, through the thin gown, and I could feel the fear seeping with every beat of her heart.

"I reserve the right to whine a lot for the next few days, but once I get over the hump, I'll be home and we'll wonder what the big deal was about."

"It is a big deal," she sniffed.

"But it'll be a little deal in a few days. And when I get home, I want junk food. If you love me, there will be Ding Dongs waiting."

She finally looked up, smiling. "Cannibal. You can have whatever you want."

"Right now, all I want is a kiss. And make it a good one because I understand I might not want one again for about a week."

The OR escort threw the door open in mid-kiss, but waited to say anything until we'd parted, and we weren't letting the interruption stop us.

"Hop up on the gurney, Mr. Davis," she said after Terry had taken a half step back. And then she asked Terry, "Do I understand correctly, that you'll be accompanying us to the surgical floor?"

"Unless it's a problem."

"Not at all. Most family goes straight to the waiting area, but there was a notation on the orders allowing you to go up."

"I'm important," I said.

Terry smiled nervously, and the escort replied simply, "Apparently so."

I eased onto the gurney and sat there while she raised the head of the bed, and then tolerated her putting a blanket over me; I didn't want to be tucked into bed, but that's what it felt like.

Naptime.

Terry held my hand in the elevator, gripping tighter with each floor we ascended. By the time the doors opened, my fingers were tingling.

Doug was waiting by the OR desk and followed us into the recovery room, where I would get the final prep before going into the operating room. He stayed close to Terry, something I was grateful for, given her nerves.

She was visibly shaking.

"What's next?" I asked him.

"Your nurse anesthetist will be over in a minute. You'll get an IV, and he'll dope you up with Versed. Once you're good and loopy, I'll take Terry to the waiting area and you'll be taken to the OR."

"No one said anything about an IV."

"Stop being such a wuss. And no whining when it goes in."

For Terry's sake, I didn't whine. I let the CRNA jab that sucker in and didn't so much as flinch, lest she begin crying.

She took a step away from the gurney when Surfer Doc walked in; he almost looked like he belonged there, dressed in scrubs, a stethoscope around his neck.

"No sneezing with your fingers in my brain," I warned. "You'll piss off the blonde if you do, and trust me, you don't want to piss off the blonde."

The CRNA injected the Versed into the IV line, and within seconds it hit me. The world went fuzzy and my tongue felt thick; sleep tickled every one of my senses, teasing me with the comfort of oozing into the dark.

"Give him a kiss," I heard Doug tell Terry.

I tried to kiss back but wasn't sure my lips were working.

And as I felt the gurney move as they pushed me towards the operating room, I felt a surge of gratitude that he hadn't told her to kiss me goodbye.

~

Terry

We occupied nearly half the waiting room, nine people crammed into a corner, but we made a deliberate effort to leave space for other families waiting for their own loved ones to come out of surgery. Kevin, Paul, and Spider agreed that if it looked like it was going to be a problem they would just sit on the floor, but none of the kids was willing to leave.

Paul assured me that Sherry would be at the house when Nicole got home from school, and Michael was with Lydia's parents. They would have, she said, been there if they hadn't been needed to babysit.

Will wanted to be there, but Chip had forced a promise from him to be at the restaurant when it opened.

My parents had every intention of being there, but relented to his plea that they stay home; my mother agreed as long as he accepted that they would be in church, praying on his behalf. She couldn't have known how much that would touch him and was surprised at the tears that sprang to his eyes.

Chip could have packed the room if he'd let more people know what was happening to him. I didn't think he realized how many of his friends and acquaintances would want to be there for his family.

The kids were all bleary eyed when I met them in the waiting room, but the first time Doug left to check on Chip's progress, they all came alive, anticipating.

He left wearing jeans and a sweatshirt but came back dressed in blue surgical scrubs with paper booties over his shoes.

"No style points," Kevin mumbled.

"He's out, immobilized, and they've made the first cuts."

"And that's all you can say?" Kris asked.

"That's all there is to tell. It'll be a while before they're drilling through the sinus cavity."

Eileen was sitting with her head resting against the wall behind her, and she sighed, "I just want this over with."

"I bet Dad wants that more," Kevin said.

Doug half snorted, half laughed. "Right now your Dad is off in lala land and doesn't want anything."

"You still have a bad feeling?" Paul asked his sister.

She lifted her head to look at him. "It's not even bad, per se. Just…something."

"This whole thing is just something," Kevin said. "We all want it over and done with."

"As long as he's okay," Katie said softly. She was sitting next to Paul, her arms folded as if she was trying to hold herself together.

"Are you feeling all right?" I asked her. She looked exhausted, and I could practically feel the nausea that was pricking at her.

She managed a slight smile. "I'm fine. I think we're all feeling the stress and just want that doctor to come out here and tell us it's over and Chip is great."

Kevin got up to get the trash can and set it near Katie. "Just in case."

"Your text message wasn't theoretical, was it?"

He shrugged. "Sorry. They're kind of shrewd sometimes. You probably didn't help your cause when you piled sliced grapes and cole slaw on top of your hot dog the other night."

She looked at me sheepishly, and I had to smile. "Katie, Chip was thrilled. We both were when we realized…"

"It's just that Nicky doesn't know—"

Paul slipped his arm around her shoulders and gave her a light hug. "He's not going to mind, Katie. He'll be a little overwhelmed at everything he's missed, but he'll understand why everyone already knows."

She didn't look as confident, but nodded anyway.

Doug checked on Chip's progress hourly; at ten thirty he reported that the surgeon was removing the tumor and estimated it would be another hour and a half. He stood near the doorway with his hands on his hips, regarding us all carefully.

"This would be a good time for you all to go get some breakfast or lunch. I'm betting none of you have eaten anything today."

I refused to go anywhere.

"Can we bring food in here?" Kevin asked Doug, who nodded. "Good. I'll order pizza."

He got note paper out of Lydia's purse and started writing down what everyone wanted. And when he'd gotten our orders, he went to everyone else in the waiting room to ask what they'd like on a pizza, and if they didn't want that, what kind of sandwich.

He was met with light protests, but my son was insistent. We'd all been waiting there since nearly dawn, and surely the people suffering in the waiting room with us were just as hungry.

By the time the pizzas were delivered and everyone had eaten, Doug was able to tell us that Chip was almost done. The tumor was out, he'd had mesh placed behind his sinuses, and they were suturing the incision under his lip.

He'd made it through the surgery, now we had to wait for him to clear the recovery room, and it couldn't happen soon enough.

~

Chip

Pain has an audible tone. It's a high pitched knife slicing through the skull, with a weight pressing down with exaggerated gravity.

I woke up in the dimly lit recovery room, my head filled with sound I was sure only a dog could hear.

It screamed through my skull and forced me back into the darkness, away from myself.

~

Doug's voice. "How's he doing?"
"Whining. I gave him morphine. It should help soon."

~

"Breathe, Mister Davis. Deep breaths. Come on, breathe for me."
I am breathing.
I am.
"That's good. Concentrate on breathing."

~

Doug. "Come on, Chip. You have to breathe."
I am, I am, I am.
"Deeper. You can do this. Breathe for me."
Breathe.
"It's the morphine." Someone new, someone I didn't know.
Then Doug. "The sooner you start trying to breathe and wake up, the sooner you get to see Terry. Come on."
Terry.
Right.
Breathing now.

~

"I need him to wake up just a little bit more."

"Breathing better?"

"Well enough."

"Wake up, Chip. I know you're in there."

Here. Somewhere.

Make it stop.

Thick fingers grasped my chin. "Chip."

"Doug," I croaked.

"There you are. Welcome back."

"Fuck. Fuck fuck fuck."

"It's going to hurt for a while."

Holy shit, no.

"Can't see," I cried.

No, no, no.

Doug's hand still on my face, gripping my chin. "Don't panic. You can see. Just open your eyes."

"Are. Open."

"Nope. Your eyes are definitely closed. Try to open them."

"Am."

His finger on my eyelid, prying it open. "See? They were closed."

"Kiss.

"My.

"Ass."

"He's fine. Don't count on the whining ending anytime soon, though."

~

Slow down. Slow down. Slow down.

It felt like the gurney was rolling down the freeway with a speed addicted teenager at the helm. Every bump, every corner, sent ribbons of agony weaving through my skull, pulsating against whatever brain cells I had left.

I wanted to stop. Leave me in the hallway. But stop moving.

I tried to open one eye but the blinding light overhead sliced through me and I snapped it closed.

I see it. I see the light.

"Mister Davis, open your eyes now. I need to take a look."

"No."

"Just for a few seconds. Come on. Let me see those baby blues."

"No."

A cool hand slid across my arm, gently caressing. "Irish. Please, open your eyes."

Fine.

For you, I will.

"All right, so they're green. On a scale of one to ten, where's your pain at right now?"

"Terry?"

"She's right here. Tell me how much it hurts, and then you can see her."

"Twelve."

"Okay, we'll get you another dose of morphine to take the edge off that."

"No." I tried to squint against the light, and the nurse reached overhead and flipped it off. "No morphine."

"Don't fight it," I heard Doug say from the foot of the bed.

"Stopped. Breathing."

"No, you didn't. The morphine repressed your breathing, but you never stopped. You'll be fine, I swear."

"Please. No."

"I promise you won't stop breathing."

Breathe.

Don't stop breathing

Don't die now.

Breathe.

~

"God. Thirsty."

I managed to open my eyes, and Terry was standing there beside the bed, pouring water from a plastic pitcher into a cup. She held it for me, guiding a straw between my lips.

"Don't be shy about asking for more to drink, Irish. They're not going to give you your DDAVP for a few days to see what happens."

"But I can't. Get up to…go."

"You won't have to. You have a catheter."

"Goddamn."

"The kids want to see you. Are you up to it?"

"No."

She brushed hair off my forehead. "All right."

"But okay."

"They won't stay long," she promised. "And one at a time."

Breathe.

~

"He slept through everyone else. Don't take it personally if he doesn't wake up."

"Of course not." Kevin was nearly whispering. It sounded like he was standing to my left, so I tried to turn my head and open my eyes, but I barely managed to move.

"Kev."

He bent over, leaning down towards me so that I wouldn't strain myself trying to look at him. "You look like hell, Dad. Like someone kicked your face in, and then punched you a few times for good measure."

"Feels…like it."

"Can I get you anything?"

"Grape juice."

"All right," he chuckled. "I'll go to the cafeteria and get you some grape juice. Anything else?"

"Make your mom. Go home. Sleep."

"There's not a snowball's chance in hell of that," she said, her hand going to my forehead. "I'm staying right here."

"Go. Home."

"He's right, Mom," Kevin said. "You need to rest, too."

"Absolutely not. Someone has to be here to make sure he keeps drinking and he can't hit the call button yet to tell anyone when he's thirsty. If he doesn't drink enough…"

"All right. I get it. And I'll go get his juice."

"Ter," I whispered. "No."

Warm lips pressed onto my forehead. "I promised you, Chip. We're never spending another night apart. I don't care if I have to sleep standing up, I'm not leaving."

~

"Just a little prick, and I'll let you go back to sleep."

"What time is it?" I asked, watching as the nurse drew blood.

"Two thirty."

"Did my wife finally go home?"

She gestured to the other side of the room. "We rolled in a cot for her a couple of hours ago."

"Stubborn woman."

"And you're lucky to have her. Now, can I get you anything while you're awake? You've got a new pitcher of water. Can you reach the call button if you need more?"

I reached a tentative hand out and determined that I'd be able to reach it.

"Now, how about the pitcher? Can you both reach it and fill the cup?"

My arms felt like rubber, but I could finally get to the water pitcher on my own, and pour it out. "I think I'm set," I said.

"Good. How's your pain right now? From one to ten?"

"Eight, maybe."

"Very good. I'll get you some Percoset for it, and when I get back we'll change the gauze."

"What gauze?"

"Under your nose. It's catching what the nasal packing doesn't."

Nasal packing.

I contemplated that while I waited for her to return, minus the tubes of my blood.

They'd shoved tampons up my nose.

~

Terry

"Still whining?" Doug asked as I dropped into a chair in the visitors' waiting room.

"He didn't whine, Doug. Mostly all he's done is sleep, but now when he's awake he can speak in complete sentences. For the most part all he did yesterday was grunt."

The fatigue was expected, but even with a head cold Chip would sleep for four days straight. He dealt with not feeling well by sleeping, and time would slip past him quietly. He would wake up later, feeling better, having no clue how long he'd been plastered to the bed.

This time the nurses weren't letting him wrap himself in that cocoon. He was being jarred awake every two to four hours by someone needing to take blood, someone trying to get him to eat, someone wanting to change his sheets. He'd been woken up twice during the night for blood, and each time the pain ripped through his head.

"Have they tried to get him up yet?"

"He sat at the edge of the bed for about fifteen seconds but couldn't stand and said he had to lie down before his head exploded."

"Not that he'd ever exaggerate."

"It would help if he'd eat. The only thing I've been able to convince him to try since he woke up is a small pudding cup."

"He's probably a little nauseated. Give him a little while. He won't starve to death."

Kevin stuck his head into the room, looking somewhat amused. "Mom? I think you're needed in Dad's room."

I was up and headed down the hall before he could say anything else; he only caught up to me because of his long legs.

"Don't freak out. Dad is fine; it's the orderly who needs your help."

There was a very young woman standing next to his bed; mentally I ticked her off at eighteen or nineteen. She had a towel in one hand and a blue plastic box in the other, and Chip was glaring at her like she'd offered him arsenic for breakfast.

His arms were crossed defiantly, and as I hurried into the room he snapped "No" at her.

"But I—"

"Absolutely not."

"Dad doesn't want a bed bath," Kevin explained. "He's pretty determined."

I pointed towards the door and gently shoved Kevin toward it, whispering, "Stay close in case I need your help."

Chip's stubborn streak was glowing, and the aide didn't seem to know what else to say to him. She had a job to do and most of her patients surely cooperated.

"What's the problem, Irish?"

"I do not need a sponge bath."

"Are you sure about that? You're getting a bit ripe, mister."

"No." He glared at her and added, "You can go away now."

I asked her to give me a minute with him, and she stepped around the bed and headed for the door, uncertainly pinging off the floor with each step.

"Irish, look at me. That poor girl has a job to do and you don't need to make her feel bad about it. Just let her give you the bath."

"No."

"Chip—"

"I'm not letting some teenager sponge me off."

"Hey now." I reached for his hand, making him uncross his arms. "I used to be a teenager and you didn't seem to mind…"

He exhaled sharply and looked away.

"Ah, that's it. Chip, you've got a catheter wedged up there and a killer headache dulling everything else. I don't think you have anything to worry about."

"No."

"Fine." His heels were dug in deep. "What if I do it? Would that be all right?"

"I don't really need it."

"Hey. That wasn't really a question. It's either me or the teenager, take your pick. I promise, you'll feel a little better after."

"No teenagers," he grunted.

I went out into the hallway and got a towel from the aide and a pack of warmed body wipes, and asked Kevin to help me sit him up. When Chip saw him he scowled and said, "He's not much better than the teenager."

"I need his help, Chip. Suffer."

Kevin held his arm out for Chip to grab onto, and pulled his father into a sitting position while I untied the gown he'd been forced to wear. "Can you hold him there?" I asked Kevin. "I might as well get his back while he's sitting up."

He sat on the edge of the bed and Chip leaned into him, holding on tight. "You okay there, Dad?"

"Barely."

He sighed when I rubbed the warm wipe across his shoulders and neck, and he grudgingly admitted that felt good. When I was done with his back Kevin helped him lie back down and then excused himself, pulling the curtain around the bed to give his father the privacy he obviously wanted.

I set the gown on the chair by the bed, and folded the blankets back. "Let me know if you get cold and I'll cover you back up."

"I'm fine. I hate that thing anyway. And you were right, I need this."

"But not from some strange teenage girl."

He grabbed my wrist and held my hand against his chest. "I'm sorry. I really don't want to be a pain in the ass."

"I don't mind. Besides, you would do this for me."

"I would."

"Then just close your eyes and enjoy it."

He closed his eyes and was asleep before I got to his feet.

~

He ate the Jello that came with his lunch tray and feigned interest in a stalk of broccoli, but he still wouldn't eat. An hour later his food was cold and mostly untouched, earning him a reprimand from the aide who came in for his tray.

"If you tell me there are kids starving in China who would eat that, I'll shove it—"

"Stop right there," I warned him.

The surgeon came in before Chip could say anything else snarky, and she rolled the cart out, the wheels squeaking down the hall.

"So, dude, how are we feeling today?"

"We feel like someone drilled a hole in our skull. Dude."

He glanced at Chip's chart. "Looks like your pain is easing up a bit. Feeling fatigued?"

Chip nodded.

"I'm amazed. Your electrolytes stayed level through the night. I expected there to be issues there. You managed to keep up on fluid intake?"

"She managed it for me. I just laid here, she held the straw."

"Awesome. We'll give it another day and if you still have symptoms, we'll start giving you your DDAVP again. Now, how about your teeth?" He clicked his fingernail against his own two front teeth. "Any feeling there?"

"Haven't really checked that."

"I had to clip the nerve. You may never get the feeling back in them."

"Great."

"I noticed your lunch being whisked away. Feeling nauseous?"

Chip held his thumb and forefinger close together and said, "Just a little bit."

"Really. Just a little bit?" He glanced at his watch and then at me. "Is he cranky? Irritable?"

"All things considered…a bit."

The doctor leaned against the wall, watching Chip closely. He had the chart in hand but wasn't writing anything down, and I wondered what he was doing until he said, "Turn to the other side of the bed, please. I kind of like these shoes."

Chip rolled over onto his side and vomited onto the floor, one large gush that painted the floor in bright red.

"Right on time." He pushed off the wall and headed for the door. "I'll get someone to clean it up, and I'll tell the nurse he'll want food soon."

~

I fell asleep in the chair beside Chip's bed; I could hear the kids as they came and went but didn't have the energy to wake up enough to acknowledge them, though at one point I was sure Katie was there and crying. I wanted to tell her Chip was fine and that she was bound to be a little emotional, but I couldn't work past the idea to actually doing it.

Then I felt Kevin's hand on my arm, and he was telling me I needed to wake up. Chip was sound asleep, and Kevin was whispering, but he wanted me awake and said I needed to come with him.

Unless it was important, he would have left me alone. I stumbled after him, trying to shake the cobwebs away, trying to not yawn rudely as I ran my fingers through my hair.

Kevin stopped at the doorway to the waiting room, waiting for me. Eileen was sitting across from the door, and when she saw me her eyes flooded with tears, and all I could think of was Katie, and how I'd just wanted to sleep instead of going to her to find out what was wrong.

~

Chip

Seven, I decided before I even opened my eyes. The buzz saw cutting through my head was operating at a seven, which had to be better than the eight I'd been holding onto. I wasn't sure how much of that I owed to the Percoset or how much was simple progression, but I'd take it. At that rate I'd be down to a six by nightfall, and with luck I'd have nothing more than a bad headache in the morning.

And I was hungry; that would make Terry happy. Up until I'd vomited all over the cheap tile floor she'd taken my lack of appetite personally and wasn't going to shed herself of the mothering impulse until I had a reasonable amount of food in me.

I wondered what time it was, but the last time I'd opened my eyes she was in the chair, asleep, and I didn't want to even fidget in case any movement woke her up. I kept my eyes closed and willed the thirst that was ripping my mouth to shreds to ease up, just for a little while, just long enough for her to get some sleep.

A mechanical *whoosh* cut through the quiet and I could feel the cuff around my right bicep tighten and then tighten some more, squeezing until it felt like I was being stuck by a dozen pins. Right when I thought it was stuck and that I was within my rights to rip the damn thing off, the air let out and the cuff relaxed.

I heard her shift in the chair, but she didn't say anything. I clenched my teeth against the overwhelming need to grab the cup that was on the tray just to my left as long as I could, but within a few minutes I was reaching out for it.

"Hey."

Blurred by sleep and drugs, I wasn't seeing quiet straight; I could make out Terry's blonde hair but her voice had dropped a few octaves.

"Paul," I guessed.

He handed me the cup and said, "Try again."

I closed my eyes and took a deep breath, fighting the stab of fatigue and the new slap of pain. "Don't screw around with me, I—"

His hand brushed over mine as he took the cup from me and set it on the tray. "Mr. Barron sends his regards."

My eyes snapped open. "Nick."

He was standing there by the bed, leaning over and laughing at me. He had his mother's blue eyes and her blonde hair, but that smile was his own. "You look better than I thought you would. When Barron told me, I half expected to walk in and find the Elephant Man."

"You'd better give me a hug, son, just so I know this isn't some side effect of too much Percoset."

He hugged me gently, and was slow to pull away.

"When did you get back?"

"Three hours ago, give or take half an hour. We landed at Travis Air Force Base and they had a car bring me here."

"Wait, they? Barron wasn't supposed to tell you anything."

"I know. But the timing was right for me to come home for a few days. He told me on the plane."

A few days. He only had a few days.

"Have you seen Katie?"

"I made sure I saw her first. No offense."

"None taken. I'd be a little pissed off if I was your first stop."

"You, I missed. Katie...I *missed*."

"Then you should go find her, and stop wasting your time sitting here staring at the swollen grump."

"I will when Mom gets back. Kevin literally picked her up and carried her into the elevator. I think he was taking her to the cafeteria."

"Good man," I said softly.

"Paul said Kevin's been pretty much taking care of you and Mom through this whole thing."

"That he has."

"Good. And Kevin says Paul has been keeping an eye out on Katie."

"From a respectful distance."

"I trust Paul with her, Dad."

"I know you do. Now quit talking about them to avoid talking to me. How are you doing, really?"

"It's been an eye opener," he said quietly. "But I've been fine. I'll be fine."

"And you can't tell me what you're doing."

"I shouldn't. I can probably get away with telling you we're looking for someone and he's slippery as fish, but he seems to be stuck in one area."

"Seems to," I said. "Be careful, Nick. The ones who seem to be stuck are the ones who are gone long before you realize it."

"I know. This guy must be important, though, because Barron has been overseeing the whole thing personally."

"If you're where I think you are, everything is important."

He wouldn't confirm or deny anything; Terry came in then, carrying a plate and drink cup. He kissed his mother and told me he'd be back in a little while, and went off in search of his wife.

Terry had tears in her eyes; she was torn between wanting to hold onto her son as tight as she could, and taking care of me. If not for the tightly wound nervous and nauseous brunette waiting for him down the hall I might have told her to go after him.

"You know," I said, "I really would like to kiss you but I don't think I'd feel it."

She leaned over and kissed the corner of my mouth, away from the gauze sling that was still under my nose, and away from the incision that was beginning to throb. "They sent him home to see you," she murmured.

"He had the time…"

"He had the time, unless it means more. Chip, those people know everything about you. What if they already know what was growing in your head?"

"Ter, Nick was on the plane before I even went into surgery. They didn't send him home to say goodbye. They sent him home because Barron is a decent guy and Nick had some time to kill."

She didn't look terribly sure, but nodded anyway.

"What'd you bring me?" I asked. "I'm starving."

"Don't tell me that to make me feel better."

"No, really, I'm hungry now. As long as it's soft, I'll eat it."

She kissed me again, a flutter of her lips on my forehead. "Any other time, coming from you, that would sound dirty. I brought you some fruit and chocolate pudding, just enough to tide you over until dinner. And grape juice, since you seem to be craving it."

I watched her stick a straw through the lid on the cup. Her eyes were still moist, but she had a little bit of a smile playing at the corners of her eyes.

"Thank you," I said.

"It's just grape juice, Irish. I didn't even make a special trip for it. Kevin actually threw me over his shoulder—"

I pushed the side rail down and reached for her hand. "Come here. That's not what I meant."

She sat carefully, and resisted when I tried to pull her into a hug.

"I won't break. Just avoid bumping your head into my face, because that would seriously hurt."

I scooted over as far as I could, my hip against the far rail, and she curled up beside me, her head on my chest. I could have fallen asleep like that, with my arms around her, but as soon as my eyes closed she was pulling away and tugging the sheet and blanket up around me.

"Spider is in the hallway," she said, "and you're naked and were flashing."

I had the thought that if he'd made note of that, he would have gone away and left us alone, but instead I took the juice from her and tried to work up some enthusiasm for my son-in-law.

~

Kevin

Nick was more than a little travel-worn; he was bone weary and looked ready to drop, wrapped in nearly as much exhaustion as Dad. Watching Katie walk down the hall, though, his eyes were bright and I could feel the hunger he was too mature to allude to.

"Not letting her run off, are you?" I teased as I came up behind him.

"Doesn't matter how much you miss someone. When Mother Nature calls, you answer."

Or, you throw up. "You should take her home," I ventured.

He was shaking his head before I could get the thought out completely. "I want to see Dad again before we leave. She understands that."

"Of course she does."

He turned around to look at me. "Sounds like you've done a pretty good job of holding everything together here, Squirt."

"I'm just the chauffer."

"How many doctors did he see before agreeing to this, Kevin? Did they even try to use chemo or radiation to shrink the tumor?"

"It's not cancer, Nick. He saw Uncle Doug, and then he saw the neurosurgeon."

"You're kidding me. You don't *know* that it's not cancer. Why the hell didn't you push him to get a second and third opinion? It's his goddamn brain. He should have taken more time—"

"He trusted Uncle Doug to choose the best surgeon."

"You," he insisted. "If you were so willing to take this on you should have done more to make sure all of this was necessary."

"Dad's a big boy. He didn't need me to decide anything for him."

"He found out he had a brain tumor, hell, yes he needed you to make some decisions. He probably wasn't thinking straight and just blindly did whatever the hell they told him to."

Nick was tired, I reminded myself. He was exhausted and taking it out on me because he didn't dare take it out on Katie. I refused to take the bait and said as calmly as I could, "He has Mom to make decisions with him. I do what they ask me to. It's not up to me to tell them what to do."

"It is when they need help."

"And they didn't need my help, not in deciding what to do. Go home, Nick. You need some sleep, and Katie needs some time with you."

"I'll go after I've seen Dad again. She understands that."

"Of course she does," I said again.

He stood there stubbornly, refusing to give even a fraction of an inch.

"Look, if you won't go home, there's a nice little café across the street. Take Katie there for dessert or something."

"Trust me, Squirt, I'll make sure we have some time alone tonight."

"Nick. Trust *me*. You need to be alone with her, and not tonight."

He squinted, considering. "I need to? Is something wrong?"

"Take her across the street, buy her something sticky sweet, and just talk to her, Nicky."

He took a step closer to me, so close I could feel his breath on my face. "If there's something wrong, you better spill it."

I was saved from his implied threat by Katie grabbing him by the arm and pulling him towards her. "And what," she asked playfully, "are you two so serious about?"

"He just wanted to know someplace he could take you to be alone for a little while," I said before he could get anything out. "I was recommending that place across the street, the one with the bagels and scones and stuff."

She slipped her hand in his, and with a light laugh said, "Awesome idea, Kevin." She took a step away, tugging at his hand. "Come on. We'll come back and see your dad in a little while."

When they got to the elevator, Nick looked back at me, and it crossed my mind that if a glare could inflict a wish, my hair would be on fire.

~

Three hours later Paul and I were alone in the waiting room; Eileen had gone home and Mom was in Dad's room trying to convince him that he wouldn't die from terminal embarrassment if he let the nurse hang his catheter bag on a walker so that he could try walking in the hallway for a bit.

I had offered to duct tape it to his leg, and was summarily dismissed from the room.

"He won't put that stupid gown back on, what makes them think he'll wander around naked with that bag hanging from his nads?" Paul mused.

"Give Mom a little while. He'll have on the gown and he'll be shuffling behind that walker, swearing under his breath. She's just as stubborn as he is when it matters."

"We could go in there and haul his ass out of bed for her. It's not like he can run and catch either one of us."

We both knew he might not be able to even stand at the side of his bed for more than a minute, but the idea of going back and threatening him with it was tempting. And we might have, if Nick hadn't come back, looking more disheveled and tired than he had before.

Katie was not with him, and neither of us wanted to ask what had happened. We sat there and stared at him standing in the doorway of the waiting room, his hands shoved into his pockets.

"We went out the wrong door, I think," he said after a minute of awkward silence. "Did you know there's a hotel next to the hospital?"

I turned to Paul. "Apparently, they serve a better scone."

"Blueberry," Paul offered.

He just stood there, and we waited.

Neither of us had intended to tell our parents, and we sure as hell weren't going to say anything to Nick.

After several screamingly quiet minutes, Nick said, "I have to go back early Monday morning."

Paul let out a deflated, "Oh, man," at the same time I cut loose with a disappointed expletive.

"I don't know how long I'll be gone." He reached into his back pocket for his wallet, and pulled out a small white business card and handed it to me. "If anything happens when I'm gone, *anything*, call that number and ask for Cooper."

"And that would be you?"

He didn't answer, but looked at Paul and said, "You have to swear you'll be there for anything she needs. I don't care if she calls you at three in the morning and wants ice cream with pickles. Promise me."

"You know I will," Paul told him.

Nick slumped against the wall by the door, crossing his arms, holding himself together. "I'm going to miss so much…"

"Dad thought you'd only be gone for two to four weeks," Paul said.

"Months," Nick said. "I meant months. And that's assuming we…finish."

Finish what, we didn't ask.

If Nick was gone that long, he was going to miss the first time Katie felt their baby move; he'd miss out on those long nights spent with one hand on her belly, waiting to feel the tiniest flutter.

If his assignment took longer, he'd miss out on seeing elbows and feet poking out at him. For sure he would miss the first time Katie got to hear the baby's heartbeat.

"You'll be home when it matters," I said, though I honestly didn't know that.

"You bonded with Michael before he was born," Nick murmured. "What if I don't get a chance at that? What the hell kind of father will I be if I'm not there for the very beginning?"

I would have told him he'd be a good one regardless. Paul would have, too. But we were stopped short by Mom, who wandered into the waiting room in time to hear Nick's agony. She put her arms around him and hugged him tightly, and then said softly, "Go talk to your father, Nicholas. He can tell you exactly what kind of father you'll be."

~

Chip

I won the battle over the walker; they settled for sitting me in the chair by the bed for a few minutes, and when the world felt like it was going to spin around me, Terry helped the nurse move me back to the bed, and then left me there to fall asleep while she spent some time with Kevin and Paul.

I was ready to drift off; given a little more time and I would have been out, but Nick was suddenly there, sitting beside me, and the tears in his eyes chased away any notion of sleep.

He was running his hands through his hair, trying to figure out what he wanted to say, his own pain bubbling just under the surface.

"I thought it would be good news," I said when it seemed like he just couldn't speak.

"It should be. It is."

"But?"

"But I won't be here. I might not be here for any of it. This is my first kid, and I might miss it all."

He wasn't even sure he'd be back in time to see his son or daughter born. He admitted to being in Iraq. The U.S. was getting ready to hand sovereignty back to the Iraqi people, and the person they were chasing after like a fly in the dark was the one person who could throw a wrench in the works. If they didn't find him and it all fell apart, Nick was sure he'd be stuck in an exponentially increasing war zone.

He was protected now; if the situation exploded he wouldn't be.

"You're a trainee," I reminded him. "Barron will send you home before that happens."

"The agency is less than half the size it was when you were active, Dad. There aren't enough people to cover everything. Out of everyone who went into training within the same year I did, I'm the only one left. They're either dead or they washed out. If I wasn't an asset"—he practically spit the word out—"I'd be on my own there."

"Look at me. You are *the* asset in this mission. You hold all the information together; you're the one they need to compute it all. Barron will protect you himself if he has to."

"It still takes time, Dad. What if I miss her entire pregnancy?

How the hell will I connect with my kid? If she gives birth while I'm gone..."

"You'll take one look at your son or daughter and you'll fall in love. Instantly. I promise you that."

"How?" Barely a whisper. Mostly a plea.

"I fell in love with Kevin and Eileen before I knew them, and I wasn't even sure they were mine." He looked up, startled; he knew the details, but I didn't think he knew my doubts. "Nick, I made a conscious decision that I would love the child your mother was carrying no matter what. Then she got so sick... I didn't even see them until they were almost three days old, but the moment I got a glimpse of Eileen's little foot slamming into the side of the bassinette—"

"It's not the same."

"If those two could capture my heart, even with all the misgivings I had, and after three days...you'll connect with your own child. It'll hurt that you miss so much, but I swear, you'll love that baby as much as if you'd gone through every single step with Katie."

I wasn't sure he believed me; I didn't think he could, not until he'd met his child for the first time.

"How long before you knew?"

"That I loved them? Before they were born, though that first look cemented it."

"No. That they were yours. Because when Mom told me the whole story, that was the first thing I wondered. If they were yours or Uncle Doug's."

"They were always mine, no matter who fathered them."

"Kevin looks just like you."

"Yes, he does. And I have to admit, if he looked like Doug, I doubt we'd be friends now."

"Then how did you know? Some kind of divine revelation?"

"Doug did a paternity test," I admitted. "While I was sitting by your mother's bed, praying she wasn't going to die, he was very quietly determining whose DNA those two had. He had his answer six weeks later."

Nick looked up and past me, to the doorway.

"I didn't know that," Terry said.

Nick stood up, and when she came to the side of the bed he

kissed her on the cheek and said, "I'd better go. I left Katie asleep in a hotel room, and I don't want her to worry."

We watched him leave, and neither of us spoke until he was several steps beyond the door.

"How long were you listening?" I asked.

"Long enough. You needed a paternity test?"

My head was pounding, I needed something to drink, and every muscle in my body was screaming at me. "Doug did, not me," I said.

"And yet you never told me."

"You didn't need any proof."

"Son of a bitch."

"Hey." I reached for her hand. "You may have been sure, but he wasn't. And since our kids wound up marrying each other, it's probably a good thing he had it confirmed long before they even realized each other existed."

"Still."

"Terry, I'm sorry. I really am sorry."

She sat down in the chair, hard. "You're not the one I'm seriously annoyed with right now."

"It was almost twenty four years ago. Let it go."

She pointed a finger at me. "Tomorrow morning, you're getting your ass out of this bed and walking. I don't care if you have to carry the catheter bag in your teeth."

There was an 'or else' there but I didn't care to push it.

I agreed just to pacify her.

My face was messed up and there was something wrong with my brain, but my common sense was still intact.

Don't tick off the blonde. Never tick off the blonde.

~

The night nurse woke me at two thirty for blood and a gauze change, the same as the night before. And like before, Terry was curled up on a cot next to me, sound asleep.

After she drew the blood and was folding up new gauze to stick under my nose, she cringed, and the smell hit us at the same time. We both looked down to the floor, watching as a pale yellow wave oozed across the off-white tile.

"The bag broke," she sighed.

"From the catheter?"

"Appears so. I'll go get the janitor."

I wanted to wake Terry, but I doubted she'd share my sense of pride over having peed enough in four hours to break a collection bag.

~

At nine in the morning, a new nurse was on duty, and she marched in with rubber gloves and scissors, and said brightly, "Good morning! I'm here to remove your catheter!"

I eyed the scissors suspiciously. "With that?"

"I'll just snip it, and pull it out."

"Like hell you will."

"Irish," Terry sighed, "just let her do her job."

"She wants to *pull* it out."

"Hon," the nurse said, a little too sweetly, "how did you think it was going to come out?"

Before I could do anything about it, she flipped the sheet back, and snipped the tube, and to my horror she yanked it out in one movement.

"Oh my God!"

"Now, that wasn't so bad, was it?"

"Yes, it was! It's not bi-directional, you know!"

"It came out in the right direction, sweetie." She flipped the sheet back down and patted the mattress. "Now, sit tight and I'll bring you some scrub pants, and we can go for a walk."

Before I could protest, Terry leaned forward. "You will get out of bed, and you will walk, mister. You will not argue, and you will not whine."

"Really," I told her, "you were a lot more fun when you were giving me a sponge bath."

~

At three thirty, after I'd walked twice in five minute spurts, Dr. Harris came in, two of his residents in tow. He pulled the gauze back and looked in my nose, and carefully looked under my upper lip.

"Good news, dude. I think the packing can come out today. And we'll put you back on the DDAVP soon after."

"Tell him how they come out," Terry said. "He'll love that."

"Oh yeah, I heard about the catheter. Dude, this is worse. But it'll be over in, like, five seconds. Each."

"Each."

"One up each nostril."

"Doug was right," Terry said after they left. "You do whine."

~

"It's simple," Doug said.

He was standing at the foot of the bed, having ushered the nurse away. She was, she told him, tired of arguing with me.

"Simple."

"Simple. Fart, and you can go home."

"After all this, it comes down to gas?"

"Pretty much. The bowels have to move one way or the other before you can go."

Kevin wandered in, looking for his mother, who was down in the cafeteria with Nick and Katie.

"Quick," I told him, holding out my hand. "Pull my finger."

He turned around and left without saying a word. Doug shrugged and started to follow him.

"Fart."

~

At three o'clock on Monday morning, they decided I could go home; anyone who could argue that much in the middle of the night, the nurse declared, didn't need their care.

At three fifteen, Nick came in quietly, defying the orderly who kept trying to tell him visitors were not welcome for another five hours. She followed him into the room, threatening to call security; when he was close to the bed he turned and hissed, "Lady, I leave for Iraq in twenty minutes. You're going to let me have a few goddamn minutes with my parents before I take off, because God only knows when I'll see them again."

She softened instantly and nodded, backing away and leaving the room without another word.

"Wake her up," I said quietly. "If you leave without telling her goodbye, you'll break her heart."

"No shit. Katie's curled up on a hotel bed crying her eyes out right now. She knows I'll be okay, but…"

"But now you know, and she wants you to be here."

"Yeah. Now I know."

He knelt next to the cot and gently shook Terry, whispering to her to wake up. He needed to see her before he left.

The moment she realized it was Nick's voice she heard and what he was saying, her eyes snapped open and she sat up, reaching for him.

"Not so soon, Nicky."

"I'm sorry. I have to get back."

She swung her legs over the edge of the cot and stood up so that she could hug him tightly; when she let go I lowered the rail of my bed and tried to sit up, my head swimming in a sudden fog of throbbing pain.

"Stay in bed, Dad."

"Just help me sit up, that's all."

I dangled my legs over the side and he looked down, chuckling at the white support hose sticking out from the blue scrub pants. "Those are definitely you."

I patted the mattress, and asked him to sit next to me for a minute. Terry stepped closer, too, her hand on Nick's shoulder, not letting go until she had to.

"I have to know. How many people are you working with?" I asked him. "You don't have to hint at anything classified. Just give me an idea what you're working with."

"Three incomplete teams, four people each."

"You're Cooper."

He nodded.

"Then you really are the keystone. They can't succeed without you."

"They can," he said carefully. "I'm not keeping any of the information I process to myself. Barron gets it all."

I got it then. "You're Cooper to the SG."

"What does that mean?" Terry asked.

"It means," Nick said, voice tinged with regret, "that I have to go. Barron is waiting for me in a car out front."

I put my arms around him and hugged him as tightly as I could. "Just keep your head down, son."

"You know I will."

He got up and reached out for Terry. "Tell Kevin I'm sorry. I was a real shit to him and he didn't deserve it."

"I will." She pulled back, and kissed him lightly on his lips. "We'll take care of her, Nicky. I promise."

"I know." He kissed her again, and then leaned over to kiss me. "With any luck I'll be back before your swelling goes down. But if not…don't let her name my kid after her father. It'd be an omen, for sure."

"Funny."

He headed for the door, raising his hand back in a little wave and said, "Love you guys," as he disappeared around the corner.

Terry sat next to me on the bed, resting her head on my shoulder. "Tell me now what all that meant, Irish. What is Cooper to the SG?"

"Cooperative agent," I said. "It's like the cog in a wheel. All those teams rely on him for intel; he gets the information, sorts it out, pieces together things that belong together, and then decides who needs to know what. The SG's Cooper gets to see all and knows all, even things team leaders don't. It means he's being groomed for much bigger things."

"More danger, you mean."

"Not necessarily. It does mean that he's honest when he says they value his brain over his brawn. Nicky will be protected, Terry. They have plans for him, and they're not going to risk losing him."

"But he still might miss the birth of his first child."

"Unfortunately." I tried to slide out of the bed, reaching for her to steady me. "Since you're up...I have to pee."

She let me lean heavily against her, my arm around her shoulder, and she guided me towards the bathroom. "No DDAVP before you went to sleep?"

"They gave it to me. And I could wait, but since we're both awake..."

She opened the door for me and helped me shuffle in and then asked, "You okay from here, or do you need more help?"

I hadn't counted on how weak I was going to feel. "I can either hold myself up with those nifty rails, or I can aim. I can't do both. I would prefer to do the aiming, but..."

"But I might not be able to hold you up and you've never been able to go sitting down. You owe me, Irish."

"Yes, I do."

"Can you even do this, mister close-the-damn-bathroom-door?"

"I lost my dignity two days ago," I assured her.

Once she had me back in bed, she started to put the rail up, but I stopped her and reached for her. "It's a small bed, but we both fit."

She snuggled as close as she could, careful to avoid bumping my face. "You'll be home tonight, you know."

"I know. But Doug warned that the ride home was going to wipe me out, and I might not have the energy to even blink at you. Unless you're just really uncomfortable, I'd like to hold you while I'm awake enough to realize it."

"For a little while. You need to get back to sleep. I'll get back up when you start to drift off."

I agreed, but two and a half hours later Doug found her still curled around me, both of us asleep.

16

Terry

Doug's warning that the ride home would be harder on Chip than the last two days in the hospital had been was an understatement. He'd walked the hall near the nurses' station with no problem, as long as he had me on one side and Kevin on the other supporting him. When the doctor signed his release Chip was bubbling with energy and eager to get home.

By the time Doug pulled his car into our driveway, Chip was enveloped in exhaustion and couldn't get up without help. He sat in the back seat, his head pounding and fatigue pulling in tight strands at him, but we needed to wait for Kevin, who was just a few minutes behind us. I didn't have the strength to help him from such an awkward position, and Doug wasn't sure he could do it without straining something.

We complained about aging while we waited. Surely even ten years ago one of us could have helped him out of the car without worrying about breaking ourselves.

Kevin got him out of the car and helped him up the three steps to the front door, and once inside and confronted with the stairs that blocked Chip's way to the bedroom, he put Chip's arm around his shoulders, put his own arm around his father's waist, and practically lifted him over each stair.

"And that," Doug said to no one in particular, "is why the boy took the week off." He set Chip's gym bag off to the side and said he'd call later to check on him, but he was a phone call away if needed.

Kevin had him seated on the edge of the bed when I got to the bedroom; Chip was trying to kick off his shoes but couldn't get leverage, and he wasn't letting Kevin help.

I pulled his shoes and his socks off and then grabbed a pair of loose shorts from the dresser. "Come on, Irish, don't fight us on this. You need to get into bed, and you'll be more comfortable if you're out of the jeans and t-shirt."

We had him down to his underwear when he moaned, "Fuck, I have to pee."

Kevin started to help him up but Chip tried to shake him off. "Suck it, old man. After the things you've said to me lately, you don't get to be embarrassed. You either let me help, or we'll slap a diaper on you."

"Your mom can help me."

"No, you're too damned heavy. I've seen you pee before, Dad. This is not a big deal."

It was to Chip, but he relented and let Kevin take him into the bathroom. When he had Chip back on the bed, I helped him strip the underwear off and get into the shorts.

"I'd rather leave those off," he grumbled.

"Nicole," I reminded him. "After you sleep for a while she's going to want to see you. You can take them off later if you want."

"Fine."

He eased back onto the bed, looking miserable and defeated, but he let me slide the shorts on. I kissed his forehead and started for the door, but Kevin stopped me.

"You need some rest, too, Mom. Lie down for a while. Lydia and I will cook dinner and I'll wake you when it's ready."

"He's right," Chip mumbled. "Just come curl up with me. You don't have to sleep."

It was like they'd flipped a switch, and the last four days drained out of me. I closed the door behind Kevin and stripped, reaching for one of Chip's old t-shirts to sleep in.

Normally he would have asked me to leave it off, but he was half asleep himself, and within three minutes we were both gone.

~

I lost all sense of time; when Kevin woke me later I had no idea how long I'd been sleeping. He had obviously crept in quietly and made sure we both had at least the sheet covering us; it was too neatly pulled up to be anything other than intentional.

Once I was awake, he went into the hallway for a card table he'd brought up from the garage, and he set it up near the foot of the bed, then went back for two chairs.

"So that you and Dad can have dinner together," he explained. "I'll bring it up in a minute so you have time to put some clothes on."

I peeked under the sheet to see just how far up the t-shirt had ridden, and immediately felt bad for him. If he hadn't already been in therapy, by the time he moved out of our house, he was going to need it.

Chip was still groggy when Kevin helped him out of bed, but he was hungry and willing to tolerate the pounding in his head and the overwhelming desire to slide under the table and curl up on the floor.

While Kevin helped Chip to the table I felt a tiny prick of worry; he still needed soft food and I hadn't thought to tell Kevin that, but when he took the Tupperware lids off the bowls he'd brought up I realized he was more tuned into what his father needed than I realized.

"Beef stew," he said simply. "Lydia cut the meat into tiny, tiny chunks, so it shouldn't be a problem. And trust me, she makes a mean stew." He reached for the paper bag he'd set on the dresser and from it pulled a loaf of sliced fresh bread and a tub of butter. "It's hot and soft, and Lydia cut the crust off, so no worries there, either."

"You two thought of everything," I said. "Thank you."

Chip took a tentative bite, trying to avoid the gauze sling under his nose. "Holy shit, this is good."

"If you want more, just holler."

He started out the door but stopped when Chip called after him.

"Where are my grandkids?"

"Downstairs. Michael is babbling at Max, and Nicole is pretending she's not really hungry. Apparently the stew looks like something she once barfed up."

"I want to see them."

"If you're coherent once you're done eating, I'll send Nicole up."

"Warn her, Kev. I'm not exactly going to win any beauty contests for a while."

"She knows. She's not worried that you're going to freak her out. I think she wants to take pictures, frankly."

He shrugged. "I might let her."

He ate almost half of his stew, and suddenly stopped, setting his spoon down carefully. He closed his eyes for a moment and took a deep breath, and then asked quietly, "Will you help me get back into bed? I don't think I can sit here anymore."

"Tired or do you feel like you want to throw up?"

"Just tired," he said as I helped him from the chair. He didn't fully stand, but stumbled, hunched over, from the chair to the side of the bed. "Why the hell am I so tired? I've been in bed for four days already."

"That was major surgery, Chip." I sat on the edge of the bed, brushing hair from his forehead, just to be able to touch him. "It was intense stress, and that much stress will wear anyone down. You'll feel a little better tomorrow, and even better the day after that."

"I know that makes sense, but will you call Doug and ask him? Just to be sure?"

"Of course I will. But before I do, are you still hungry? You can eat in bed, you know."

"No, but make sure Lydia knows I really liked it and she'll be expected to make it again when I can kill off three or four bowls of it."

"All right." I kissed him on the forehead and got up, picking up as much of our dinner as I could. "I'll go call Doug. Are you ready to see Nicole, or do you want to go back to sleep?"

"I'd like to see my granddaughter, as long as you're sure she'll be all right with how I look."

"You look a lot better than you did even yesterday. She'll be fine, Chip."

Truthfully, she'd been so overly warned about how swollen and bruised Chip's face was that I thought she might be a little disappointed with how nearly normal he looked.

~

Chip

Just a few minutes after Terry left the bedroom, I heard Nicole's feet thundering on the stairs and Kevin's voice trailing after her, warning her to be quiet and to be gentle with Grandpa. He stopped her just outside the door and said, "Remember, he's very tired, so if he seems grumpy, it's because of that and not because he's mad at you. He really wants to see you. And if you hug him, you have to be very careful not to bump his face with your head or your shoulder, because that would hurt a lot."

"I'll be careful," she promised.

When he let her in she bounded for the bed and nearly jumped up on it, but caught herself at the last second and stopped near the foot of the bed.

"Hey, sweetheart," I said, my voice sounding thick even to me.

She tilted her head and laughed, a deep chuckle that sounded nearly evil. "Grandpa, you look like a Teletubby."

"A what?"

"Tinky Winky," she giggled. "Can I get on the bed with you?"

I scooted over a little to make room for her. "I'd give you a kiss, but my lips aren't quite working yet."

"That's okay. I can kiss you instead."

"On the cheek," Kevin told her. "And carefully."

"You," I said to my son. "Go away. Give me some time with Nicole, and then bring me my grandson."

"Ten minutes," he told Nicole. "Grandpa needs to rest."

"He's bossy sometimes," I said after he left. "He's not trying to be mean."

"I know. Daddy says Uncle Kevin is pretending to be your mother so that he makes sure you get better."

"He's kind of ugly for a woman, don't you think?"

That got me a giggle.

"So what did you do for four days? Did you get to do anything fun?"

She sat cross legged on the bed, and regarded me the same way she did hamsters at the pet store. Curious and amused. "Daddy's friend Sherry came over and I got to swim, and we went to play miniature golf and got pizza, and we watched some DVDs. It was kind of fun."

"Just kind of?"

"Well, I had school on Friday but it was the last day so that wasn't too bad."

"School's out for summer now?"

"Yep and you know what? I have to go to a new school next year."

Paul hadn't been sure what he was going to do about Nicole and school when we moved; he'd taken her out of the neighborhood public school after Monica died and sent her to a parochial school, but he wasn't sure he wanted to make that drive every morning and the church bus wasn't going to pick her up from Vacaville.

"Does that make you mad?"

She shrugged. "Daddy says I'll make friends that live near our new house if I go to a new school and then I'll have friends right there to play with. That would be fun."

"I think so, too."

"Oh! And you know what else?" She leaned forward and whispered, "I saw Daddy *kiss* Sherry! I was supposed to be in bed but I wanted to ask him something and they were by the front door and he was *kissing* her!"

I had to bite back a smile. "Did that bother you?"

"No, but I don't know if she's his girlfriend or not. He shouldn't kiss her if she's not."

"You let Daddy worry about that, sweetheart. He might have a lot of girlfriends over the next couple of years and he might even kiss one or two of them."

"I know." She looked down at her legs, fingers grasping at the hem of her pants. "Did it hurt, Grandpa?"

"After I woke up it did. It still hurts a little bit."

"Did they give you medicine for it?"

"Yes, they did. And it worked pretty well. It made me sleep a lot."

"That's good."

She wasn't looking at me, so I tucked a finger under her chin and made her look up. "What's wrong?"

"Was it cancer?"

Carefully, "We don't know yet. But the doctor got the whole tumor out and he'll send it to another doctor whose job it is to cut it open and look at it, and that's the doctor who will be able to tell me what it was."

"Okay."

"Remember the penny in the pool, Nicole."

"Okay."

Kevin was at the door again, this time with Michael. Nicole got up on her knees and very carefully leaned over to hug me, taking great care to keep her head away from mine. "I'll probably be able to go downstairs tomorrow, Nicole. We can spend more time together if you want."

"You can help me walk him," Kevin said as she slid off the bed. "We need to make him get up and move."

"Like a dog? Can we put him on a leash?"

She laughed all the way down the hall, until she was in her room.

"Mom," Kevin said as he handed me my grandson, "will be up in a minute. She's talking to Uncle Doug right now."

I sat him on my stomach, and his hands immediately shot toward my face, which caused Kevin to lunge for him.

"It's all right," I said. "I can keep him from grabbing my nose. He's just curious about the gauze."

"Ba!" Michael said when I pulled his hands away. "Ba! Ba!"

"Bottle?" I looked up at Kevin.

"Beats me. He just ate, so he shouldn't be hungry."

"Baba!"

"Hey, kid," Kevin said. "It should be 'Dada.' Piss Mommy off and say 'Dada' first."

"Baba baba baba!"

"Maybe it's babytalk for Tinky Winky. Apparently that's who I resemble right now."

Michael kicked his legs out and caught me in the chest, prompting Kevin to reach down and pick his son up. "No kicking Grandpa."

"Baba!" He was working his hands, fingers stretching and clenching, arms straining towards me.

"Holy shit." Kevin looked at Michael, and then at me. "You're Baba."

"It's just a sound. It doesn't mean anything yet."

"Like hell." He smiled and pulled Michael in close, kissing him on his cheek. "Is that your Baba, little man? Did you miss him when he was gone?"

I felt a kernel of near-panic catch in my throat. His first real sounds should be annoying one parent while making the other one happy. He should be squealing 'Dada' or 'Mama' and we should be pretending that he knew exactly what he was saying.

"Mommy," Kevin said, "will be very happy to hear something other than the emergency broadcast alert coming out of you."

"Don't be so sure of that," I warned. "In fact, don't even tell her you heard that. Don't make her miss her baby's first sort-of word."

"No, we wouldn't want her to think that. Come on, kiddo, Grandpa needs his rest."

He headed out the door, and before he hit the stairs I heard one last "Baba!"

A few minutes later Terry was back, a water bottle in one hand and a round foil covered hockey puck in the other. "Doug," she said, setting the water on my nightstand, "says this is all perfectly normal, and that tomorrow you'll feel much better, but he's coming over to check for himself."

"That's good. I have to be mobile tomorrow because Nicole is going to tie a leash around my neck and take me for a walk."

"Okay," she laughed, unsure. She held out the foil hockey puck and said, "Ding Dong, as promised. If you think you can eat it."

I set it next to the water bottle. "Maybe later."

"Sleepy?"

"I don't think I can sleep. I wish I could, just to stop the tiny people that are tap dancing inside my head."

She offered a backrub to help me relax, but there was no way I was going to be able to roll over and push my face into a pillow. She settled for me rolling onto my side, and brushed her cool fingers lightly over my spine. It would either relax me, she said, or do things to me, and she was fine with either.

"Doug might not agree," I sighed.

"He'd get over it, I'm sure."

Fifteen minutes later he was knocking on the half-open door, his proverbial little black bag hanging from his free hand. Terry grabbed one of the card table chairs and moved it to the side of the bed for him, and then went to the other side the crawl up onto the bed with me.

"Your timing is wonderful," I said. "Another five minutes and I might have gotten lucky."

"I'm sure that's exactly what you feel like doing right now. Tell me how you're feeling, Chip. And don't pretend it doesn't hurt."

No pretense was possible. "I feel like I've been run over by a truck. And then it backed up and did it again, just to make sure I felt it the first time around. Even my feet hurt."

"I'm not surprised. You had your head drilled into but your body is going to take sympathetic offense. Add to it the fact that your own natural response to not feeling well is to shut down, and you have the recipe for feeling this bad."

"But I should be able to get from the bed to the bathroom by myself. Doug, I can't even stand there without help. I get up and feel so drained that it feels like I'll collapse."

He opened the bag and took out a blood pressure cuff and then wrapped it around my arm. "You're a little more wiped out that I thought you'd be but I don't think it's anything to worry about. How much pain are you in?"

"From one to ten? I was at a six when I left the hospital, now I'm back to an eight."

"Your BP is right where I'd expect it to be." He put the cuff away and pulled out a thermometer and stuck it in my ear. "No fever, either."

"So I'm a being a wuss."

"No, not this time."

Next he pulled out rubber gloves, and I flinched. "You can keep your hands to yourself this time. They're the same size they were last week."

"Funny. I just want a look at the damage. I'll be gentle." He pulled the sling away from my nose and peeled back the gauze, inspecting it before tossing it aside. "All right, tilt your head back a little. I'm going to lift your lip and check the incision, so it might hurt a bit."

Terry grimaced when he did, but my lip was mostly numb and it didn't bother me.

"Looks fine. What did they send you home with for pain?"

I shrugged; I had no clue.

"Ibuprofen," Terry told him. "One every eight hours."

Doug scowled and said, "Seriously? That's it? Did Harris prescribe it or did his resident?"

She pointed to the bottle on the night stand and he picked it up.

"His resident. No wonder you're feeling worse. This is barely going to touch the pain for a couple more days. I'll go get you something a little stronger so you can sleep tonight. By tomorrow it should ease up, and in two or three days you'll be mostly mobile."

"If he feels like it, can he get out of bed tomorrow?" Terry asked. "No one was really clear on what he can and should do. It was like sign the paper and get out."

"You can do anything you feel like doing," he told me. "Just listen to your body and don't overdo it."

"Nicole wants to take me for a walk tomorrow."

"Maybe around the back yard. Just make sure Kevin sticks close by in case you need help getting back into the house. But getting up and moving is a good idea as long as you don't try to do too much."

"So anything I feel like doing?"

He glanced at Terry and got up. "Okay, the caveat is you can do anything that's not going to raise your blood pressure too much. It won't kill you but I guarantee you'd have a bitch of a headache afterwards. I'll be back in about half an hour with your meds. If you *are* tempted, please be done by the time I get back."

~

An hour and a half later I was well into a nice Percoset haze, and Terry was stretched out beside me, her head on my shoulder and fingers gently stroking my chest. Doug's caveat aside, it was relaxing but that was it. Neither of us felt remotely inclined to do anything else, and if not for the noise coming from down the hall—one crying baby and one fussy eight year old who didn't want to go to bed—I would have fallen asleep.

"Did you know," I said thickly, trying to think past the fog, "that Nicole spied Paul kissing Sherry?"

"I had no idea they were dating."

"I don't know if they are. But Nicole seems pretty sure that if she's not his girlfriend that he shouldn't be kissing her."

"Let's hope she still feels that way in about five or six years," she said lightly.

"Who knows? Eileen evidently did unless there was some boyfriend we never knew about. Did she date anyone other than Spider?"

"There were a few crushes, but Spider was her only boyfriend. First kiss, even."

"Hm. She must get that from your side of the family."

"At least I influenced one of our kids."

"Two," I reminded her. "Katie was Nick's only girlfriend."

"So it's your fault Kevin and Paul both dated their little heads off?"

"It's my fault that Paul slept around, I think. Kevin was just killing time, waiting for Lydia to break up with her boyfriend of the semester. I'm pretty sure she was his first kiss, too."

"How the hell did we pull that off?"

"Dunno. I'm just glad they didn't turn out like me. Paul might have broken a few hearts, but at least his past isn't going to be littered with them."

She lifted up onto an elbow. "You really think you left a trail of broken hearts behind you?"

"I think I crushed a few women along the way. And we know what happened to the last one."

"That might not have been totally your fault, Chip. She was pretty messed up before you hooked up with her, wasn't she?"

"She was seriously messed up," I admitted. "But I broke her."

"From everything I know, you were just honest with her. Maybe not as gentle about telling her as you could have been, but you were marrying her for the hell of it and you didn't want kids with her. Not telling her that would have been more unfair than admitting the truth."

"Maybe. I doubt we would have really gotten married, Terry. I don't know what would have happened, but I regret not trying to save her life instead of using her."

"That's not who you were then."

It took Brenda Webb dying to make me realize I was not the person I wanted to be. It took Terry five seconds and a smile to convince me that I really could be a better man. If they were part of some cosmic conspiracy to get me where I was, flat on my back in bed with most of my family in the same house, all of them mostly happy and healthy, I could live with whatever shadows of guilt I still had.

I listened to Michael wail in the next room; whatever he was unhappy about his parents weren't fixing it fast enough for him.

"When I'm feeling better," I said, trying to get my arm around my wife, who was pulling back lest she hurt me, "We owe some serious babysitting to those two. Did Kevin ever leave the hospital during the day?"

"No. He and Lydia decided he would stay there and be my backup, and she would make sure things here were all right. She took care of Max, cooked for Paul and Nicole, checked in with the dojo… I thought he'd be bored out of his mind in the waiting room for so long, but he had a notebook and did a lot of writing."

"Seriously? He's still writing?"

"He won't let anyone read it, but Lydia says he's been working on something since Michael was born."

"Why the hell is he so shy? He would never let us hear him play the guitar or sing. I know he writes well; mention sex and he freaks…"

"I don't know. It's enough that he still does the things he likes."

"And what happened to his plans to go back to school?"

"He opened a dojo and had a son."

"Can I bribe him into going back? I'll pay for it."

She laughed and reached out to touch my cheek, fingers feather soft. "He can afford to pay for school if he wants to go. Right now he just wants to teach karate and raise a family. Getting a degree isn't going to make him more successful."

"But damn, Terry, he could be *anything*."

"He's a business owner. He teaches. Maybe that's everything for him."

"Nick and Kevin both have these *brains*…why aren't they using them for more?"

"Nick is trying to save the world. What more could he do? And Kevin…Kevin is trying to save people from pain. What they do is good enough, Chip. I never would have thought you'd be disappointed in that."

"I'm not."

"Then what?"

"Kevin—if anyone could find the cure for the common cold and cancer, it would be him. Nick would be far better suited to be a teacher. He wanted to; he wanted to get a teaching credential."

"As a cover," she reminded me. "He was going to get a teaching credential so that we wouldn't know he'd joined the agency. The same way you opened a restaurant and why you were ready to marry a hooker. For the cover. The restaurant wasn't what you wanted, Chip. If it was you wouldn't have shucked it off onto Paul as soon as you could."

"If Paul doesn't want it, I'll close the damn thing."

"That's my point. The kids are doing what they want. Nick wants to follow in the shoes you shoved aside when he was a teenager because he admires you and wants to make a difference. Paul wants to run your restaurant and I think he'd consider branching out if the economy was better. Eileen loves teaching music, and Kevin…"

"Kevin teaches karate out of some subconscious need to keep other people from suffering what he did. He doesn't love it, Terry. He does it because he feels like he has to. He replaced one calling with another."

"And that's not such a bad thing. He has Lydia, he has Michael, and he has a sense of purpose. He loves to write, and even if he never does anything with it, he's *doing* it."

"I'm not disappointed in my kids," I said, afraid that was how she would take it. "I'm anything but."

"I know. You love them and you want them to be happy, and you're just high enough on the Percoset that your filters are down. You wouldn't be questioning them otherwise."

"Maybe."

"Anything you want to change about me, while you're in a forgivable state of being able to blame the pain and the drugs?"

"No. Is there anything you want to do that I don't know about?

Like go back to work, or run your own business, or start fostering stray kittens? I wouldn't have a problem with two out of the three."

"Then I'll forgo the idea of going back to work. How many kittens would you like?"

"If you bring kittens home, Max will eat them."

"Quite possibly. You know what I would really like to do?"

"Yes, I would."

"When you're better, and we've moved, and life is not all chaos, I would like for you and I to go on a long vacation together. Somewhere requiring a passport. You've seen the world, Irish, but I haven't."

"We could do that. You've never wanted to stray too far from home before."

"I know. And I might only want to go once. But I want you to show me the places you've been that you fell in love with."

"The places I've been have been violent and nasty. Maybe we should go someplace neither of us has been. Hell, even just go to Hawaii and play on the beach. Or take a cruise. Anything you want."

"Irish, right now I really want to kiss you."

"Just be gentle."

She leaned over and kissed me on the lips for the first time since we'd been interrupted by the OR escort.

"What's the smile for?" I asked when she pulled away.

"You're making plans, Chip, and it's not 'if I'm okay.' It's 'when.'"

For a few minutes, I hadn't considered the looming potential bad news. I was simply moving forward and trying to take her with me. If it made her smile, all the better.

Whatever was going to happen, whatever news we got later, that wasn't going to change.

Life had to go on.

17

Chip

Two weeks later we were sitting by the pool, while Kevin and Paul played tag in the water with Nicole, and we watched Lydia carefully wade in the shallow end with Michael. He was slathered in 75 spf sunscreen and she'd put a floppy white hat on his head; he was squealing, his hands slapping at the water as she spun him around slowly.

I was still tired; it was measured in moments of not wanting to do much, and of occasional twinges if I sneezed or if Max head-butted my face in the middle of the night, but it was enough to remind me that I wasn't up to one hundred per cent. I hated the feeling of listlessness and the toll not being able to work out was taking on my body, but I trusted Doug's assurances that what I felt was normal and that I'd be back in the gym in two or three more weeks.

The kids were amusing each other, but Terry and I were there to distract ourselves. We'd both woken up that morning with sadness brushing the edges, yet neither one of us had admitted why. She'd been quiet all day, keeping herself busy with laundry and scrubbing bathroom floors, and I stayed out of her way, knowing I couldn't do a single thing to help.

Still, one of us had to mention it, so I cracked through the silence by quietly saying, "It's Nick's birthday."

She didn't look away from the pool, where Nicole was trying to dunk her father. "I know."

"Twenty eight years ago—from right about now, actually—you were threatening me with grave bodily harm if I even thought of ever touching you again."

The corner of her mouth twitched against the smile she was determined to not have. "I do recall threatening to rip your lips off."

"Among other things. Remember that first time he really looked at you?"

"He was so annoyed." She finally smiled, and let slip a laugh. "Like he was demanding to know who the hell I thought I was and why did I push him out of that nice warm place."

"Kind of set the tone for his personality."

"Even if he was home we might not have spent much time with him today, but him not being here just feels wrong."

From birthdays lost to the agency, I was fairly sure that Nick and the people he was with would find a way to celebrate; in the worst places in the world, even where alcohol was forbidden, there was always a case of beer to acknowledge and annoy someone who was ticking one more year off their calendar. It probably mattered more to his parents than it did to Nick.

"We can celebrate anyway," I told her. "Give Kris and Doug a call, see if they want to go out for dinner tonight. And not the Charybdis, someplace where I actually have to pay."

"Not that you're cheap. Are you sure you're feeling up to it?"

"I've been taking it easy for two weeks. It would be nice to get out for a while. Hell, even if they can't go, you and I still will. As long as I can get dessert."

She started to get up, and leaned over for a kiss. Very gentle, still worried about hurting me. "All right, I'll call them. You can tell the kids they're on their own for dinner tonight. If they're inclined to cook, there's chicken thawing in the refrigerator."

I watched her walk into the house, and decided I definitely felt a whole lot better.

I went over to the side of the pool and glared, making sure they all understood I'd better not get splashed. Nicole was still trying to push Paul's head under water, but she stopped and slid off his back, looking at me like '*you* can't yell at me, because *he's* my dad.'

"Your Mom and I are going out tonight, so dinner is up to you. The cook will not be home."

"I'm going to Aunt Eileen's!" Nicole happily informed me. "I get to spend the night!"

"Good for you, sweetheart. I assume the rest of you are capable of feeding yourselves."

"Isn't that why I got married?" Kevin asked sweetly, a safe distance from his wife, who raised one eyebrow and then told him he was having cold oatmeal.

"I won't be home anyway." Paul glanced at Nicole and then heaved himself out of the water, and walked over to the lounge chair I'd been in. I took the hint and followed, and Nicole turned her attention to her uncle.

"Work or something else?"

"When do I tell her I'm seeing someone?"

"That depends. Is this just a date or is she spending the night with Eileen because you very well might not come home tonight?"

He looked just past me, watching his daughter push Kevin under water. "If I come home, it was just a date."

"But you're hoping not to."

He shrugged lightly.

"How long have you been seeing this girl?"

"I've known her forever, Dad. We've been tap dancing around each other for over a year. I'm not exactly rushing it, just finally catching up to what I've wanted for a long time."

"She's our best hostess," I reminded him. "Don't screw that up."

He couldn't cover his surprise. "How the hell?"

"Nicole saw you kiss her when I was in the hospital. I think it's safe to tell her that you're dating, though I wouldn't tell her any more than that. She was not happy with the idea that you kissed Sherry and might not consider her your girlfriend."

"I'm sure as hell not going to tell her that I might spend the night."

"You've got a hell of a balancing act to learn, Paul."

"Nicole likes Sherry."

"Now she does," I agreed. "But when she's positive she has to share you…there's no telling. And be willing to move very slowly with Sherry if you think this is a relationship that will last."

"Amazing, you sound just like her."

"Good. And while I love my granddaughter, I hope you learned your lesson there."

"Trust me on that one, Dad."

I turned and headed for the door. "Night stand on the right side of my bed. Take as many as you want. Three flavors, even."

~

"He's twenty eight," Kris said, awed by the realization. "That means Spider is only a couple of months from turning twenty seven."

"I'm not old enough to have a kid that age," Doug grumbled.

"Bullshit. You're old enough to have a kid turning thirty seven," Kris snorted.

"If you'd started when Paul did," Terry added to his humiliation, "forty seven."

"I am not that old."

"Face it," I said. "You're that old. You're what, sixty five now?"

"Kiss my ass. I turned sixty this year. If I'd had one when Paul did it'd be younger than Blondie here."

"Not by much," Terry teased.

"I hate you all."

Kris leaned in her chair and kissed him. "If it makes you feel better, I'm older than you, and you don't look nearly your age."

"True," I said. "In reality, you only look fifty nine."

"You know for someone who turns fifty this year you're sure as hell glib."

"Doug, I'm glad to be turning anything, to be honest."

"Still no report?" Kris asked.

I shook my head, and Doug said, "That could come at any time. Typical lately seems to be three to four weeks for non-urgent cases."

Kris seemed surprised. "A brain tumor isn't urgent?"

"Not for something that tends to grow as slowly as a pituitary tumor. They got it all, so even if it grows back he has plenty of time to do something about it."

Unless it metastasized.

I sure as hell was not going to bring that up.

"Guys," I said, "can we find something else to talk about? It's been nothing but my brain for weeks now. We all have to be tired of it."

"We're allowed to be worried," Kris reprimanded.

"Still tired?" Doug prompted, not caring if I wanted to talk about it or not.

"A little," I admitted. "And I'm happy to report, peeing is now a solitary activity."

"Thank you for sharing."

"Hey, if you people are going to keep talking about it, I'm going to share the nasty details." I looked at Kris. "Want to know what it looked like the first time I blew my nose after the surgery?"

"Oh God," Terry sighed, "it's bad enough that you showed me."

Doug shrugged it off. "I'm sure I've seen worse. You'd be surprised what people shove into body openings and expect me to fish out. Sometimes it's gross, sometimes it's just amusing."

"Like gummy bears?" I asked, remembering the patient he'd seen just before he decided I might have a tumor.

"Gummy bears, toys, vegetables."

"Vegetables," Terry uttered.

"A few years ago I had a woman who came in crying her eyes out because she had part of a cucumber stuck."

"I think I'd cry, too," Kris said.

"She was only crying because it wasn't her husband who put it there and she was afraid he'd find out."

"Wait," Terry said, backtracking. "Only part of it?"

"Looked like someone had eaten off the other part. Once the external part of the cuke was gone, it was like this sucking vacuum and the rest of it just disappeared."

He and I were howling; Kris and Terry decided that was a good time to head to the ladies room.

"Don't make me laugh like that again," I said. "Makes my head hurt."

"Badly?"

"Marginally. Seriously, I feel fine. I get tired easy but that's getting a whole lot better. I'd probably get my wind back quicker if Terry would let me do things around the house. I think she's still sure my head will explode with any kind of exertion."

"So you still haven't...?"

"I think that's off the table until I've had my follow up with Surfer Dude Harris and he deems me perfectly fine."

"Hell, I'm a doctor. I'll tell her you're fine. I could even stress that it might be very helpful to your recovery, what with the release of endorphins and all. And if you start with a headache, well hell, that might cure it. See how helpful I am?"

"And if I wind up with an even mildly worse headache, do you really want to suffer the wrath of that little blonde fireball? She'll come after you with fangs and claws bared."

"So test fire that thing by yourself. See if you get a headache."

"I'm not twelve, Doug. I can wait."

Terry slid back into her chair, her hand brushing over my arm. "What is it you're waiting for?"

"Dessert," I said simply.

Doug chuckled and asked where Kris was.

"She's trying to figure out how to answer a text message from Spider. He wanted to know if it was really all right to let Nicole talk to friends online or if she was trying to pull a fast one."

"Where's Eileen?" I asked.

"I didn't ask, and I'm not going to. I'm just happy Spider cares enough to double check before he takes Nicole's word."

"Is she allowed online?"

"With supervision."

"Kind of like you," Doug said. "Did you ever go online to see what a PA is?"

"I'm still not sure I want to know."

He and Terry both laughed and he said, "Get dessert first. Trust me on this."

~

When we got home Michael was asleep and Kevin and Lydia were stretched out on the sofa together, watching the news. Seeing them tangled around each other like that reminded me of all the evenings Terry and I had spent there just like that after the kids were in bed. I'd lie down and she would relax on top of me, my arms around her, and we'd watch whatever happened to be on.

It was quiet and kid free, a way to connect when we were too tired for anything else.

I decided to give them privacy in case they wanted it, and steered Terry up the stairs. We could, I reasoned, go back down later if we needed to.

Once inside the bedroom she kissed me lightly and then kicked off her shoes. "I needed that tonight, Irish. I hope it didn't wear you out."

"Nope. I needed it too, I think. Any time I can yank Doug's chain about being old is a good time."

"Be nice. He's getting touchy about it."

I knew that and I couldn't blame him. I had obsessed over the idea that I might not have many years beyond fifty, and he was wrestling with the reality that retirement for him could be just around the corner. Neither one of us had ever planned on getting that old, and we were unprepared for the unpleasant shock of it.

I sat on the edge of the bed and watched as her clothes came off. She had no idea what she was doing to me; this was simply what she did, changing out of nice clothing into something comfortable. I was sure she intended to get into shorts and a t-shirt, after which she would pick up a book to read or she'd flip the TV on.

When her bra came off I sucked in an audible breath and she turned, concern flooding her face.

"I'm fine," I said before she could ask.

"Sudden headache?"

Normally I would tease, or she would, and the euphemisms would be flying. But she looked worried, and I was filled with enough sense of want that I decided to cut through the usual preliminaries and answered, "Sudden erection."

Caught off guard, all she managed was a quiet, "Oh."

"I'm fine," I stressed. "I'm not too tired, my head will not explode, and I want you. And truthfully, if you say no I won't be upset but I'll damn well lock myself in the bathroom and take care if it myself."

The smile I was hoping for tugged at the corners of her mouth. "Well, there's one I haven't heard before."

"You can call Doug and ask. He says I'm fine and this isn't a problem."

She stood there, mostly naked and with her hands on her hips, and regarded me with a pretended coolness. "Well, *we* have a problem, mister."

"An insurmountable problem?"

She stepped closer, and gestured for me to get up. "The problem as I see it," she said once I was standing in front of her, "is that I'm not really wearing anything and you are."

I pulled my shirt off and realized she was already working on getting my belt off, and when I was down to just underwear she took a step back and said, "There. That makes us fairly equal."

"I don't have to be equal." I stripped the boxer briefs off and tossed them aside. "You win. Name your prize."

"Just get me where I want to go, Irish. And you'll have to lead the way, because I really don't want to hurt you."

"Just kiss me gently," I said. "You can abuse me all you want from the neck down."

She wrapped a hand around me, squeezing gently. "I'm not sure you can take much abuse. In fact, I'm pretty sure that with a well placed tongue this could be over for you in less than a minute."

"Then I ask that you avoid licking anything you might set off prematurely. In fact, avoid touching anything. If you want me to take the lead…just let me roam."

"Are we actually negotiating how we make love?"

"Tonight, we are. You've taken care of me for over two weeks; you've fed me and bathed me and given me long back rubs…let me take care of you. At least this way you won't worry about bumping my face or kissing me too hard. Lie back and just let me. You can tell me what you want me to do, but just let me."

She stretched up on her toes and kissed me very gently. "I can hardly say no to that. But…"

"What?"

"This ends with you inside me, Irish. If you feel like you're getting to that point before I do—"

"I'll let you know."

She flopped down on the bed and held her arms out to me. "And kiss me if you can. You have no idea how badly I've wanted a long, deep kiss from you lately."

I had an idea because she wasn't alone in that want, and decided I didn't care how much it hurt; she was getting what she wanted.

~

Kevin

Forty five minutes after Mom and Dad came home we headed upstairs; forty seven minutes after they came home we were back on the sofa in the living room with the television turned on and the baby monitor on the end table.

"I did not," I grumbled, "need to hear that."

"Come on. You don't know exactly what you were hearing. Well, other than an apparently religious experience."

"Sure, that's it. My mother was just in the middle of one hell of a prayer and was working overtime to get God's attention."

"There you go. A perfectly reasonable explanation."

"You know, I'll accept that just to get the truth out of my head."

I was flipping through channels, looking for anything halfway decent to kill half a hour; I thought it would be about that long before we could safely go upstairs and not have to hear a repeat of one parent or the other in mid-orgasm.

Lydia set her hand on my thigh and leaned back into the sofa cushions. "Please tell me we'll be like them when we've been married as long as they have."

"I would hope we'd be a little more discreet with kids in the house."

"I mean the affection, Rabbit. When Michael is twenty three I don't want it to be a shock for him to see me grab you and kiss you. If my mother did that…I'm sure my parents still get it on, but I'd never know from any evidence they've graced me with."

"Your parents are affectionate. They're just not grabby."

"I have never seen my father kiss my mother. I don't want that for us. Or for Michael."

"I will always be affectionate," I promised her.

I didn't want our kids growing up wondering if their parents loved or merely tolerated each other. The fact that we stayed together wouldn't be enough; they'd want proof.

"You are," my dad reminded me out by the pool, when I was so mortified I wanted to shove him in and hold him under, "Michael's only example of married love. If you're squeamish about it...kids sense it, son. Half your problem is that right when you hit the age where you would start to understand what Mom's and my affections meant, we weren't speaking to each other. You learned too much from watching Paul, and you didn't like what you saw."

"I didn't like what I heard, either," I admitted. "Paul...he was a pig when he was fourteen and fifteen."

"And he told you everything he was doing," Dad guessed.

He had; I was twelve and didn't need to hear any of it.

The front door creaked open and then closed quietly, the lock turned with deliberate care. Paul shuffled in, surprised to find us there in the living room in the middle of the night.

"Obnoxiously loud parental units," I explained. "You're home late. Party at the restaurant?"

"Date," he sighed, slumping into the overstuffed chair near the fireplace.

That got my attention. "First date gone wrong?"

Before he could answer, Dad walked in, headed for the kitchen. He was wearing nothing but flimsy blue nylon shorts, and Lydia leaned over to kiss me, whispering "I'm going upstairs, Rabbit. You might not want to hear your parents going at it; I don't want to sit here with your Dad pretty much naked."

"I'll be up in a little while," I told her.

Dad came back from the kitchen with a bottle of water and he dropped onto the couch next to me. "So. Just a date, Paul?"

"Apparently so."

"Wait, was this a first date or not, and what the hell would you expect of a first date?" I asked.

"Not a first date," he replied thickly. "And I suspect I'll be buying Katie that minivan."

"You're buying Kate a minivan," Dad pondered. "Can't Katie buy her own minivan?"

"They have a pseudo-bet," I said. "And Katie cheated anyway."

He waited for an explanation.

"My wonderful siblings were picking on me about my lack of a social life," Paul said. "Long story short, I bet Katie that I would have sex before she had a baby. *Then* she tells me she's three months along. I figured I had a year, year and a half. So I'm buying a minivan."

"If you have sex just to win a bet, I'll personally cut your pecker off." He stopped for a moment to think about it and then asked, "What do you get if you win?"

"Sex!"

"But not tonight," Dad chuckled, getting up.

"Not for a long time, if I intend to try to have a relationship with her."

Dad stopped at the doorway. "Don't use her, Paul. If those are her terms and you're determined to win that bet, walk away."

Paul leaned his head over the back of the chair and looked at Dad. "I don't care about a stupid bet. I do care about her. I can suffer the disappointment."

"Good."

"It would have been kind of awkward to whip out fruit flavored condoms anyway."

"Heh."

"Spill it," I said when Dad was out of the room. "I'm glad you're seeing someone because Nicole was right and Sam's not an option...but how long have you been seeing her, and is it serious?"

"It's definitely serious, but damn, until tonight I had no idea that she's someone who will definitely hold out for some kind of commitment before anything will happen. She made that crystal clear."

"Is that a deal breaker?" I asked. "Are you looking for sex or looking for Ms. Right?"

He was conflicted. He cared about the girl, he really liked her, but he *really* hoped for something more. "If I can harness my inner horny teenager...it'll go somewhere. But damn that teenager is dying to be cut loose right now."

"To quote Dad, 'God gave you two good hands. Go use one of 'em.'"

"That got old a long time ago, Kevin. And it's not just sex that I want. If that was it I could get laid tomorrow."

"But you're not looking for a wife."

He paused for a beat, considering. "I think I am, but right now what I want is someone I can trust. Face it, all of my so-called experience was as a teenager. A young teenager."

"Come on. You and Monica had sex."

"We did, but I know it wasn't great sex and I'm not sure it was even good sex. We never let ourselves get much past that back seat groping kind of thing. When we could have, we were so pissed at each other that we weren't talking and when we weren't talking we were cheating on each other. And when I was cheating…I didn't give a fuck who I was with or if it was any good. I was in it for myself."

That he was in it for himself didn't surprise me.

"I'm not proud of it, but there it is. I need someone I can trust, because honestly, I suspect I suck at sex and whoever she is, she's going to have to be very patient for a while."

"Then whoever this girl is, *you* should be patient and wait. If you can see her as part of your future…she'll understand."

"Hell, she probably knows more about my miserable marital failures than I do. Surely Monica confided in her."

"Awesome. You finally sucked it up and asked Sherry out."

"It's more like we fell into it. I don't know, Squirt, a year ago the idea felt wrong, like I was cheating on Monica again just by considering even being friends with another woman. Sometimes it still does."

"But you're lonely, and you want a girlfriend."

"I want sex, Kevin. Again, I'm not proud…"

"Shit, you are conflicted. If you just want sex, call one of your old hookups. If you want someone you can trust, be patient."

"I resent that I'm even mildly disappointed that tonight didn't go the way I thought it would."

"If you want someone who can sympathize, talk to Lydia. You know how long she had to wait for me to come around."

He knew, and he'd given me ten tons of crap for it.

"I'd rather not admit my depravity to your wife. In fact, I don't even want to talk to Dad about it again, and if Nick was here… no way in hell."

"You're allowed to be horny beyond belief and want to do something about it, and still be determined to respect the girl whose bones you really do want to jump."

"Yeah, but Nick would tell me to push the point because God knows no one should suffer the way he did when Katie was giving him the cold shoulder, and Dad would lecture. I don't need to hear about how badly I fucked up and that they don't want another grandchild under those particular circumstances."

"He wouldn't."

"He already did. It wasn't a lecture but it was a pointed reminder. 'I love my granddaughter, *but...*' Like I didn't learn that lesson the hard way."

"You got Nicole out of it. It was worth it, wasn't it?"

"It was."

"I hear a 'but' in there."

"But." He carefully weighed his words, as if he was saying them in his head to make sure they didn't sound horrific on the way out. "I know I've said before that marrying Monica was the right thing to do and that I was glad I did. It kept us from walking away more than once. And I did love her. Do love her. But."

"Giant but, it sounds like."

"If I could go back, knowing what I know now, feeling what I feel..." He sucked in a deep breath. "I'm almost ashamed to admit it, but I think I would have fought her for custody and raised Nicole on my own. I wouldn't have married her."

"You wouldn't have cut her out of Nicole's life."

"No, that's not what I meant. Look, I know I would have gotten custody. It's bitchy to say so, but money goes a long way and I would have won. I had Mom and Dad on my side and she had an abusive father and spineless mother on hers. Nicole would have always been safer with me. And the truth is that if I hadn't married Monica, she might be alive now."

"Paul."

"I've thought about it backwards and forwards. If we hadn't been so busy hurting each other, and if she hadn't been determined to suffer the agony of that last, incredibly painful affair she had... I honestly think we would have grown up better if we'd been apart, and she would have been with someone who made her happy. Someone who would have been there to see the pain that was starting. At the very least she would have realized it was physical pain and not a broken heart."

He swallowed hard. "She really thought it was a broken heart,

Kevin. She thought it was pain she deserved so she sucked it up and didn't say anything to anyone. And dammit I know it's selfish, but if we hadn't gotten married I would have had the chance to grow up without a wife, and I might be with the right woman now."

"Or," I said, "Monica might have died an ugly and lonely death and you'd still be alone. Or you never would have gotten out of that sex-with-anything-that-moves rut."

"I doubt it. I really doubt it."

"Did you know," I said carefully, "that Mom and Dad have actually talked about what would have happened if they hadn't separated when they did? They think that if Dad had been around, you wouldn't have been jumping girls like a horny bunny, and never would have gotten Monica pregnant."

"That may very well be."

"And as painful as that was for them, they'd do it again if it meant having Nicole. They would suffer everything again, even the pain of losing the daughter-in-law that they truly loved, if it meant Nicole."

"I admitted it was selfish," he groaned, throwing his head back. "But it is what it is. I wouldn't change having my daughter; I would just change marrying her mother. And I know that sucks. I know how it sounds. And you have to believe me, I loved Monica."

"I know you did. I know you still miss her."

"Would you change anything, Kev? If you could go back, would you?"

"Yes, but not what you think."

"You'd still go to the seminary?"

"I needed to be there."

"You were freaking raped there."

"I know. But if it's a choice of none or all, I'll take all. The importance of those three years was not wiped out by one horrible night."

He lifted his head. "Then what would you change?"

"I would ask Lydia to wait for me."

"And if she said no, even knowing you'd eventually wind up together?"

"Then I would have risked a Nicole of my own. And that makes me as selfish as you."

"So we're selfish. I suspect that won't surprise anyone. At least you're in a good place now, Kevin. You've got the right woman, the kid, and at least one hickey a week. I can't imagine it being any better than that."

"It is good."

"Now I'm hearing a but."

"Everyone has their problems, Paul. You have regrets, I have hang-ups. Life goes on."

"Yeah, but at least in your life, there's sex."

"Okay, so I have hang-ups, where you're just hung up. And I think you're mixed up."

He sighed hard. "Fine. Straighten me out."

"I don't think it's necessarily sex that you want. If it was, you really would just hook up with someone, even if you are worried that you suck at it. That never stopped you before."

"I freely admit that I want a relationship," he allowed.

"You want *it*, Paulie. And I'm not sure you can articulate what it is, if your marriage really was what you say it was."

"It was mostly a black hole of suckage."

"You know, I'm not kidding when I say I have some hang-ups. I have some odd ones. Yet even with those my sex life is great."

"Well, thanks for rubbing it in."

"That's not my point. And I'm not bragging. The sex is great, Paul, but it's what comes after that's better. You know how connected Mom and Dad are? It's not because she has the libido of a seventeen year old boy."

"I'm sure that helps."

"All right, point taken. But it's after that. When you're done and you're sweaty and tired but you don't want to *be* done. Everything's quiet and it's just the two of you…"

I stopped, suddenly feeling like the dork of the month, but Paul leaned forward, listening.

"It's not the sex. It's everything that happens after. The laughing. The whispering in the dark. It's that you've totally exposed yourself to this person and been about as vulnerable as you can be…and she still wants to be there. You open yourself up until you're raw and bleeding, and she doesn't make you feel stupid for being too drippy."

He didn't look away. There was no smart ass remark poised just so on his tongue, no teasing about embracing my inner fourteen year old female; he didn't look away and his eyes went red with the strain of trying to not cry.

"The only time I've even come close to that was just before Monica died. And it only happened because she was saying goodbye. We were never like that. We just did it and I either went to sleep or got up and went out for a beer."

"But isn't that what you really want?"

"I am afraid," he said deliberately, "to want something more than what I had."

"You're afraid you won't get it."

"Probably."

"If your cell phone rang right now and it was Sherry, and she said you could go right back over there and get laid tonight *or* wait a year and have a long relationship, what would your gut reaction be?"

"You know I would wait, Kevin."

"You'd wait because it's Sherry, or because you just want a relationship with someone?"

"Because it's—" His eyes fluttered closed for just a moment, and he almost smiled. "I want *her*, Kevin. More than anything."

"So tonight wasn't just a date."

"No. It wasn't."

"So tell her everything you told me. And that you'll wait as long as she needs you to, because you're in it for the long haul. You are in it for the long haul, aren't you?"

"As long as I don't blow it with massive coital ineptitude."

"She'll forgive that if you're willing to try harder. Trust me on that."

"Didn't you just say your sex life was awesome?"

"I also said I had hang-ups. We're working through them. The beauty of that is we probably have the next fifty years to fix me."

He snorted out a laugh and got out of the chair. "Squirt, I think I'm gonna go call her, and apologize for leaving the way I did. She probably thinks I'm an ass."

"Well…"

"Go work on a hang-up or two."

"Not gonna happen tonight. I'm not opposed to going upstairs and just stretching out on the bed and talking to her. You should try that sometime, just spend a few hours knowing there's no way in hell you're getting laid, so you might as well just talk."

"What do you think I've been doing?"

I got up and followed him up the stairs. "I think you've been trying to figure out when it would be acceptable to cop a feel. Stop thinking with your dick and start using your brain."

"I've been told they're one and the same."

"That was years ago. You're a big boy now, Paul."

"Whoopee. That doesn't make me feel any better. I just realized, I'm the only adult in this house who's not getting any."

"Sucks to be you," I said, opening the bedroom door.

I'm pretty sure he flipped me off.

~

"The only thing coming from your parents' room now is talking," Lydia assured me. "Your poor little ears are safe until they catch their second wind."

"They're old. Surely they'll fall asleep before then."

"You stayed downstairs a long time. Was Paul that interesting or did you really want to avoid hearing your parents again?"

"He needed someone to talk to."

I gave her the condensed version; Paul was a horny boy with a girlfriend who was holding out for, if not the ring, at least the assurance that he had that in his future plans. I didn't share his doubts about whether or not he was any good at it, just that he really wanted it. And I suspected that part of what was holding her back was knowing far more about his marriage than he would ideally like her to; he was a serial cheater and she had no guarantee he wouldn't fall back into old habits.

"Paul's not the same person he was even a year ago," she said. "Surely she can see that."

"I'm sure she can, but why risk it? She doesn't want to be used, Lydia. He can hardly blame her for that."

"It's almost a shame Debby is so into Topher. You could have hooked them up for a night or two."

"That was mean," I said lightly.

"You know she would have."

I did know she would have. If not for Topher, Debby would not have had a problem with the idea that Paul would be interested in only sex. And she probably could have taught him a thing or two.

"How much longer until Topher wears her down?" I asked.

"Unless she finds a better job I don't think he will. She's determined to match him paycheck for paycheck."

"Stupid."

"She's not going to listen to me, Rabbit. She'll listen to you."

I really didn't think that was a conversation I should have with Debby. I avoided being alone with her; not because I was worried she might make a move that would piss me off and break Topher's heart, but mostly because I didn't want him worrying about it.

"So we'll corner her together," Lydia said.

"Why are you so interested in whether or not they get married?"

"Because I really do think she's right for him. And because I care about Topher. Don't be threatened by that."

"I'm not. He knows how badly I could hurt him with just a whim and an index finger."

"You know," she said as she slid her leg over mine, trying to get closer, "he's actually interested in learning some self defense from you. Debby says it's a mix of wanting to be a little badass and wanting to get into shape."

"He can take classes. He'd be Sam's student, though, not mine."

"What about Brandon? He actually showed up while you were off."

"Only because Sam warned him that if he didn't he was fired. Give him a few more weeks, he'll be back to his old lazy ways and he'll call late one afternoon because his dog died for the fifteenth time."

"Are you still seriously considering the second school?"

"I've pretty much decided. You are going to move there with me, right? I'm not going to lose my office manager."

"Whither thou goest," she laughed. "But if you're going to open another school, you could solve Debby's dilemma."

"She's not moving with me."

"Hire her, Rabbit. Sam will need someone to run the front. You can pay her more than the minimum wage she gets right now."

"You don't think the hours will bother her? Topher works days and she'd be working until nearly nine o'clock."

"I think if it got her what she really wants, which is Topher, she'd suck it up. And it might only be temporary, until she realizes that a paycheck doesn't mean equality."

"Who'd have ever thought you'd want me to give Debby a job."

"Who'd have ever thought I'd want her anywhere near my life? Or that you and Topher would wind up being best friends?"

There were a lot of things in my life I never thought would happen, and one of them rolled over and slammed his head into the side of the crib.

"I'll get him," I said as I slid out of bed. "We need to have a little talk about practicing that rolling over thing so this stops happening."

"This coming from the man who doesn't want his own father to talk to him about things that happen in bed," she teased.

"Don't mock me, woman," I said when I was the door. "You benefitted from my extreme embarrassment."

"Now if only you'd let me return the favor."

"If only you didn't have cramps."

She shrugged lightly. "So take care of our son and come back. I never said I wouldn't do things to you tonight, just that I had no desire to have things done to me."

I walked the floor with my son until he stopped crying, and then stood there by his crib, rubbing his belly until he fell asleep.

"You will not have my hang-ups," I whispered to him. "I will not make you feel weird or awkward about the things you might want. Remind me when you hit puberty...I promised to be a good example to you. If Mommy and I are all you got, kiddo, I'm going to make it shine for you."

18

Kevin

"Ninety per cent," Builder Guy said. "Kitchen cabinets and appliances go in this week, and the flooring will be done next week. Your pool is ready to fill."

Dad and I stood in the middle of the court, watching as construction crews streamed in and out of the houses. From the outside they looked ready; landscaping was in place, they'd been painted, and the playground was already up at the foot of the street. The tall wrought iron gate was partially constructed at the head of the court.

"We could close in three weeks," Dad guessed.

It was mid-July and the builder had until the end of August to meet the incentive-laden deadline. We'd probably all be moved in long before then.

Builder Guy was more optimistic. "Two weeks. You'll be in by the end of this month, I guarantee it."

Dad turned to me and said, "I'd better hire a moving company then. And you'd better start shopping. I'm assuming you'll want a place to sit once you have the house."

"I can't just walk off with some of your stuff? Like the living room TV?"

"He's cheap," Dad told Builder Guy.

We were there because Dad wanted to inspect construction progress and I tagged along for the hell of it. I hadn't seen the model home that Mom had liked so much and I was curious; once inside I was blown away by how different it was from the house I'd grown up in.

"We didn't need anything that big," Dad said. "Hell, we don't need anything this big, but I still harbor hopes that your grandparents will buckle one day and move in."

"Never gonna happen."

"If it was me, I'd move in with you," he said, almost a threat.

The thing was, I was certain he would. If Mom died first, Dad would fold up and wouldn't fight me if I tried to haul his ass next door and set him up in a spare bedroom. Presuming I won, anyway. There would be a family squabble: who gets Dad? We'd all fight for him. Chances are we'd wind up taking turns, making him hate us in the process.

If Dad died first? She would stand on the front porch with a whip in hand to keep us all at bay.

Their house had mirror master suites. Giant mirror master suites. There was a gas fireplace on one wall, and a huge flat screen high definition TV bolted to another wall. The walk in closet was bigger than the bedroom Lydia and I were currently in, and the bathroom was designed to accommodate their horny aquatics. They had a sunken bathtub big enough for four people, and with some leverage you could get five into the separate shower. The dual vanity countertop was glossy black granite, the cabinetry a deep red mahogany.

"It's what she wanted," Dad said simply. "I thought she'd go for something a little lighter and more girly. She likes wood."

"You can swim in your freaking bathtub."

"It's an option."

All the little touches, I realized as I wandered through the rest of the house, those were for her. She'd spent nearly their entire marriage in the house Dad had lived in for all but six or seven years of his life and it was her turn. She wanted light hardwood floors, she got them. She wanted deep red stone counter tops in the kitchen and professional grade stainless steel appliances, she got them. He didn't care where he lived, only that she finally got what she'd probably wanted all along—a really nice house, but one that didn't scream *I only married him for his money*.

The house Dad inherited screamed *Envy my wallet, suckers*.

It didn't quite mesh with Mom's innate middle class sensibilities.

We took a cursory look at everyone else's new homes and then headed for mine. We headed for the master suite and once I was satisfied that the colors were what Lydia had picked out, the closet big enough to house all her future shoes, and –score– the bathtub was nearly as big as Dad's, we moved onto Michael's room.

"Sure you want him right next to your room?" Dad asked.

"It's the nursery. We'll move him when the next kid rolls around."

"So I'm definitely getting more grandkids out of you."

"She wants three. As long as one of them is a girl, I'm fine with that."

"And if you don't get your little girl?"

"I think I'll be disappointed. I really want a daughter."

"What if you have three kids and Lydia decides she wants another one?"

"Then I suppose we're having another one. I don't want to field a whole baseball team but if she wants four or five I can handle that. I just don't want them as close together as you did."

"Having you kids so close is probably why you get along so well."

"Didn't you tell me before not to pile them one on top of the other? And having us so close is probably why Mom nearly died when Eileen and I were born."

"That wasn't just because we had four kids in four years, Kevin. She was pre-eclamptic and under a hell of a lot of stress that year."

"Still…we'd like about a year and a half between them."

He just wanted grandkids, and he wanted them to all be born while he was alive and still able to play with them.

After we left the court we headed for the construction site for the new Charybdis. Ground broke three weeks after his surgery with the goal of being able to open before New Year's Eve. It would have twice as much seating, but there would be fewer tables intended for only two people. The bar would be twice its current size; people weren't paying through the nose for fine dining, he said, but they were paying for alcohol. Menu prices would be slashed nearly in half with the hopes of making up the difference in volume.

It would look high end, but that was it.

He got copies of the plans from the construction trailer, and we headed for the Charybdis, where he spread them out over a bar table.

He'd included everything about the restaurant that made it popular: the bar, the dance floor, and the stage for live music. Paul's office would be twice as big, and in this version of the restaurant there would be an actual employee break room instead of a table crammed into one back corner, away from customers.

"Why so much space for Paul's office? He needs a desk, filing cabinets, and a computer."

"For the same reason your office is twice the size you probably need."

"Paul doesn't need crib space."

"Not yet, but hopefully someday. And in the meantime, he has room for the sofa. For emergencies."

"Is that what you told Mom about the custom furniture when it was your office? You needed it for an emergency?"

He shrugged. "I wasn't always married to your mother. And I wasn't always a nice guy. I'm sure once or twice I thought it was an emergency."

"I really don't want to think about you doing someone else, Dad."

"I haven't since it mattered, kiddo."

"She'd burn the sofa if she knew."

"She knows."

He had a beer in hand and was staring at the blueprints, but I don't think he was seeing them anymore. "When did it start to matter?" I asked.

A near whisper. "The moment I laid eyes on her."

"So what, the night before you met her you had some poor girl pinned to that monster sofa in your office and the next day Mom bats those blue eyes at you and you're some kind of angel?"

"No. But from the minute I met her…no one else, Kevin."

I admit it; I was curious. He'd alluded a few times to a pre-Mom past that he wasn't proud of, but I never had the details. I wasn't even entitled to the details, but that didn't keep me from wondering if there was anything Mom wrestled with when it came to knowing what he'd done before they got married.

The difference between us was that she hadn't known Dad for most of her life and hadn't loved him longer than she knew what love was. She could accept his past because she wasn't a part of it. I had a hard time accepting Lydia's because I'd been there and wanted it to be me.

"Did Mom have any wayward boyfriends to apologize for?"

"To apologize for? No." He sighed and looked up from the plans. "We were both engaged to other people before we met. Hers ended badly and mine…"

"Changed her mind?"

"Let's just say it was my fault."

"I totally can't picture Mom hanging off anyone else like she—"

"She didn't. If that boy had laid a finger on her your Grandfather would have mowed him down in the middle of the street with his station wagon. Double standards were the norm. I could screw around all I wanted and no one blinked."

"Cripes, how many girlfriends did you have?"

"Actual girlfriends? None."

"None. What about the girl you were going to marry?"

"That's complicated. I was not in love with her. I'm not even sure I liked her."

"Well. At least we know where Paul got it from."

"Paul has nothing on me, Kevin."

"Jesus, Dad, Paul probably slept with twenty different girls in high school and ten more when he was married."

"Hm. Yeah."

"Are you serious?"

"You don't want to know."

"Maybe I don't, but I kinda do." I gestured to Will to bring Dad another beer. "I dated at least forty different girls in high school. Not that I did anything with them, but there you go. If I'd been Paul—"

"You would still have a long way to go to catch up to me."

"You slept with more than fifty girls. Women. Whatever."

I could see it poised on his tongue: *lie to the boy*. Make something up; absolutely don't tell him the truth.

He slugged back what was left of his beer and then sighed, "Your mother guessed four."

"Four what? Four hundred? Are you freaking kidding me?"

He looked up at Will when he brought the next beer, but never looked anywhere near where I was.

"It was more?"

"Haven't you ever wondered why I tried to hammer into you how well you should treat the women you're with? Why I told you to consider how you'd feel if one of your friends was doing to your sister what you were thinking of doing to your date?"

"I assumed it was to keep us from hurting anyone."

He sipped at the beer, taking time to consider what he was going to say. "I hurt a lot of people, Kevin. I was thirteen the first time I had sex, and I was such a jaded little bastard that I didn't care what the girl I was with thought of herself afterwards. I jumped from one girl to the next and I probably never slept with any of them more than twice. You figure two or three different girls a week from thirteen until I met your mother, and you have a really messed up person."

I did the mental math and damn near spit out my soda. "Jesus Freaking Christ, Dad. That's somewhere around a thousand different women."

"I told you that you didn't want to know. I don't think it was quite that many, though."

"I'm not sure if I'm impressed or horrified."

"Be horrified. I am."

"Yet one of them tripped you up enough to want to marry her."

"One of them was convenient and I was at a point with the agency where I needed to expand my cover. Being engaged to her didn't mean I was giving up anything or anyone else. Marrying her wouldn't have changed that, either."

"Yet you changed for Mom."

"I had started to change before I met her. It was a clusterfuck of unbelievable proportion. I broke that poor girl so badly…"

His soul clenched; I could feel it from across the table and decided it was a good time to shift gears. "What about Mom's fiancé? She was only nineteen when you met her. How serious could it have been?"

"It wasn't. They dated in high school and I guess thought it was the next logical step. He proposed, she said yes, but when she wouldn't put out, he bailed."

"Jerk."

"I was that kind of jerk, Kevin. And I never wanted you to treat a girl that way."

"I didn't. I was honest with the girls I dated. They knew which direction I was headed."

"Good." He rolled up the blueprints, no longer interested. "Look, I know I'm an intrusive and a nosy son of a bitch and I don't have a right to stick my nose in the things that I do. And I never mean to actually embarrass you."

"I know that."

"But I do. And I did. I'm sorry for that, I really am."

"It wasn't wasted information, Dad."

"Maybe after hearing all this you'll understand better why I'm so willing to bulldoze my way into your personal matters. You're a better man than I ever was, but because of it you may not learn some of the harder lessons I did. And some of the more gentle ones."

"Mom taught you to be gentle."

"When I tried to point out to you the difference between what Lydia did with her old boyfriend and what she does with you...I knew a lot about sex and more than your mother will ever want to consider, but that's *all* I knew. I didn't have that light bulb moment until we—"

"I understood the difference when you said it."

"It's huge, Kevin. And if in that she wants to try something that doesn't involve another person, why not?"

"I'm working on that. You'd be proud of me."

"Would I now?" He let out a low chuckle, looking past me to where Paul was at the end of the bar with Sherry. "Would I be as proud of him?"

"I think so. He wants her in the worst way and he was just pissed at himself for having unrealistic expectations."

"So he wasn't upset with her?"

"I think he appreciates where she's coming from."

"And that would be?"

I looked over my shoulder at them. "She's riding in the slow lane. If he wants to speed up, he'll have to just pass her. He doesn't want to do that."

Just before I looked away, I saw Paul reach out to touch her hand. It was tentative, his fingers making contact in a way that suggested he was asking permission, but she didn't pull away, not until the front door opened and customers walked in.

Dad picked the blueprints up and asked me to wait while he took Paul into the office to show him the plans. He could have called Paul over to the table to show him the lines that would eventually become his place of future employment, but half of what he had to say to my brother had nothing to do with the restaurant. There was physical distance between Paul and Sherry, and he was going to pounce on it, steering Paul away and behind closed doors where he could grill him about the love life he may or may not have.

Sherry was showing an older couple to a table in the bar, and I watched her. I could see everything Paul was attracted to: the long black hair and eyes so dark he could stare into them for hours just trying to figure out what color they were; she was nearly his height and thin without being skinny, fit without being overly muscular. Even her polite smile, the one reserved for customers who were feeding her lines they thought were clever but in reality were stale, rehashed, and repeated to her every day, that smile was bright and one he would contort himself to see.

She smiled at me as she headed back for the front, but I reached out and touched her arm and said, "Take a break. It's not busy."

"It will be in about half an hour, Kevin."

"Come on. Sit down for a few minutes."

She slid into the booth where my dad had been, the expression on her face a mixture of curiosity and irritation. I'd never spent much time with her before; we talked here and there and knew enough about each other for a short conversation to not be awkward, but we weren't friends.

I was either going to make her my friend or my enemy, and she sensed that.

"Did he apologize to you?"

"For?" she prompted.

"For being a giant tool. He said he was going to call you…"

"He called me."

She wasn't giving anything up; this was none of my business and she was making sure I knew that.

If there was even a remote chance Paul would wind up with her, she needed to know that we were a nosy bunch and I wouldn't be the last person to put her on the spot.

"You know he's crazy about you."

"He certainly knows what he wants."

I heard disappointment in her voice instead of anger and wasn't sure what to make of it. "Whatever happened, however out of line he got—that's not all he wants. In fact, in the list of things he wants, that's probably ranked four or five."

"He told you?"

"He told me he made some pretty moronic assumptions and stupidly didn't make sure you knew that's not all he's after. He felt guilty and frustrated and probably didn't tell you how he feels about you."

She was practically willing the office door to open and for Paul or my dad to rescue her. I knew I was making her uncomfortable; I didn't really care.

"I'm not sure I want to talk to you about this, Kevin."

"I'm sure you don't. But the ugly truth is that I don't trust my brother to be able to say to you what he's admitted to me. I think he'll get so tangled up in trying to make sure that you hear him that he won't even listen to what you have to say. He's out of practice when it comes to communicating, and he wasn't very good at it to begin with."

"I know. I was there for the worst of it."

"You were there to see a couple of unhappy teenagers pick at each other because they didn't know how to be married. Paul is not that person anymore. He grew up."

"It's hard to forget having to be there for your best friend when she's broken in half."

I didn't doubt that, but I knew it was also revisionist history. "She cheated first. She was determined to prove that she didn't deserve happily ever after, and she flaunted it in his face. If she was broken in half, then half of that was her own doing. But he's not going to remind you of that because he's not going to betray Monica's memory. Yeah, he was a serial cheater, but if she had held up her end of the vows, he probably wouldn't have been."

A bare shrug of her shoulders.

"Come on, Sherry. He's falling in love with you. Either give him an honest chance or end it before his heart gets broken."

"I don't want to be his rebound."

"And he doesn't want to date thirty different women just to see if one sticks. He wants to date one woman, and he wants to date her with the idea that someday they might get married. That's his end game. Marriage, babies, everything. And he's wanted you for a long time, but until now it didn't seem appropriate."

"It's that whole wanting thing. What he wants right now he could get with anyone."

"He wants *you*. And if it means he'll have to be held at arms' length for the next year, then he'll wait."

"And then what? I give in, he gets bored?"

"Do you care about him?"

"God, Kevin."

"Simple question. All right, if you didn't know the ugly details about his marriage—"

"Dammit," she hissed. "This is none of your business. It's mine, and it's his."

"He's my brother, and even though he's a giant tool sometimes, I love him. I don't want him hurt."

"And you think I do? I don't want to be his rebound because I want to be *it*. I want to be the last woman he ever wants to be with. Don't you get that?"

I got it. "You're in love with him."

"He's falling, but I *fell*. I've loved him for years, and no, it was never appropriate and I'm not convinced that it is now." She was fighting tears, but she wouldn't look away from me, looking at me so hard I could feel the weight of her stare. "But you nosy son of a bitch, I love your brother and all I'm doing is trying to make sure that neither one of us gets hurt. But I do love him."

I heard him before she did and I looked up; he was just behind her, and Dad was behind him, looking a little sheepish and not especially apologetic for sneaking up on us.

"Clock out," Paul choked. "This just isn't going to wait until later."

She shot an evil look at me before she got up; we watched her leave the bar and head for the time clock at the back of the restaurant, but as soon as she was out of sight Paul turned to me and said, "Congrats. You're the hostess for the next hour and a half and your pay goes straight to her."

"You're welcome."

"Jesus, Kevin, I didn't ask you to talk to her."

"But I did, and now you know that she loves you. And before you wander off to have this huge talk, you need to know. She doesn't want to be the mistake you make after realizing your wife has been gone long enough that it's all right to start seeing other women. She wants you to mean it, Paul."

She waited by the host stand for him, and as they headed out the door Dad said, "Later on he's either going to hug the crap out of you, or he's going to kill you."

"Like you weren't talking to him about the same thing in there."

"Yes, but I was talking to *him*, not the woman he's yearning for."

"I doubted he was going to without tying his own tongue in knots."

"Yeah, well…now you're stuck working here and I don't have a ride home."

"So I guess you're stuck here, too. You can pretend to be the manager for a while."

He looked out into the dining room. "I can do that. Who can I pick on? Who's newest?"

"Why don't you try getting to know them instead of trying to scare them? You can start with James. He's hiding from you at the other end of the bar."

He looked down to where James was and then back at me, and groaned. "When did you turn into such a dad? You're no fun at all anymore, Kevin, no fun at all."

~

Paul

The splash when I shoved Kevin into the pool was not half as satisfying as I had hoped for. I think I wanted to him to belly-flop; I wanted to hear the sting that would wrap around him as he sank to the bottom of the pool, I wanted to see him sputter for air when he finally kicked his way to the surface.

Instead, he went into the water neatly and bounced back up as if he'd jumped in himself, and he only looked mildly confused.

"Oh shit, Paul. I thought you were Lydia."

His wife was pacing the living room with a crying baby while he was outside staring into the swimming pool with Dad.

"Sorry to disappoint you."

"Sorry to be disappointed."

He was in a good mood; I wasn't going to be able to crack that with one shove into the deep end.

I wasn't angry, exactly; I was annoyed that he'd taken it upon himself to talk to Sherry, and I was irritated because he'd been able to tell her what I couldn't manage to get out of my mouth the way I intended it.

Dad tossed a spackle blade and a tube of sealant to Kevin and said, "Since you're in there, you might as well dive down and see if it really is cracked."

"Can we thrown giant rocks on top of him?" I asked once he was under water.

"I take it things didn't go well?"

I wasn't sure how to answer that. We left the restaurant feeling their stares burning our backs, but once out in the parking lot I didn't know what to do. I didn't want to sit there in my ancient minivan trying to convince her that we had a future, not with so many reminders of my daughter cluttering her view; she was already wrestling with the idea that somehow my dead wife, her best friend, was hovering over us, ready to drop between us like an ethereal wall.

You just don't try to convince a woman that you want a future with her while surrounded by Barbie dolls and with a Britney Spears CD perpetually stuck in the stereo.

It was her idea to leave in separate cars; I followed her to her apartment complex and we left my minivan there and then headed for downtown Vacaville. There we could walk along the quaint store-fronts, a throwback to small towns everywhere, or we could take the path along Ulatis Creek.

Either way we went we had the privacy to talk; either way we went we might walk away crushed.

I had a mantra running through my head during the entire silent ride from the apartment complex to the park entrance. *She loves me, she says she loves me, she loves me...* I didn't know if that was enough to make up for everything she already knew about me, and I didn't know if it was enough to give me a chance to prove myself to her.

I didn't blame her for how she felt; when the insults were flying fast and furious, when Monica and I were practically shoving our infidelities in each other's faces, she stuck by her best friend. She defended Monica to me; she berated me every time she thought I was even considering sleeping with someone else. She was loyal to a fault and had no problem pointing out my massive stupidities.

And yet she told Kevin she had loved me for years; I would have guessed that she merely tolerated me as the person who had a legal right to reside in the same apartment as her friend.

She parked her small Hyundai near the park entrance and we got out of the car, our doors slamming shut simultaneously; I wasn't sure which way she wanted to go, so I waited by the side of the car. If she headed right, we were going downtown. If she headed toward me, we were walking along the creek, or perhaps in the park.

She came around the side of the car toward me, but before I could take a step in her direction she fell against me, burying her face between my head and my shoulder. She wasn't crying, but she made it clear she needed to be held. I stood there, back pressed into the searing heat of the car, with my arms around her, until she was ready to move.

And still, she didn't say anything.

She led and I followed. The stairway down to the creek was blocked off, so she headed into the park and for the paved path that wound around it. We walked without speaking for a long time, head-ing for the part of the park that was shaded with tall trees, both of us looking for some way to start.

I reached for her hand, hoping she wouldn't jerk it away.

I could apologize a dozen times for how I'd acted and it wouldn't be enough. There was no excuse for pushing past the first "Not now," until she had to snap "I said no, Paul, and if you don't back off, I swear, I'll push you off the balcony."

In that fraction of a moment, she meant it.

I was used to hearing no, no, no, and then yes. The total of my experience was facing that initial resistance and then getting my own way. Everything up to that moment had told me that with a little time, some persistence, and saying all the right things, I could get anyone's clothes off.

But not hers.

Not that way.

We'd been walking for nearly half an hour when she finally said, "You'll break my heart, Paul."

She had every reason to think that I would; before there was Monica there were all the girls in high school I had used and then shoved aside. If not for Nicole, there was a chance that somewhere along the line I would have set my sights on her, and hurt her terribly.

"I won't." Yet we both knew that even with best intentions, I couldn't promise that.

I'd probably started the first tiny crack, when, after being told to stop, I asked what the hell the problem was. And when she told me it would never get that far, not until we had some kind of commitment between us, I said that was fine. And then I left.

She had opened the door for this talk then, and I had slammed it in her face.

Why should she trust me?

"What did my brother say?"

I felt her fingers squeeze mine just a bit tighter, and just for a moment. "That doesn't matter. What is it you wanted to tell me?"

"That I'd give anything to take back what happened? That I wish I had stayed and made sure you understood that I don't just want you to be some stupid bedpost notch? That I have no intention of seeing anyone but you, for any reason?"

"You were mad as hell."

"Not at you. I was upset with myself for assuming anything and then falling back into old habits. I shouldn't have pushed for that much this soon."

"Then you don't want to sleep with me."

"Oh hell, yes, I do. But I've wanted that for nearly a year, and I'll wait that long again if I have to."

She fell quiet again and we kept on walking, through the thick of the trees, around the playground, and we were very nearly where we started from. I didn't know what else to say. If I'd known, I wasn't sure I'd know how to say it. We left the park and headed down Main Street, detouring into the Creekwalk Café for something to drink.

The table we were seated at looked over the park and the creek that wound its perimeter, and on the high creek bank was a splash of brightly colored mixed flowers, and I sat there wondering if someone planted those intentionally or just a stroke of luck.

"What Kevin said," she started, pulling me away from my gaze out the window, "was that he doubted you would be able tell me everything you'd already told him. And that you told him you're not interested in playing the field. You want to be with one person, and hope that you end up married again."

"He had the gist of it."

"I told him I don't want to be your rebound. And I don't, Paul. I don't want to be the woman you start dating just to see if you've grieved enough to move on."

"You're not."

"But how can you know?"

"I just know."

She was holding one of my hands in both of hers; my hand was open, knuckles on the table, and she was tracing lines across my palm with her fingers. "I feel like I'm dragging you into something you may not want."

She had to be kidding.

But she wasn't.

"Did you know that last year Kevin threatened to tell you that I wanted to jump your bones? In those exact terms. I had come out of that fog I was in and he realized who I was focusing on. If I'd needed a rebound relationship I would have started one then. But I didn't. I wanted to wait until I was sure there wasn't going to be any…weirdness…between us."

"A year ago we would have just been hooking up." Quietly. A realization.

"I made the commitment back then, Sherry. I don't want anyone else and I'm not going to. So I'll wait for however long it takes you to trust me."

She wrapped both hands around mine then. "Your brother—"

"My brother has a good heart and he means well. But you're going to have to get used to him and everyone else in my family because they're just as pushy and nosy as he is."

"You heard me tell him that I love you."

"I didn't mean to eavesdrop, I swear. We were coming back to the table…it was timing, that's all."

"That's not the way I wanted you to hear it for the first time. And if you say it back now, I won't believe you."

"If I tell you I'm almost there, will you believe that?"

She could accept that; I couldn't tell her I loved her, not just because she wouldn't believe it, but because I wasn't there yet. I could feel it just within my reach, right at my fingertips, and with a little more leverage, I would have it.

We resolved nothing, other than deciding we needed to breathe; she drove me back to my minivan and kissed me goodnight, and I went home and shoved my brother into the pool.

"I think," I answered Dad, watching Kevin's air bubbles pop on the water's surface, "that I still have a lot to learn about women, and I really wish I'd paid more attention to everything you were telling me when I was a kid."

"Then you didn't break up?"

"No, but I really have to learn where the lines are drawn."

Dad gestured to the water. "He drew his own lines. And look what he's got now."

Kevin resurfaced, gasping for air. "It was a freaking twig," he sputtered. "A long, skinny, freaking fake-crack twig."

Dad picked it up after Kevin tossed it onto the deck and said, "It looked a whole lot bigger when it was at the bottom of the pool. Funny how that happens, these little things that seem so big until you get a good look at them."

Kevin hauled himself out of the water and when he was on his feet, I shoved him back in.

"Big? She loves me and I don't want to screw it up."

"Slow down and you won't. If this is really the woman you want to spend the rest of your life with and the woman you want to be a mother for your daughter, then slow down and let it happen. It doesn't have to be complicated."

Kevin was treading water and sputtered, "If you shove me back in I'm pulling you with me."

"Fine, I won't," I promised.

He got out of the pool again and I stepped back, a sign of good faith. But then Dad shoved him and as Kevin hit the water he chuckled, "I never agreed to that."

~

Chip

If Paul was truly upset with Kevin, he let it go. At midnight I glanced out the bedroom window and they were sitting by the pool, bottles of Doug's home brew on the table between them. The only thing missing from that picture was Nick, and the odds were that he wouldn't make it home to share a beer or two with them before we moved.

Nick was missing everything; Katie was showing and she'd felt the baby move. She was buying the house without him and sold her compact car for something more practical. She was moving through all the important parts of their life alone and I could feel her resentment radiate in loud pulses of choked back tears and swallowed frustration.

I might see all of my sons sitting by my pool together again, but it would be somewhere new, and they probably wouldn't be talking about Nick's terrors of facing parenthood for the first time, or Paul falling in love and being afraid of screwing it up.

I'd left Paul standing by the pool laughing at his younger brother and went inside where I would be safe from retribution. Michael was wailing in the other room and Terry was on the phone, the glare in her eyes making me wonder if I might not be better off going back outside and letting Kevin have at me.

When she hung up, she stood there for a moment with her hand curled around the receiver, knuckles white with effort. I expected her to either throw it or break it, and I had the thought that if I wanted to duck for cover I'd better do it fast.

"They lost your pathology report," she finally seethed. "Doug called them today because it had been too long, and they lost the fucking report!"

"Who lost it? The lab or the neurosurgeon?"

"The lab. Supposedly they emailed a copy to the surgeon, but he never got it. When they went to send another one, they couldn't bring up the file. Your report and a dozen others were on a sector of a hard drive that corrupted. They may be able to retrieve it, they may not."

"So what, then? It's not like they left any of the tumor in my head for a do-over and I'm not sure I'd let them back in even if they had."

She softened a bit and put the phone down. "They kept tissue samples. You'll get a new report, but it could be another month unless they recover the data from the hard drive."

"Another month of potential treatment lost."

She nodded. "In the meantime Doug wants another MRI."

I'd expected that; Surfer Doc had mentioned post-op imaging so they could see how things looked a month or two out. Now they'd be looking for any signs of re-growth, anything that could scream out what the tumor was.

She was as angry as I'd ever seen her, as angry as she'd been the night she went down the hall and slammed the guest room door closed on the next two years of our marriage.

We could wait; it was aggravating but we'd been waiting.

She needed to smile.

"You said 'fucking'," I teased.

"Oh, very nice, you would pick up on that."

"You're not an f-bomb kind of girl."

"Tonight I damn well am."

"Having to wait isn't going to change the results, Ter. It'll only drive us nuts if we let it."

I tried to get her mind onto other things: deciding how we would move our furniture, do we sell this house or rent it, was she going with Katie to her next doctor's appointment to see the ultrasound, watching Michael being up on his hands and knees and trying to figure out the mechanics of crawling.

It was midnight and none of it had worked very well.

I thought about trying to distract her with sex, but then the idea that I risked being mauled by an angry horny woman hit me, and I wasn't sure she wouldn't inflict unintentional damage.

While I stood there and watched two of our sons in animated discussion she was changing clothes, a sure sign that I was better off not laying a hand on her unless she started something first. She flitted between the bathroom and the closet, chucking her shoes in the latter and brushing her teeth in the former; even the buzz of the sonic toothbrush sounded ticked off.

When she crawled into bed, though, she seemed to have lost a little of the fire and asked me quietly, "What are you looking at so intently?"

"Paul and Kevin." I slipped into the bed and propped myself up on pillows, hoping she would scoot across the mattress and put her head on my shoulder. "I suspect they're talking about Paul's blooming love life. Your second oldest is falling hard and fast, woman. I hope you like the girl because six months from now she's liable to be a part of this family."

That brought a gentle smile to her face, and she relaxed against me, one arm pulled tightly across my chest.

"I like her. I don't know her very well, but so far I like her."

"He's not allowed to blow it. If he does she'll probably quit and replacing her would be a bitch."

"It's nice that you have your priorities straight, Chip."

"It kills two birds with one stone. He gets the girl and we don't lose the hostess. I'd say I have excellent priorities."

"That's more like one bird with two stones. And kind of a gross way to put it."

"Not too gross, as long as you think in bird terms and not that we're chucking rocks at her head."

She lifted her head and looked at me. "All right, now you have the image in my head of poor Sherry running from you because you're trying to stone her to death. Let's leave that thought for if they ever break up."

Whatever worked.

She was no longer obsessing about my pathology report, and now wanted to talk about Paul and the girl he had his sights on.

~

Three days later I was sitting in Doug's office; he'd arranged another MRI for early morning—we didn't need him or Kris to hold our hands through that one—and wanted to see me afterwards to go over results from blood the endocrinologist had drawn a week earlier.

"I've got her notes," he assured me. "I won't screw you up too badly."

She was off for the next eight weeks but left Doug instructions on the care and medicating of Chip Davis. With or without the pathology report, we were pressing on.

"The DDAVP is a given," he said, looking at my file. "You'll be on that for the rest of your life. But what she wants to add..." He flipped through the pages, double checking. "A low dose of Synthroid, because your thyroid is sputtering and it's just a matter of time before you'd really need it anyway. Testosterone replacement, your choice of a cream or patch. And she recommends an insulin stress test."

"I'm becoming diabetic?"

"No. No, that's not what it's for."

"Put the damn file down and talk to me, Doug."

He glanced up, surprised, and then sheepishly tossed it onto his desk. "Sorry. I hate it when people do that to me, too. The insulin stress test is to see if your brain is producing any growth hormone now. You come in having fasted, we take baseline blood sugar levels, and then inject you with insulin to drive your blood sugar down. That stresses the brain, and when the brain is under stress it releases growth hormone. Over three hours we keep checking your blood sugar, and when it bottoms out we take a few tubes of blood, and then you get to eat sugary crap to drive your blood sugar back up. Another check of your blood sugar, and you can go home."

"That's an awful lot of jabbing me with needles."

"Tiny little finger sticks to get the blood sugar levels. You'll have two IVs for the rest."

"And I need to do this?"

"It's optional. But you complained about lean muscle loss and struggling in the gym; if you're not making any HGH on your own, this will prove it, and you can then go on a replacement."

"Sure, what's one more pill to swallow."

"Yeah, about that, Superman. It's a daily injection. Think you have the stomach for it?"

I wasn't sure about it but I nodded anyway. "And what about the testosterone?"

"Gel or patch. I'd recommend the latter because you don't want Terry routinely touching it."

"I can keep her away from a tube of gel."

"Typically applied to the scrotum."

"Oh. All right. The patch then."

"I thought so. You can place the patch on your arm or hip and it shouldn't be a problem if her hand grazes over it. But it should help with the sponginess she complained about."

"She wasn't complaining."

"Chip, it's just a phrase we use. 'Patient complains of testicular atrophy and spongy erection.' It just means you said that's what you had. Don't get so defensive."

"I'm not. But she wasn't complaining."

"Or maybe she was."

"I think she's happy as long as it works. And doesn't shrink."

"Lose much more of the testosterone and it might. And fair warning, if she does happen to come in contact with the patch regularly, it might increase her libido."

"If that happens I'm moving in with you."

Without thinking he said, "If that happens I'm going to borrow a patch and slap it on Kris's ass."

"Really now."

"Never mind," he sighed. "This is about you and your medical woes, which we are addressing. I'll write the prescriptions and we'll set you up for the stress test."

"Fine. Are we done then?"

"We're done."

"Awesome. So shove Doctor Stone up your ass and let Doug come out to play. If you need to talk…"

"I don't."

"All right. Then clock out or whatever it is doctors do and let's go get a beer."

~

Halfway into his third Long Island Tea, he put Dr. Stone back where he belonged and let Doug ooze out onto the table. We were in the booth farthest to the back of the bar, where I could keep an eye on anyone approaching; after my second beer I switched to iced tea and he never noticed. He slid right past the buzz into drunk off his ass, and when he did the floodgates opened.

"I warned you about menopause," he groused. "It's like someone clipped all the goddamn wires and then shoved sandpaper into her joints so that I'd have all this guilt over just wanting."

"Wanting what?"

"Anything! It was bad enough when all she had to deal with was some arthritis, but you pile on that whole post-menopausal insanity and you might as well cut your dick off and throw it away, 'cause you're not gonna need it anymore."

"Yeah, but where does the guilt come in?"

He sighed like I was stupid. Draw the slow kid a diagram, maybe he'll finally get it.

"She hurts," he said. "All over. All those years of running to hell and back and the combat training…she's got arthritis in just about every joint and dropping a hundred and sixty pounds of me on top? Just. Doesn't. Work. Then she whines about how much weight she's gained, like I should automatically shut down because she got fat. I don't care. She's still Kris. So yeah I feel guilty as hell about wanting sex once in a while."

"So where does the menopause fit into that?"

"Before that we…I mean, she tries, but still…"

"So slap a patch on her ass if it's that simple."

He glared at me over the rim of his glass.

"It's not that simple," I guessed.

"She's gotta want it, Chip. She knows she can medicate for the pain and then lose some weight to help it out, and find ways around the way things just fucking dry up with age. But it's too damned hard and I'm tired of feeling like I have to beg for it."

I had no idea what to say to him.

"You've got time. Terry's only what, forty eight? And I don't think she's even perimenopausal."

"Oddly, she was looking forward to menopause."

"She's looking forward to amenorrhea. She doesn't want the rest of what comes with it and for all your pathetic whining neither do you. Sometimes I fucking hate you when you complain."

"And yet you listened to my complaining and found a brain tumor."

"Shut up. I'm wallowing in my misery here. I don't want to feel smart."

"Fair enough. Let's just get you nice and stupid. Kris will appreciate it when I bring you home lit up like a Christmas tree."

"Fuck her."

"You'd like to, I'm sure."

"Do you know how many *years* it's been since she really wanted it, Chip? Since I didn't have to talk her into it or work so damned hard—?"

"Not a clue."

"With the exception of one sympathy blow job, a drunken blow job New Years Eve nineteen ninety nine, which I remember because I convinced her the world was going to end at midnight and she decided we needed to go out with a bang—she was *really* drunk—it was right around the time Spider and Eileen started dating."

Eileen was fourteen, almost fifteen, when she started dating Spider; now she was three weeks away from turning twenty four.

"Think of it this way, Chip. I was about your age. How would you feel if you had to practically beg or if Terry cut you off now?"

"I don't know. It would depend on why. I'd sure as hell try to talk to her about it."

"How? How the hell do you do that without being whiny and sounding selfish?"

"I suppose the same way I did after the twins were born and I thought she'd just forgotten about it."

"But *how*?"

"I told her I loved her and I missed her, and that we could start slowly, but I needed to be with her again."

I'd also gotten Doug and Kris to babysit for the weekend and had taken her to the beach where there were no small children thundering through the house to distract her. To her it started out as a couple of days to catch up on sleep; to me it was a mission to get laid.

We both came home happy.

I wasn't sure that would work for Doug.

"If I tell her I need it, she'll roll her eyes and tell me I don't *need* anything."

"Maybe she's just protecting herself, Doug. If she's in that much pain sex might be one of the most frightening things you can ask from her."

"Yeah. Maybe. Probably. I know it is. I am an ass and I know it."

"You're not an ass."

"I do miss her."

"No one can blame you for that."

He was well into his third drink and close to sliding under the table. When Will came over to ask if we wanted refills I told him Doug was cut off and if he asked for anything else to only bring him ice water.

"Would Terry still love you if you were impotent?" he wondered, slurring half the words.

"She would."

"She'd give up sex for you."

"Me being impotent wouldn't mean we'd give up sex. It would just limit our options."

"I just want—"

"I know what you want. And it's not what you think it is."

"How can I need something that hurts her?"

"Because you love her and can't imagine not wanting to be with her."

"If you could have all the sex you're having now knowing you only had a couple years with her, or never have sex again and know you'd have twenty, what would you take?"

"I'd take the twenty, Doug. And I'd resign myself to a lot of frustration and self abuse."

"Kris is sixty four. Do I have twenty left?"

"You just might. Hell, you might have thirty."

"If you promise me I have twenty years left with her I'll stop caring."

"All right." He wouldn't remember it in the morning, so why not? "I swear, you have at least twenty years left with her. And they'll be good ones, too."

"Fucking right."

"Ready to go home?"

"Nope."

"Ready to pass out?"

"Maybe."

"You're a lightweight, Doug."

"I almost hired a hooker, Chip. I almost did."

"But you didn't."

"Have you ever hired a hooker?"

"Now why would I need to do that?"

"Before Terry, you moron."

"I was engaged to one, Doug. You know that."

"That doesn't count. Did you *pay* for it? Ever?"

"Once or twice, when I was a teenager."

"Remember the redhead in Amsterdam? I think you were sixteen and already had two women hanging off you and you sent her my way."

I didn't remember, but I said I did anyway.

"I was twenty six. Twenty six. Twenty fricking six. And I'd never had sex before. I couldn't understand a damn word she said and it was a fucking disaster but she gave me another chance. By morning I almost knew what I was doing."

Then I remembered. We were in a hotel a good five miles from where we were supposed to be, with Kris and the rest of the team combing the streets for any sign of us. Doug was supposed to keep me out of trouble, but instead I pulled him right into it with me.

"You will never tell Terry about that," I warned him. "She already thinks I was a perverted little shit."

"You *were* a perverted little shit. I *still* don't know how you did two women at the same time. What the hell do you do with two women at the same time?"

"Jesus, Doug, just watch a little porn sometime."

He folded his arms on the table and rested his chin on them. "Sometimes I really miss all of that."

"I miss the people, not the work. And I really don't miss what a little shit I was then."

"But you were a fun little shit. My God, all those women…"

"I need to get you home. You're too close to passing out."

"Yeah. Maybe. I'm sorry about your brain, Chip. If you die I'm going to kick your ass."

"I'm not going to die. The tumor is gone."

"Unless it's not. But if it's not I swear I'll do everything possible to save your life."

"I know you will." I got out of the booth and helped him up, trying to hold him steady as we headed for the door.

"You're my little brother, you know that, right?"

"I know, Doug. That's why I wanted you to be my kids' uncle."

"And I'm a fucking awesome uncle!"

"You're also very, very drunk. Your wife is going kick me square in the nads."

"Well, good. Now I won't be the only one not getting any tonight."

~

Michael was up on his hands and knees, rocking back and forth, trying to work up the momentum to move. There was a bright pink stuffed rabbit ten feet in front of him and he wanted it but wasn't quite sure how to get to it. I wanted to egg him on; Terry made me sit on the sofa with her and just watch. We were not, she determined, going to get that baby to crawl without his parents there to see.

He'd finally started to make obvious sounds and there was no doubt as to his meaning. Lydia knew who he meant when he said "Baba" and he added "Mama" to his list soon after that. Terry had not yet been anointed but she didn't seem to mind. He almost always smiled when she looked at him, and that was good enough.

We were babysitting, she informed me when I got home after facing the Wrath of Kris, because Kevin had given Sam the night off and was teaching five classes back to back while Lydia trained Debby to take over the front desk. With their attention divided, they didn't think trying to keep an eye on him was their brightest idea, and Terry jumped at the chance to watch him before they could call Eileen.

I certainly didn't mind. Another month and he'd no longer be under our roof, and we'd miss out on those odd middle-of-the-nights when he'd wake up and we'd get to him before his parents. We wouldn't be waking up to the sound of him squealing happily in his swing in the next room, or even his cranky, disappointed crying when Lydia put him down for the nap he was fighting.

Kris had called her before I could get home, complaining about Doug's extreme state of inebriation; what the hell was I thinking?

We were at opposite ends of the sofa, feet bare and touching. "I was thinking," I told Terry, "that Doug needed to go out for a beer. I didn't think he'd hit the hard stuff but since I'm not his mother..."

"They had a fundraiser to go to, Chip."

"Was Doug speaking at it?"

"No, but—"

"Then it's not my problem. If going was that important to him, he should have said something and shouldn't have gotten drunk."

I was right and she knew it. I also wasn't going to tell her why Doug was getting drunk, though I suspected I'd hear about it later. He was unwound enough that I had a feeling Kris was going to get an earful, and once she did, Terry would.

Still, not my fault.

Michael gave up on the rabbit and flopped to the floor, rolling over to look up at us.

"It's pink," I said to him. "Probably a girl rabbit. If you don't go after her she'll never know that you're interested."

"She's a progressive rabbit, Grandpa. When he least expects it, she'll come to him."

"Probably after he's given up and is looking at some other hot little stuffed number."

She slid her bare foot up my leg and over my hip, hooking her toe into one of my belt loops. "So if I ignore you for a day or two you'll start checking out my competition?"

"You have no competition. Besides, I know you're interested."

"I might be, but one of us has to keep an eye on your grandson."

"You'll survive until he goes to bed. Where's my granddaughter? We could toss them both in the car and go for pizza or something."

"She's upstairs, but I already have chicken marinating."

"And that won't keep? Come on, how often do we have both the grandkids and none of their parents around telling us to not let them have junk?"

"You're using your grandkids, Chip."

"I'm tired of chicken, your majesty."

She unhooked her toe and shifted, leaning over to kiss me. "All right, that's fair. But we take them out for something reasonable, and if you behave, you can get dessert."

"Pizza is reasonable."

She snickered, kissing me again. "You're twelve years old, aren't you?"

"I had better erections when I was twelve. But I have a prescription for that now."

One more kiss, and she got up, heading for the stairs. "Then I guess we're going to the drugstore before we go for dinner. The sooner we get you on that, the better."

"Now see there, Michael?" I said, reaching for him. "She thinks I'm twelve but she's the one with raging hormones."

"Ba!"

"That's right. But we're not complaining, are we? We may never complain about that again."

~

"'Apply directly to the testicles, alternating left to right every twenty four hours, between eight p.m. and midnight,'" Terry read from the box.

"Holy hell no." I grabbed the box from her and started to read, but she was already laughing.

"It says to stick it to your lower back, abdomen, thigh, or upper arm. If it falls off before noon, apply a new one. If after noon, wait."

"You're mean, you know that?"

"But you love me anyway."

"That I do. Where do you want me to stick the patch?"

"Less hair on your lower back. And I'd be less likely to accidently pull it off."

I peeled the paper backing off the patch and slapped it into place.

"Did Doug say when you could expect results?"

"It's been five seconds, woman. Give it a day or two."

She tried to say she didn't mean right that minute, but we both know she did.

~

Two days later we were woken by the sound of the pocket door between our room and the nursery rattling, followed first by the sound of little hands and knees scraping across the carpet, and then by a frantic Kevin whispering harshly, "Sorry, sorry, sorry…"

He snatched his son up and zipped back into Michael's room; Terry and I both sat up and looked at each other.

"Was he crawling?" she asked sleepily.

"He was, indeed."

"Time to block off the stairs."

"Time to move."

19

Paul

Closing day was a flurry of hurry up and wait; Mom and Dad closed on their house first thing in the morning, and then Dad made himself available for the rest of us. He sat quietly at one end of the table in the title office, ready to jump in and explain in plain English anything we found confusing.

The only one who really needed him was Katie. She sat there, swollen and miserable, signing her name over and over, trying to choke back tears, only half listening to everything going on around her. I stayed with them—I promised Nick I'd look after her—but I was nothing more than an observer to her pain. I couldn't say anything that would make her feel better about doing this alone; I sat next to her while Dad explained every line she signed her name to, and mentally tried to will her into feeling better about this.

She wanted the house; she wanted to move and shook off a few notions of waiting until Nick was home before moving. He didn't care where home was, and after the impulse to wait hit she realized that when he did get back she didn't want to waste time she could be spending with him boxing up everything they owned and hauling it away.

Kevin, Spider, and I were going to pack for her and then move it all; Dad stepped in and hired professionals to take care of it.

In the end, Mom and Dad rented a twenty four foot long truck and moved only part of their furniture. It was old and had been through too many kids and their friends, and if they left it in place they could rent the house out as furnished. Nicole and I shoved what little we had into their truck, along with Michael's crib and toys.

I'd forgotten, until we were packing, that Kevin and Lydia had lost everything they owned when her apartment building burned down.

We both now had fairly large homes and nothing much to put in them.

Eileen and Lydia dragged us off to shop; I would have bought a sofa and TV, new beds for the two of us, and a few lamps. I never considered linens and towels and actual pots and pans or utensils and dishes for the kitchen.

"I don't cook," I informed my sister.

"You won't be living with Mom," she reminded me. "Your daughter will need to eat. I suggest you start cooking."

They forced me to buy a washer and dryer with the slice of news that I was doing laundry from now on, too.

The evening after closing I sat shoulder to shoulder on the bare living room floor of my new house with Sherry, wondering how something so obvious could have escaped me.

My mother had been cooking and cleaning and doing a large bulk of the caring for my daughter. At the very least I'd need to feed her, and beyond opening boxes of cereal and slapping peanut butter on bread, I wasn't sure how I'd accomplish that.

I could bring home dinner from the restaurant every night, but I wasn't sure that would be the healthiest option.

If I called out for pizza more than once a week my mother would notice, and she'd find a way to ground me.

"Get moved in," Sherry said. "I'll teach you to cook a few things. I can even cough up some dishes with stealth vegetables if there's something you want Nicole to have that she refuses to eat."

"She doesn't turn her nose up at much. But if you can get me to eat a parsnip, my mother will love you."

She took that as a challenge.

Most of my furniture would be delivered over the next two days; I still had to help Mom and Dad move heavy stuff around their house, and I promised Katie I would help keep an eye on the people packing her and Nick's things, but after that she was free to find anything parsnip I might like.

"You have a birthday coming up," she mused.

"Kevin and Eileen and I figured we'd celebrate together since our birthdays are so close. Kind of a 'happy birthday and welcome to the new digs' party next week."

"I can find something parsnippy by then."

"You'll be there, right?"

"I'm not intruding on a family thing, Paul."

She had no clue. "If you're not there, my parents will be disappointed, and they won't give me my birthday present. And I'm pretty sure this year I'm getting that skateboard I've been begging for since I was eleven. So you have to be there."

"I'd hate to deprive you of your skateboard. I'll be there on one condition."

"Anything."

"You have to tell Nicole you're dating. I don't want to show up and surprise her, especially if it might upset her."

"She knows."

"But does show know it's me?"

I'd picked Nicole up from her karate class a few days earlier and decided to approach the subject. I had Dad's warning in my head— she might like the idea of me dating but not the reality—so I decided to soften her up with ice cream before going home.

I'd catch hell from Mom; what was I thinking, ice cream half an hour before dinner?

I was thinking that I'm her father, dammit, and I can take her out for ice cream if I want.

It was only after we were sitting at a table in Baskin Robbins that I realized if Nicole was ticked off she could chuck that ice cream cup right at my head.

For a few seconds, I think she wanted to.

"Do you remember a few weeks ago when you said you wouldn't mind if I started dating someone?"

"Yep."

"Are you still okay with the idea that I might have a girlfriend?"

"Do you?"

Carefully, trying to weigh her reaction, I said yes.

She set the cup down, and her eyes narrowed when she looked up at me. "That's just mean, Daddy. You *kissed* Sherry, I saw you. You shouldn't have done that if you have a girlfriend because now

Sherry thinks you like her!"

"I hope she does like me, sweetheart, because Sherry *is* my girl-friend."

"Really?"

"Scout's honor."

She brightened and picked the cup back up. "Then it's okay if you kiss her."

"You're okay if I go out with her a lot?"

"Sure. I like Sherry. I've known her since I was really little, you know."

"Funny, kiddo, so have I. I was younger than you when I met her. I think we were five years old."

"Really?"

"Yep."

"You used to be five?"

"Eat your ice cream, smart ass."

She asked questions; when did I know I liked Sherry, was I sure that she liked me back? Did Sherry live with her Mom and Dad, too, and was she allowed to go out with someone who had a little girl?

Another reason to move, I realized; she found it perfectly normal that I lived with my parents.

"She knows it's you," I told Sherry, getting up. I held a hand out to her, helping her off the floor. "She's happy it's you. In fact, if I'd said it was someone else, I was getting mint chocolate chip ice cream shoved up my nose."

"Then I'll be here for your birthday. Presuming my hard ass boss lets me off."

"I'll bribe him. I hear he's cheap."

"I heard he was easy," she snickered, giving me a quick kiss. "Do you realize that in just a few weeks we've had our first fight, I've been grilled by your brother, I've cried buckets over you, and now not only have you told your daughter we're dating but I'm going to be dragged out in front of your entire family?"

"This is us, taking it slow."

"It almost makes me wonder what you do when you're taking things fast."

I'd tried that; she threatened to throw me over the balcony.

~

I'm not sure what we all were thinking, trying to move at the same time and get it all done in a week. We loaded not quite half of what Mom and Dad owned into a rented truck, shoved the crib and boxes filled with Nicole's and Michael's toys in it, and moved that in a day. Uncle Doug and Aunt Kris had twenty eight years of crap to be boxed and hauled away, and while Katie had professional help we still had to place everything for her and move boxes from room to room.

In between deliveries of furniture, we unpacked for parents and for Katie, and still had to plan for the party to which we'd already invited a couple of dozen people.

It would be outside in the court; none of us would have a house ready for visitors, although Mom and Dad, and Kevin and Lydia opened theirs up for the inevitable restroom needs. Dad laid carpet runners from his back door to the hallway bathroom for those coming out of the pool, and he set up portable lights that would turn on at dusk, bathing his yard and the court in brightness.

Sherry fretted over the party for the entire week. While she helped me hang pictures and figure out where in the kitchen I would have less trouble finding things, she worried about birthday gifts for Kevin and Eileen—it wasn't that kind of party, I assured her, we weren't even giving each other anything—she worried about Nicole finding some deep well of resentment when she saw us together; she worried about whether or not my parents would like her outside of the restaurant, she worried about how co-workers would react when they found out the manager was dating the hostess.

That last one was the only thing I was concerned about. A few times over the years I'd been hit on by employees and politely declined with a firm "I don't fraternize" policy; suddenly I'd reversed myself and was more than willing to go out with the woman who had men melting with a simple polite smile.

I wasn't worried about the rest of it; Nicole was excited that for once Daddy wouldn't be the odd man out at a party and I was more worried about her saying something inappropriately suggestive than I was that she'd get upset if she spotted a wayward kiss or me with my arm around Sherry. My parents were just glad that I was willing to put myself out there, and my siblings—they liked her already and had hopes almost as high as mine that it would work out.

The invitations were for three p.m.; pool party, dancing in the street, Dad and Uncle Doug firing up their grills. By four it was in full swing but Sherry refused to take off work early—that would smack of favoritism—and she showed up at five-thirty. I was beside the pool with Nicole, threatening to throw my daughter in for the crime of having shoved a cold soda can against my bare back, when she came around the corner of Dad's house. Her long hair was tied back and she was dressed in white shorts and a red t-shirt that clung to her like a second skin. I looked up and saw her smiling at me, and felt my breath catch and my heart start to pound.

There was no more "I'm getting there." With that one smile I fell the rest of the way, and I fell hard.

Kevin took one look at me and shoved me into the pool, and when I surfaced he asked, "Water cold enough?"

"Just about," I sputtered.

"You're welcome."

~

Chip

It was loud; the music was a mix of rock, hip hop, and just plain awful, and two hours into the party I was ready for it to be over. The kids, on the other hand, looked like they were just getting warmed up. Doug and I wondered if they'd all leave after we fed them, but Kris and Terry laughed at us and said we needed to resign ourselves to the fact that our nice quiet court was going to be loud and crowded until at least midnight.

I didn't know who most of the people there were. My in-laws declined the invitation for the very reasons I was ready for the party to be over; I recognized Topher and Debby and a few students from the dojo, but beyond that I had no clue which guest was friend to which kid, and I couldn't even be sure the party hadn't been crashed by complete strangers.

Early on the kids circulated, making sure their friends had beer or soda and they made introductions; after the grills had cooled off and everyone was subsisting on soda and chips the kids seemed to gravitate towards their best friends. Kevin and Eileen sat in a semi circle with Lydia and Spider, Michael in a stroller next to Lydia, with Topher and Debby bouncing between them and Katie, who seemed content to sit in one spot on Kevin's front lawn while her friends came and went.

Paul and Sherry sat with her for a while, until the music slowed from headache-inducing rap to something slow; they jumped up and Paul grabbed her by the hand, leading her onto the street where several other couples were dancing.

Even at his own wedding reception he hadn't been so singularly focused. Paul danced with his new wife then, but he laughed and talked to friends on the dance floor; when he pulled Sherry close to him, I could feel the rest of the world drain away and I could hear his heart pounding, the blood rushing in his ears.

He had her in his arms and no one else existed.

Nicole was curled up on the grass between Terry and I, watching them dance. I waited for the flicker of annoyance, some sigh of derision, but her eyes lit up and her lips curled in a half smile. She watched as Sherry's arms looped possessively around Paul's neck and as she moved in closer, and when Paul kissed her Nicole tugged on my shirt and whispered, "Grandpa, Daddy has a girlfriend!"

"Looks like it, angel," I agreed.

Katie was struggling to get up and Kevin shot out of his chair to help her up, laughing with her as she headed towards his house. She was rubbing her back as she walked; not quite waddling yet, but now big enough that there was no hiding her pregnancy.

Less than three months to go, I realized.

Instead of going back to where he'd been sitting Kevin walked over to us and knelt on the grass in front of Nicole. "Having a good time, kiddo?"

"Pretty good."

"Wanna dance?"

"With you?" she squealed.

"Hey, I'm not bad. Come on. I really do want to dance with the second prettiest girl here." He added in a mock whisper, "I have to say Lydia's the prettiest, you know."

She took Kevin's hand, giggling as he walked with her onto the court and bowed to her before taking the lead.

"Just think, Grandpa," Doug said, "in a few short years she'll be out there dancing with some teenage boy."

"Shut up."

"You thought it was difficult seeing Eileen when she was fourteen? I bet that'll be harder."

I waved him off. "Eileen was with Spider. That wasn't as hard as it could have been. He had no doubt what I'd do to him if he got out of line."

"He certainly knew what her brothers would do," Kris pointed out.

I still had the picture in my head of Eileen in the back yard, standing on the end of the diving board with Spider; I watched from the house, certain he was going to push her into the pool, silently cheering him on. Eileen was signing at him frantically, not only to avoid being dunked but to get him to hear her. When he reached up and gently touched her face and then kissed her, everything changed.

He was no longer cousin to my sons; in their eyes he shifted roles and was Eileen's boyfriend. Any leeway they would have given him with another girl didn't apply; if any of them had caught Spider doing anything to their sister they found inappropriate, he would have been running for his young life.

It wasn't until she was halfway through college that Nick and Paul began to relax where their baby sister was concerned. By then she was engaged to Spider and there was no doubt that they'd get married sooner or later. After that it was up to the happy couple, and still Spider kept a respectful distance.

"I never would have guessed when he was a teenager that he really did know how to treat women well," Doug mused. "I thought he was screwing around every chance he got."

"He dated," Kris said. "He just wasn't ready for anything more."

If he'd had the notion, Paul nipped that in the bud. Where his friends might have admired the numbers he was racking up, they did not think highly of his marrying at sixteen and having a daughter to care for.

I wasn't happy about it, but I did admire my son for stepping up and trying to create a family where one should not have existed.

Now he was dancing in the street, one step closer to starting over.

Paul and Sherry moved closer to Kevin, and when he was within arms' length Paul scooped his daughter up, her laughter cutting through the din of the party. Kevin politely backed off and Paul danced with his daughter on his hip and his arm around his girlfriend.

"Look at that," Terry said quietly. "If that doesn't look…"

"Right?" I finished for her.

"My God, look how happy he is."

"They remind me of you two," Kris said, gesturing towards Terry and me. "When I see the way Paul looks at her it's like watching you look at Terry thirty years ago."

"Except I'm blonde and have better boobs," Terry snickered.

"Give it a few years and they'll be bouncing off your knees," Kris told her.

Terry glanced at me."Better than shrinkage."

"Hey. I'll show you shrinkage."

"God, I saw it already, I don't need to hear about it, too" Doug groaned.

"You saw what?" Kris asked, confused.

He was about to answer when a taxi pulled into the court a little too quickly for my tastes. I jumped up, ready to tear into the cab driver and into whoever had called for it, when the back door opened up.

He was dressed in military BDU pants and a black t-shirt, hair cropped close, and had three days beard growth. His wrist was wrapped in heavy bandages and he had obvious cuts and bruises; scrape marks were scattered across his cheek and neck, and he had a fist sized black and blue mark on his forearm. He looked tired and surprised, and as soon as he stepped out of the cab I knew who he was looking for.

Quiet settled over the party like a fine mist; Kevin's front door opened and Katie stepped out, and from behind me I heard her squeak out, "Nick?"

He shot across the court and over Kevin's front lawn, scooping her up in a tight hug, until he realized there was more of her to hug than he expected. He took a slow step back, his hand very gently going to her stomach, settling there lightly, tentatively, and he breathed, "Look at you."

I felt Terry melt into my side, her forehead pressed to my shoulder, and her breath caught as she tried to not cry. We all wanted to run to him, yet no one wanted to take that moment from Katie.

Out of the corner of my eye I saw Doug at the cab, paying the driver.

Paul had put Nicole down, and after Nick had kissed Katie she couldn't contain herself anymore. She launched across the pavement and over the grass, throwing herself at her uncle; he turned and caught her and hugged her tightly, looking over her shoulder at his mother.

I nudged Terry in his direction; in the murmuring that formed behind me were quiet expressions of relief, and friends telling my kids that the party was great, but it was obviously time to leave.

I waited until Nick had been hugged by everyone else, and when I had my arms around him I whispered in his ear, "You got him, didn't you?"

"You know I did," he whispered back.

"Welcome home, Coop."

When the excitement calmed and Nick was seated in a lounge chair with Katie on his lap, we fired the grill back up and tossed on what was left of the chicken and ribs. Doug stood behind me, ostensibly putting more beer on ice, and he asked me, low enough so that Terry wouldn't hear, "Did I hear you call him 'Coop'?"

"You did."

"And he was working directly with Barron?"

"Yep."

"Holy shit, Chip."

"I know."

We both looked at my Nick, who was sitting there with one arm around his wife, and one hand on her belly, feeling his first child kick out at him. We saw the same thing: a kid who didn't really know what he was in for, a kid who would likely be, by the time he was my age, the Secretary General of the government's most fringe agency.

~

Paul

Kevin held out his beer bottle in toast to Nick. "Dude. Best birthday ever."

Nick touched his bottle to Kevin's and snorted, "What? You mean the party wasn't for me?"

"If only we'd known…"

Nick was humoring us; he didn't want to sit out there and drink beer with his brothers and sister, and he didn't want a late dinner with the family. He only wanted to go home and spend the night with his wife, but she seemed happy enough to sit there curled up on his lap. He understood Mom needed to see him for just a little bit longer, and she was going to make damn sure he got some food in him before she let him out of her sight.

Nicole asked him what the rest of us wanted to, but weren't sure we should: "What happened to you, Uncle Nick? Did you get in a fight?"

He shook his head and said, "Naw. I'm kinda clumsy. I fell down some stairs the other day."

She believed him.

No one else did.

After he'd eaten and spent enough time with everyone to at least pretend to be polite, Nick admitted fatigue and jet lag, and started to get up, but once he was on his feet he looked around with a touch of confusion.

"Where the hell do I live?"

Katie took his hand and tugged him in the right direction, across the court, house closest to the playground. "Come on, Mister Nick. I'll show you the way home."

Once they were inside Kevin snickered, "Think he'll get the grand tour tonight?"

Eileen had a reply ready and her mouth was open, but Dad shook his head, nodding slightly toward Nicole.

"And it was such a good one," she muttered.

Once Uncle Nick was no longer there for her to stare at, Nicole slid out of her chair and trudged over to me. "I think I need to go to bed, too, Daddy. I'm tired."

"All right, sweetheart. You go in and get ready and I'll be there in a few minutes to tuck you in."

I could feel Sherry's hand tense in mine, as if she was about to pull away.

"Will you read to me tonight?" Nicole asked her. "I'm reading a book that I don't think Daddy will like."

"Aren't you reading that Judy Blume book?" I asked.

She shot me a look that could have exploded my brains right on the spot.

"I love Judy Blume," Sherry said. "Sure, I'll read to you."

Nicole grinned and headed into the house, and I was fairly sure I heard a maniacal little laugh in her wake.

~

I knelt by Nicole's bed and listened to her prayers, the same as we did every night. But this time she crawled into bed and summarily dismissed me, waiting for Sherry to come in and read with her.

We were past the typical bedtime story, snuggling in bed while I read to her, but I wasn't ready to give it up. Instead we took turns reading out of the books she was most interested in, some of the same books Dad had read with me when I was her age.

This night I waited in the living room while someone else got to read the next chapter, and I was a little annoyed that I wouldn't find out what was going to happen unless I snuck into her room and got caught up while she wasn't looking.

"She kicked me out," Sherry marveled fifteen minutes later. "It was a short chapter and I was going to read the next one…"

"Further proof that she approves of you."

"Kicking me out is proof."

"She knew I was out here waiting for you."

She started to sit next to me on the sofa but I pulled her onto my lap.

"I won't get grabby," I promised.

"Not with your daughter still awake."

And if Nicole was asleep, I wondered. What then?

I was not going to push it, not again.

I settled for a kiss, and said, "Thank you for coming to the party. It would have sucked without you."

So would everything else.

"I think your brother coming home would have taken the suckage out of it."

"Maybe," I allowed. "But still, as much fun as Nicole is, you're the better date."

"Well, that makes me feel special. I'm better than an eight year old."

She was trailing a finger down my arm, very softly, making my hair stand on end. Intentional torment; she knew exactly what she was doing to me and knew I'd stand by my promise to keep my hands to myself.

The most I could allow myself to do was tighten my arms around her waist and I closed my eyes when she kissed me, very slow and soft, her tongue darting lightly over my lips.

"Don't," I moaned, hating the words bubbling out of my mouth. "You can't kiss me like that."

Her lips still grazing mine. "Like what?"

"Like you mean it."

She pulled back a little; I opened my eyes and she was looking at me sheepishly, trying not to smile. "This is a little backwards, isn't it?"

"I can't do the whole 'let's make out and then stop' thing, Sherry. I want to but I can't."

"I know."

"Kiss me like that again and you'll be looking for the nearest balcony to chuck me over."

It was then I realized she was trembling against me and I could feel hear heart beating against my chest.

"I saw the way you looked at me today," she murmured. "It wasn't just…want."

"No, it wasn't."

"No one has ever looked at me like that, Paul."

"Of course someone has. You just weren't looking at him at the right moment."

"No—"

"Sherry…surely at some point someone has looked at you and realized just how much they love you. Maybe you didn't see it, but that's what they looked like. Me, just before Kevin shoved me into the pool."

She shook her head lightly. "I've seen horny determination. I've never seen that look before."

"You'll see it again," I swore. "Every time I'm completely blown away by how much I love you, you'll see it. Because I do love you."

She kissed me again, sweetly, and was trembling even harder.

"This isn't where you tell me you just realized that you don't love me?"

"No. This is where I tell you I'm scared out of my mind."

"I won't break your heart, I swear."

"Paul," she breathed. "We'll break each others' hearts a million times. And that does scare me, but…"

I waited. Her hands were on my face; she was trying to not look into my eyes, and her cheeks flamed red.

"I don't have nearly the experience you do," she finally said.

"That's a good thing. I'm not exactly proud of mine."

"I don't want to disappoint you."

I leaned my head back, trying to look at her face. "You don't have to worry about that. I've suspected for a long time that I suck at sex. You're probably a lot better at it than I am."

"That's weirdly sweet."

"You think it's funny, but I'm serious."

She slid off my lap and stood up, reaching for my hands. When I was standing in front of her she said the two words that caused all the blood to rush from my head.

"Prove it."

~

"This does not constitute the walk of shame," I assured her at six the next morning. "This is just you trying to escape before my daughter wakes up."

"I'm wearing yesterday's underwear. It's the walk of *something*."

She woke me up at four thirty, warm lips pressed just below my ear, with the bathroom light shining on the bed. I struggled through the fog and forced my eyes open; it didn't matter how tired I was, if she was awake I damn well wanted to be, too.

"You gave me a hickey," she accused lightly.

"You bit me. We're even."

I was flat on my back, squinting against the light, and she leaned into my chest, her hair tenting around my head. "What time does Nicole usually get up?"

"Depends. I'm guessing sevenish today since she went to bed so early."

"I need to be long gone by then."

"Why?"

"She might be all right with us being together, but she doesn't need to be beat over the head with it."

"Fine. I'll herd her out the door and send her to Grandma's before she sees you."

"I don't think so."

I knew she was right; that didn't mean I wanted to admit it or that I wanted her to just get up and go.

"You can't leave yet," I said, half pleading.

"I wasn't planning on jumping up and running."

"Good. Because you've got your hand on my junk and that's as good as a promise, you know."

"You're a master of foreplay, Paul."

"I told you I sucked at this."

"You do not," she said, fingers teasing me. "Except for the hickey."

Truthfully, I didn't remember giving her one, but the evidence was undeniable.

An hour and a half later I was walking her to her car at the end of the court, assuring her that this wasn't the same as some college girl traipsing her way back to her dorm room after spending one wayward night with a frat boy. I opened the gate for her and stole one more long kiss before she got in and drove off, and when I turned around Kevin was sitting on his front porch with the newspaper in hand.

"What the hell, Squirt? Don't you ever sleep?"

"I have a six month old. What's your excuse?"

"There's this girl," I replied sheepishly.

He looked over the edge of his newspaper, eyeing me pretentiously. "Wandering around outside in nothing but baggy shorts," he noted. "Mad case of bed head, bite marks on your shoulder, and you have a stupid-assed smile plastered on your face…methinks you had a decent night."

"You thinks correctly."

"And what would your mother say if she saw some poor girl sneaking out of your house at the crack of dawn?"

"Yay for Paul?" I guessed.

"Probably," he chuckled, folding the newspaper. "Lydia's making muffins. Do you have something to feed Nicole for breakfast or should I bring some over?"

"Shit," I swore softly. "I really will go grocery shopping soon."

"Father of the year, you are," he muttered as he headed inside. "Father of the year."

~

Chip

I rolled out of bed early to avoid waking Terry with my tossing and turning, and followed Max into the kitchen; he stomped ahead of me and marched up to his empty dish, looking up at me as if he wanted to say "Well? Do your job. Get me my food, you worthless waste of skin." I scooped out the quarter cup of kibble that Terry had determined was enough, and then watched as he sniffed it.

"More," he meowed. I didn't need a translator; I knew exactly what he meant.

"Sorry. You're fat. So that's it."

I didn't wait for the look that was designed to melt my face off; I left him in the kitchen and by the time I was in the living room on the couch, I could hear his name tag pinging off the side of the dish. I reached for the remote but before I could turn the TV on I heard voices outside, and the grinding slide of the gate, so I looked out the window, wondering which of my spawn was up so early.

Paul was walking down the sidewalk wearing nothing but white satin basketball shorts and a smile. I wasn't sure if I wanted to go out there and throttle him for having his girlfriend stay the night with his daughter right there or if I wanted to congratulate him for having enough sense to get her out of there before Nicole was up.

I could hear Kevin's voice; surely he was giving his brother a hard time, and if he was up and mentally awake enough to do it, there was no point in me bothering to open the front door.

Max padded his way back from the kitchen and sat on the floor in front of me, his head chocked to one side.

"I know," I said. "It's too damned quiet in here. And you can't find Nicole, can you? I hate to tell you, furball, but you're going to need to find someone else to sneak crunchy treats to you."

He had walked the halls most of the night, as restless and unsettled as I was. This still felt like being a guest in someone else's house; nothing was where it was supposed to be, and it smelled wrong. I'd walked into the laundry room once thinking I was headed for the bathroom, and turned right at the end of the hall instead of left, forgetting which of the master suites we'd decided on as ours.

And the quiet…I noticed it that first night, when there was no trying to ignore Michael crying or the sound of water rushing through the pipes when Nicole took her bath or one of the kids showered. Music from Paul's stereo didn't drift on the night air and the dark wasn't peppered with Lydia's giggles or Kevin's deep voice droning two rooms away.

It was just us.

At three in the morning I was sitting out on the front porch, Max perched on my lap with my finger hooked through his collar, and a dull ache forming in my head. The grills were still at the end of the driveway and most of the lawn furniture was scattered across the asphalt. Kevin and Eileen had started to put things away after Paul went inside to put Nicole to bed, but we waved them off. It could wait.

Nick's living room light flicked on, and I wondered which one of them it was; Katie, not able to sleep because she was uncomfortable, or Nick because his entire timeline was screwed up and he was in yet another strange place.

He'd been gone a little over three months; unless things had changed, he was out of the bucket and safe from being tagged for anything overseas for a good six months.

Things had changed, though. Barron and Nick had both hinted of it. The agency was half the size it had been thirty years before and operated on a shoestring budget. Less manpower might mean he would get a week or two and then disappear in the middle of the night.

They want my brains, not my brawn.

"They want it all, Mister Cooper," I whispered.

Max looked up at me and then tugged his head, trying to free his collar from my grip.

"In a minute. We both need the fresh air. You're a lonely kitty and I—"

I didn't know what I was, exactly. Displaced, uncertain, a little bit nervous; I knew that half of what I felt had nothing to do with being in new surroundings. That half was across the street and apparently awake.

Max tugged harder, and I gave up. I took him back into the house and locked the door, and then crept into bed. Terry stirred but she did didn't wake up, not until I got up for the second time and fed the cat.

I heard her soft footsteps coming down the hall and Max made a beeline for her, trying to wind his body around her legs but she sidestepped him neatly. Sleep was still clinging to her in wild wisps, and she ran her fingers through her hair, trying to tame the wayward tufts that were sticking out in odd ends.

"Why are we up so early?" she groaned as she sat next to me.

"Go back to bed. I didn't mean to wake you."

"I rolled over and you weren't there. It gets pretty cold without your body heat, mister."

"I'll go back to bed with you if it helps."

"I'm not sure I'm awake enough for that."

"I meant so you could go back to sleep." I stood up, pain stabbing at my temples, and I winced.

"What?"

"Headache. Just let me take something for it and I'll keep you warm."

She sighed. "I doubt I'll go back to sleep but I can hardly refuse the offer to cuddle."

She followed me back into the bedroom and slid beneath the sheet while I went into the bathroom and swallowed some Tylenol. By the time I was in bed beside her, my head was pounding.

"Hell, maybe I will sleep," I mumbled, pulling her against me. "Unless you have other plans."

"Just hold me. You can fall asleep and do that."

I tried to fall past the drum beating steadily in my head, rhythmic pounding that thundered in tandem with my heartbeat. It seemed like every time I was just past it, the pounding got harder and jerked me awake, until finally Terry was shaking my shoulder.

"Chip, wake up," she urged.

"Not asleep."

"Open your eyes. Come on, you have to wake up."

I barely opened them, but the light bleeding from around the drapes stabbed at my eyes, adding new pain to the agony already swirling around me.

"Chip."

"What?"

"Jesus, Chip, your nose is bleeding like crazy. There's blood everywhere."

I barely turned my head; the pillow case was streaked with red, and I could taste it dripping over my lips. Blood ran in a thin stream past the corner of my mouth and over my chin, pooling at my neck; when I sat up, it spilled across my chest in a dark surge.

As soon as I sat up the pain knifed through my skull and I choked on blood that was dripping down my throat; Terry had a warm wet washrag under my nose before I could think straight, and the phone in her hand before I could protest.

"Don't even," she warned when I opened my mouth.

She grabbed clothes from the dresser and starting putting them on as she spoke with Doug, and by the time she hung up she was dressed and had clothes in hand for me.

"He's already at work," she said, trying to wrestle briefs onto me. "We'll meet him there."

"I can dress myself," I moaned, though truthfully I wasn't sure I could.

"Guess what, mister. You don't get to give me shit right now. Hold the washrag to your face and don't fight me on this or so help me God, I'll drag you out the door by your sense of humor."

~

Kevin

Eileen and I were stacking lawn chairs when Dad's garage door creaked open and Mom backed her car out of the driveway so fast that I wasn't sure the gate would slide open before she plowed through it. We watched her peel out, leaving a black smear of rubber on the street and the garage door wide open.

"What the hell is that about?" Eileen wondered.

By the time the gate closed Mom's car had disappeared around the corner. "Was Dad with her?"

"Hunched over in the passenger seat."

"That can't be good."

"I hope they're just late for something."

If there had been something wrong with our grandparents, they would have stopped long enough to say something. If Dad's pathology report was finally in, they would have said something. If it was a heart attack, there would be EMTs crawling all over the place. So, I reasoned as I punched the number on the keypad outside the garage door to close it, it couldn't be all that bad.

Eileen wasn't so sure; anything that would get Mom to lay rubber had to be *something*.

We had the chairs stacked and I was pushing Dad's grill up the driveway when Paul's front door opened and Nicole bounded out, a backpack in one hand and half a muffin in the other. Paul followed, locking the door behind them. He had changed from his baggy white shorts into a suit, and if he wasn't my brother, I might have said he looked presentable.

Nicole ran across the lawn shouting, "Thank you for the muffins, Uncle Kevin!"

"You're welcome. Where are you headed off to, cupcake?"

"I have to go to work with Daddy," she sighed.

"You get to," Paul corrected. "You get to go to work with Daddy. I thought you liked hanging around the restaurant."

"I do when Grandpa is the boss."

"Does Daddy make you work?" Eileen teased.

"Yes! He makes me fold napkins and I have to count stuff, and stuff!"

"Yes I do," Paul admitted. "Last time you went to work with me I had you count a box of chocolate mints, and oddly enough out of the one hundred that should have been there, you only found ninety five."

She grinned. "Mints are tricky."

"Too lazy to pick up the phone and ask one of us to babysit?" I asked Paul. "She can't go to work with you all summer."

"It's only until a slot opens at the day care center. And I'm not asking Mom to pick up my slack."

"Good, because Mom and Dad just tore out of here like their collective ass was on fire."

"Day care?" Eileen asked. "When we would happily watch her?"

Nicole was looking up at us, soaking in the exchange.

I didn't understand why, either. "We'll watch her, and then she can go to the dojo when I open in the afternoon. She's headed there every day anyway."

"Or I'll watch her and I can take her there when I open for piano lessons at four," Eileen offered.

Paul sucked in a deep breath. "I appreciate it, but I want her in day care during the summer. She can meet the neighborhood kids, and then when school starts she'll already know people."

"Oh," Eileen and I said together.

"See, I do tend to think ahead sometimes."

Nicole snickered, and Paul shot her a look.

"What about today?" Eileen asked. "Does she have to go with you? Spider has summer school and I'd like someone to hang with. We can go check out the outlet stores."

"Up to you, kiddo," he said to Nicole. "Go with me and count mints, or go with Eileen and shop."

She scrunched her nose up and asked, "Will your feelings be hurt if I wanna go with Aunt Eileen?"

"No, sweetheart, my feelings won't be hurt." He crouched down next to her, fishing his wallet from his back pocket. "Tell you what; I'm going to give you forty dollars..."

She tried to snatch it from him but he pulled it back.

"...but you have to take Aunt Eileen to lunch and pay for it. If there's anything left, you can spend it, all right? And no borrowing money, you spend what I give you."

"Okay!"

He kissed her on the cheek and stood up. "And be good. No letting Aunt Eileen talk you into something that will get you arrested. If I have to post bail it's coming out of your allowance."

"Well, hell, you're no fun," Eileen said.

He leaned over and kissed her, too. "Thank you. And don't let her talk you into anything. She's getting sneaky."

"It's nice that we have influence over her."

I watched Paul's minivan turn the corner. "Well, now, if I give you money, too, will you pick something up for me?"

"Whatcha want?"

"Chocolate truffles. There's a place right across from the food court that sells them. Think you can remember to get them for me?"

Nicole eyed me suspiciously. "Is this like when Grandpa tries to get me to sneak candy to him when he knows Grandma will get mad?"

I fished my wallet out of my pocket and handed her another forty dollars. "Nope. It's a surprise for Aunt Lydia."

"Wow." She looked at the money clenched in her hands. "Aunt Eileen, I think you better hold this for me."

"I think Uncle Kevin wants an awful lot of chocolate," Eileen mused.

Nicole nodded in agreement. "I think he's gonna sneak some to Grandpa."

"Maybe for both Grandpa and Grandma," I said. "After the way they took out of here, they might need it."

~

Chip

Doug's receptionist took one look at me and asked why we hadn't gone straight to the emergency room. My t-shirt was splattered with blood and it was stuck to my whiskers and the gold chain around my neck. At best my eyes were half open, partly from the pain and partly from the lights in the waiting room, and I probably looked like I'd run face first into a brick wall after a night of drinking and drugs.

Terry's hand was on my arm and I felt her tense; she managed to avoid snapping at the woman but said evenly, "This was closer, and Doctor Stone is expecting us."

I was in pain and she'd threatened my gonads; there was no telling what she would threaten that poor woman with if she talked back at all.

Doug spared his receptionist by opening the door and ushering us in; he took us to the first exam room just past the entry way, pointing to the exam table as I entered.

"I'm not displacing some kid with gummy bears up his nose, am I?" I grunted as I slowly hoisted myself onto the table.

"Not even a woman with wayward vegetables," he assured me as he gloved up. "I was doing paperwork today. What started first, the headache or the bleeding?"

"Headache. Off and on all night but it got worse around six thirty."

"And the bleeding?"

"I noticed it about twenty minutes ago," Terry said. "He was in bed and mostly asleep; I rolled over and realized there was blood all over his face and pillow."

"Scale of one to ten on the headache?" he asked as he wet a blue hand towel.

"Fifteen," I groaned.

He wiped away as much of the blood from my face as he could and then swabbed out my nose with gauze. "No chance you two bumped heads in your sleep?"

"My face is still sensitive. I would have noticed that."

He grabbed a scope and looked into my nostrils, then told me to open my mouth. "You're definitely bleeding from your sinuses."

"Why?" Terry asked.

"Not sure yet." He picked up the BP cuff that was on the desk and wrapped it around my arm, quiet as he pumped it up. He scribbled the numbers down and then took my temperature and listened to my heart, and the entire time Terry sat perched on the edge of her chair as if she might need to spring up and help him.

"Blood pressure is a little high, heart rate is elevated."

"Cause or effect?" I asked.

"Response to pain, most likely. Where in your head did you feel it first?"

"Behind my eyes and the top of my head."

"And now?"

"Whole freaking head hurts."

He grabbed his clipboard and sat on his stool, scratching out notes. "I looked at your last MRI just before you got here and it came back clean, but let's get a cat scan to back it up." He tore the paper off the notepad and handed it to Terry. "Do me a favor and take this up to the front desk. Marjorie will make the appointment and should be able to get him in sometime today. After she has it, come back and let me know. I might be able to take off and go with you."

She glanced at me—she didn't want to leave—but she took the paper and left.

Once the door was closed I said, "That was slick. You always do that crap yourself. What's up? What's wrong with me?"

"I suspect your eldest son is what's wrong with you, Chip. You've had a hell of a stressful summer and capped it off with Nick showing up last night all banged up. You know what he's headed into and it scares the hell out of you. I'm guessing you didn't sleep at all last night."

"Not really."

"The more you thought about it, the more worried you got. The more worried you got, the worse the headache became."

"And the nosebleed?"

"It's actually very little blood. Coming out of the nose it just looks worse. You either spent some time picking the hell out of it, or your blood pressure shot up suddenly and caused blood vessels that were already fragile to break."

"And Terry couldn't hear this...why?"

"Because of Nick," he explained. "You can't tell her what being the SG's cooperative really means, because if you do that means you have to explain exactly what he's being groomed for. You need her to keep believing that for the most part he's just Barron's favorite desk jockey."

"That's an understatement."

"I'm finally starting to understand what my father went through when I signed on," Doug said. "It aged him, and I couldn't understand why. After all, I was going in as medical backup. I wasn't an actual agent."

"Yeah, right."

"You and I survived it, Chip. Nick is smarter than both of us combined. And frankly, I'm pretty fucking smart. You know the training he's getting is head and shoulders above what we got. Barron is seeing to that."

"Intellectually I know that." I started to sit up, struggling against a sharp stab that felt like a spike had been tapped into my head and a wave of nausea. "Doug, I think I'm gonna hurl."

"Roll onto your side," he instructed, reaching for the trash can.

He held it to the edge of the exam table while I retched up the blood I'd swallowed. When I spit out the last of it, he set the can down and reached for another towel, soaking it with cool water.

"Put this over your eyes. The light can't be helping. I'm going to get you something for the pain and see if Marjorie got that appointment for you yet."

"Do I really need the cat scan?"

"It wouldn't hurt to have it for confirmation. I really think what you have brewing here today is a stress induced migraine-scale headache with sinus hemorrhage due to a sudden spike in your blood pressure. But I'm not infallible, so we'll get a peek, if for no other reason than it will ease Terry's mind."

I waited with the wet towel over my eyes; Terry came back in quietly, her hand sliding gently across my chest to let me know she was there. She stood by the table, fingers absently rubbing lightly over invisible lines on my t-shirt while we waited for Doug to come back. I wanted to peel the rag back and look at her, make sure she wasn't as worried as I thought she might be, but I knew if I let the light in, the pain would ratchet up and I might be back at square one.

Next thing I knew Doug was warning me "Just a pinch" before he stabbed me with a needle.

"All right. You have a walk in appointment at a radiology clinic downtown. Head there from here and they'll get you in within half an hour or so. There's a radiologist on staff, so we'll get an answer almost immediately. I may be able to tell by watching the images come in."

"You're going?" I mumbled.

"Gets me out of paperwork. I don't think we'll find anything on the cat scan," he said for Terry's benefit. "I want it mostly as a backup. I think your real problem is the summer from hell and moving this last week didn't help matters. You may need to back off the day to day dealings with Whatever The Hell Chip Does Enterprises for a while and rest a little more, and we'll keep an eye on your BP."

I peeled a corner of the towel up. "You don't know what I do?"

"I'm not even sure what you do," Terry said.

"I know," Doug decided. "He's got a massive pot farm in Napa disguised as a winery."

"Real estate acquisitions and management, you moron," I mumbled.

"Aww. He's almost like a mini Donald Trump."

"I have better hair."

"And a hotter wife," Terry added.

"Come on, hot stuff," Doug said. "Let's go peek inside his head."

~

Three hours later we were sitting in the restaurant bar; my headache had faded to a dull and manageable throb, the bleeding had stopped, and I felt almost human. The only downside at the moment was Doug's insistence that anything I had to drink not be alcoholic. We ordered sandwiches, which was sure to annoy the I'm-Not-Just-A-Damned-Cook day chef, and soft drinks, which was sure to annoy tip-seeking James.

"I didn't see anything and neither did the radiologist," Doug said. "You can cross that worry off your list."

"That worry doesn't get crossed off until we get the pathology report," Terry said. "How much longer are we supposed to wait?"

"Until it comes in," he replied. There wasn't much else we could do. It wasn't as if any of us could storm the lab, find the tissue samples, and work on them.

Terry would try if she could.

"I've got the MRI and the cat scan telling me there's nothing growing there right now," I reminded her.

"Nothing either of those can see right now," she countered. "We don't know that whatever it was isn't still clinging on by just a couple of cells that could suddenly explode. I want to know so that you can start whatever treatment you need to."

"But it's something. At least we know I'm relatively fine for the moment."

"Relatively being the key," Doug snorted.

"You be quiet," she said, poking her finger at him. "And how often should I expect him to have these wonderful nosebleeds?"

"Daily if he doesn't quit picking his nose."

"Doug."

"I want to keep an eye on his blood pressure, just for jollies. It could have been a random spike, and he'll never have another one like it, or he could have two or three a week until those blood vessels have completely healed. Pick up a digital BP cuff on the way home and take it two or three times a day and keep track of it."

I looked up over Doug's shoulder; Paul and Sherry were standing outside his office door, looking at each other awkwardly, almost shyly. His hands were stuffed into his pockets and she had her arms crossed, both determined to not reach out and touch, not where co-workers and parents would see.

"That's so cute I could just about hurl again," I said, pointing them out to Terry.

"I wanted to hurl a lot when you two were first dating," Doug said.

"Bullshit. You were too busy trying to run from Kris, screaming like a little girl. 'Oh no! The big bad married lady wants to have her way with me! Save me! I must remain pure!'"

"Damn right," he chuckled. "Hell, your anniversary is right around the corner, isn't it?"

"Twenty nine years next week," Terry said. "Or twenty seven, depending on how you look at it."

"We were married the whole time," I reminded her.

"There will be a party, right? Lots of drinking and junk food?" Doug asked.

"Maybe next year," Terry replied. "Thirty is a major milestone. Twenty nine just sounds like someone's fake birthday."

"Besides, the party the kids just had was enough for a while."

"Christ," he muttered. "You two really are getting old."

Paul was leaning on the doorjamb, grinning. "Him," I said, nodding toward my son. "Twenty six tomorrow. Kevin and Eileen are twenty four. They're getting old. Us, we're already there."

"Speak for yourself, Grandpa," Terry said.

"If you're old, what the hell does that make me and Kris?" Doug groused.

"*Really* old."

Terry slid out of the booth. "While you two bitch about who's getting old and falling apart, I'm going to go talk to my son and find out where Nicole is today."

"Now see, we are getting old," Doug said. "We used to be able to run her off in about five minutes, now it takes half an hour."

"Takes me longer to do a lot of things."

"Speaking of which, how's the patch working out?"

"She's not complaining."

"She wouldn't. Have you noticed any difference?"

"Holy shit, Doug. You want to run into Paul's office and try to turn me on so you can give it a good squeeze and see for yourself?"

"I'd have nothing for comparison and contrast," he said dryly.

"Funny. And to shut you up, yes, it's working."

"That's all I wanted to know. DDAVP letting you sleep through the night?"

"Thankfully. Getting up three or four times was getting old."

"Any breakthrough?" Does it seem to wear off in the afternoon or evening? Do you wind up feeling especially thirsty before taking your next dose?"

"Sometimes. Why are you asking this now? Shouldn't you be doing this when you're at work?"

"I'm always working, Chip."

Terry plopped back down next to me. "Nicole is with Eileen today, and tomorrow Paul is taking the day off and taking her to Six Flags, and I just totally interrupted, didn't I?"

"Doug was obsessing about the quality of my erections," I said. "Does this mean I'm working here tomorrow?"

"No, I already told him to not even think about asking you. Will is working instead. You get to spend the day taking it easy."

"I'm moving furniture around, aren't I?"

"I was thinking more along the lines of lounging by the pool or going to a movie, but sure. That works, too."

Someday, Doug pointed out, I would learn to keep my mouth shut.

Yeah, I doubted it, too.

20

Chip

The bar was packed, an unexpected crush of mid-afternoon customers sitting elbow to elbow at the bar; Kevin and I grabbed the only open table, surprised at the crowd and the noise they were generating. I'd wanted to go over a breakdown of my business structure and my assets with him, away from where his mother would overhear, and away from the possibility that Nick would wander in and take unintentional offense to learning that I was trusting his younger brother with this instead of him.

Kevin had his own motives for going with me.

"It's not a party," Kevin said, "just your kids and grandkids. And Grandma and Grandpa. And Uncle Doug and Aunt Kris."

"And…?" I prompted.

"And Paul's girlfriend. But that's it. Family."

"So basically—on our anniversary—you want your mother to cook for fifteen people."

"What? No. We were thinking of coming here. Next year this will be in a new building and you can have the major blowout there. But this might be the last family-type thing we do in the existing building. And since Nick is home…"

"All right. You don't have to oversell it. I'll have to talk to your Mom and see if she's willing to change our plans…"

"You had plans?"

"It's our anniversary, of course we had plans."

"What, you were taking her to play miniature golf?"

"You're not entitled to the horny details. Now quit stalling and open the damn folder. It's lesson one in how the money is spread out and how I deal in business."

"I thought I only had to do this when you died."

"You might as well start learning it inside out now, Kevin. If I drop dead five years from now, it would be nice if you were able to step in without any transitional hiccups because you need time to figure out what you're doing. The only thing I ask is that no matter what you do with everything—whether you sell it all off or try to build it up—your mother is taken care of."

"Five years. Do you know something?"

"I pulled that out of my ass. But I will feel better knowing none of this will get dropped onto your mother's lap if the worst happens. This is nearly thirty years of investments and business ventures and she's never wanted to know about any of it."

He opened the folder and flipped through the first few pages. "Scylla LLC," he mused. "I'd almost give you points for cleverness there, Dad."

"I should note that the Charybdis is not a part of that. It's a separate entity, and it becomes Paul's problem sooner or later."

"Thinking about giving it to him while you're still around?"

"He's got control of day to day operations as it is, and as you pointed out a few weeks ago, I'm more and more out of touch with the people who work there. But no, I won't give it to him. I'll sell it to him."

"I presume you'll keep the land it's on and the structure itself?"

"He would get a generous land lease agreement."

"Out of curiosity, since I'll find out while I'm poking around in this anyway, what's your net worth?"

"We're comfortable," I told him.

"No shit, Sherlock. And I'm not completely nosy; having an idea gives me a benchmark to work with here, how much I'm taking on."

I suspected he was completely nosy. "Somewhere around a hundred, maybe a hundred ten."

"Million."

"The numbers aren't what matter, Kevin. It's keeping all the balls in the air without losing sight of potential ways to throw something else into the mix. It's my own odd little game, how diverse can I get without spreading too thin. Your grandfather played the stock market, invested in real estate, and did a hell of a lot of venture capitalism."

"And you decided to follow his path."

"When he died he left an estate that was spread out over a dozen different business ventures and hundreds of investments, and it took me a while to figure out how he managed as much capital growth as he did, but once I did... I was hooked."

"You depleted that by fifty million with trust funds, Dad. How the hell—?"

"Your trust landed in your lap with ten million. How much of it do you still have?"

"Before or after investments?"

"Before."

"All of it, less the cost of buying and rebuilding the dojo."

"After?"

"Thirteen, give or take a few thousand. Well, minus the house. I didn't want a thirty year mortgage."

"Well, there you go. You have positive capital growth, and at a decent rate. That only reaffirms my wanting you to take this on. And it answers your question. Whatever you're doing, that's how the hell."

He closed the folder. "All right, this isn't exactly light reading and it'll take me a while to plunge through it. And you still have my word; if something ever happens to you I'll try to keep it all going for Mom. And when she goes, with any luck it'll be with every dime you left her, and then some."

"Hopefully you have at least thirty to forty years."

"And hopefully I won't be trying to keep some leech—"

"I was serious before, Kevin. I want her to push on and if finding someone makes her happy, then support her."

"I will, but she won't be supporting *him*."

"She can, to a certain point. If she's truly happy, and part of that happiness is supporting someone she loves..."

"We can talk about the hypotheticals all we want Dad, but you and I both know that if you die first, she won't even consider being with anyone else. So sure, let's pretend she'll find a boy toy and shower him with cash and gifts, and they'll both get Mohawks and tattoos and see the world on his moped. We can say it, because it won't happen."

"Your mother has an awful lot of love to give, Kevin. I don't think she can live long without someone in her life."

"She'll have her kids and her grandkids, and I suspect that will be enough for her. If she doesn't have you to worry about and do whatever horny little things you do that I really don't want to think about, she'll shower her grandkids with attention, and by then there's liable to be a lot of them."

"I hope so."

"By Thanksgiving you'll have your third. After Michael turns one we'll probably start trying for another. I know Paul wants more kids, and sooner or later Eileen is going to spawn. Hell, that's a lot for *you* to stick around for."

"Trust me, I'll do everything I can to be here and make you all miserable."

He held up the folder. "This is certainly a start."

"You're up to it."

He begged out of the bar because of the noise and the distraction, and as we climbed into his car he muttered, "I wish I had your faith in me."

"Kevin. I was never half as smart as you, yet my father trusted me with it. If anything, you'll do better."

"Do you realize that you never refer to Grandpa Davis as your dad? It's always 'my father.'"

"He never got the chance to be a dad to me. It took years for me to stop referring to him by his name. And I still have to stop once in a while to remember that the man I thought was my father wasn't…all very muddled in my brain."

"Wonderful family dynamics you grew up with. Come to think of it, you rarely mention your mother. If at all. I'm not sure I've ever heard you talk about her."

"I have mother issues," I said.

"Obviously."

"And I don't want to go there."

"Then what about your brother? I never hear anything about him, either."

"I barely knew him. The last time I saw him alive he was fourteen years old and terrified of being sent to a boarding school. The next time I saw him he was seventeen and I was identifying his body."

"Shit."

"That brain you've got, that was David. He was so damned smart. I wish to hell I'd been more aware of what going on with him when he was little. I left home when he was ten or eleven and hardly saw him after that."

"How'd he die?"

"Drug overdose," I choked out. "Stupid, fucking drug overdose."

"Dad, I'm sorry, I didn't mean—"

"My brother is one of my regrets. I could have done a lot for him, and I didn't. I shouldn't have ignored his existence when he was away at school. And damn, I look at Paul and see pretty much what David would have looked like…"

"Does that help or hurt?"

"Both. And I can see parts of him in each of my kids, little traits and personality quirks you must have gotten from him. Paul looks like him and laughs like he did, you have his brains, Eileen has his sense of humor, and Nick…Nick has that arrogance he was just coming into when I left home."

"Yeah, I don't think I'd share that with Nick," Kevin chuckled.

"It's not necessarily a bad thing. That arrogance is wrapped around a deep determination to make sure everything is all right for everyone he cares about. He might irritate the hell out of you sometimes, but his heart is always in the right place."

"Speaking of whom…" Kevin pulled up to the gate and hit the remote. Nick was sitting by the swing set with Katie, and they were watching Nicole and two of her friends play.

"Nick," Kevin observed, "must have spent a hell of a lot of time while he was gone working out. He got freaking huge."

"Muscles on muscles," I agreed. "He probably had a lot of down time and not much else to do. When you're stuck in the middle of nowhere and bored out of your mind, you either sleep or exercise. He obviously chose the latter."

He parked in his driveway and cut the engine. "He always has been a little odd."

I got out of the car and Nicole shouted "Hi, Grandpa!" from the swing. Nick turned and waved us over, the grin plastered on his face piquing my curiosity.

"Look at this," he said, picking up a stack of photos that had been scattered over his and Katie's laps, thrusting them at me. "We got a three-d ultrasound. Meet your next grandchild."

"Holy…" I could barely breathe the word out. The images were so clear and perfect that I could see every detail on the baby's face and count the fingers and toes. "This is amazing."

Kevin examined the pictures as I held them. "Beautiful," he said in a near whisper. "Obviously this kid is taking after Katie."

"Do you know what it is yet?" I asked. "Do you want to know?"

"I'd like to know," Katie offered.

"The tech said she couldn't tell us, but she'd send the images to Uncle Doug and he would. She didn't want to be liable for any disappointment if she was wrong."

Kevin took the pictures from me and flipped through them again, picking out one in particular. "Any preference?"

"Hell no," Nick said.

"Do you really want to know?"

"You can tell?" Nick stood up and craned his head to look at the picture Kevin was holding.

Kevin snatched it close and held it against his chest. "Do you really want to know?"

"Seriously, Kevin, if you can tell…" Nick glanced at Katie. "Do you want his best guess? Even if he might be wrong?"

She nodded.

"Spill it, Squirt."

Kevin looked at the picture again, and then pulled another out from the middle of the stack, the perfect image of the baby's face. "Say hello to your son, Nick."

Nick took the picture from him and sank back onto the bench slowly, leaning into Katie. "Oh my God," he murmured. "Our son."

Kevin was still flipping through the rest of the pictures. "Now I can't tell you what the other one is, but—"

They both stood up at the same time.

"Other one?" Katie sputtered.

Kevin pointed to a blur on the picture he was looking at. "There's either another one, or your son has four arms and four legs. It does explain your size, Katie. Nothing personal, but you are kind of big for only being six months along."

Nick snatched the picture from Kevin's hands. "God, Katie, look…"

They stared at it in awe, long enough that Nicole jumped off the swing to come over and see what was going on.

"I hope those arms and legs belong to a second baby," Katie said. "Otherwise we might have a problem."

Kevin fished yet another picture out of the stack and rotated it, practically squinting as he stared. "Ah, there it is. Can't tell what it is, though. This one is obviously a little more modest."

He held the picture out for Nick and Katie to see, his finger running down the middle. "Your son is on the right side, your shy one is on the left."

"How the hell can you tell, Kevin?" Nick asked, almost in a whisper.

"I read a lot."

Nicole was standing on her toes, trying to see. Nick picked out the clearest picture and handed it to her. "Check it out, short stuff. That's your cousin."

"Wow."

"It's one of them, anyway," Nick added. "Kevin thinks we're having twins."

"Really?" she squealed. "One of them better be a girl because if it's not then there'll be *three* boys and just me!"

"A little girl would be nice," Nick told her. "But it might be two boys, you know."

She sighed and looked at Kevin. "Well, then you need to have another one and make it a girl next time!"

"I'll try my hardest," he chuckled. "Nick, has Mom seen these?"

"Not yet. I went in to show them to her but I think she was in the shower."

"Well, come on then!"

Nick reached for Katie's hand, and with a reminder to Nicole to not open the gate for anyone, not even her own father, we headed into the house. Terry was at the kitchen table making a grocery list, and barely looked up when she realized I was there.

"Got something to show you, Grandma," Nick said sheepishly, pulling a chair out for Katie.

He set the pictures on the notepad she'd been writing on, and it took her a moment to realize what she was looking at.

"Nick...oh God, how beautiful!"

"Keep looking."

She went through the entire stack, marveling over the image quality, and kept coming back to the picture of the baby's face.

"You can tell exactly what the baby looks like," she marveled. "And in this one—you've got a thumb sucker."

"Show her, Kevin," Nick said.

Kevin reached down and picked out a picture, running his finger down the middle like he had for Nick and Katie. "Baby number one on the right, baby number two on the left."

Her eyes went wide and jaw slacked for just a moment, then the grin caught up with her. "Twins?"

Katie looked up at me. "I blame you for this."

"It's Terry's fault," I said. "Twins run in her family."

Nick touched a finger to the first picture. "This is your grandson," he said quietly. "At least Kevin seems sure."

"The other one seems to be a bit shy," Kevin said. He dug through the pictures and pulled out the one he'd shown to Nick earlier. "Hopefully this is not indicative that your son is going to spend his life flashing people."

"He's just proud," Nick laughed.

"Apparently he's got something to be proud of," I said as the phone rang.

I took the four steps across the kitchen needed to reach it. "For you, Nicholas," I said after I answered. "You weren't home and Doug decided to try here."

Nick jumped up and was across the kitchen in a single leap. Katie stayed at the table but watched him hopefully, smiling when he did, her breath catching when his eyes filled with tears.

"You," he said to Kevin when he hung up, "are too fucking smart."

"It really is twins?" Katie asked hopefully, looking up as he came back to the table.

"We're really having twins," he answered. He bent over to kiss her and added, "Nicole is going to be so disappointed."

"Both are boys?" Kevin asked.

Nick put a finger to the picture Kevin had decided was a clear shot of twins and said,

"Apparently Uncle Doug got more images than we did, and this one gave him a clear view of the goods. He says they both look healthy and are developing just how they should be."

Katie turned in her chair, reaching for him. He got his arms around her and helped her up, holding her close when she couldn't fight back the tears anymore.

"You're going to be an amazing mother," he whispered against her hair.

A year ago he hadn't wanted to face the idea of becoming a father; he'd dropped out of law school and was floundering, wrestling with the offer the agency had made. He resisted Katie's urge to start a family, resisted hard enough that we weren't sure he'd ever want kids, and hard enough that I worried what his reaction would be when he found out she was pregnant.

Nick held his wife, and all I could think was that he was only half right. Katie would be an amazing mother, but he was going to be amazing right along with her.

~

Paul

"This is so many levels of awesome," I said, looking at those first baby pictures. "I don't even think sonograms like this were possible when Monica was pregnant."

"We need another word besides 'awesome'," Spider said. "But damn, yes, this is awesome."

Nick and Katie were curled up together on a chaise lounge in Dad's back yard; even though we'd moved it was as if nothing had changed. Evening rolled in and the entire family gravitated to his back yard, the deck littered with pool toys and grown kids, Michael's playpen a safe distance from the water.

Mom and Dad didn't seem to mind.

"Almost makes me want one," Eileen said absently.

Spider blinked rapidly, not sure he'd read her lips correctly. "Say that again," he signed.

"Almost," she repeated, signing with gross exaggeration. "Let's wait and see how we feel when these two get here and we can play with them."

Spider already knew how he felt; hell, I suspected Eileen did, too, but she was so tired of being badgered about having kids that she'd resist just to be stubborn.

Sherry had an arm around my waist and was looking at the pictures with me. "That is amazing," she said.

"I wish I'd had pictures like this of Nicole." I handed them back to Nick, to who immediately started looking at them again.

Nicole stomped up to me, put her hands on her hips and said, "Someone around here better have a girl soon."

"I'm not exactly equipped, darlin'," I reminded her.

"Hmph." She pursed her lips thoughtfully and glanced at Sherry, but kept her mouth shut as she walked away.

"Well that could have been awkward," I mused.

"She's teasing you and you know it."

"She's teasing a little bit," I allowed, wondering what Sherry would have said to Nicole if she hadn't walked off after dropping the hint.

Three months ago, not wanting kids would have been a deal breaker for me.

Now, I ached to know if this woman I had fallen in love with had any desire to have children of her own.

If she said no, I didn't think I could walk away.

If she said no, I wasn't sure I could live with it.

I wasn't sure I could ask.

Before I could finish the debate going on inside my head Dad brushed past and asked me to help him drag the grill from the garage to the back yard.

I was saved by his not wanting to tear up the new grass with the grill wheels.

"You had a panicked look on your face," he said once we were in the garage. "I wasn't sure if you needed rescuing or not."

"I think I did," I admitted.

He opened the grill and peeked inside, partly to make sure Kevin had cleaned it after the party, and partly to give himself time to decide if I wanted to talk.

I leaned against his car, and talked.

I wanted another child. It felt like it was part of the package; I wasn't dating just to date, I was dating with the express intent of finding a wife and the mother of my kids. I didn't want to guess my way through it, but when you've only been with someone for such a short time, how do you ask?

"Kind of late for worrying about that now, isn't it?" he wondered. "If you ask her if she wants children and she says no, you can't just walk away. You'd break your own heart."

"We haven't been dating that long."

"Bullshit. You're already connected, Paul. We can all see it. If she doesn't want kids of her own, you'll suck it up the same way your mother did when I said I didn't want any more."

"You what? I thought you didn't have more because she couldn't."

"She had notions of adopting," he said. "I didn't want to. We had four healthy kids and Nicole was on the way…I just didn't want to."

If Nicole was on the way, that meant they discussed it right after reconciling.

"Yeah, I know," he said, catching the look on my face. "The timing would have been all wrong. But she loves kids and always wanted more. If I'd said yes, you'd probably have two or three more brothers and sisters and Nicole would have some readymade playmates."

"Telling her no wasn't a deal breaker in getting back together?"

"It could have been, if she'd let it."

If she'd let it, Dad would have been broken. So would she, for that matter.

We lifted the grill over the grass and carried it to the back yard. Nicole and Sherry were in the pool together, splashing at Kevin.

I set my end of the grill down and then jumped in the pool, pulling Sherry away from the water fight Kevin would intentionally lose no matter who was there to help my daughter. We sat on the pool steps and watched them, Nicole's arms pumping wildly to make sure she kept Kevin doused.

If I'd asked Kevin for advice, he would have told me to stop guessing and ask her. The worst thing she could do was tell me no, and the world would not end.

Maybe not, but a small part inside me would.

Nicole dove under the water and went for Kevin's legs, upending him and forcing his head under water.

"Do you want kids?" I asked suddenly.

She turned to look at me. "Are we speaking theoretically or what?"

"Specifically, actually," I decided to just go for it. "With me. Can you see yourself having kids with me someday?"

She put a wet hand on my cheek and kissed me. "I can't see me having them with anyone else."

For a half second it felt like the world slipped and spun a little differently. "You want kids," I sputtered.

"If they're yours. I was never sure about it before, but there's something about you that makes me think it would be a very good idea."

"Mine." I felt dumber and dumber as the seconds ticked on.

She laughed lightly and reached for my hand. "Relax, cowboy, I'm not asking you to marry me. But if we do ever get there, yes, I want kids with you."

"We are getting there," I said quietly, not wanting anyone else to hear.

"But we haven't been together that long," she said.

"So? We've known each other forever, and I've wanted you for a very long time."

"And you got that," she snickered.

"That's not what I meant. I didn't mean I just wanted sex with you, I wanted *you*. And I'm pretty sure you wanted me, too, we just couldn't—"

"Bad timing."

"I wanted to be absolutely sure that I wasn't trying to prove something, not even to myself."

"You needed to be sure you weren't trying to replace a piece of Monica. I get that, and it's all right. I was hesitant for the same reason, until I finally admitted that I've been in love with you since high school."

"That long?"

"That long. But there was no way I was going to say or do anything, not with the way you were back then."

"And then I knocked up your best friend."

"That did put a damper on things." She shifted on the step so that she was facing me. "I wanted your marriage to work. Don't ever think I tried to steer Monica in another direction just so that I'd have a chance. She and I fought constantly over how she treated you."

"I would have guessed you two sat around bitching about how badly I treated her."

"There was some of that," she admitted, "but mostly I just wanted her to stop and think about what she was giving up every time she cheated on you. She got it, she really did, but she simply never thought she deserved to be as happy as you could make her."

"I know."

"And then she was gone…I couldn't do anything then, Paul. It felt wrong."

"But it's not."

"Not now. Now it feels…"

"Appropriate?"

"It feels like it was supposed to be."

"It was," I murmured. "Sherry, I can see us twenty years from now. I walk through that house and I can already feel you there. If we both know this is meant to be and it's what we both want, what the hell are we waiting for?"

She nodded towards Nicole. "We'll wait to be sure she's as okay with us as she seems to be. And we'll wait to be sure that this isn't just us feeling warm fuzzies about being together and obviously…compatible."

My daughter came first. Even in her eyes, Nicole was more important.

If I hadn't fallen in love before, I would have dropped like a rock right then.

"New Year's Eve," I said. "If we both feel like this on New Year's Eve, I swear, I'll propose."

"We're planning when we'll get engaged?" she asked lightly.

"Yes. We're engaged to become engaged. Face it, a year from now we'll be sitting in this pool, talking about my parents' upcoming thirtieth anniversary, but I'm betting we'll be married by then. So why not plan when I'll propose? At least you won't be wondering when the hell I'll grow a pair and ask."

"The trick," she said with another kiss, "will be to keep you from asking before then."

"I won't...but we are free to discuss the future since we know we'll be together."

"Like how many kids we want."

"And when. That's something we might as well agree on, because the second you've said 'I do' and have a ring on your finger my dad will pull you aside and start begging for grandkids. And he'll tease you with 'even though you're not Irish, I still want grandkids from you.'"

"Then I'll make your father very happy. Not only will he get grandkids from us, but I'm third generation Irish on my father's side and fourth on my mother's."

"Oh my God, if I *don't* marry you I'll be disinherited."

"We wouldn't want that, now, would we?"

"New Year's Eve," I reminded her. "I swear."

~

An hour later, when the chicken was coming off the grill and Nicole was sitting on the grass next to Michael's playpen while he babbled at her, Kevin looked at me, and then at Sherry, and asked my daughter, "Hey, short stuff. How would you like to spend the night with Aunt Lydia and me?"

"Can I read a story to Michael?"

"Sure. I think he'd like that."

"Kev," I said, "shouldn't you ask your wife before scheduling a sleepover?"

"Spontaneous sleepovers are the most fun. I'll ask her, but she won't mind." He started toward the house and as he passed me he whispered, "You are never gonna make it to New Year's Eve. I don't think Nicole heard, but since I did…you never know."

He was laughing as he went into the house in search of his wife.

"Is it okay, Daddy?" Nicole asked.

"If Aunt Lydia says it's all right, then it's fine with me."

She jumped up off the grass and ran over to me, throwing her arms around my neck.

"You have to be good and not keep Michael up too late," I reminded her. "Or Kevin and Lydia for that matter, because Michael will be waking them up early."

"I know. I'll go to bed at my usual time."

"That's up to your aunt and uncle."

She leaned in close and whispered, "Is Sherry going to spend the night at our house?"

"Why would you ask that?" I asked just as quietly, though from where she sat, Sherry could hear everything.

"Because you like her," she reasoned.

"Yes, I do."

"Do you love her?"

"Yes, I do."

"Are you gonna marry her?"

"Someday, kiddo."

"So it's okay then." She let go of me and looked right at Sherry and said, "You can put his foot through the wall now, if you want to."

She skipped off into the house, leaving us there to watch Michael.

"What was that about?" she asked.

"That," I explained, "…that was my eight year old daughter giving us permission to have sex."

~

Chip

"Come on," Kevin urged, "tell us what your plans were."

Nick and Katie left shortly after dinner, Paul and Sherry not too long after that; they told Nicole he was driving her home and would probably stay long enough to watch the news, but she rolled her eyes and grunted, "Yeah, right," before turning her attention back to her baby cousin.

Now she was in the spare bedroom with him, crawling on her hands and knees as she chased him around the room. He was squealing with joy over all the attention she was giving him, looking back every other second to make sure she was still there. She promised to shout out if the baby needed anything and swore she wouldn't leave him alone, not even to go to the bathroom.

"I won't take my eyes off him," she said earnestly.

Lydia agreed that she was old enough to watch him back there, mostly because the room was empty and there was nothing for either of them to get hurt on.

We spread out across the living room, and I was a bit surprised that we all fit. I'd thought it was smaller than the one in the old house, and the kids practically tripped over each other there. Spider and Eileen were curled up together in the loveseat, Kevin was stretched out on the floor, and Terry and I sat on the sofa with Lydia.

They were trying to get us to tell them what we'd planned for our anniversary, but Terry cut me off with a death glare and hissed, "Don't you dare."

"Man, we really screwed up something good, didn't we?" Eileen asked, laughter tinting each word.

I simply smiled and shrugged, and assured them whatever we'd thought about doing we would do another day.

Truthfully, the only things we'd planned were a ferry ride from Vallejo to San Francisco and lunch at Fisherman's Wharf; she didn't want to tell the kids because she didn't want anyone else to tag along. If they thought we had especially kinky plans, that was fine with her.

Fine with me, too.

"Paul set aside the back of the restaurant, everything to the left of the dance floor," Kevin said. "There will even be live music. He hired Four-Twenty to play."

"He hired a stoner band?" Eileen asked.

"Technically. But they also play elevator music when the situation calls for it. Those guys clean up really well."

"This was supposed to be a family dinner," Terry reminded them.

"It is," Kevin said. "It's not like the band is going to eat with us. And Paul didn't close the place down for this party."

"We should take Nicole shopping for a dress," Lydia said to Eileen. "I'm not sure that's something Paul would think of."

"Wait," I interrupted. "We have to dress for this dinner?"

"Would be nice if you weren't naked, Dad," Eileen mocked.

"We don't have to wear suits and ties," Kevin said. "They just want an excuse to go shopping."

"Exactly! Oh, and we should invite Sherry along," Eileen added.

Spider, who I was certain had been falling asleep, nodded and said, "You need to start teaching her to sign. Someday I might have to talk to her."

"Well that's a nice way to put it," Kevin snorted. "You'll never *have* to talk to her, numb nuts. But it would nice if you wanted to."

"Kiss my ass. You know what I meant."

"Kiss him on the cheek for me, Eileen," he chuckled. "And where are your parents tonight anyway? It's almost no fun picking on Dad without your mom helping me."

"Yeah, thanks for that," I grumbled.

Spider grinned. "Dad asked her out on a date. He said they'd never really done that, so they're doing it now."

"No, they never really did," Terry told him. "They worked together and fell in love, but I don't think they actually dated. Good for them. Better late than never."

"Dad just wants to get lucky," Spider said.

"God," Kevin moaned, "more old people sex. What is it with your generation? Don't you know you're supposed to stop when your kids are getting all freaky on their own?"

"Yeah. About that. I'll remind you when Michael is a teenager and thinking about everything he can possibly do to the cheerleader two seats over in English class."

"Better her than the English teacher," Terry snickered.

Kevin sat up sharply. "You totally did not," he said, looking straight at me.

"We're talking about Michael, and how you have to stop having sex when he's seventeen and crawling all over some poor girl under the bleachers."

"He knows about the bleachers?" Lydia blurted.

"Well, he does now," he replied, tilting his head as he looked at her. "Can I tell them how you dragged me under there in spite of my protests? All I wanted was to go to the snack bar, but no, you had all these impure thoughts and wanted to act on them."

"And I pee out rainbows," Terry chided.

Lydia snickered. "He's not exactly lying. He was headed for the snack bar and it was my idea. It was also where he broke my heart for the first time."

"All I said was that I might have a vocation. No one said that meant Stop. You're the one who got all 'oh no! He's going to be a priest and I just let him touch my boob!'"

"You two just tormented the hell out of each other all through high school, didn't you?" Terry asked.

"Yes, we did," Kevin said. "It was good practice for the self denial that comes with having a kid who starts crying at the most inconvenient times."

Lydia cocked her head, listening. "Speaking of whom, it's gotten awfully quiet back there."

Kevin started to peel himself up, but I waved him off and got up to check on Nicole and Michael.

Max was sitting in the doorway, watching them suspiciously. Michael was sound asleep on his stomach and Nicole was lying on her back, staring up at the ceiling. When she saw me she sat up and whispered, "I didn't leave him alone, not for a second."

"Good job."

She yawned and said, "I'm really tired, too, Grandpa."

"Do you just want to sleep here? You can crawl into the bed in the other room."

"But I promised Uncle Kevin…"

"He won't mind," I assured her. I reached a hand out and helped her up. "I think Grandma has pajamas for you in the top dresser drawer, and you have a toothbrush in the bathroom. It's the red one."

"Are you sure it's okay?"

"It's fine, sweetheart. You can spend the night with Kevin another night."

"Okay." She hugged me and stumbled off to the bathroom, leaving me to gently pick Michael off the floor and carry him to the living room. His weight sagged in my arms, and he snuggled in tight, head in the crook of my neck and drool dripping onto my chest.

Lydia started to reach for him, but I shook my head and sat down with him. "I don't get this every day now," I whispered. "You're letting me hold him for a while."

"He's all yours for now," she said, rubbing his little arm.

"And Nicole is staying here tonight. She's half asleep already and just wanted to crawl into bed, but she's worried you two will be offended."

Kevin pushed himself up. "Is she in bed?"

"Not yet."

"Then I'll go tell her it's all right and give her a kiss good night."

Spider gestured to Michael and said to Eileen, "Tell me you really don't want that."

"Not tonight."

"Tomorrow?"

"Ask me then," she said with a sigh.

He raised a playful eyebrow. "I might be winning!"

"Actually she was saying 'shut up or I'll cock punch you,'" Terry mused.

"Oh my god, Mom!" Eileen doubled over laughing, and took a few deep breaths before adding, "You did not just say that!"

Terry shrugged lightly and Kevin trotted down the hall and asked, "Did I just hear 'cock punch' come out of my mother? More importantly, did Nicole?"

She put her hand over her mouth and murmured, "Oh no."

"You people." Kevin pointed at all of us. "You're a wonderful example for these kids."

"We're evil," Eileen agreed.

"Just so long as you know it."

Eileen patted Spider on the leg and got up, turning to him to say, "Come on, mister. When my mom starts throwing around the c-word, it's time to go home."

He was laughing as he got up, and then leaned over to kiss Terry.

"Sometimes," he signed, "I really wish I could hear, because that was golden."

"And sometimes," I whispered to Michael as they closed the door behind them, "I wish you were old enough to potty train, because you just peed on me again."

"Time for us to go then, too," Lydia said quietly. She got up and carefully lifted her son out of my arms and cradled him close. "You really are sopping wet, aren't you?"

"I'll be there in a minute," Kevin told her. "I promised Nicole I would come back and say goodnight."

I peeled my wet shirt off and headed for the laundry room; from it I could hear Nicole giggling quietly, and the low hum of Kevin's voice as he told her that Grandma had just said something naughty, and that Michael peed all over Grandpa.

I tossed the shirt into the sink and started back for the living room, but rooted in place when I heard Nicole ask Kevin if Daddy was going to marry Sherry for real.

"Would it bother you if he wants to?" Kevin asked by way of an answer. "It's okay if it upsets you."

"No, I want him to."

"Then you like Sherry?"

"Uh huh. But if she marries Daddy, will that make her my mom?"

I nearly held my breath, hoping he knew what to say.

I'm not sure I would know.

"I think," he said carefully, "that if they get married, for a long time you'll keep calling her by her first name. And maybe someday you'll want to call her Mom, but she's never going to make you do that. She knows you love your mother, Nicole. She'll never try to replace her."

"I don't want my real mom to get mad if I get a new one," Nicole said, nearly whispering.

"Sweetheart, no. She would never be mad about that. More than anything in the world she wanted you and your dad to be happy, and I know for sure she wanted him to find someone who would love you both just as much as she did."

"Did she tell you that?"

"Yes, she did. And if he marries Sherry, if she can watch from heaven and she'll be so thrilled for you both that she'll cry the way Grandma does when something makes her really happy. Your mom loved Sherry first, you know."

"Really?"

"They were best friends in high school," Kevin told her. "Your dad knew Sherry all the way back when they were in kindergarten, but it was your mom who loved her first. So I'm sure that it already makes her happy that your Dad loves Sherry, too."

"I hope she loves him back."

"I think she does, cupcake. I think she loves him a lot. You ready to go to sleep now?"

"Yep."

A kiss on the cheek, and he said softly, "I love you, kiddo. Sleep tight."

He stopped in the hallway when he realized I was in the laundry room, and I shrugged and signed, "I didn't want to make any noise, in case she stopped talking to you."

"I didn't screw that up, did I?"

"You did good, son. I couldn't have done better myself."

I followed him into the living room and watched him kiss his mother goodnight, grateful that he was light years ahead of where I had been at his age.

21

Kevin

If everything went according to schedule, Paul said, the restaurant would close down on December 24th and reopen in its new location on the 31st. All but two employees were planning on moving with it, so training would be minimal; a couple of days to learn the new layout and computer system, and we'd be good to go.

"We," I repeated. "You mean you'll be good to go. There's no 'we' here."

"Block off a couple of days, Squirt. You're still technically on the payroll as a fill in, and you need to learn where everything is, too."

Apparently one does not quit the family business even when one has his own to look after.

We were sitting at the bar, waiting for our parents and sister to show up; Lydia was in Paul's office with Michael and Nicole, and Sherry was still working, showing early dinner customers to their tables, but everyone else was still half an hour from arriving.

Paul kept rotating on the barstool, watching her move between the dining room and the host stand; his attention was seriously divided and every time he looked at her I could see Dad looking at Mom, and I could feel the way want caught at him the same way it tugged at me nearly every time I looked at Lydia.

"Why don't you just go for it, Paul?"

His gaze was still on her, standing near the front door, waiting for the next customers to walk in.

"I have a promise to wait for," he said.

"What's the point?"

Nicole, he reminded me. For whatever they wanted, his daughter came first. Throw on top of that the fact that they'd been seriously dating for all of about three months, and it meant waiting.

"Bullshit. I can see it, Mom and Dad can see it…even Nicole sees it. She's not going to suddenly throw the brakes on and decide she doesn't want you to have a life. She likes Sherry."

"That doesn't mean she's ready for what comes next."

"She also doesn't get to dictate the terms by which you get married, Paul. She's eight. She doesn't get that kind of power. If you have no doubt that Sherry's the one, then follow your heart and do it."

He finally turned and looked at me. "I have absolutely no doubt. But waiting a few more months is fair. And seriously, we haven't been together that long."

"Mom and Dad," I pointed out. "Look at them. They only *met* six months before they got married. You met Sherry when you were both practically embryos."

He snorted a laugh through his nose.

"Wouldn't it be a kick to open the new place with a wedding reception instead of a proposal?"

His eyes flicked wide for a second, the idea knifing through his brain and settling there.

"Just something to think about," I said, getting up.

I headed into his office and left him there alone, knowing he would spend the fifteen minutes until she was off watching Sherry work, knowing that the woman he was seeing in his mind's eye was not dressed in black slacks and a black dress shirt, but all in white.

~

Twenty minutes later we cleared out of the office so Sherry would have a private place to change out of her work clothes, and we headed for the back of the restaurant. Paul had set aside the two largest tables for us, and the band was beginning to play a short warm up set.

The stoner band, as Eileen kept calling them, left the electric guitars and amps behind and set up as dual pianos with one acoustic guitar and drums, and instead of the grunge-wear they were usually in they were all dressed in dark blue suits with pale blue t-shirts underneath. The last time I'd heard them live they opened with a wonder tune called 'Weed for Momma,' but tonight I heard a soft melodic version of 'Tonight' from *West Side Story*.

Michael was fussy and Lydia was pacing between the tables with him, bouncing him lightly while she tried to calm him down. He wasn't screaming yet, but as he amped up that was the next stage, and we both hoped Sherry was out of the office by then so we'd have a place to take him.

"If he winds up being a pain in the ass we can take turns with him in there tonight," Paul told her. "He won't be heard from the dining room unless the door is open."

"I can babysit him," Nicole offered. "After we eat, this thing is gonna be boring anyway. We can watch TV or maybe cartoons if there's still the DVDs in your desk."

Paul gestured for her to come over to him, and he pulled her into his lap. "It won't be too boring, I promise. But even if it is, you have to be good and not whine, because this is important to Grandma and Grandpa. You know what today is, right?"

"Their anniversary."

"You know how long?"

"A long, long time."

"Twenty nine years. So we all have to be on our best behavior, even Uncle Kevin."

She giggled and looked at me. "You're gonna get a time out in the office tonight aren't you, Uncle Kevin?"

"No doubt."

She turned back to her father and put her hands on his cheeks. "You have to be good, too, Daddy, but you can still kiss Sherry if you want."

"Thank you for the permission, sweetheart. I'll try to not embarrass you."

"I'm not embarrassed," she said earnestly. "I like it when you kiss her."

"Do you now?" He tilted his head back just a touch, as if he was considering her from a whole new angle.

"You're really happy when she's around you, you know. You

smile a lot more."

"Didn't I smile a lot before?"

"It's not the *same*, Daddy. Sometimes when she's next to you, you smile for no reason or maybe it because she smells good or something, and I like that."

"So do I."

Nicole's hands slipped from his cheeks to his chest. "When are you going to marry her?"

Paul pursed his lips thoughtfully, looking for the right thing to say. "That's something Sherry and I have to decide for ourselves, Nicole. I can't answer that yet."

His eyes flicked over her shoulder and she turned to see what had caught his attention, and we all looked to see Sherry walking towards us. She had changed out of the black shirt and slacks into a sleeveless pale yellow dress that hugged every curve, and as she got closer Nicole slid out of Paul's lap so he could stand up, and she whispered loudly, "I *told* you she made you smile."

"Best behavior," he reminded her in the same whisper, "and that means no picking on Sherry about marrying me, you understand?"

"That's okay. That's what Uncle Kevin is for."

As Paul leaned over Nicole to kiss Sherry, I winked at my niece. Truthfully, if I wanted to corner Sherry, there wasn't much he could do about it.

Michael was ramping up, and I was about to take him from Lydia when Paul reached over and asked to hold him. He lifted Michael up high, planting tiny knees against his chest so that they were nearly face to face and murmured, "You get no respect, do you, little man? Here you are trying to tell them something and they just think you're cranky and need to be locked away where no one can see you."

"He's going to start upsetting the paying customers," I warned Paul.

"There's always a reason, isn't there?" he asked Michael, pretty much ignoring me. "If you're not wet and you're not hungry and you don't want to be bounced, there's always something else that can make a guy cranky. You're not tugging at your ear and you're not rubbing your eyes, so what's making Michael an unhappy little boy?"

He stuck his finger in Michael's mouth and ran it along his gums.

"And that would make a guy cry, wouldn't it? You've got a whole bunch of Ouch and no one listened when you said so."

Lydia pulled Michael's chin down and looked into his mouth. "Oh my God! Kevin, he's got two teeth poking out!"

While we gawked over our son's new teeth Paul told Nicole to go into his office and look in one of his desk drawers for the tube of gel the dentist had given her the last time she had a toothache.

"I feel bad now," Lydia said as Paul handed the baby back to her. "I just thought he was tired and cranky."

"I walked the floor with Nicole screaming her head off for almost an entire day before Mom came over and pointed out some obvious toothy little nubs," Paul said. "Don't feel bad about it. You've never had a six and a half month old baby before."

We both felt bad about it, but within a few minutes Nicole was back and the rest of the family was trickling in. Paul swiped his gel-slicked finger over Michael's gums, and within seconds he relaxed, smacking his lips against the numbness. When he caught sight of his grandparents he broke into a wide grin, held his arms out with his hands opening and closing and squealed "Baba!" loud enough that they heard.

I whispered into his ear, "Dada" but all that got me was spit on my face when he turned his head and thrust his tongue out of his mouth with a rush of formula-scented baby breath.

"Yeah, I love you, too," I muttered, wiping my face off with the sleeve of my shirt.

"Get used to it," Paul said. "From here on out, they're the good guys. You're just Daddy."

"That'd be fine if he would just say it."

"You can do that, can't you?" Paul asked his nephew. "Come on. Say 'dada'."

Michael grinned at him, looked at me, and then tilted his head backwards until the top of it was pressed into Lydia's chest. He threw his arms out again, and with a squeal that said he meant it, he shouted, "Mama!"

~

"They didn't have a reception," Kris told us as our parents melted into each other on the dance floor. "They threw the wedding together so quickly that this would have been the only place for it, but all they really wanted to do was say their vows and head off for their honeymoon."

Grandma Stevens pointed at Nick and said, "You. If someone had made me the offer, I would have bet cash that you were showing up within seven months."

"They bribed me to hang onto one of her ribs and wait inside for an extra three months," Nick teased.

"You did not like Chip," Grandpa reminded her. "Not one bit. When Terry said she was marrying him I thought you were going to hurdle over her and claw his eyes out."

"He's like a fungus," she explained. "Give him a while and he grows on you."

Kris had something to say but stopped when Dad dipped Mom low and was very slow to get back up.

"Getting old sucks, doesn't it?" she said, just loud enough for them to hear.

Dad cocked an eyebrow at her—if we were anywhere else he probably would have flipped her off—and guided Mom to the other side of the floor.

She was laughing and kept touching his face, a thumb trailing over his ear, fingers brushing over his lips.

We could have turned how many times they kissed into a drinking game. She kisses him; take a shot. He kisses her, take two. If it lasts longer than a second, slug from the bottle.

We'd have been plastered by the third song.

"Your parents are adorable together," Sherry told Paul.

"Don't tell any of these guys that their parents are hot, though," Lydia said. "They get all flustered."

"I have a hot son-in-law," our grandmother declared. "If you kids don't like it, tough."

"We don't exactly need to hear about it," Paul said as he got up. He held a hand out to Sherry and added, "I may not dance as well as my father, but I look better doing it."

"No one spoil his delusion," Eileen snickered when they were out on the floor near our parents.

"I like her," Grandpa said. "She's quiet, but there's something very nice about her."

"She makes Daddy smile," Nicole informed him.

"Well, now. I supposed I like that quite a bit."

"Remind you of anyone?" Kris asked, gesturing to both couples on the floor. Paul had his arms wrapped around Sherry and they were dancing close, moving together as if by thought alone. Mom and Dad weren't nearly as close, but she had her arms around his neck and was stretching up to kiss him.

Paul was five inches shorter than Dad and as blonde as Mom, and he gazed at Sherry nearly the same way our father was looking at our mother.

"Very much so," Grandma said.

Michael leaned over in his high chair, craning his neck to see past Lydia. He watched his grandparents and uncle for a moment, and then stretched out his arms and started crying, "Baba! Baba!"

Without missing a beat they drifted across the floor and Dad lifted him up, carrying him in his arms while they continued to dance. Michael snuggled close, setting his head on Dad's shoulder, one hand grasping his shirt and he jammed the thumb on his other hand in his mouth.

"Now that's hot," Aunt Kris declared. She looked over at Uncle Doug, who had moved to the far end of the table and was alternating between making phone calls and reading emails off his cell phone. "That's not so hot."

"What's he doing?" Nick asked.

"He's got a patient emergency. Don't be surprised if he has to leave, and then one of you has to drive me home."

"No, Mom," Spider signed. "We're making you walk back. Along the Interstate. In high heels."

"You're mean, Uncle Spider," Nicole said. "I think Aunt Eileen should make you dance. That'll teach you."

"I thought you liked dancing," he said.

"I do, but watching you is just funny."

He stuck his tongue out at her and made her giggle, and then asked Eileen, "Is the music loud enough that I'll feel it out there?"

"No, but it's slow. You can follow me."

He squinted at Nicole, trying to not smile. "You better not laugh at me."

Grandma Stevens watched them for a minute and then turned to Aunt Kris. "Did you ever think you'd see him dance?"

"When he was Nicole's age, no. But once he fell in love with Eileen... Now I can't imagine him not dancing with her every chance he gets."

"That girl brings music wherever she goes," Grandpa mused.

Mom and Dad wound their way to the edge of the dance floor and then back to the table, taking the seats Eileen and Spider had vacated. Michael was half asleep and I started to reach for him but Dad shook his head.

"How do you feel about cutting in on your brother and asking your potential future sister-in-law to dance?"

~

Paul

Kevin was the last person I wanted cutting in on us, but Sherry said yes to that little boy smile and I found myself headed back to the table. Anyone else would have been fine; Kevin was sure to drop far too many not-so-subtle hints and I wasn't sure she would feel comfortable enough to blow him off.

Before I could sit down, Mom was up and had grabbed me by the hand, telling me to follow. She wanted to talk, and it wasn't a request. She led me into the office and closed the door quietly, leaning against it for a moment before sitting on the sofa.

"Just hear me out, okay?" She patted the empty space next to her.

I hesitated.

'Just hear me out' usually does not end well.

"Nick and Katie were so young when they got married, but I still felt good about it," Mom said as I sat down. "I had absolutely no doubts about Spider and Eileen, and when Kevin married Lydia—"

"Meant to be," I finished for her.

"It was. And funny enough, when I married your father I don't think anyone was certain about it except for us. My father didn't argue because he knew I loved Chip, but my mother…you would not believe how angry she was."

She kindly did not point out that when I married Monica the best anyone really hoped for was that the eventual divorce would not be messy and protracted, and any children would not be fought over.

"So you have a gift for knowing," I ventured, hoping she was not wandering into You-Got-The-Wrong-Girl territory.

Over this, I would not have a problem walking out on my mother.

"I think I do." She spun the ring on her right hand around, and then slipped it off. "Your father gave this to me a few months after Kevin and Eileen were born. We had decided that we wanted to renew our vows in the church, and even though we had four kids and a lot of history between us…he wanted there to be an engagement ring."

She reached for my hand and pressed the ring into my palm.

"As sure as I felt about your brothers and sister, I never felt the desire to give them this ring. But I'm more certain about you and Sherry than I think I've ever been about anyone."

"Mom—"

"Even about your father and I, Paul."

"I can't take this. I know how much it means to you."

"And that's exactly why I want you to take it. This ring meant forgiveness, and it meant a promise for a forever I was too stupid to pay close enough attention to. The love that came with it means everything to me…and I want you to have it because you'll be able to promise her not just forever, but faithfulness and patience, and I know you'll honor your promises with your soul."

I looked at the ring setting in my hand; it was a thin gold band that held three small diamonds; it wasn't flashy and it wasn't expensive, but it felt like my mother had given me the most valuable thing in her life.

"Renewing our vows was about starting over, and it feels like that's what you're doing."

"It feels new," I agreed.

She touched a finger to each diamond. "Past, present, and future. Every day that ring is on her finger, you'll have all three."

"I told her I would propose on New Year's Eve," I explained in a near whisper.

"You'll propose when it feels right," she said, kissing me on the cheek.

She got up, ruffling my hair a bit before she walked out of the office, and left me there with the weight of the world burning into the palm of my hand.

~

Kevin

"My brother is in love with you, my father is well past being in like with you, and my grandfather says you're smokin' hot. My grandmother thinks you're sweet, my mother wants to adopt you, and my niece has given you her stamp of approval. The rest of us…we frankly think you're too good for him."

"No pressure there," she said lightly.

"It's not 'Paul, and his girlfriend Sherry.' It's PaulandSherry. You've been reduced to one name, so you might as well not fight it."

"I'm not fighting it," she assured me. "We have plans."

"Plans were made to be broken." The music stopped, and as the band was announcing their break, I added, "Just remember; it could take you forever to be sure that you're ready, and he'll wait for you. But don't make him wait that long. Don't make *us* wait that long. Like it or not, you're family."

~

We got back to the table at the same time Mom did, but before Sherry could ask where Paul was Mom nodded towards Aunt Kris and Uncle Doug, wondering what they were talking about so deeply.

Dad shrugged; Doug had been on his phone off and on for the entire evening and Kris finally decided to pull him off to an empty table where she could talk to him in between calls and messages.

They sat with their chairs close together, turned just enough away from us that Spider wouldn't be able to read their lips.

"It's obviously private, so we're leaving them alone," Dad said.

"Imagine that," I mocked. "Respecting someone's privacy. What a concept."

"You shut up," he said. "Tonight you have to be nice to me, Not only is it my anniversary, but I have your son, and I might be inclined to keep him for a while."

"Um, not tonight, you're not," Mom warned.

"Oh, geeze," I muttered.

Dad smiled brightly at me. "There you go. You're turning about three shades of red. Now you can have your son back."

"I can't believe how big he got while I was gone," Nick said as Dad carefully slipped Michael into my arms.

"You were gone for nearly half his life," Mom pointed out. "He went from hardly being able to sit up in someone's lap and not flopping over to crawling and calling your father 'Baba.'"

"And now he's got teeth." I added happily.

"With which he can bite you," Paul said from behind me. He bent over to kiss Sherry before sitting down. "Sorry about that. Just a little business I had to take care of."

"Sometimes business shouldn't wait," Dad offered.

Sherry peered at Paul. "Something wrong?"

"No, not at all. Just something unexpected."

If they'd been alone she probably would have pressed for more, but in the middle of his nosy family, she let it go. Nick and Katie were telling our grandparents about their twins, Spider was signing something slowly to Nicole, who still sometimes struggled with sign language, and Lydia was digging into the diaper bag, asking me if I'd seen Michael's toy keys.

The din was enough to distract Sherry and give her a taste of what to expect.

It was almost enough to distract me from the nagging voice that told me I'd looked at Uncle Doug and missed something, but I heard it tapping at me and looked back; he and Aunt Kris were both staring at Dad.

I tapped his arm to get his attention. "I think whatever Uncle

Doug has been doing all night has to do with you."

Everything stopped. Lydia dropped the diaper bag to the floor, Nick stopped in mid-sentence, and everyone turned to look at Uncle Doug. His eyes were tinged with red, and he stole another glance at the email glaring back at him from his Blackberry.

From the corner of my eye I saw Mom reach for Dad's hand, and could feel the way her fingers curled around his, a soft squeeze, her thumb rubbing his absently. She looked up at him, but he kept his eyes on Uncle Doug.

As he got up, Sherry leaned over and whispered to Nicole, who nodded and then took her hand as they walked towards Paul's office. Doug slipped into her chair, across the table from Dad, and said softly, "Your pathology report is in."

22

Chip

As he sat down, Doug was staring at his cell phone. I tried to gauge his expression—Disbelief? Anger? Fear?—but I wasn't sure. I waited for signals I could trust; if he exhaled slowly, it was disbelief. If he swallowed hard, it was fear. Anger would have him slapping the phone onto the table with a crack that might make Michael cry.

Nick quietly moved over so that Kris could sit beside Doug, her hand snaking through the crook of his arm.

Moral support?

Thickly, so low I had to strain to hear, he said, "We never even considered this. This is so rare—"

I could feel Terry twitch beside me, and her grip tightened on my hand.

Remember the penny in the pool, Nicole, that's how rare this kind of cancer is.

"I mean, seriously... Remember Kevin told you that there have only been roughly a hundred documented cases of pituitary cancers, ever?"

All I could do was nod, and clench my teeth in an effort to steel my nerves.

My entire family was witness to this; I was not going to blink more than I needed to lest it upset them.

My heart began to pound hard.

My head was not far behind it.

It can't be cancer.

No one gets pituitary cancer.

"This is even more rare than that," Doug went on.

Kevin shot forward, one hand clenching his son to him, the other splayed out on the table. "What the *hell*, Uncle Doug? What could be more rare—? The worst case scenario was a craniopharyngioma. Treatable. What the fuck?"

"We considered everything except this," Doug went on, ignoring the anguish in Kevin's protest. "I've never seen this, Chip, and other than maybe one or two cases, it's never been seen in men."

I watched Kevin's hand slide back.

"Usually we only see it in young women who are pregnant with or who have just had their first child. And even then, it's very rare."

"Oh holy…" Kevin breathed out.

"Your tumor," he went on, glancing at Kevin, "came back in all resections as autoimmune hypophycitis. It's—"

"You bastard," Kevin hissed.

"—a collection of cells comprising an infection."

I waited for the other shoe to drop.

Doug's eyes were red and damn near filling with tears, and I didn't want to ask.

Did my pool just drain of all but the one thing I can't deal with?

"You had a brain zit," Kevin finally said. "You had a fucking zit in your brain."

"Wait. I what?" I wasn't sure I heard either of them correctly.

"It was just a mass of infection, and the likelihood of recurrence is pretty much zero," Doug said. "It's gone, Chip. It's not coming back."

"Then why—?" I started to ask what the tears were for when Terry buried her face against her arms and started to cry. I looked at Paul and said, "You go tell your daughter now. Make sure she understands that I don't have cancer. I don't have anything."

~

Kevin

Paul sprinted towards his office. Mom's arms were folded on the table and she rested her forehead against them, sobs tearing at her so hard the entire table shook. Dad slid his hand across her back gently and then set his head next to hers, his lips near her ear as he whispered to her.

I couldn't hear him, but I could guess.

It's all right. We're fine. I love you and you have me for the next thirty years.

Relief spilled across the table in choked back tears, and within a few seconds Mom sat up and turned in her chair to put her arms around him. She was still crying, but a smile tugged at the corners of her mouth, and as she pulled his head towards hers for a kiss, Nicole bolted across the dining room shouting, "Grandpa! Daddy said you don't have cancer and you're not gonna die!"

The restaurant fell quiet, all eyes on the little girl leaping at her grandfather.

The guitar player on the small dance floor stage glanced at us, and then the dining room, before reaching for the microphone.

"Good news, everyone," he said in a deep, melodious voice. "Our host for the night is *not* going to die. Everyone raise a glass in salute, and then hit the dance floor because this is now a party!"

He turned to his band mates and nodded, and the air swelled with the loudest music of the night, drum-beat pounding a distraction from the mixture of laughter and tears coming from our corner.

"Grandpa, is it true?" Nicole asked over the din of the music.

"Uncle Doug just found out. The tumor wasn't cancer, and since the doctor got it all, I don't have to worry about it anymore."

"Are you sure you're sure, Uncle Doug?" she asked.

"I'm positive."

"Do you *swear*?"

Dad pulled Nicole into a tight hug and said, "It's all right, sweetheart. We promise."

"Good." She wiggled away from him and stood in front of him, her hands on her hips, and said, "Now all the grownups have to go dance like that guy said to. It's a party!"

"Wait," I said. "Does that mean I have to stay here?"

"Uncle Kevin," she groaned.

Katie leaned back and put both hands on her belly. "I'll stay with the kidlets. She's right, everyone who can should go out there and dance."

"What about Uncle Nick?"

"I'll stay here, too, munchkin. I haven't spent much time with you since I got home, so now's my chance."

Nicole scrambled over to the chair next to him and waved the rest of us off.

We were dismissed by an eight year old.

~

Paul

We practically filled the dance floor; Eileen and Spider wound through us until they were close to the stage where he could better feel the beat of the music, and my grandparents barely ventured past the table, but Nicole got what she wanted: nearly all the adults that mattered to her were paired off and dancing close. She'd forgive Katie for not wanting to dance for no other reason than she got to sit there with her hand on her aunt's growing belly and feel her cousins turning and kicking.

Aunt Kris and Uncle Doug held each other lightly, too busy laughing with each other to pay attention to the music, but Kevin was glued to Lydia and my mother had her arms looped around Dad's neck, and even with tears still pooling in her eyes, she couldn't stop looking into his.

Sherry moved closer to me, so close I could have almost kissed her without moving my head. I could feel her breath skip across my face as she said, "Your parents have had a wonderful anniversary, I think. I don't think I've ever seen anyone so happy."

Take a closer look. Look at me.

"They deserve this."

"Somehow I think you mean more than just getting good news on their anniversary."

"They fought for their marriage," I told her. "I don't think it was easy, but if anything, they love each other more now than the day they got married. They adore each other, and they have an especially close family."

"You're each other's best friends," she observed.

"Most of the time. They've got the grandkids they always wanted, and two more on the way. And everyone's happy. For the first time in years, I think every single one of us is happy."

Her smile was so warm that it nearly buckled my knees. "Your parents deserve seeing that happiness," she mused. "It's the cherry on top of the whipped cream on top of layers of ice cream and cake."

The song we were dancing to ended and I saw Kevin approach the stage, whispering to the guitar player.

"I'm not sure they've gotten the cherry yet," I told her, feeling the weight of my mother's ring in my pocket.

Kevin was reaching for Lydia when the next song started, and as he spun past he sang under his breath, intending for us to hear, "When I fall in love…"

"So, is the cherry some ideal they have to keep reaching for?" she asked, amusement with my brother touching every word.

"No. It's just one more thing that would make something already nice a whole new level of awesome."

"I hope they get it then."

"I do, too." I led her away from Kevin, who looked like he was about to lean over and start singing to both of us. "Are they overwhelming you tonight?"

"Hardly. I'm having a very good time, and Kevin made it a point to tell me I have their approval."

"They have absolutely no doubts about us, and frankly, considering it's me, that's saying a lot."

"Give yourself some credit, Paul."

"I do. I know I'm not the same little creep that slithered around campus in high school. I know what matters." I gestured to my parents. "What they have, that matters. My daughter matters. And you matter more than just about everything."

Her hand slid to the back of my neck, squeezing gently. "Paul…"

"Nicole loves you, and even if six months from now she has an attitude adjustment, she doesn't get to pick the woman I fall in love with. Hell, in five years you're going to tell her to do something and she's going to roll her eyes and hiss 'you're not my mother' no matter what we do now. We know where this is going. What are we waiting for?"

I was acutely aware that we were no longer dancing, but standing in the middle of the floor with my family moving around us.

"New Year's Eve," she said simply.

"And then what? Give Nicole another six months to get used to something that's going to happen anyway, whether she likes it or not?"

"This isn't just about Nicole," she said. "It's about us and the fact that we were going to take it slow."

"My parents, the ones who are celebrating twenty nine years today? They only knew each other for about six months before they got married. Yet we've known each other forever. You know as well as anyone what kind of person I was and you know what kind of man I want to be. You know *me*. And yet, you love me."

"Yes, I do, very much."

"Then tell me what we're really waiting for."

"Right this moment, I'm not really sure."

My mother's ring exploded in weight, and I reached into my pocket for it. "My father gave this to my mother as a sort of second engagement ring," I said quietly, watching her eyes go wide. I let the weight push me to my knee and I held it out carefully, looking up at Sherry's eyes.

"I want forever with you, and I want it to start now. I love you, and that's not going to change. Don't make me wait until New Year's Eve to hear yes. Marry me on New Year's Eve, and say yes tonight. Please. Will you marry me?"

No one was moving, collective breaths waiting.

She nodded, just slightly, and as I came up off the floor she reached for me and sobbed, "Yes."

~

Kevin

Dad sat in the bar booth, running his hands through his hair while staring at a beer he wasn't going to drink. Mom was by the front door waving to Aunt Kris and Uncle Doug as they left, and

Lydia had taken Michael into Paul's office for a bottle and change of clothes.

The restaurant was quiet other than the background noise of servers prepping for the next day, and the bartender clinking glasses together at the bar.

"I didn't even want this party. I wanted to take your Mom into San Francisco instead."

"And think of everything you would have missed out on."

His wallet wouldn't be so light, for one thing. Sherry said "yes," and we exploded around them, the noise so jarring and loud that one server dropped a tray and the guitar player stopped playing mid-song.

Paul scooped her up and spun her around the way Dad had Lydia the day we told him we were getting married. By the time he'd set her down and kissed her, the band recovered, and he and Sherry both turned toward Nicole, motioning for her to join them.

She bolted toward them, but it wasn't Paul who got her first hug.

When the rest of us managed to quiet down, Dad asked the guitar player to thank the customers for their congratulatory applause and for their patience with our family, and to then tell them that their meals were on the house, including gratuities. He wanted everyone to share in our joy.

I suspected the evening cost him close to five thousand dollars, and he would tip the staff at well over thirty percent, but I also knew he thought it was worth it.

The happy couple spent the next hour dancing, and when Dad suggested that they keep their grubby hands off each other until the wedding, Paul made excuses to leave. Sherry wanted to call her mother, he said. They needed to wind down from all the excitement.

Katie thought the idea of going home and turning in was a good one. Her feet were swollen and she had world war three being fought inside her; Nick helped her up and then told Paul he was taking Nicole with him.

"So you two can dance a little longer," he said. "But your daughter will probably fall asleep in my house, so you might as well let her stay the night."

"You." Dad pointed at Nick. "You're an enabler."

When everyone else left we moved to the bar, staying long after closing.

"I thought Doug was going to tell me I was going to die," Dad admitted. "I saw the look on his face and the tears he was fighting, and I was sure he was going to tell me there was nothing they could do."

"He was overwhelmed," I said. "He got to give you incredible news and it made him happy."

"I can't even tell you what he said it was; all I can remember now is hearing him say was that the tumor was never coming back."

"You have zits for brains," I said. "The rest of the details we can fill you in on later, after it's sunk in."

"And Paul… while your mother and I were dancing we talked about giving him her ring for when he was ready to propose, but I didn't think it would be tonight."

"I hoped."

"Son," he said, pushing himself up, "I think tonight is a night that will go down in family history as, 'Remember that night?'"

It could have become that no matter what the news Uncle Doug had delivered or the answer Sherry gave Paul; but he was right, this was going to be 'Remember that night?' but instead of saying it with gravity, it would be with wonder-tinged lightness.

I followed him towards the front where Mom was waiting with Lydia. She'd changed Michael's diaper and put clean pajamas on him so he could be dropped into bed when we got home; Mom was inspecting his two new teeth, lavishing praise on him for being such a big boy.

Part of me wanted to tease her for it, but the greater part of me thought he deserved it.

It was a big night, after all, and teeth were something to celebrate.

"Happy anniversary," I told my parents as they were about to get into Dad's car. "But remember, this was just a practice run for the big three-oh."

Dad leaned against the car, regarding me over the cloth top. "Son, the only way you can top this year is if for the next, one of you has quintuplets and another one of you gets a sex change."

I looked at Lydia and shrugged. "We'll get right on it."

"Funny man," she sighed as she clicked the car seat into place. "So who gets to transgender?"

"Uncle Doug. I was thinking that you and I could work on quints."

She looked up from Michael, pretending to glare.

"What? You don't want to make their thirtieth memorable?"

"If you ever," she said as she buckled up, "suggest quints to me again, I swear, I will pin you down and bite your dick off."

"Ow. You're mean."

"If all you want is another child, then we can talk."

"Now?"

"I think we should wait until we get home to actually do it, but why not now? It would put nearly sixteen months between kids, and that's presuming we got lucky right away."

"What happened to putting at least a year and a half between them?"

"I think that flew out the window with Paul waiting for New Year's Eve. Sometimes waiting is an exercise for the sake of exercise. We know we want another one and it might take us a while."

"So we want another baby. Soon."

"I'm ready to start trying if you are."

I started the car and headed towards home, my father's convertible just half a mile ahead. "We'll end up with two kids under two," I pointed out.

"We have a whole lot of people to lean on if we need help," she countered. "But I'm serious, if I have quints, you're losing a body part."

"I think I determine gender, but if you have a litter, it's probably your own fault."

"You're just aching to get shoved into your dad's pool, aren't you? I can have that arranged you know." She peered ahead of us, squinting against the dark. "Your dad is in an awful damned hurry tonight."

"Can't say as how I blame him. He's only got an hour of today left, and if I was him, I'd be barreling home to make sure I made love to my wife on our actual anniversary."

"And that doesn't embarrass you?"

"No. Now if you try to tell me he's speeding because she's giving him road head…that would embarrass me."

She laughed lightly and reached over to touch me, one finger tracing lightly over my ear. "I don't think your parents' horny impulses bother you nearly as much as you pretend. I think that deep down you love them for that, and you hope that when we're their age I'll still reach for you the way your mother reaches for your father."

I will always be affectionate.

"But not at seventy five miles an hour," I said.

Her hand was resting on my shoulder, fingers brushing the back of my neck. "Forget about doing anything in the car; I'm just happy that you're holding still in stationary positions. You don't flinch anymore."

"Well, there's a ringing endorsement for my manhood."

"But it is. You made an effort to like something you didn't think you would, simply because I wanted you to try. Now the only thing is getting you to admit that you do."

"I like everything we do," I assured her. "If you want proof, we'll be home in about three minutes. Toss the kid in bed, let me take a shower, and I'll show you."

"You don't have to prove anything to me, Kevin. I'll put Michael to bed and you can jump in the shower, but anything else that happens…I don't need proof."

"What do you need tonight?"

"I need," she said thoughtfully, "to take some time to unwind, and then to just be grateful that your father got the news that he did. I am so thankful…"

"We can do that," I said softly. "Tonight doesn't have to be anything sweaty. We can put Michael to bed together, and then if you want we can offer all the thanks we can that Dad's going to be all right."

I pulled up to the gate and hit the remote as her hand slid from my shoulder.

"You're pretty private about prayer, Rabbit."

"I know. But tonight my brother asked the woman of his dreams to marry him and she said yes, and tonight my mother got the gift of what I hope will be another thirty years with my father. You're right, we need to be grateful about that, and prayer is the first thing I turn to when I want to give thanks."

"But…"

I cut the engine, and turned to her. "My privacy where faith is concerned is just one more hang-up to get past, Lydia, and you're really the only want I want to work on that with. If you want me to, I will pray with you."

She pulled me close to kiss me, fingers in my hair, the gearshift digging into my thigh, and our son babbling happily in the back seat.

"I think he approves," she said against my lips, amused.

"Someday," I said to Michael, "we're going to do this and you're going to gag, but remember, I spent years gagging at my parents when I actually approved of what they were doing."

She kissed me again and I felt Michael's feet on his car seat as he pumped his legs, the wild little thump of his joy pulsating in a drum beat on leather, and when she finally let me up for air he giggled and finally squealed for me.

"Dada!"

~

Chip

Neither of us could sleep; at three a.m. we gave up and went outside, sitting by the pool with only the underwater light to see by. We sat with our legs dangling into the water, Terry's foot absently stroking mine, her heel fitting neatly into my arch.

If she could have, she would have wound her toes through mine.

She had barely been able to let go of me in the seven hours since Doug had given us the good news; she managed ten minutes away from me as she said goodnight to Doug and Kris at the restaurant, but otherwise she kept finding ways to make contact. Even on the ride home she kept one hand on me, her fingers playing at the back of my neck or rubbing across my thigh.

Sitting by the pool, both tired and spent yet not willing to go back to bed, she quietly said, "I feel like I've been holding my breath for nearly three months, and finally got to let it out. Now my heart is pounding and I'm almost a little dizzy."

She was afraid that if she fell asleep, come morning she would find out it was only a dream. We had too many good things happen at once, so how could it be real?

I offered to stay awake, to hold her while she slept, so that when she woke up I could promise her she hadn't been dreaming.

"Just give me a little while longer, Irish. I'm not ready for tonight to be over."

"We can stay out here as long as you want. This has definitely been a hell of a night. Forget the pathology report. When you decided to give Paul that ring, I never actually thought he would propose tonight."

"Yes, you did," she teased. "Why else did you get Kevin to distract Sherry long enough for me to give it to him?"

"I certainly wanted him to have the option. But no, I thought he would be stubborn enough to wait."

"I think without everyone telling him how perfect she is for him, he would have waited until New Years' Eve like they planned. He's so worried that it looks like he's pushing her to the altar or that they're moving too fast…"

"They are moving fast. That doesn't mean it's the wrong thing for them to do."

"The oddest thing…" She slipped into the water and reached for my hands, pulling me in with her so that she could get her arms around my waist. "When Sherry said yes and Nicole ran to her and hugged her, the first thing that went through my mind was that I wished Monica could see this."

"That's not odd. She wanted Paul to find someone."

"And more than a small part of me thinks she wanted him to find Sherry."

"I don't doubt it. I've had the notion that even if Monica had lived, eventually Paul would have found his way to Sherry. I loved her, Terry, but the more I see Paul now, the more certain I am that he was never meant to be with Monica forever. He was meant to save her from that life she was barely surviving under her father's thumb, but I don't think they would have or even should have seen ten years together."

"Should we have let them get married?"

"I don't know. I wish we had given Paul more options and more time to think about it before we agreed. And I know that was mostly my doing. I wanted him to have a chance to be a father, and in my mind that meant being married to his baby's mother. But I'm not sure it was the right thing."

"If Paul announced in the morning they intended to drive to Reno and anyone who wanted to be there was welcome to follow?"

"I wouldn't hesitate."

"I think I might ask him to consider that she's never been married before and might like a big wedding and reception."

"They'll wait for New Year's Eve and we'll have one hell of a holiday season this year. All the wedding excitement, Michael will be old enough to be terrified by Santa and fascinated by all the Christmas decorations...and Nick's kids will be here."

"Nick's kids," she sighed. "I wasn't sure I'd ever be able to say that."

"David and Mark, unless they get a surprise at the last minute."

Her hands slipped from my waist and she took a step back. "They hadn't told me. Chip..."

"David Mark." I swallowed against the lump in my throat. "Nick never even knew him, but he wanted to give his sons my brother's name. And goddammit, I wish David was here for all of this. He'd be forty five years old, Terry."

Her eyes filled with tears for at least the fifth time that night, and she reached out to place a wet hand on my chest. "You've missed him a lot lately, haven't you?"

"All I knew was the little kid. I never gave the teenaged David a chance. But the last couple of months...yes, I miss him. Everyone's gone. My mother, David, Ron, then Grant. I never had a chance with any of them. I'm the only one left."

"And for a few terrifying moments, you thought you might die, too."

"As screwed up as my family was, I miss them all. But I'm in no hurry to join them."

"I would have liked to have known your little brother, Irish. Just from the pictures I've seen, I think he would have been fun to have around."

"Until he blew up something you liked, you might have thought so. The kids would have loved him, I think. Just to have an uncle…"

"You gave them an uncle," she reminded me. "Doug might not be your blood, but you love him like he's been your brother all along."

"I've hated him like it sometimes, too. But all in all, he's been a very good brother to have."

"He was just as afraid as everyone else that we might lose you. He knew more than anyone that the odds were in your favor, but you saw his face tonight. He was so relieved he wanted to cry."

"Like someone else I know and love."

"It hit me all at once. I'm not sorry about it, even if it embarrassed everyone."

"No one was embarrassed," I promised. "They understood, and I was touched."

"But you shouldn't be surprised."

"My hair is falling out it in places it shouldn't, I'm pretty sure I'm never going to be able to lose this nice layer of body fat that has destroyed my six pack, my junk is shrinking, and I damn near dropped you on the dance floor tonight. Maybe I should be surprised that you still seem to want me so badly."

"I kind of like the way some of your hair has fallen out," she snickered. "And your body looks awesome, even if you have an extra half a per cent of body fat. You're not spongy anymore and I don't care if the boys shrivel up to pea sized as long as the rest of you works. And even if that broke…"

"I thought I saw crying tonight—I'd probably hear wailing then."

"We'd figure something out," she guessed. "No matter what, Queen Gumby loves her King, and she'll take him any way she can get him."

"Will the queen promise me something?"

"Tonight you can have anything you want."

"Rein the kids in on my birthday. I don't want to be surrounded by people I barely know and by business associates, and I especially don't want to grit my teeth through the ass pounding music they played at the last party."

"They'll want to do something for you, Chip. So will I, for that matter."

"Keep it to family only. There's nothing I want more than to just spend a quiet day with my wife and my kids."

"It won't be quiet. But basically you want a day pretty much like any other."

"Yes, but with presents. And cake."

"And grilled chicken."

"You hate me, don't you?"

"It's my job," she said, placing a warm wet kiss on my chest, "to keep this beating for as long as possible. And as well as it's beating, I just might be torturing you with chicken and fish for fifty more years…but I'll let you have steak on your birthday if you want. Ice cream, even."

"Wow. You must like me or something."

"Or something. And I think I'm ready to head back in. Just please don't let this be a dream."

Before we crawled back into bed I scribbled a note and taped it to the bathroom mirror. *It wasn't a dream, your majesty. The King promises.*

23

Chip

I stood in the middle of the beach house living room, looking out the window, wondering if I'd made a mistake. Kevin was sitting on the porch railing, staring out at the water, his shoulders slightly hunched over and his elbows digging into his knees. He'd been sitting there for over an hour, watching while Nicole played in the sand and as Nick dug a pit for the fire he wanted to light when it got dark.

Terry was in the kitchen, clearing away accumulated dust and Katie was asleep; the house was eerily quiet except for the sound of paper towels being wiped across old Formica countertops. Lydia had taken Michael into town with her while she shopped for groceries; she'd been eager to get out of the house but wanted to go alone, leaving Kevin to sit on the porch and stew.

When I told the kids I wanted to spend my birthday at the beach, I hadn't stopped to think that the last time Lydia had been in this house it had been with a knife constantly pointed at her, the threat of imminent demise hanging just inches in front of her for over forty eight hours. I hadn't stopped to consider that this was where Nick killed Kevin's seminary roommate, where Kevin made a nearly fatal mistake of pulling the trigger on a blank-loaded gun just inches from his own head.

"We should leave," I told Terry. "This was probably the dumbest idea I've had in years."

"Everyone else is on their way, Chip. Give Kevin and Lydia a chance to relax before deciding anything. Once this house fills up with the noise of their family instead of those two horrible days, they may want to stay."

"Birthday or not, if they're both uncomfortable by tonight, we're all going home."

"Fair enough."

Because of Michael, they couldn't take Kevin's upstairs bedroom, and the only room big enough for his portable crib was the master; Lydia took one step towards it and turned around, taking Michael from Kevin as she mumbled that she would do the grocery shopping, and no, she didn't need any help.

That was where Jake had kept her when he wasn't walking her up and down the beach, tied to the footboard of the king sized bed, while he pretentiously prayed and tormented her with the details of what he'd done to Kevin, little slices that Kevin hadn't shared with anyone, and things he hadn't even known because he had been drunk enough to black out.

I jammed the crib into one of the rooms in the converted garage; the bed was hardly big enough for the two of them, but it came with fewer ghosts and I didn't think they would mind it as much.

Kevin hadn't moved at all; it felt as if he was holding his breath while he waited for Lydia to come back. I opened the door quietly, not wanting to startle him, and then climbed over the railing to sit beside him.

"I'm sorry," I said after a minute or two. He hadn't looked at me; I wasn't sure he had even blinked. "My brain was not engaged when I thought about coming here. We can go—"

"No, we can't," he murmured. "And it's all right. We needed to face this place sooner or later. We probably should have done it a long time ago."

It had only been a year; I thought they should have more time if they needed it.

"I'd understand if you never wanted to come here again, Kevin."

"We talked about it, how it was going to feel walking into the house…I don't think either of us realized it would be so hard."

I should have.

I'd felt how hard it might be months earlier, but I shoved that into the back of my brain.

"Your mom and I came here a few months ago, and it hit me then, too. I walked the beach and that's all I could think about. I just didn't stop to think about it when I decided I wanted to spend my birthday here. I really am sorry."

He finally turned to look at me. "You don't have anything to apologize for, Dad. I don't want this house to be someplace we avoid. I want it to be someplace we bring our kids every summer, and I want them to have as much fun as Eileen and Nick and Paul and I had when we were growing up. This is just a bump Lydia and I have to get over, but it'll be all right."

"If you're both still feeling squirrely about it tonight, we'll leave. Seriously, son, I can spend my birthday anywhere. The whole point was to have the family together and to have some fun. We can do that somewhere else."

"We'll be fine," he said.

"You're a stubborn son of a bitch."

"I get that from my old man. It'll be better when everyone gets here, Dad. Once we're all down there on the beach sitting around the fire, I think Lydia and I will both realize that it's more fun than awful. When it gets right down to it, by the time we leave I think the only downer will be that I don't get the room with the view."

"Michael—"

"I know. But you might want to consider getting a better railing upstairs and real stairs instead of that ladder. This family is going to explode with kids in the next few years and we'll need to be able to shove them up there."

I gestured towards the house next door. "I keep offering Patterson a nice chunk of change for his house. I think he's close to accepting it as long as his family can spend a couple weeks there during the summer. We can bridge the space between them with a giant common room and turn that house into nothing but bedrooms."

"Isn't that renovating past the price point of the neighborhood?"

"You've been doing some reading," I mused.

"It takes a lot of reading to figure out where all the pieces to your business puzzle are. It took me a while to realize you weren't doing high end renovations to all your properties just in case you sold them someday."

"You can renovate the hell out of something you're sure you'll keep forever; rental property you keep within the midpoint of the area comps. The tricky one is figuring out when and what to do with the apartment—"

"Oh, I get it. You only wanted me to start learning about all of this so you'd have someone who would be willing to talk about it. Mom doesn't give a crap, so let's get Kevin get excited about granite counter tops and Travertine tile!"

"Sorry. But you might be on to something there."

"I'm just giving you a hard time. I'm enjoying poking through all that stuff more than I thought I would. I may need you to help me wade through the commercial side of your businesses, though. I had no idea you owned as many as you do."

"Diversification. And you really enjoy it?"

"It's complex. That interests me. And Lydia likes it because it keeps me out of her hair in the morning."

"Just don't stop writing, Kevin. I'll bring you into every aspect of the business if that's what you want, but I don't want you to give that up because of it."

He leaned back a little and squinted at me, "Where'd that come from?"

"You have talent, son. I wouldn't want you to stop writing because you're so busy trying to learn the things that I'm interested in."

"I won't," he promised. "I still write, and I have ideas simmering in my head. Someday I want to write the family history…I'd like to get everyone to sit down and tell me their version, from the moment it started."

"It started with a dead hooker," I said absently.

"Well, there's something to tell your grandkids."

"If you're going to do it, you're going to have to do it warts and all. And this family wouldn't exist without a dead hooker named Brenda, and a slightly psychotic ex-boyfriend named Matt."

"He was the guy that kidnapped Nick when he was a baby."

"That would be him."

"And if I do this, you'll be willing to open up about everything? Your parents and your brother? Kris's first husband? The agency?"

I spun on the railing and slid my feet down to the porch. "I'll tell you anything you want to know."

"It could be painful. I know Mom had an affair with Uncle Doug. And I know when you two split—"

"It was a one night stand, and you'd have to talk to them about it. There's a lot of pain in my past, Kevin, but you have to believe me when I say your mother has more than made up for it all, even the things she was responsible for. If I had to do it all over again, I'd take it all if it meant that I'd wind up right here with her still beside me."

He slid off the railing, a slight grin on his face. "That's what makes it worth writing, Dad. Most people would have walked away, but you…if anything you love her more than you ever have. That's what I want my kids to know. Even when you were hurting each other the most, you still wanted each other. I want my kids to see that even when the hormones are flying wild or when it seems like everything is wrong, the biggest part of love is choice. You chose her. You chose to honor your commitment to her, even when you weren't sure the children she was pregnant with were yours, and even when she locked you out of the house. You still choose her every day, no matter what."

I didn't know what to say.

"I know you had doubts about Eileen and me, and yet you stayed. When you and Mom separated, you had a line of women in that apartment complex that would have been happy to spend a night or two with you. You could have lived a life a lot of men dream about. But you chose *her*. Don't think your kids didn't notice that. And it's what I want our kids to understand. And our grandkids. Our parents loved each other and stayed together by choice."

"I don't think I really had a choice, Kevin."

"But you did. The same way I had the choice to marry Lydia or find another seminary, you had the choice to stick around to make it work or walk away. I would have been happy as a priest, but can you really see it now? The woman is my soul mate, but yes, I made that choice. So did you."

"Then I keep making the right choice," I said.

"Most definitely."

"It doesn't feel like a series of choices, Kevin. It just feels…normal."

"You're the King and Queen of normal," he chuckled, "if normal involves being nosy and pushy, and slightly kinky when you think no one is looking."

"Hey. I'm not kinky."

"But you are nosy and pushy. And that's not a complaint. You turned out to be a better therapist than the woman I was paying two hundred bucks an hour."

"Paid as in past tense?"

"She was a big help getting through some anger issues, but honestly…you know me better. You don't care about embarrassing the hell out of me and you don't tip toe around what you know to be the problem. If I need to talk to someone again and I can't talk to Lydia, I'll come to you."

"Then I didn't make the problem worse?"

"You made me realize I can talk to my wife about anything. I thought I knew that before, but…"

"Just a heads up—if you have a complaint about your wife, it's usually better to bitch to your best friend before even thinking about talking to her."

"Maybe."

"Unless he's the issue…I know she has a history with Topher."

"I'm learning to get past the details I'd rather not even be aware of."

"And that takes time."

He nodded. "How, Dad? How did you get past it being Uncle Doug? It's one thing to know that Lydia had a relationship before, but…"

"It didn't happen overnight. I didn't talk to him for months. When she told me…If I'd laid eyes on him then I honestly think I might have killed him. Anyone else would have hurt, but he was supposed to protect her while I was gone. And Kris—she shrugged it off like it was nothing. I couldn't do that. I couldn't explode at your mother because she was pregnant and I couldn't face Doug without killing him…it wasn't until just before her birthday that it occurred to me that Doug screwed up, but he wasn't the one who had taken vows with me. I focused all my anger on him, but he wasn't the one I was the most pissed off with."

"Mom."

"No. Me. I blamed her, but I was angry with myself for putting them in that position in the first place. Once I realized that, I knew I could face him again."

"So what, you called him up and said 'Sorry I put you in that awkward position'?"

"The only thing your mom wanted for her birthday that year was for Doug and me to try to mend fences. They were dealing with finding out that Spider was deaf and we still wanted to be a part of his life…and yeah, I missed my best friend. We managed a very tense politeness for about half an hour before I beat the holy hell out of him in the backyard. I don't think he even tried to defend himself, he just let me wail on him until he had four broken ribs and a bloody nose and black eye."

"Cripes."

"And that was it. I let it go as much as I could and we got drunk." I tapped my chest, right where my tattoo was. "That was also the night we walked over to this little place near the restaurant, and I got the shamrock. Even drunk I knew your mother would like it."

"Did Uncle Doug get one?"

"He got Kris's name scrawled onto his ass."

"She was thrilled, I'm sure."

"Slapped him on the ass every chance she got, until it healed. That night cemented him becoming your uncle, by the way. Nick was already calling him Uncle Doug, but…somewhere in the middle of that fight I spit out that you just don't do your brother's wife. I realized when I was trying to choke the snot out of him that somewhere along the line he had truly become my brother…and that's probably why it hurt as much as it did."

"But you didn't exactly forgive him then, did you?"

"That took years, Kevin. I don't think I finally exorcised that particular ghost until Spider and Eileen had been dating for a couple of years and we all realized they were in it for good. So it took nearly seventeen years for me to get from trying to forgive him to knowing that I honestly had."

Kevin was looking through the window; Lydia was back with Michael and she was helping Terry put groceries away. I could hear them both laughing, and Michael was crawling across the floor, trying to get to the window.

"And yet you loved her through all of that," he said quietly.

"Apparently I chose to."

"And I'm grateful every day for it, Dad." Michael was at the window; he had pulled himself up and was standing there, smearing his fingers across the glass. "Someday, he will be, too."

~

"It's midnight," Terry said as she slipped her arms around me. "Happy birthday."

Nick's fire was still going strong and the kids were lounging around it, the chatter and laughter louder than the music filtering through the old boom box Paul dragged out of a closet. Doug and Kris had taken Michael inside at nine and Nicole followed half an hour later, leaving the rest of us outside where quiet was merely a concept for inside the house where the grandkids were trying to sleep.

"Technically I'm not fifty for a few more hours," I grumbled. "Let me hang onto my forties as long as I can."

"That's too bad. I was about to take you inside and offer you a happy birthday blo—"

I clamped my hand over her mouth. "Not where they can hear you. Or read your lips."

"Kind of late for propriety," Kevin droned. "We all know where she was going with that thought."

"Son, I swear to God, you have ears like a cat."

Eileen leaned over to look past Spider at Kevin. "Who was going where with what?"

I pointed at Kevin and snapped, "No."

"I hope you see all the little shades of irony here," he said with a grin.

"I don't care if you embarrass me. Don't embarrass your mother."

"I'm not embarrassed," she offered. She pushed herself up off the blanket and held her hand out to me. "Come on. Take a walk with me."

She led me down the beach, walking two steps ahead, until we were a couple hundred feet away. When she stopped she turned around, and I followed her gaze.

It was a snapshot moment, all of our kids sitting around the fire pit; Nick and Katie were huddled together on a blanket, propped up against one of the three six foot long logs the boys had once cut and kept stored under the beach house porch for the nights just like this. She looked drained but happy, and was snuggled up against him, his arm around her protectively, lips on her cheek.

Spider and Eileen were in deck chairs with a small table between them, slapping playing cards down. She was laughing wildly and he was shaking his head in wonder; neither was signing but they were still finding a way to talk, falling into that place the rest of us were never invited, a small sliver of Them that they'd discovered long before they got married. They learned to speak to each other through small gestures and smiles, something neither of them could—or wanted to—explain.

Paul and Sherry sat on one of the logs across the fire from where we stood; they straddled it so that they were facing each other, their conversation deliberately low so that they would have to lean in close to hear each other. He kept inventing reasons to touch her: a stray hair, his hand brushing against her leg, his hands on hers as he showed her how to sign the alphabet.

And Kevin was stretched out on the sand, his back biting into the third log. Lydia was next to him, her arm strewn lightly across his shoulder, one foot set gently on top of his feet. They both kept looking up to the house, and I could feel their sense of being torn between wanting to go inside to be with their son and wanting to stay there on the beach with the rest of their family.

After dinner I'd made the offer to him again; if they were uncomfortable, we could leave. I'd be just as happy to sit around the pool with my kids as I would be sitting out on the beach.

"And miss Sherry's introduction to Pyro-Nick?" he asked. "Not a chance. When she sees those flames shoot six feet out of the pit she might turn around and run screaming from Paul's lunatic family. I want to see that."

I hoped he felt as relaxed as he looked.

"Now that they're distracted, do you want to sneak back into the house for an early birthday present?" she asked, leaning against me.

"Maybe in a little bit. And if we do, I'd prefer full participation on both our parts, not just me getting my sense of humor nibbled on. Perhaps the queen could go for a pony ride."

"I'll get my spurs."

"Damn, woman."

"Fine. I'll be gentle. But what are we waiting for?"

"I was just looking at the kids…feeling very grateful none of them turned out to be like me."

"Now why would you say that?"

"Come on, I used to be such a little bastard. I'm just glad that none of them decided to follow in my footsteps, so to speak."

"You need to take another look at your kids, Irish. Your daughter used you as the measuring stick for whether or not Spider was good enough, and she probably will until they're both old and sitting in rocking chairs, picking on young nurses in a retirement home. You set the bar pretty damn high for Spider, but she expects him to get over it because you always did. And every one of your boys followed in your footsteps."

"Paul tried, when he was young and stupid."

"Not that. Paul was a horny little teenager with no impulse control, but he grew up. But look at Nick. Of all the things he could have done in life he decided to pick up where you left off at the agency. And don't kid me—I suspect he's damn good at it and will make it work, even with a family. You may have fallen into it, but what he understood was that you were ultimately working for the greater good, and he wants to carry your work onward. He wants to save the world, and he's doing it by picking up where you left off.

"Paul—he never had to keep working at the restaurant. He could have gone to school to study something else, but what he wanted was to do exactly what his father had done for all of his life. You dropped the restaurant into his lap, and it wasn't much different than the way you got it. It was necessary to live on for a while, but in the end you both stuck with it because it served a purpose. He'll make it his life's work because he saw the joy you got out of making other people happy in hour and a half slivers. He saw you giving your employees a leg up and benefits they would never get anywhere else, and he wants to keep that going because it makes a difference for them.

"And Kevin. My God, Chip, he's the most like you. He's what you would have been if you'd been raised differently, but when it comes down to it, he's so much like you that I sometimes look at him and melt a little. He has your sense of humor and your depth of kindness, and he's interested in the same things you are. He's Irish two-point-oh. He even took back the family name.

"They *all* followed in your footsteps. It's just that they stepped into them at a later point in your life. They'll never be what you were before I met you because they don't know that man. The man they know is someone that they admire and are proud of."

"Don't make me sound better than I am," I said quietly.

"Don't keep thinking you're the same person you were even the day before I met you. The night you walked into my apartment— neither of us has been the same since the moment I opened the door."

"You have definitely been good for me."

"I've also broken your heart more times than I care to admit—"

I opened my mouth to protest, but she held up a warning finger.

"—but the biggest thing is that we were good parents to those kids, and truthfully I'd be a little disappointed if they hadn't turned out like you, because whether you see it or not, you're worth following. You're a good man, Chip. You might have been a horrible teenager, but you became a good man."

I pulled her into a tight hug. "Thank you."

"You think if we hadn't done so well with those kids that they would have hung around the hospital waiting for even tiny bits of news during and after your surgery? When you peed without the catheter for the first time I thought they were going to cheer."

"Then clearly they lead boring lives."

"Nick flew all the way from Iraq just to see for himself that you were really going to be all right. They were all as terrified as we were…"

"And it was just a zit."

"I know you hate the idea of being fifty, but this is one worth celebrating. You're *here*, and you're as healthy as you've ever been. We get to keep you around, Irish. *I* get to keep you around, and I'm not done with you yet."

"Let's see how happy you are in when you turn fifty."

"That's different."

"Somehow I knew it would be." I gestured towards the kids. "If they're the price I have to pay for getting old…I suppose it's worth it.

I'm still not happy about getting fat."

She poked one finger into my gut. "Will you stop it? You're not fat. You're not even in danger of bending over and having a third of an inch hang over your belt. You still have the six pack, Chip, it's just not like seeing flesh colored plastic wrap glued onto muscle. And frankly, I like this a lot more."

"If you like it so much then why the hell do I have to eat chicken and fish all the time?"

Her hand slid from my belly to my chest. "Because of this. Because sometimes I'm just as afraid as you are of your family history. I don't want to lose you in a few years to a heart attack. So I'm going to keep playing the part of the Food Nazi, because selfishly, I want to keep you around."

"I still get steak for my birthday, right?"

"Giant T-bone, grilled medium rare," she laughed as she fell against me. "You even get cake."

"And ice cream?"

"Chocolate."

"Ah, you do love me."

"And don't you forget it." She slipped out of my arms and reached for my hand, pulling me back towards the kids. "Let's go say goodnight to the monsters. And I don't care if they know what I'm considering doing to their father. If Kevin is embarrassed, tough."

"He wants to write the family history," I told her. "He already knows a lot about us…how much more do we want him to know?"

"It wouldn't be true if we held anything back."

"The little shit read my journal when he was fourteen. I'm not sure how much more there is to tell him."

"We fill in the blanks for him, then. We've done some horrible things to each other, but there's nothing I wouldn't tell my kids if they asked. Kevin is asking."

"I'm not sure it's our history he's looking for. But if you're on board with it, I'll tell him anything he wants to know."

"What is it you think he's hoping to hear?"

I stopped just short of the fire, and took another long look at our kids. Nick's hand was resting on Katie's growing belly. Paul and Sherry had stopped the sign language lesson and were wrapped around each other just past the far log, dancing to slow music. Eileen and Spider were in deep discussion, not caring if everyone else was eavesdropping, and Kevin had his arms around his wife, and his face was nuzzled in the crook of her neck.

What he wanted was right there in front of us.

"He wants more than the history of how his family started, Terry. He wants what he'll get. He wants a love story."

~

I woke to the sounds of Michael squealing with delight and Nicole's high pitched laughter drifting from the living room below. We slept in Kevin's old room, having given up the master bedroom to Nick and Katie, and even with the door closed I could hear my family downstairs.

Looking out the near floor to ceiling window at waves lapping the sand, I finally understood why Kevin loved that tiny room, so cramped that two people could barely turn around at the same time in it.

Part of me was tempted to spend the day there, watching my kids on the beach, but Terry slapped a gentle hand on my backside and told me I had to get up. I wanted to spend my birthday at the beach; that obligated me to peel myself out of bed and go outside where the beach was.

We spent the day digging in the sand, building castles with Nicole and tossing a football back and forth with the kids. Michael crawled reluctantly from one adult to the next, preferring to sit in someone's lap rather than risk wet, grainy sand clinging to his knees. I got exactly what I asked for, a day with my family on the beach, filled with those punctuated moments of perfect normal Paul had spoken about.

After dinner, when everyone was tired and quiet and I was on the porch waiting for the grill to cool down so I could put it away, Kevin slipped out of the house and asked me to follow him to the beach, where the logs were still seated around the fire pit. He had a notepad in hand and a pen stuck behind his ear, but when we sat down on the log furthest from the water he left it in place.

"I still want to write your story," he said, staring out at the water.

"Our story. I thought about it for a good part of the night, and the longer I thought about it the more I wanted to get started."

"As long as you understand it's not always going to be pretty."

"I lived through your separation. I know there's a whole lot of butt ugly there."

"You're going to find out more than you really want to know," I warned. "Our marriage could have fallen apart more than once."

"Uncle Doug, I know," he said.

"Before then, even. Remember when we were at the lake and I told you your mother and I had gone out there to reconnect? It was my first last chance with her, Kevin."

"Your dad had died. You were a little bit lost."

"I also had come within a few wayward breaths of cheating on her in the back of a van with an old hookup. Our story is peppered with a lot of stupid things on both our parts. If you write this, you may never look at us the same way and I don't want to lose the relationship you and I have."

He turned and looked at me for a moment, pursing his lips thoughtfully. "I understand that my parents are human, and that in spite of everything they're still together and still in love. Whatever else I learn about you can't top that."

"Then you're absolutely sure you want to do this?"

He gave a bare nod. "Even in the ugliest moments you've given us some beautiful things to see. If not, I sure as hell wouldn't be living right next door to you, and Lydia and I probably wouldn't be adding to the family—"

"Wait. You're trying to have another baby?"

"I'm shooting for those quints you requested, but she swears she'll bite certain things off me if that happens."

"You might want to scale your ambitions back a little. Your house might not be big enough."

"I'll settle for one healthy baby, preferably a girl."

"Since it's my birthday, I get to pry," I said. "How long have you been trying?"

"Long enough that every time she says she doesn't feel quite right, I get a little excited. I think Lydia is, too, at least excited enough to start throwing names around. I'm pretty sure your thirtieth anniversary party is going to have lots of little kids crawling around."

"Names."

"Aubrey if it's a girl. 'Hey You' if it's a boy."

"Then it better not be a boy."

"You know, last night Spider and Eileen were talking about kids…and she wasn't threatening him with bodily harm."

"Rude to eavesdrop, son."

"Then they should have gone inside. But I'm pretty sure that she agreed to stop not trying to have one and to just let it happen when it happens. So figure on four tiny ones crawling around at that thirtieth celebration."

"That would be nice."

"Paul and Sherry, I wouldn't count on them for a couple of years. But you're going to get your court full of grandkids, Dad, and sooner rather than later."

"Happy birthday to me."

"I thought you might like that better than the book I got you."

"Son, the only thing that would make this day better is if you knew absolutely for sure that Lydia is pregnant. I'll settle for the possibility."

"She's a week late. There you go."

"My preoccupation with grandkids is a little bit nuts, isn't it?"

"You grew up in a crazy family, Dad. You were alone even when you weren't alone. Now you have a mostly normal family and you want to see it grow. Nothing wrong with that. And you're not pushy about it, just obvious. We're sure as hell not going to have kids just because you want us to."

I was alone even when I wasn't alone.

He could see that when I hadn't.

I pointed to his notepad. "Last chance to change your mind about hearing it all, Kevin."

He pulled the pen from behind his ear.

"Before I say anything else, you have to know that above all, I love your mother more than anything else. She comes first in everything, even over my kids. No matter what you hear from either of us, or from Doug and Kris, that woman is my life and I will love her long past my last breath."

"Way to state the obvious," he chuckled.

"How far back do you want to start?"

He considered it for a moment and then said, "I think you have two complete stories to tell, but the one I'm most drawn to right now is the one that begins with you and Mom."

"I'm not sure I'm ready to pick through the detritus of my childhood, anyway."

"Maybe someday," he said. "For now, I just want the story of my parents. How you met, when did you know she was the one…?"

"Kris set us up, blind date. I walked into her apartment—but that's not where it really started. It started a year before that, when we both had hurt and been hurt."

I stared out at the ocean, watched as wave after wave lapped the sand, and tried to think back to the moment I knew I needed to change. The day when Kris found me abusing the piano in the restaurant and decided that I needed a push to head in a new direction, and knew the perfect person to help me turn around.

I looked at the sun sinking into the horizon and saw that teenager's blue eyes, and the wicked smile that pulled me in with the first *hello*.

I saw the moment when my heart was hers, before I even realized it.

I could see it all stretched out in front of me, glittering in the wake of waves that lapped the sand.

We could have thirty more years together, easily, but it started just before she opened that door and owned me.

I sucked in a deep breath and blinked, and began to tell my son the story of his family.

"The hooker I was going to marry was dead…"

About the Author

K.A. Thompson is a writer[1] living in Northern California with a Spouse Thingy and two crackhead cats[2]. When not writing, she spends her time playing online, or can be found touring the back roads on her spiffy Piaggio MP3 scooter. If you see her, please wave, it makes her feel good.

Thumper Thinks Out Loud
http://kathompson.blogspot.com

---

[1]One would think that was evident by the production of a book, but apparently some people enjoy having this spelled out in black and white.

[2]This would be Max the Psychokitty, and Buddah Pest; they're both far more popular than the author. In fact, Max has several books of his own that regularly outsell everything the author has ever written.